KEVIN BRIDGES

THE BLACK DOG

WILDFIRE

First published in 2022 by
WILDFIRE
an imprint of HEADLINE PUBLISHING GROUP

First published in paperback in 2023 by
WILDFIRE
an imprint of HEADLINE PUBLISHING GROUP

3

Cataloguing in Publication Data is available from the British Library

ISBN 978 1 4722 8907 0

Typeset in Dante MT by CC Book Production
Printed and bound in Great Britain by Clays Ltd, Elcograf S.p.A.

HEADLINE PUBLISHING GROUP
An Hachette UK Company
Carmelite House
50 Victoria Embankment
London EC4Y 0DZ

www.headline.co.uk
www.hachette.co.uk

Having started performing stand-up in 2004 shortly after his seventeenth birthday, Kevin Bridges has ascended the ranks and is now regarded as one of the UK's top comedians. He has made numerous television appearances on shows such as *Live at the Apollo*, *The Jonathon Ross Show*, *Graham Norton Show* and fronted his own BBC One series *Kevin Bridges – What's the Story* and the stand-up special *Kevin Bridges: Live At The Referendum*. He has won multiple awards and performed four critically acclaimed, box office record-breaking tours. His most recent tour *The Overdue Catch-Up* included a staggering sixteen-night run in his home-town of Glasgow's twelve thousand capacity OVO Hydro Arena. He was presented with the SEC Platinum Artist award by the Hydro, marking a staggering 63 solo performances in total at the venue. Kevin has also released four chart-topping DVD's and his 2014 autobiography, *We Need to Talk about Kevin Bridges*, was a *Sunday Times* bestseller.

Praise for *The Black Dog*:

'Brilliant'
Sun

'A thought-provoking literary story full of heart'
Scottish Field

'Edgy, dark, funny and perceptive. . . and very sharply observed'
Herald

'One of the funniest stand-up comedians in the world and now the author of a brilliant novel. Kevin's talent is starting to annoy me now'
Rob Beckett

Dedicated to Liam John Bridges

PART 1

'It's Sharm El-Sheikh, Ryan, "Sha-rm-El-Shake" shake, like a milk-shake, not "Sha-mal Shook".'

She's got her big grin on and lookin' roon the livin' room, makin' sure they're aw laughin', makin' sure every cunt is laughin'. EVERYCUNT.

Ah've went that nauseous, lightheeded way, the room's spinnin' and their faces go aw blurred and distorted, pixelated tae fuck, like when ye watch the fitba at Wee Steesh fae the work's hoose. The Rage is overwhelmin'. Over-fuck-ing-whel-ming. The rage that ye only get when yer bird corrects ye in front eh everybody.

Ah can just aboot make oot her face, then the two sisters, the wee brother and his new bird, the granny's there, tae, and then there's the wank of a da', pourin' his wee can of Holsten Pils – or whatever pish he's drinkin' noo – intae his glass n lookin' up, laughin', aw chuffed. He's huvin' a fuckin' great wee night, sniggerin' away, a right wee shitey laugh tae, his face doesny suit it, like wan of they cunts that doesny deserve tae laugh. 'Sha-mal Shook,' he's repeatin', sittin' admirin' the froth in his daft tumbler.

'Sha-mal Shook up, mm, mm, mm, yay, yay.' Her granda's got up aff his chair noo. Whit the fuck. He's up oan his feet, tryin' tae dance, makin' oot that he's Elvis.

'Eighty years old and he's sharp as a tack, aw happy birthday,

Granda,' her sister's hittin' oot wae and then puttin' a big kiss on his cheek.

Aw the voices are slowin' down, muffled, ah canny make oot words, just noise, distorted. It's like ah'm under water or sumhin, chucked intae the Clyde and every single cunt that's ever put me doon is there, every cunt that's ever hud a go at me, they're aw there, pointin', laughin', pishin' thereselves at who ah huv become.

Ma eyelids are flickerin', sweat pishin' aff me, ma heeds went cloudy and ah canny think. It's like ah'm floatin'.

Maybe this is wan eh they oota body experiences like they American cunts on YouTube that wee Steesh is always on aboot.

'Get yersel together, Ryzo. Screw the nut,' ah say tae masel, like a fitba manager watchin' his side aboot tae capitulate under an early onslaught eh pressure.

'Where will you be staying, Ryan, the Heartbreak Hotel,' the old cunt's just hit oot wae, no a bad bit a patter, al gee him that. They're aw fuckin' roarin' but, man. Cunts are hawdin' thur sides. Greetin'. Tears. Hawns in the air like thur tappin' oot. Holsten Pils runnin' doon the da's nose.

'Here, yer takin' it tight, Ryzo, surprised at ye, mate, surprised yer letting yersel get took fur a cunt here,' Ah'm sayin' to masel.

'Fuckin' settle doon, Ryzo. Settle,' and fae naewhere ah'm back in the room, ma fight or flight receptors huv kicked in or whitever the hing Wee Steesh is always sayin'.

The auld cunt's dancin' aboot, the life and soul.

Ah just fuckin' fly fur 'um. Bang, ya cunt.

That wee split second that done it fur 'is. The wee split second ah seen it in his eyes, seen it register that it wis fuckin' Ryzo he wis windin' up, goadin'.

Ah land a heavy blow, cunt flies right back tae where he came fae, intae his chair but his chair canny take the impact cause eh the pace ah've sent 'um travellin'.

The wumman are screamin', especially her – delighted she's got somethin' else to get on ma case aboot.

The wee brother jumps up aff the couch – wee cunt 'hinks he's a ticket, stays up tae watch the cagefightin' – doesny eat breed and aw that – he's comin' right fur me, fast, wirey wee cunt, fast but no fast enough. Fuck ye.

Walkin' stick right aff the face. Bang.

Am standin' there like Bruce fuckin' Lee. Enter the Dragon. ENTER THE FUCKIN' RYZO. Am eggin' maself on fae inside ma ain heed whilst they're aw trying tae pick the chair up wae the auld cunt still in it, sparked clean oot. 'Watch his hip, watch his hip,' her sister's screamin'. 'Fuck 'ees hip, tell him tae watch 'ees mooth.' Ah lean over the toppled chair and get right in his face. 'WATCH YER FUCKIN' MOOTH.'

Ah look aboot the room, everycunt greetin'. Different mood noo eh. A great fuckin' time when it wis 'let's aw rip the pish oot Ryzo' though.

Ah decide it's best that ah make ma excuses n leave cause ye willny hear the end eh this wan.

The wee man's in the living room noo, wantin' tae know whit's goin' oan.

Ah gee him a wee pat on the heed. 'Yer old papa was bein' a bully, son, but Daddy sorted it, away back and play, pal.'

Ah want tae let him know the auld cunt husny got long left n then we'll aw get weighed in but ah show some decorum n keep that tae masel.

The wee man looks as us guan 'Are we still going on an aeroplane to Egypt?'

Fuckin' heartbreakin'. 'Ah don't 'hink we will be, noo, pal. No anymare, Mummy's no gonny let us.'

He looks at her as if 'Whit the fuck's that aw aboot then?'

The wee man knows ah love him and that ah wid dae anythin' fur him, got 'ees name tattooed doon ma neck, the lot, mare than can be said fur her, obsessed wae gettin' him intae aw the Disney pish. 'If I don't go to bed Mummy will turn into a pumpkin, Daddy,' he wis geein' it the other night. 'If ye don't go tae bed the cunts that leathered yer uncle Barry will slap you aboot anaw,' ah said, see ah'm a realist, ah teach him aboot real life, no fantasy. Ah dae like Cinderella though, ah will admit, especially the wee fat moose cunt, Gus, ah 'hink.

Ah nod tae the wee man and stick ma jaiket oan, ah get ootside the hoose n ah phone wee Steesh n head doon the boozer tae get him.

He's sittin' wae a couple eh cunts fae doon his bit, thur fulla shite, daft cunts, no the brightest. Intae motorsports n aw that but fuck it, ah sink a coupla jars and there ah um, back, hawdin' court, tellin' everycunt the story.

'False teeth flyin' across the livin' room, then the dug wis aff wae thum.' Ye need tae add a wee bit oan artistic licence, that's whit makes me who ah um, a good laugh, a crackin' cunt.

They're aw pishin' thurselves, there's some gear goin' aboot noo so we're aw in the cludgie, me, Steesh and two other cunts, rackin' thum up. 'Whit a laugh, Ryzo, some fuckin' boay, mind that night ye . . .'

Ah come bouncin' oot the bog 'hinkin' how ah like wee Steesh, always pays a tribute tae 'is, a real pal.

See that's ma idea eh a night oot, a right good swally n everycunt tellin' Ryzo stories.

Fae fuckin' naewhere but ah just burst oot intae tears, fuckin' greetin', thur aw gaun 'Whit's wrang, Ryzo?' Wee Steesh tries tae gee me a cuddle kinda hing, am tempted tae nut the cunt but before ye know it am doon on ma knees . . .

Ah get ma phone oot, ah cut across the pub on ma fuckin' knees, everycunt starin', ah get tae the bit where ye get a signal n ah phone her. Before she can lecture 'is ah'm away . . . puttin' a few hings straight . . .

SHAM EL SHEIKH!! SHAM EL SHEIKH!!!!!!!!! ah'm screamin' doon the line . . . FUCKIN' FUCK YER SHAM EL SHEIKH . . .

AAAAHHHHHHHHHHH! Ah feel numb, ah feel nuttin' bar ma own pish runnin' doon ma leg. Canny stoap greetin'. Greetin' n pishin' masel in the fuckin' boozer. This is the end. Ah'm done wae it aw.

Ah walk oot intae the street. Ah hear wee Steesh n a few other cunts shoutin' me back but it's done noo. It's aw over wae.

Goodbye ya cunts and fuck yees. Everywan eh yees.

Declan knew he'd misread the room. He'd honed a heightened sense of self-awareness over the years, a personal transferable skill acquired through an abundance of similar humiliations: from primary school, to high school and college, to the group interview which had denied him a job at Asda – their loss, Morrisons' gain, though.

He'd held his shelf-stacking job for close to three years, which was a relative success, it could be argued – but Declan had served his apprenticeship in failure and he knew exactly when he had fucked up again.

After his 'solo performance of an original spoken-word piece' he had remained standing – he knew that sitting down would be a signal for the feedback to commence, and no one was ready for that yet.

His gaze was fixed slightly above the heads of his seated audience. He knew not to look down, to allow them at least a few seconds of privacy to adjust to the change in atmosphere.

The audience reciprocated this reverence and no one looked up at Declan, but he could sense the sets of eyes below him, looking around to make contact with each other, to confirm the tension.

Relative strangers in the class were bonding through the awkwardness, like the big rugby player type guy, Ross, who'd been coming to the class with a view of getting into acting, and a girl called Lauren, or maybe Laura – she'd corrected Declan on the second week and he was since reluctant to take the 50/50 gamble and commit to a direct addressal – who both nodded an embarrassed apology at Declan after her high-pitched cackle perforated the ephemeral yet excruciating stillness that his recital had sprung on the class.

Their contrite faces acknowledged their minor betrayal of Declan, as, being the three youngest, and all non-smokers, they'd been exchanging small talk during the brief break in the two-hour classes over the past few weeks.

The conversations hadn't progressed from the superficial: drama, documentary and film recommendations – assumed shared ground given the theme of the class – and some fatigued commentary on current global affairs, opinion-free, of course. Any slight deviation from the neutral was halted by a generic 'The world's gone mad' or the ubiquitous post-Covid 'It's all a bit *Nineteen Eighty-Four*', the latter often accompanied by the quick self-satisfied glance of someone who's seized on a relevant moment to reference a book they've never read.

Their exchanges were fairly rigid but they served a purpose in passing ten minutes without any lulls and with minimal screen time.

If they'd clicked more and reached the point that they could take the piss out of each other, then maybe the blatant mockery of Declan and his performance wouldn't have seemed as deceitful.

It wasn't clear what Ross had done to elicit such a piercing laugh, but during the first-week introductions he'd confidently told the class that he often entertained his workmates and that they loved his facial expressions and compared him to Jim Carrey.

He'd tried to showcase a couple of his favourites and do a few impressions during class exercises. He wasn't very good, although it didn't discourage him. You got people like that, Declan knew, people with unwavering self-assurance built upon zero merit – a personal transferable skill acquired through years of having never been punched in the face.

'Come on now, Lauren, it's not an easy thing.'

Alex, the tutor, brought the focus from a mortified-looking Lauren back to Declan's car crash of a performance and its ill-judged content.

'Lauren, Laur-en, Laur-en, Ralph Laur-en.'

Declan's memorising of her name was futile as he knew he'd probably never see her again. This was his last week of coming to the class, he vowed.

His dad had seen the advert in the arts-type pull-out of a

Sunday newspaper and mentioned it to his mum, and they'd paid for the 'writing and performing for pleasure and profit' course as a Christmas present to their first-born, who had long been interested in writing, television and film.

The guilt he would feel from abandoning it a little over halfway would serve as a strong argument for his return, but, for now, the liberating thought of walking out of the arts centre door and never having to see these people again alleviated his dread of the looming group discussion on his work.

Lauren looked genuinely remorseful and ashamed, and even though she had laughed at him, Declan felt bad for her. This was his fault. What was he doing coming here?

Tuesday nights in an arts centre?

Two fucking buses. It was a bastard to get to, the blanket term for anywhere without direct transport links from one's front door. Two buses and a fairly challenging walk, gradually uphill and about a half-mile or so, not the type of terrain or the distance that would ever raise funds for a charitable cause, but demanding enough to leave Declan self-conscious about his arse marking a visible equator of perspiration on the centre's dark-grey plastic seats.

Lauren and the rest of the class had probably all been to university. Some of them even had writing and acting credits, Declan remembered, from the opening night's initial meet-greet. He hadn't heard of any of the publications or productions that were mentioned, but he'd managed to look impressed enough as the CVs were rattled off. This wasn't his world. This was their world.

'I found it a little, I don't know . . . toxic? One for the lads maybe?'

The voice sounded like a headteacher, a senior police officer, a Scottish conservative politician. It was that sort of voice and that sort of tone. A voice and tone incompatible with saying anything positive to someone like Declan.

The story hadn't gone down well, fair enough, leave it there, Declan thought, hoping to switch off before being offered some 'constructive criticism'. The worst fucking kind, he thought, and this dose sounded certain to be administered with the self-satisfied smugness of someone convinced that they're the most interesting person in the room and that they've observed what no one else has, like they're breaking an exclusive, like it hadn't already crossed Declan's mind that he had fucked up quite catastrophically.

Declan wasn't from a background where criticism was a means of constructing anything: its purpose was to hurt, to ridicule, it was a power tool used to alleviate one's own insecurities and failings by emphasising – and often exaggerating – those of the subject.

Constructive criticism had blighted his life for as long as he could remember. He loved football, but constructive criticism had led to his early retirement from the game at the age of twelve. A heavy touch in his own penalty box resulted in his team's early exit from a mini-European Championships tournament held as part of the end-of-term activities in his first year at high school.

'Fucking shite! Ya useless, fat bastard!' – the voice of an exasperated Scott Lawson echoed in his head as he'd replayed the goal. That Scott Lawson was said to be a drug addict now, currently serving a custodial sentence for attempting to rob an Esso garage, armed with a Stanley blade, didn't offer any satisfaction.

Declan had long dropped any charges – he had said worse to himself and he knew that Scott Lawson had been correct, and, in a way, Declan appreciated his honesty – it had caused him to stop embarrassing himself on a football pitch and to try and watch what he was eating, at least in the weeks that followed. It had been more bullying than constructive criticism, perhaps, but that was at an age when a bit of bullying – in moderation – could be beneficial for your development. Not now though, not now that Declan was his own biggest bully and any criticism – constructive or scathing – only served as a fortification, holding him captive in his own head.

Declan realised his mind had gone elsewhere, like he had trained it to do when he felt under attack, when his heart rate would speed up and that feeling in his stomach came back, the feeling that had a superpower to transport him back to any other stage in his life when he'd felt similarly feeble and useless.

At twenty-four he'd familiarised himself with the assembly points to get to during these episodes, which anything he per-ceived as a confrontation could bring on, the safe houses in his head where he could try and get comfortable and drift off to his own hard-luck story.

A supermarket worker, brought up and still living in a low-income household, sleepwalking through a second crack at completing an HNC at an underfunded college in a neglected building on the outskirts of the city centre.

What chance have you got in a room of artistic, middle-class creatives, these thespians, these wankers? It would always take this course, the voice in his head, it would lure Declan in by consoling him and reminding him of how he was up against it, of all the obstacles in his path. He'd recently picked up the potentially destructive habit of letting this inner monologue dictate to him, unchallenged. It would turn nasty, everyone would be called a prick, life itself would be deemed meaningless, and then it would get to its favourite subject of Declan himself.

He was fat, ugly, he'd no real qualifications, no trade, no career prospects, he'd never get a girlfriend. The voice would be off on one, like a United States marine sergeant mercilessly reprimanding the tenant of an unmade bed.

Declan jolted himself back into the room, noticing that he was still standing as more of the group were contributing to the conversation about *Ryzo* and the 'disturbing themes' that had been addressed. Some found positives, most found flaws, some found it offensive, but it didn't matter now.

The confidence and the conviction that had carried Declan to the end of his performance had abandoned him, and whoever that self-assured, flamboyant showman that had stood up and taken centre stage for those five or six minutes was had bailed – fucked off – leaving the real Declan to deal with the debris.

He'd felt like someone else for a while. He hadn't quite managed to 'immerse himself in the character' or whatever, but he had felt like he was acting at least.

He'd thought about it all day at college, on the bus there,

the bus home and on both buses here. He'd never spoken in front of an audience before, let alone 'performed', and let alone performed his own work.

He'd been in negotiations with his nerves all day – everyone else is going to have to do it, face your fears, what's the worst that can happen? – all those adages had culminated in him printing off one of his short stories in his college library, writing he'd never shown anyone, and presenting it to his class.

He went over his performance in his head – the tones, the intonations. He'd really tried to sell it, he had attacked it with a fervour, like someone with rock-solid belief in their material, which made him cringe even more.

Even if he'd narrated it in a monotone drawl, like rugby Ross had done, he wouldn't have left himself so open, so exposed, he thought, as he felt his arms folding – defensive body language, he remembered someone telling him.

His hands nestled under his armpits, which were soaked. He glanced down to see the sweat patches that had appeared on his dark-grey round-neck jumper. He'd sweated through many a T-shirt and his work polo shirt, but a jumper was a first.

It wasn't the satisfying sweat of physical exertion or honest labour, either. This was the unique special blend the human body distils exclusively for occasions when one makes a colossal cunt of oneself.

Declan felt a second wave of mortification come over him as he imagined if any of his pals had been present to witness whatever the fuck he'd just done. That they'd probably be in the pub watching one of the Champions League games made him think of the safety of the familiar surroundings, the same faces and the conversations that would only be as intellectual as he made them. There had been confirmed sightings of Declan reading a book, so he was regarded as a savant in his social circle.

He felt a pang, like homesickness. He was only maybe seven or eight miles from where he grew up, from the only house that he'd ever lived in, but he felt like he was in a distant land, the hostile unknown. He felt like he'd volunteered to fight in an unwinnable war and found himself taken hostage.

He glanced to his left at rugby Ross's watch and saw that there was a quarter of an hour left of the class. He started to think of the outside and his plans for his release whilst words like derivative, vulgar, crude, and terms like toxic masculinity, were being fired around the room.

It would be about fifteen quid in an Uber, he remembered from the previous week, when he'd considered getting one but decided to keep the money and take the soaking. This was different though, he just wanted his old life back, so the price of the convenience was justifiable, even if it more or less equated to working the first two hours of tomorrow afternoon's shift for free.

He had his exit plan in place and thought of the commiserating feeling that the first drink of a cold pint would provide, and of ditching this strange speaking voice that he'd unconsciously developed. Again he felt himself squirm as he thought of his pals.

Where could he tell them he'd been? He couldn't dare mention that he'd been attending this sort of thing – he'd even sought an assurance of confidentiality from his own parents and his younger sister, Ciara.

Writing was the only thing that he'd ever felt mildly competent at and he wanted to study it more to develop and see if it could take him anywhere, even if he didn't have one single word published. He knew he was at his happiest writing, when he could disappear over the hills behind the new-build houses to the back of his street, with just his music, his notebook and Hector, his seven-year-old black Labrador cross.

That's why he was here. He'd got this one wrong, but he wasn't a performer, that didn't interest him. Maybe if he'd printed individual copies of his original spoken-word piece and handed them out, to be read, the class would have taken more from it.

Not that there was much to take, but Ryzo was an interesting enough character, a composite of the sociopathic, deeply flawed lunatics Declan had met in his short life. His home town was full of guys like Ryzo and the poor women who feel stuck with and imprisoned by them. A 'writing and performing for pleasure and profit' class in an arts centre wasn't the correct demographic for Ryzo, he accepted. It wasn't their fault they didn't like it: he'd brought a bare-knuckle brawl to a Centre Court Wimbledon crowd.

Ultimately, it had been meant to be a comedy piece – as dark as it was, Declan only intended to draw a few laughs from the deranged world of young adult male insecurity and the perceived injustices felt by those being forced to grow up and enter the real world against their will. He'd tried to make some semblance of a point too, but what that was he didn't quite know himself.

'What is it that they say, we learn from failure not from

success?' Declan felt rugby Ross's hand slapping his knee. Alex, the tutor, looked at Declan with a smile and nodded at Ross's quote, as though to confirm that yes, he was correct, 'they' did say that. It was patronising but nothing to be taken personally, and at least the class was about to move on and the last couple of speakers were to get up.

Declan felt a bit of confidence come back to him, and before he could tell himself just to let it go, he was challenging Ross. 'A great quote and do you know who said it?'

He was surprised to stumble upon a trace of defiance that had lain dormant inside of him as the firing squad took shots at his work. He realised these were the first words he'd spoken since Ryzo signed off with a *'fuck yees. Everywan eh yees'*.

'Oh, I think it's just a general thing. It would be hard to credit it to anyone in particular.' Ross looked round at the faces of everyone else in the group except Declan's as he answered his question – as though Declan's performance hadn't been enough to affirm that it was them against him. 'You see it on Instagram, a lot,' he added, turning to Lauren for verification.

'Bram Stoker, mate. Professor Abraham Van Helsing, in *Dracula*, he said it.'

Declan felt a round of applause break out in his head and rare shouts of encouragement. He'd got himself back in the game: *'Fucking superb, son.'*

It had come from nowhere. He'd stood his ground and salvaged something from the evening. 'I've literally just finished reading *Dracula*, that is so weird, I take it you've read it? It's actually so good.' Lauren quickly put her hand over her mouth, and turned to Alex, her face apologising for her excited digression.

Declan smiled and, unfolding his arms, he leaned forward and pulled his seat a few inches further into the shape of the class and waited for Alex to call forward the next turn.

He looked at Ross's watch again. The traffic wouldn't be bad, so he'd probably make it to the pub for around 9.30 he calculated whilst a poem was being recited. He didn't have college the next day and his shift wasn't until 1pm. Doof Doof had Wednesday off so no doubt he'd be in the pub and a few pints in by now.

Declan had stopped in to buy a bottle of Coke from the Co-op on the walk here, partly to kill time, so as not to arrive at the arts centre early, a lesson learned from the week before, when he'd had to stand trying to take part in conversation with two of the senior class members as they reminisced about time spent in New York and London, on Broadway and in the West End.

He could go back to the Co-op, buy a quarter-bottle of vodka and pour some into his half-empty Coke bottle. He'd buy another bottle of Coke to top it up with and replace the missing Coke from the new bottle with the rest of the vodka. Perfect. It was the sort of mixology he'd mastered from when he used to go to the football, on the supporters' bus.

It would pass the Uber journey and also help cut the inebriation deficit on anyone who'd been in the pub since seven. If anyone had asked where he'd been he could say he'd gone out for a drink with a few people from his college class, an alibi that the effects from the rapidly consumed quarter-bottle of vodka would corroborate.

His plans were sealed just as the poem came to a sudden, theatrical end and Helen, the retired GP, was thanking the group for listening and explaining how much the words had meant to her.

After Alex praised Helen's work and prompted the rest of the class to come forth with their analyses and their interpretations, and all of that, he began wrapping up the class and thanking everyone for coming. Declan managed to restrain himself from leaping up with too much enthusiasm, but it was like the school bell had rung on a Friday afternoon.

He stretched his shoulders back as he stood up from his seat – cautiously checking back for any streaks of sweat – and folded his sheets of A4 paper over, the word 'everycunt' catching his eye a couple of times, which made him writhe with shame as he glanced round at his class again, watching them pack away their Pukka pads and their Moleskine notebooks into their tote-bags and satchels.

He picked up his Coca-Cola bottle from under the chair, checking that the lid was tightened, and then he crushed *Ryzo* into the back pocket of his jeans whilst looking at the bin across the room, on the opposite side of the door that Ross and Lauren were leading the class out of.

He wanted to discard the evidence but not at the scene of the crime.

Alex was apologising to a couple of the students who hadn't got the opportunity to showcase their work. He didn't need to explain why, and it hadn't escaped Declan that his performance had been by far the longest of the evening – why didn't someone stop him? He squirmed again, but a few drinks of vodka and lukewarm Coca-Cola in the back seat of an Uber were only minutes away. The negative voices would take a back seat of their own and he could find some temporary solace.

'Oh, we're all going this way then?' he heard Ross announce, through a bellowing, hearty chuckle, seeming to find it genuinely amusing that he'd said goodbye to some of his classmates only to be heading off in the same direction.

'Fuckin' wank,' Declan whispered, for his own entertainment, furtively stepping on to the pavement, relieved that Ross and the rest were walking in the opposite direction to the shop.

He pounded along the road with his head down, looking forward to trying to erase the past two hours from his memory. He entered the shop and grabbed a bottle of Coca-Cola from the fridge and made his way to the counter, studying the different prices of the different sizes of the different bottles of the different spirits, despite knowing exactly what he was going to ask for.

'You know that stuff's no good for ye!' the shopkeeper announced, smiling, the same guy who'd sold him the bottle in his hand. 'Aye,' Declan laughed, 'I might as well take a quarter-bottle of vodka as well then.'

'Why not, pal, life is for livin', eh,' the shopkeeper replied, surveying the shelves behind him and repeating 'quarter-bottle, quarter-bottle' with the emphasis on quarter, implying that he didn't sell many of them. It was a nice enough part of the city, Declan thought, hesitating to specify 'Glen's vodka' but confident that it would be the only one the shop sold by the 200ml volume.

'That's the only quarter-bottles I've got,' the shopkeeper

said, nodding to the bottle that he held with only his index finger and his thumb, the label facing Declan, awaiting his inspection and confirming his premonition. 'Ideal,' Declan said, whilst the shopkeeper went for the up-sell. 'I've got half-bottles of Smirnoff and full bottles of some other one, that Grey Goose, I think.' Declan rolled his eyes at the shopkeeper's turned back – wanting out of the shop, fearing the arrival of someone from his class – as he watched him study the labels of the spirits that he stocked, as though it was the first time that he'd ever paid them any attention.

It's only for a quick dunt to catch up with whoever's in the pub, mate – an equaliser – Declan thought, telling the shopkeeper, 'No, that's fine', and holding his debit card out in front of him, waiting to be presented with the machine.

'Do you need a bag?' the shopkeeper asked, knowing the answer, but it was something to say whilst they waited on Declan's card processing.

Declan shook his head and placed the bottle in his jacket pocket.

'That's you, pal, take care.'

'Cheers, mate,' Declan said, pulling the shop door open with his left hand and reaching into his jacket pocket, for his phone, with the other.

His Uber app confirmed with him that Filip would be arriving, in a Skoda Octavia, in three minutes, which was sooner than expected, he thought, diving to the side of the shop, substituting his phone for his quarter-bottle of Glen's, clicking it open and pouring a generous measure on top of the tepid Coke that he'd brought to the class.

He then opened the fresh bottle, pouring some on the ground and pouring some into the other bottle, to try and take some of the sting out of his potent double, maybe even triple, vodka. He filled the fresh Coke bottle with vodka and, noticing there was some left, took a sip from the room-temperature bottle, to clear space.

His head immediately turned warm and he felt his whole body contract, his mouth and eyes opened as wide as they could, and he let out a liberating 'wah!' noise, like he'd just executed a karate move.

He ditched the empty quarter-bottle into the bin outside the shop, which must have been emptied recently, judging by the satisfying crash of the glass bottle hitting the bottom.

He took a quick scan of the main road, towards the arts centre, making sure there were no stragglers approaching that he'd have to exchange awkward pleasantries with. He'd have to talk in his class voice too – fuck that, fucking idiots, he thought, taking another sip, this time from his new Coke bottle, which was chilled but even stronger than the first. He shook his head again, closing his eyes until the shudder had passed through him. He tightened the lid of both bottles and placed one in each of his jacket's side pockets, taking out his phone to see a message from Filip saying that he'd arrived.

He walked along the pavement a little, in the direction of the arts centre, just as he heard a single toot of a horn. He looked over the road and saw the car pulling up and its hazard lights reflecting off the window of a closed estate agent's. Filip had been a tad premature in confirming his arrival, but it didn't matter, he was out of here.

He slid his phone into the front pocket of his jeans, before remembering that he should text his mum, who'd probably be expecting him home in about half an hour.

He rapidly composed a text, checking through the windscreen as the car pulled away, and then checking Filip's Google map, displayed on the phone in the corner of his dashboard, making sure they were headed in the right direction to the right location.

He let his mum know that the writing class had gone well again, and that he was going out for a drink with a few people from the class. He'd fulfilled the last of his duties for the evening, his class was done, his mum could sleep easy, and he could now step down and surrender himself to the power of alcohol.

He knew his mum would like the idea of him hanging about with – well, 'socialising' with – creative types, people who were intelligent and well-to-do. She took comfort in the fact that very few people got beaten up or stabbed in arts centres, on Tuesday nights, so this was one night she didn't overly worry about her son.

His Coke bottle opened with a pop, which made Filip look into his mirror, smiling. 'Is that ok?' Declan asked, pulling the bottle back from his lips, holding it up for Filip to see, as though the label provided full disclosure of the contents.

Filip laughed – in polite approval – seemingly aware that his passenger's pre-purchased, in-car refreshments contained alcohol, even complimenting the proactive ingenuity when Declan explained that he had to catch up with his mates, who would already be 'Very drunk, very drunk. In the pub. Watching the football.'

'Of course!' the driver laughed, as Declan turned to the window, taking the largest gulp yet from one of his bottles, noticing he was already desensitising to the strength. He enjoyed the cooling sensation of the car's window on the side of his forehead, which was now radiating warmth from the vodka.

He knew they would pass his house on the way to the pub and that he could ask Filip just to drop him home, a sensible suggestion but one that another sip from the bottle dealt with easily, sending that part of his brain retreating, its hands up in submission, aware that it wouldn't be needed for the rest of the evening, but that it would be putting in a solid shift tomorrow.

He knew already what kind of drunk he was going to be – frustrated, angry and sad – but, still, it would feel better than being sober and frustrated, angry and sad.

A couple of clicks of his thumbs and a short, few minutes' wait, that's how easy it was to go from the arts centre to the pub – to go from the creatives, the thespians and the budding artists to the hard-luck stories, the alcoholics and the felons. Declan rolled his eyes, bored at himself and abandoning the process of trying to formulate some sort of metaphor out of this.

He looked at his first bottle of Coke, studying it before throwing the rest back in one go, condemning the night to its fate.

At least he'd tried, he thought – rewarding himself by taking the first gulp from his second Coke bottle – he could spend his years in the pub now with everyone else who believed that they too had tried. He could join the support networks and drink and discredit the success stories of the area's modest-sized list of alumni who'd made something of themselves.

A few professional footballers would get it. 'I played against him in an under-sixteens game, he never got near me. Four-two we won; I scored a header. Now he's on twenty grand a week?!' Then there was James Cavani, actor, writer and director.

'His new movie looks shite anyway. He's stole a living. I haven't watched his Netflix thing yet but I've heard I'm not missing much.'

Declan had read James Cavani's autobiography and enjoyed his story.

It was surreal to see his school spoken about, their local shopping centre, swimming baths and other places that had since closed down but that he'd heard people go on about.

He'd spoken to people who grew up with James Cavani, older guys. Most of them claimed to have been his best pal at some point, but when fame came calling, he'd ditched them. They spoke as if he owed them something, money or a staggering fall from grace; a return to the pack.

Doof Doof had met him though, and he'd tell the story every time James Cavani appeared on the screen when Declan, Connor, Connor's older brother and whoever else were sat in his flat, smoking weed and watching films, or if his name came up in conversation.

Doof Doof had about five or six hits in his set list but his James Cavani story was one of his favourites. He could be a bit of a fantasist – he was the victim of too many great weekends, during his teens and early twenties – but he did have a non-fiction section.

Declan was the only one who'd still pay attention, in part because he hadn't known Doof Doof as long as Connor and his older brother, his friend since they'd started primary school in the early nineties, so he felt obliged to be courteous and attentive when he was talking, especially when Declan was a guest in his flat.

That Declan enjoyed watching the evolution of Doof Doof's stories also helped though.

He'd always known of Doof Doof but only as Connor's big brother's pal, the one who used to be a raver, his onomatopoeic nickname deriving from his penchant for blasting bass-heavy techno music from his flat.

Declan had accompanied Connor to his flat a couple of times over the years when they were buying some weed. Their friend Jordan would come too, before he'd progressed on to cocaine and the scene and the crowd that comes along with it. He'd developed a borderline alarming habit and was said to have begun selling it in and around the area, Connor had told Declan.

Doof Doof had asked about Jordan a few times, sensing that Declan and Connor no longer hung around with him. Declan sensed that Doof Doof had never quite taken to Jordan – not that he'd ever say anything though – and he knew first hand that Jordan saw Doof Doof as a loser or a weirdo or whatever else.

Doof Doof, like Declan, was a keen reader, which was a key factor in their ever-strengthening friendship. Declan thought of a night in Doof Doof's house, when *Question Time* or some other current affairs show had been on, whilst everyone sat, their heads distracted, fearful of checking the time and trying not to contemplate the following day at work – or college, in Declan's case. Doof Doof had announced to his lethargic late-evening living room that the proletariat needed to 'remove the adjectives and they'd get the facts'.

Only Declan understood that he'd meant it as a reference to demagogic politicians and their glib rhetoric, and recognised that he'd paraphrased a quote from *To Kill a Mockingbird*.

'Atticus Finch,' Declan had said, nodding, confusing Connor and Connor's brother even further and cementing their decision that it was home time.

Declan remembered this had earned him a respectful 'What's your name again, wee man?' from Doof Doof on the way out.

This was always a good feeling as an insecure adolescent, when something you'd said or done had impressed a senior figure enough for them to deem you worthy of a fresh introduction, having previously presumed you to be just another wee dick.

James Cavani's appearance was the most exciting thing, by quite some distance, that had ever happened in Doof Doof's decade-long tenure as a greenskeeper at the local municipal golf course.

The component consistent in every telling of the story was that James Cavani had been directing a scene which, to the best of Doof Doof's knowledge, had never featured in anything that he or anyone he'd asked had seen.

A local council boss had been liaising with the production crew and Doof Doof and a couple of his co-workers were briefed that filming would be taking place and that they were to carry on with their jobs as normal. There were a few release forms to be signed, requesting consent, in case any of them made it on to camera.

Doof Doof even ironed a fresh council polo shirt for the day and got a haircut especially. If the camera caught him at work, he wanted to look his sharpest, he'd admitted.

James Cavani's work tended to be quite edgy 'gritty dramas' and 'dark comedies', to use blanket, synopsis terminology. He'd acted in a few bigger-budget films, but anything he'd written and directed himself had more of an underground feel to it, so the location of the filming made sense. Doof Doof's municipal golf course was a hive of illicit activity, from substance abuse to underage drinking to more serious, violent crimes.

The lack of surveillance and the vast woodlands that segregated the fairways, along with the access road that ran from the car park below three hostile-looking high-rise flats made it a desirable location for local gangland figures looking to issue reminders of any outstanding payments, or whatever.

Doof Doof had found weapons before – a baseball bat that had broken in two, in his hands, when he'd picked it up, to put it in the bin bag on the back of his buggy. He'd said he'd remembered feeling nauseous, as he imagined how hard the final blow must have landed to have snapped the bat itself. On two other occasions he'd found ceramic kitchen knives, one of them with a blade he'd said must have been about twelve inches long.

After a few hours, Doof Doof had said, word must have got out that James Cavani was home and in town filming. A golfer or a dog walker had put it on Facebook, or something.

Doof Doof said James Cavani had been patient with the small crowd as they trickled across the fairways, congregating at the light rough on the edge of the seventh tee that led into the trees where Doof Doof had found the smaller of the two kitchen knives.

It was there that cameras were positioned and a few Portakabins – trailers, they were maybe known as, but they hadn't looked like the ones you'd hear actors talking about on chat shows or journalists describing when interviewing the stars of an upcoming release. Doof Doof said the Portakabins were similar in size and design to the ones that you'd give blood in or the little mobile library that used to come to their local shopping centre every couple of weeks.

The lack of luxury didn't bother anyone, not even Cavani, according to Doof Doof, and the set was frantic with energy, with people looking at monitors and making notes, huddled together, confiding.

There were make-up artists walking around, revealing who the actors were, as no one out of the entire crew stood out as obvious stars. He didn't recognise anyone from anything that he'd seen before and neither did the crowd, which meant James Cavani was assigned a solo mission to placate their need for autographs and selfies and to record videos saying happy birthday and get well soon, or to quote his lines from his more mainstream movie work, for their friends and relatives who were his 'biggest fans' and who 'wouldn't believe' this chance encounter.

It was all fine and both parties seemed content from what Doof Doof could observe, and it was only when Cavani and another guy had announced that the scene was to begin rehearsing that one of the production crew had alerted him to a small group of teenagers who'd been hanging around and who'd started filming on their phones.

Cavani himself walked over to ask politely if they wouldn't mind putting their phones away. They all agreed that they would and, after posing for a few more photos, he walked back to where he'd been set up to watch the scene, only for one of the wee guys to pull his phone out again, holding it up in the air and facing it, shouting 'I'm gonny be famous' or 'I'm gonny be on the telly' or something.

Doof Doof said James Cavani became a different guy. He slammed his bottle of water down on the grass and the notes he'd been holding blew everywhere, prompting one of the crew to scramble about trying to gather the individual sheets of what was presumably the script.

He started walking back towards the wee guys. Doof Doof said he looked furious, like characters he'd played on screen before. Doof Doof thought he was about to witness the latest celebrity scandal, in real time, live from his work: 'Movie star James Cavani boots a wee guy up and doon a golf course' was Doof Doof's imagined headline, Declan remembered, from the most recent version of his James Cavani story.

It had amused Declan as he contemplated that, in his local vernacular, the word 'wee' could often be a reference to age rather than size. Declan had thought of how to concisely articulate what Doof Doof meant – somewhere between the teenage years and adulthood is a 'wee guy' phase. Too old to back down from a reprimanding elder and to be content simply with the thrill of running away, of being chased – but, sadly, too young to be jabbed.

James Cavani must have reminded himself of this – Doof Doof would tell of how the initial fury in his walk dissipated with every step he took towards them – just another grown man realising that he's, ultimately, powerless to resolve a confrontation with obnoxious wee guys.

Doof Doof had watched as this predicament registered on James Cavani's face and he'd walked over himself, with the naïve notion that his council polo shirt would carry some authority and that he could spare Cavani the tense, futile, unwinnable stand-off with the defiance of youth, and, most importantly, restore some order to his fairways.

Doof Doof said his intervention had only made things turn aggressive, and the smallest of the wee guys started verbally abusing and then threatening him – 'lanky bastard', 'skinny prick' . . . The standard stuff – Doof Doof had an appalling diet though, maybe even worse than Declan's. Declan put their weight difference down to some genetic injustice as he probably expended as much energy – probably more – unloading lorries and stacking shelves as Doof Doof did during his shifts on the golf course.

The smallest and mouthiest wee guy – no doubt unaware that he was conforming to a cliché – had moved from the physical to the socio-economic and had started taunting Doof Doof about his presumed low income: 'This bike's worth more than you make in a month', which was new, a generational thing maybe, Doof Doof had surmised.

It was then that James Cavani told him to fuck off and

threatened to throw his bike in the burn. Which rattled the little prick, Doof Doof had said, as though James Cavani had leaped out of a television screen to put him in his place.

Doof Doof, who'd confessed to having been starstruck himself, always got passionate at this part of the story – he'd felt humbled that someone as well known, revered and acclaimed as James Cavani had stood up for him, even if it was only against a wee guy, a wee prick.

'His dad's Eddie Reynolds,' one of them was shouting. Eddie Reynolds was a serious name, not one anyone used liberally – the folly of youth was at play in this case – and even the apparent Reynolds junior shot his pal a cautionary glance before straightening the handlebars of his bike in preparation for their departure.

Eddie Reynolds was a notorious gangster – a drug dealer and all the rest of it – a man who headed up his own criminal empire, or as close as the area got to one.

Everyone in the area had their own stories about Eddie Reynolds. Some were true and some had been cut and mixed with as much shite as the cocaine and heroin that Reynolds and his associates flooded the streets with.

'I'm going to the papers about that,' the one wee guy who had yet to speak shouted, directly to James Cavani. Doof Doof mentioned how this had made all of their faces light up, excited, like this was a more pertinent threat than name dropping a notorious career criminal.

'One minute yer gangsters, next yer grasses, eh? Get tae fuck,' Cavani snapped, before walking back to one of the Portakabins as the wee guys left, shouting and laughing at

32

him, eager to update their social media friends and followers on their afternoon run-in with a celebrity.

Doof Doof said Cavani looked gutted, not even that angry, just despondent, and that he'd felt sorry for him, the way council workers aren't supposed to feel sorry for multi-millionaire celebrities.

Only Doof Doof and the crew member of Cavani's had been close enough to hear the entire exchange, so the crowd were confused but aware something had gone on. A few of them shouted encouragement and some were disappointed not to be seeing a scene getting filmed – they hadn't paid for or been promised anything but felt short-changed and let down.

A guy who'd got a selfie shouted to Cavani that he'd acted like a 'diva' and told him to remember where he came from. Doof Doof confessed that if he hadn't witnessed the entire episode, he'd also have assumed the narrative of the big-time film star, having a petulant hissy fit with local kids, from the area he grew up in, but this was a lesson, he supposed.

Doof Doof told of how a few of the crowd stuck around, a few left and a few new faces arrived. He continued with his work – altering pin positions, cutting grass, raking bunkers – but he'd kept looking over at what still looked like a set, to see if anything would be filmed.

After about an hour Doof Doof noticed a guy who was with the film crew approaching his buggy, which prompted him to take three or four rapid draws of his joint before flicking it into the long grass behind him and stepping on to the fairway to meet him.

The guy told him that James Cavani would like to speak to him, when he had a minute.

This was a sentence Doof Doof never expected to hear in his life.

Doof Doof had jokingly nodded at his buggy, asking if the guy wanted a lift. He smiled and they walked back towards the set.

He admitted that he'd felt paranoid that he was stinking of cannabis, but he knew that James Cavani was supposed to be a bit mental and that he wouldn't mind.

When they got to the set Cavani was leaning against a table and blowing into a polystyrene cup, trying to cool its contents, and laughing and joking with two guys who were sitting on two camping chairs, eating.

He had a new energy about him and seemed to have composed himself, and when he saw Doof Doof, he carefully sat his cup down on the grass and put his hand out.

'Mate, I just want to say thanks for earlier and sorry if I was a bit off, this thing is sending me fucking bonkers. I'm James, what's your name?'

Doof Doof said he'd felt nervous, he'd never even seen anyone famous in the flesh until this day, which was why he had hesitated between the formal and the informal, between Raymond and Doof Doof, but he'd decided it would be respectful to give his real name and it would spare him having to tell the story of how he used to be a bit of a raver. He was far enough out of his comfort zone and the half-joint he'd just smoked hadn't done him any favours, so being put on the spot and having to explain the origins of his nickname was the last thing he needed.

He explained that Cavani had an aura but he was also disarming, and as they began talking Doof Doof wanted to correct him every time he'd said Raymond. It seemed unnatural and it made him think of his late mum or his bosses, or the police, or any other authority figures.

Doof Doof commented that the only thing that stood out about Cavani was how healthy he looked. This was to be expected: women loved him, he was in his mid-forties but he looked like he'd only been a couple of years above Declan at school, he had tanned skin, dark hair and a sharp, well-defined jawline – his Italian roots providing strong insurance against his west of Scotland upbringing.

'Not much changes about here, eh? Eddie Reynolds . . . His son seems a lovely wee guy.'

Doof Doof had laughed and said, 'Tell me about it' or something like that, something he'd never said before, admitting that he'd felt like a dick as soon as the words left his mouth, as though he was trying to get into the character of 'Raymond'.

Declan always enjoyed Doof Doof's self-deprecation and he continued on the theme, confessing that he'd said, 'Do you know him?' As though Eddie Reynolds was a big name himself, of all the A-listers to ask James Cavani if he knew, he'd asked about a local crook.

Cavani didn't mind though – he was probably enjoying the break from conversations about showbusiness, Doof Doof figured.

'Same school, same classes. He went out with my sister for a while – dumping him was the only smart decision she ever made.' Cavani had laughed, adding, 'He wanted me to write a film about his life. They love all that.' Doof Doof had nodded, struggling to think of what to say, but he'd been relieved that his question was being answered and not ridiculed. Cavani had taken a cautious sip of his coffee before continuing.

'How the fuck do you pitch that? – Well, it's like *Goodfellas* but it's a Scottish remake – *"As far back as I can remember, I always wanted to be a bit of a dodgy cunt."* Scottish *Goodfellas*, write that down, BBC Scotland will be well up for it.'

Cavani had laughed again, shouting across to the guy who'd come over to meet Doof Doof.

It was true though, Declan thought to himself – lifting his head off the window of Filip's car, noticing that they were approaching the street where James Cavani grew up – that for all the great movies and series made about organised crime and gangsters, when it was real life and close to home, and the carefully curated charm of the paradoxical characters and the glamour and appeal of the lifestyle were stripped away, it was depressing, and fucking boring.

Declan thought of Jordan and how he'd apparently got himself involved with these sorts of people, albeit the lower echelons. He'd always been impressionable and loved anyone who was popular, for whatever reason, and he'd do anything to hang around with them.

Connor had recently sent Declan a video of Jordan slapping himself in the face, in someone's living room, as an older crowd shouted for him to put more force into it, finding it hysterical. Declan and Connor hadn't told Jordan that they had seen the video and that they'd found it alarming, and sad above all – as much as Jordan was turning into a dickhead, he was still, in theory, their friend and it was sad to see videos of anyone being degraded like that.

They figured he would have mentioned it first, seeing as it was widely circulated, but he never did. His pride probably wouldn't let him. He saw Declan and Connor as beneath him now anyway, and the last people who he'd want to concede his vulnerability to.

Declan and Jordan had known each other since they were toddlers, their mothers being close friends, but Declan had felt them growing apart for a while now – all they had in common was the past. If they'd only just met now, at twenty-four years old, then they probably wouldn't have become friends, Declan had hypothesised and made peace with this inevitable part of life – people change, and you change.

Doof Doof always wrapped up his James Cavani story by telling of how Cavani had told him to help himself to the spread that the catering team had put out for the crew's lunch. Doof Doof initially declined, he said, his manners overruling his appetite, but Cavani insisted, commenting on the smell of cannabis and laughing and telling him to try a donut, that it would be all going to waste anyway.

He told Doof Doof they were going to go again and try and get the scene done and asked if he wanted to be in it. Doof Doof declined, horrified at the prospect of seeing himself on screen, regardless of his new haircut and fresh polo shirt.

They shook hands. 'Nice to meet you Raymond and cheers for having our back over there earlier.'

Doof Doof told him he didn't want to bother him for a photo – as a way of asking him for a photo – and one of the crew took one of them together, after an initial struggle with operating the camera on Doof Doof's relic of a phone. A phone that had only recently been put out of its misery, the photo of Doof Doof and James Cavani along with it.

It had stuck with Doof Doof and subsequently Declan – who knew the story verbatim – how normal Cavani had been, how he was authentic, a human being.

His parents had passed away and the only family connection he had to the place was his younger sister, Siobhan, who was a recovering heroin addict and had lived in their childhood home until recently. She'd been seen around the shopping centre a few times, Doof Doof said, so she couldn't have moved too far away. James Cavani didn't mention her much in his book, Declan noticed, but everyone in the town knew about her and Declan had seen her around.

Siobhan Cavani had been a few years above Doof Doof at high school, and by his and several other accounts she'd been incredibly good-looking – everyone fancied her, and if it had been an American high school, like in a movie, Doof Doof had once explained, she'd have been the undisputed prom queen. Despite all her troubles and how her life had turned out, Doof Doof said that hearing her full name still brought back the nostalgic connotations of his youth and the feeling of first realising that you fancied someone, his first 'crush' as he put it, unsure if 'the kids' still said that now.

Cavani had a house in Glasgow, but he'd stated before that he preferred the relative anonymity of living in London, and occasionally New York – cities where people were too caught up in their own thing to care about anyone else.

The one certain truth Declan took from the autobiography, and from Doof Doof's and other locally sourced James Cavani stories, was that it sounded shite to be famous – at least when it began to interfere with the work that made you famous in the first place. But away from all of that side, what inspired Declan and drew him to the world of creative writing was how incredible Cavani made it sound to be able to turn your own ideas, thoughts, experiences, and your fears and neuroses, into content that so many people enjoyed and connected with.

Declan thought of the fulfilment of seeing something you'd once scribbled down on a scrap bit of paper or a bus or train ticket become the basis of an award-winning film, or to have millions of people watch the finale of a drama series that had brought you close to insanity with writer's block, before the answer came to you in the shower and you manically used your finger to write the buzzwords in the condensation of the bathroom mirror, petrified of the solution tormenting you further by not hanging around in your mind long enough for the appropriate stationery to be procured. He remembered finding Cavani's stories like these in the autobiography nothing short of exhilarating, and it was in these moments that Cavani said he came alive. Chasing those feelings of fulfilment – and escapism – was, Declan figured, what made him so prolific and devoted to his work.

Declan had tried and it wasn't for him. 'Thanks, mate,' he announced to Filip as he stepped on to the pavement. 'It was nice to meet you,' he added, leaning back inside the car with his thumb in the air – as though their initial good-natured conversation had been sustained for the duration of the journey.

He felt a buzzing sound in his ears and his eyes squinted as the glow from the vodka was introduced to the fresh evening air, the street lights and the neon sign from the sunbed salon opposite the pub.

There was still time to abandon his plan, he could still walk home and grab something from one of the takeaways en route. He looked at the pub again, trying to gauge how busy it was, watching as the bar door opened and a man with a cigarette in his mouth stepped outside on to the pavement, playing with his phone before feeling around his tracksuit pockets for a lighter.

'Fuck it,' he whispered, hearing the sound of the back door of Filip's Skoda Octavia slam shut as he crossed the road, back to the life that wouldn't be going anywhere, that would always be there waiting for him – to the life he'd thought he could have done better than, the voice in his head sneered, a defiant reminder that it needed more than a quarter-bottle of vodka to be silenced, especially after tonight, especially after everything.

His strides towards the pub lengthened and he opened the door to the sound of an advert playing on the televisions, confirming that the football had finished and that he was here with the sole intention of obliterating the evening from his mind, along with all the, by now familiar, feelings of being totally fucking lost which it had evoked – and the fresh feelings of hopelessness too, now that his writing dream, or whatever it had been, had taken a bullet straight to the head.

He'd given these feelings and the voice that spoke to him on their behalf an evening to remember, and it could probably still get worse, but at least the alcohol could take him away somewhere, distracting him whilst the rest of the damage was done.

He hurried himself straight to the bar, aware that a pint would disable the alarm that rang inside his head, telling him that he should have gone home, that he was drinking for all the wrong reasons.

'What is this, a nightclub?' Georgie looked at her watch, smiling.

Declan forced himself to try and smile back as he leaned himself over the bar, using his left hand to steady the bar stool that his thighs had knocked off balance and looking to the selection of draught lager pumps to allow his head to go over the final checks of his alibi as to where he'd been all night.

'I was out with a few people from my college class,' he told Georgie, surprised at how slurred his speech already sounded and at how he'd made a perfectly plausible explanation for his late arrival sound so doubtful.

He was relieved that she'd let the subject pass, that she hadn't asked where he'd gone with his college pals: she knew the city centre well and she was always recommending good pubs and music venues. She was a student herself – a real student – at the university across the road from his college building, the one that Declan could have gone to if he'd applied himself at school, if he had fulfilled his academic potential . . . Aw, so fuck, he thought, desperate now for his head to be unplugged at the mains, wishing, for the first time, that it was someone other than Georgie serving him, so he could order himself a vodka and Coke too.

'Ah, fuck.' He pushed himself back off the bar, standing up straight, placing his hands on their corresponding shoulders as he looked from left to right, at the wet patches on the sleeves of his jumper.

'Aw aye, don't lean there, it's wet,' Georgie said, her face encouraging him to laugh and join her in a sincere smile this time. Declan shook his head, his face stretched tight from what he hoped passed for a smile as he nodded to Georgie, who held an empty pint glass under the Heineken tap awaiting his confirmation.

'You should sit up on the bar stool, complete the burned-out American police detective look.' Georgie winked, tipping some froth out of a frosted-looking pint glass and topping it back up. The wink confirmed that she was aware that there was something bothering Declan and that she was only trying to cheer him up, that she hoped he was all right.

Declan appreciated this, wishing he'd had something witty to say back to her joke, to riff like they usually did. But for everything he thought of there was a feral pack of savage negative thoughts waiting to pounce and rip it apart, that critical voice which was always on guard, ready to take aim at anything upbeat or positive that dared trespass through his head.

'Doof Doof's still here somewhere,' Georgie said, bailing Declan out just before the silence became uncomfortable and would need to be addressed, which could easily result in Declan having to admit that there was something wrong but he didn't have a fucking clue what exactly it was. Maybe it was nothing, maybe it was everything.

'The lounge is like the Bada-Bing.' Georgie nodded to her right. 'A lot of fake teeth and Hugo Boss.'

Declan laughed, repeating Georgie's line in his head. 'They

were all in for dinner, your pals there, Jordan Langford, it was his treat.' Her eyes rolled, acknowledging that she'd noticed Declan wasn't in the pub with Jordan as much nowadays and that Jordan preferred the company of drug dealers over his lifelong pals. The drug dealers probably enjoyed his company too, or at least exploiting his sycophantic nature.

'Fucking muppet.' Declan tried to roll his eyes too, like he cared about anything other than the immaculate-looking ice-cold pint that Georgie placed in front of him – it was one that deserved to have its photograph taken but aesthetics were irrelevant tonight.

'Cheers,' Declan said, feeling himself come alive again after the first gulp.

Georgie checked over her shoulder to make sure no one was watching, forcing her forehead into a cartoon frown at Declan to put his debit card away.

'Naw, don't be daft, please . . .' Declan tried to put some energy behind his protest before shaking his head in a grateful surrender.

'Shut it.' Georgie smiled again.

Using the railing at the bottom of the bar, Declan lifted himself on to the bar stool, embracing Georgie's suggested burned-out American police detective look as he wondered who else was in the pub – he hadn't bothered to check his surrounds, the procurement of a pint having been assigned priority over any parochial small talk.

Anyone who knew him would recognise him from behind, he figured, wondering where Doof Doof was, and if he'd maybe just missed him.

'Thanks, man,' Declan said, making a conscious effort to take a more elegant second sip of his immaculate Heineken, to look as though the lager was being savoured, that his palate was being considered and that there was a sociable element to his visit.

'You're welcome, man.' Georgie mimicked the stress in his voice, which made him laugh, his real laugh, the one that let a warm smile take control of his face. It was the first time he'd felt this smile all night, all day, probably even yesterday too. Fuck knows.

It was a nice feeling. He recognised it as the way he usually felt when the pub wasn't all that busy and he'd get some time to speak to Georgie and it was like nothing else was happening – either in his head, or anywhere else – when he'd felt like he could talk to her for hours. They always seemed to laugh at the same things and they were always recommending bands and films and shows for each other to watch – they were on each other's list of reliable sources when it came to endorsing a series to commit to in the saturated world of streamable entertainment.

Declan had thought of asking her out – not even on a date or anything, but he would have enjoyed spending more time in her company, especially away from the pub, which was, ultimately, her workplace.

He had been reminded by everyone who'd noticed the rapport – or whatever – between them that she was out of his league or that she was gay. The latter rumour could perhaps be attributed to the resident drunken creeps who she easily put down with her dry and sometimes cutting sense of humour.

Declan didn't know if she was gay but he did know it wasn't any of his business, and that if she was straight, she could do a lot better than him. But in his more confident moments he'd often thought about the two of them together, just talking and laughing.

He sipped his pint again, hoping that those confident moments weren't gone for ever.

He felt himself squirm at the delusional thoughts of them ever being a couple as he glanced over at her scribbling something in a notebook. She didn't just look beautiful but cool as fuck – assured. It was a different kind of beautiful, the kind only possessed by someone who seemed like they belonged bang in the centre of themselves.

Doof Doof had told him to go for it a few times, to ask her out, to find a gig that was coming up or something, but he'd always found a way of changing the subject.

It was fucked now though, he reminded himself as Georgie was walking back over to him, prompting him to alter the angle at which his pint glass met his mouth so that it was a few degrees more civilised. Georgie smiled, handing him some blue roll for his sleeves which he declined with his eyes, placing his pint on the bar, coughing on his lager and wiping his mouth as she turned her back, to look occupied, to give him his dignity during his spluttering fit. 'Na, it's all right. Cheers though,' he answered, rolling his sleeves up so that the wet patches were hidden.

'I've got something for you – another record – if you still use your player.' Georgie smiled, spraying and wiping the bar top.

'Aye, still use it, aye, brilliant, thanks, man.' Declan realised he'd said 'man' again. 'I don't mean "man", man – fuck sake, I've said it again.' He laughed, the worst laugh yet, insincere, forced – angry, false, pathetic, sad. He took a nervous mouthful of his pint and jammed his eyes shut, firing a fuck off into the ceiling of his head.

'It's in the back but I'll bring it over before I finish.' Georgie smiled, overlooking the flustered mess Declan had got himself into.

Declan threw another mouthful of his pint into him, noticing that he had just under half of it left as Georgie wandered over to the staff door that separated the lounge from the bar, to help a guy in chef whites fill out a form.

'There he is!' He turned to look over his right shoulder that had just been gently massaged, turning back as Doof Doof appeared on his left.

'Sleeves rolled up already, man, you in lookin' for a scrap?' Doof Doof looked behind the bar for Georgie or another member of staff.

Declan jumped on the opportunity to try to empty the rest of his pint into him, sensing that if Doof Doof had been about to go home he would now stay for at least one, so it was an astute tactical move to synchronise their drinking, so that they'd go into a round and he'd have someone to drink with for at least two more pints.

'Two Heineken, please, mate,' Doof Doof announced to an older guy that Declan had never seen working before and that Doof Doof didn't seem to know either.

'I was out with a few people from my college class, just thought I'd come in and see if you were about,' Declan began, exculpating himself before Doof Doof had a chance to ask where he'd been and why he'd come to the pub so late.

Declan turned round to feel Doof Doof examining him, probably sensing, like Georgie, that he wasn't really himself.

'That wee Jordan is next door – him and a few unsavoury characters.'

Doof Doof accompanied his word choice and the middle-class accent he'd used with a laugh, checking Declan over again, wondering if there was something he wanted to tell him.

'Aye? Who?' Declan asked, taken aback by the confrontation in his tone.

'Just all the usual, man.' Doof Doof looked around the bar, almost whispering as he relayed a menacing-sounding team sheet.

'The two Keoghs, Gary Tanser and that Barry Merson, no fucking about, man. They were in for food, celebrating something, fuck knows. I was only in quickly to see wee Connor and Nicole – you've not long missed them, they were in for food too. That wee Jordan pretty much blanked him. A shame, man.'

Declan watched as Doof Doof went into his pocket and removed a ten-pound note from the grips of a twenty and placed it on the bar, collecting the two pints and nodding towards a table in the corner beside the door where he'd sequestered himself.

'Are ye sure ye don't want another one?' Doof Doof asked, his voice calm and polite as he stood over an old man who was sat underneath a television that showed a replay of a goal which Declan pretended to take an interest in as he took the first drink of the evening's second pint. The old man thanked

Doof Doof, telling both him and Declan that he was fine and that he was heading off after he'd finished what looked like a whisky, joking that it was long past his bedtime.

Declan took a seat, watching Doof Doof remove the cellophane from a fresh pack of Marlboro Red as the old man picked up on a conversation they must have been having before Declan had arrived, before, Declan presumed, Doof Doof had run out of cigarettes and gone across the road to the garage.

The old man must have recognised Doof Doof from the golf course, as he made a joke towards Declan about the greens being to blame for why he no longer played. Declan smiled, looking for Doof Doof to return a good-natured comment, grateful for the distraction as he thought of Jordan blanking Connor, wondering if he'd blank him too, processing the full extent of Jordan's transition into a drug dealer or a gangster or whatever he'd like to be known as.

Declan didn't know the people he was going around with, only the names and the reputations and, in Barry Merson's case, the face. The Keoghs were twins who were probably slightly younger than Connor's brother and Doof Doof.

They ran a café, a few sunbed salons, dessert and ice cream parlours – the usual shite – but their primary source of income was, clearly, the selling of illegal drugs as part of the wider Eddie Reynolds empire. Gary Tanser was in Doof Doof's year at school. Doof Doof didn't have many dealings with him but he had mentioned that he was a bully, that he abused his reputation as being the best fighter. A made man all through his teenage years – the first to drink alcohol, the first to smoke, the first to have sex – he'd become all he was ever going to be by the time he was sixteen, one of those poor pricks who found their optimum age far too early. His adult life was merely a continuation of school. He was feared locally so that's where he would stay, but maybe one day it would all catch up on him and the real world would introduce itself, catching him untrained and off guard in the same way it did with every other poor prick who didn't anticipate that life would eventually transcend their postcode.

Barry Merson was their boss. He was slightly older and originally from Liverpool – he had a strong scouse accent but he'd lived here for years. He was the only one Declan had ever spoken to on one of his first ever times in the pub – he'd been shouting at the television when Everton were playing and then celebrating when they'd scored a last-minute equaliser.

Declan, who was sitting on a chair that touched the back of his, in his innocence, had commented, over his shoulder, as a replay was shown, that there had been a foul in the build-up to the goal.

He remembered Connor booting him under the table and Jordan – who hadn't looked up from his phone for the entire game – shouting that there was no way it was a foul, and that Declan was a dick, whilst looking at the back of Barry Merson's head, hopeful of his approval.

'Clear as day a foul that, lad, but we'll take all the luck we can get,' Merson had replied, turning himself round fully, like he'd appreciated that someone else in the pub had at least taken an interest in the game. Declan, who'd been confused at the change in Connor and Jordan's behaviour, laughed and said something like 'Exactly, mate' or 'That's it, mate', hoping that any potential conversation would be halted, turning back to face the two of them, curious about what was going on.

They both got busy typing on their phones and Declan felt his vibrate in his pocket as they placed theirs on the table and looked up at the television, which was Declan's cue to check his messages. He'd picked up his phone and begun reading, feeling like he'd clicked on Barry Merson's Wikipedia page – discovering that he used to be a boxer but his career was cut short after he'd done jail time in Liverpool for possession of firearms 'or something like that' Connor's version went, whilst Jordan had gone for the hyperbolic – citation required – 'AK-47s in his boot, the fuckin lot'.

He now lived up here, where he worked for Eddie Reynolds – who he'd known for nearly twenty years and had been best man at his wedding – as an enforcer type and ran a few of his larger businesses: a nightclub, a security company, that sort of thing. Jordan had detailed some of the punishments and warnings he was said to have given out to people, faces slashed, legs broken and then eyes gouged out, fingers and ears cut off, the standard stuff that people like Jordan seemed to get a buzz out of making up, or at least embellishing and passing on, Declan remembered thinking.

He'd shrugged his shoulders and pulled his chair in slightly, to avoid it hitting off Merson's again, as it had done a couple of times, when he'd got up to go to the bar or toilet. He appreciated the heads up, despite doubting whether it had been necessary, sceptical about there ever being violent gang-land retributions carried out on a guy from the pub who'd commented that a last-minute goal had been a tad fortunate and largely down to a refereeing error.

'It was a foul though,' he remembered saying as he put his phone away. Connor had laughed and Jordan had mimed for him to just fucking shut up.

It was obvious, even then, that Jordan dreamed of a 'What's your name again, wee man' from people like this.

Connor, like Declan, was aware that Jordan was growing into someone they barely knew, and it was only time and its memories that bound them. Jordan's relationship with both Declan and Connor had grown undeniably tetchy but it had never escalated into anything other than an unspoken taut-ness when they were together, and they'd both spoken about how uncomfortable it was to be in Jordan's company without someone else present.

It was like they couldn't acknowledge who he thought he was. To them, he was Jordan, their friend since primary school – since nursery, in Declan's case – and despite his efforts to rebrand himself and despite beginning to be known locally as a bit of a shady character – or at least as someone who ran errands for shady characters, an apprentice shady character – Jordan's pseudo-gangster façade wasn't authentic to them. Jordan knew this and it probably frustrated him.

Doof Doof slid himself along his seat, standing up to help the old guy who'd stumbled upon rising to his feet, assisting him with putting his arms into his jacket sleeves as the old man made light of his misstep, assigning dual culpability to his advanced years and his inebriation levels, joking that he couldn't drink like he used to.

Doof Doof leaned over Declan to pick his cigarettes up from the table and, throwing his head back towards the old man, he excused himself and turned to open the bar door with his right hand, the old man thanking him as he made his way outside.

Doof Doof watched him with caution, shuffling behind him with his hands outstretched, poised to pounce on any further staggering.

'Two minutes, man,' Doof Doof told Declan, closing the bar door behind him and stepping on to the pavement alongside the old man.

Declan looked around the bar, feeling his focus drawn towards an old guy who looked well into his seventies, sat closest to the bar, smartly dressed and alone in his own thoughts, his eyes staring at nothing as they pointed to the opposite wall, at the door that led through to the lounge area. The old man looked sad but it was a sadness he seemed comfortable with, a sadness he'd grown used to, maybe even content with.

Aware that he was perhaps being intrusive, Declan looked away, granting the old guy his solitude to take another gentle, unhurried sip of his pint glass, his eyes staying fixed to the wall, where his thoughts had parked them.

Seeing that it was the new guy behind the bar and Georgie was still next door or on a break or getting ready to finish her shift, Declan swung himself out from under the table and walked towards the bar again.

'What kind of shots have you got, mate?' he asked, coughing in acknowledgement of the unnecessary volume at which he'd shouted.

'Just the ones you can see there, pal,' the man answered, looking at Declan, his thumb tilted behind him, to a chalkboard with the names that Declan didn't bother to read.

'I'll just take any two, you decide, four in fact, any four.' Declan nodded to the chalkboard, turning to look over at the door as Doof Doof and the old man walked back in. He looked at Doof Doof's pint glass which had barely been touched and then at his own.

'Same again?' Declan asked – his voice more sensitive to the pub's subdued vibe.

Doof Doof took a large sip of his pint in resigned preparation for the arrival of a fresh one, sitting back down, placing his cigarettes in front of him and watching to make sure the old man got back to his seat all right.

'One for the road,' he answered Declan, shooting him a warning to calm it down.

Declan noticed that the man had already placed two Heineken glasses under the pump. 'What's your name again, mate?' Declan asked, impressed that the rest of his order had been anticipated.

'Kenny,' the man responded, his tone blunted by experience, careful not to overly commit to a conversation with an intoxicated customer, especially one buying shots.

The old guy who'd been staring at the wall was now looking at him. Declan smiled but the old man looked away, taking another sip of his pint.

Fair enough, Declan thought, studying his fairly aggressive drinks order, accepting that he definitely wasn't someone the old guy wanted to end up in a conversation with.

'Brilliant, cheers, mate!' He tapped his card on the reader, grateful to be handed a tray to save him two trips over to Doof Doof.

'Fuck sake, man, that's a disgrace . . . drinkin' primary colours on a Tuesday night,' Doof Doof told Declan, forcing a shot down to appease him, shaking his head and studying his eyes.

The old man who'd been outside smoking with Doof Doof rushed the rest of his whisky back. His advanced years had probably taught him to anticipate danger. He seemed to leap into the air this time, waving to Doof Doof that it was all right, that he needed no assistance.

'I'll catch you, Raymond, son – and thanks for the cigarettes, you're a star.' The old man zipped up his jacket and grabbed Declan's shoulder, making him turn as the old man leaned in. 'You watch yourself, son,' he whispered into Declan's ear. His look to Doof Doof to take care of him – to take him home, probably – wasn't as subtle as he'd intended it to be but Declan appreciated the concern, which was justified, he thought, looking at their table.

'What the fuck, man.' Doof Doof held his palms out as he surveyed the table like he'd been left with no choice but to explicitly ask Declan what was going on, why he seemed so on edge, so distracted, so keen to make the night something that it didn't need to be.

They both looked ahead as the door from the lounge area swung open and Jordan led the way, his head turned as he walked, speaking intently to a man who was playing on his phone, distracted. He looked like a child who'd just been picked up from primary school, excited to be telling their dad every triviality of their day.

Declan recognised Barry Merson and it was fairly obvious who the Keogh twins were, so it must have been Gary Tanser who Jordan was fawning over.

'Just leave him, man.' Doof Doof gave Declan a deterring but friendly glance, nudging his knee under the table.

'Known him for over twenty years, he's my best pal,' Declan answered, lying to himself, looking at Jordan's snapback hat with the word 'ICON' emblazoned across it and then at his skinny-fit jogging bottoms, his immaculate-looking trainers and skin-tight designer shirt that revealed the long hours spent in the gym, working on the vanity muscles.

Doof Doof took another drink of his pint and tried to change the subject, his head nodding to the telly. 'Is that tomorrow night, more Champions League games?' he asked.

Declan didn't bother turning round. 'What's happening Jordy?' he shouted over to Jordan's back as he stood at the bar, ordering a round of drinks.

Barry Merson had joined Gary Tanser in playing with his phone. Only the Keogh twins looked to Declan – and then at Jordan, who offered a half-turn and a reluctant nod.

'He fucking blanking me?' Declan asked, pretending to be surprised, or offended, or hurt, his voice at a volume slightly too loud to be addressing Doof Doof but not quite loud enough to be addressing Jordan, at least now that the bar had got a little busier as the lounge was closing and a few more stragglers trickled in to catch the extra hour or so of drinking.

'Calm it, man. I mean it,' Doof Doof warned, watching as

Jordan made the first of what would be two journeys from the bar to the table, carrying pints and a can of Coke for himself, the designated driver.

Declan shook his head and looked to Doof Doof, his eyes shooting straight back to the table as it erupted into a loud, collective laughter. An aggressive kind of laughter, the kind of laughter where the joke had a victim. It brought back memories that Declan couldn't quite remember but that he hadn't quite forgotten.

He noticed that Georgie was at the till but her jacket was on and she had a tote bag over her shoulder, finished for the evening.

The old man who'd been sitting by himself stood up and placed his pint glass on the bar; it still had a few drinks left in it but the arrival of Jordan and the rest had obviously curtailed his melancholic midweek meditation.

'You all right there?' Barry Merson stood up, his voice booming with all the authority that a non-native accent needed to be taken serious in a small town, as the old man waved him away.

'Watch your back, there, lad,' Barry Merson snapped at Jordan, who'd cut across the old man's path, almost barging into him, holding a pint each for the Keoghs.

'Sorry about that,' Barry Merson told the old man, glaring at Jordan, who was busy placing the pints down, preoccupied with ensuring that all his new friendships grew four pound stronger.

Barry Merson turned again, shuffling his stool towards the table to make sure the old man's path through the pub was clear.

Declan watched the old man struggle through the pub as Jordan sat laughing at the end of Gary Tanser's story, a story that he hadn't been listening to.

Fucking prick. Declan shook his head, a thought that Doof Doof seemed to have read. 'Here man, turn round.' He pulled Declan by the elbow. 'Stop staring over like a nutter,' he laughed, hoping his tone would make light of the situation.

Declan felt his head spinning a little, which made him concentrate and focus on the here and the now. 'All good, man,' he announced, taking a sip of his pint, challenging his eyes to read the warning label on Doof Doof's cigarette packet.

'Can I steal a fag?' Declan asked.

'Aye, go ahead, man,' Doof Doof told him, sparing him a reminder that he didn't smoke. Declan removed a cigarette from the packet and stood up. 'Let me get that for you,' he told the old man, leaping forward to open the door, like it had been a coincidence that they were both going outside at the same time.

Declan didn't know why he wanted to talk to the old man or what he wanted to say, he just wanted him to know that someone else gave a fuck about him – or something – to know that the world hadn't passed him by.

The old man pulled out a packet of cigarettes of his own as Declan realised that he didn't have a lighter, so this was as natural an in as he could have hoped for.

'Sorry to bother you but can I borrow your lighter?' Declan smiled, hoping to seem disarming, to seem respectful, different from the crowd that had just arrived.

The old man held the flame towards Declan, who leaned

in, stifling a cough as he inhaled. 'Dolan, is it?' the old man asked, which surprised Declan.

'Aye, Declan Dolan, that's me,' Declan answered, watching the smoke leave his mouth as he spoke. He took another draw, conscious of how laboured the whole routine felt – the holding, the inhale, the exhale, whilst trying to intersperse conversation through it all – it wasn't as easy as the carefully curated performances of veteran smokers made it look.

'I used to work with your grandad, now I'm going way back, when I was a youngster myself . . .' The old man laughed, his face alive. Declan couldn't see any vulnerability in his eyes, no sadness and no age, really. Declan's whole perception of him changed. Maybe he was just in for a fucking pint. Declan wondered why he had done this, found sadness where there was none. He worked hard to hide the feelings he felt inside of him, so maybe he looked for it in other people, like, if he couldn't help himself, he could help someone else, something like that, maybe.

Declan didn't remember either of his grandads – they'd both died shortly after he was born – but he tried to seem interested, enthusiastic, aware that he was now representing them and that he owed it to their memory to try and show their old pals that their grandson hadn't turned out to be an arsehole.

'Was that in the shipyards? It must have been a different place around here . . . back then . . .' Declan realised his tone sounded insincere and probably reminded the old guy of his age and the way everyone else probably now spoke to him. Maybe that's why he drank alone, to get a break from that sort of shite.

Declan let whatever he'd been saying trail off, acknowledging – by the way the old guy glanced at him and looked away, suddenly uninterested – how drunk he was.

'Same old place and the same old faces – just younger versions.'

The old man's concise summary had at least managed to extract something from Declan's dull clichéd supposition, which was impressive. Declan watched as he stubbed his cigarette out on the front wall of the pub and placed it in the bin beside the railings which stopped anyone staggering on to the road at closing time.

'Your grandad, he didn't suffer fools, let me tell you that.' The old man looked at the road ahead before setting off. 'Mind yourself, pal.' He patted Declan on the arm as he passed.

'You too,' Declan shot back, realising how much more he had to say to the old guy and realising that he hadn't asked his name. He'd probably see him again though, and he still had nearly a full pint waiting for him.

He stubbed his own cigarette out and walked back inside.

'When did you start smoking?' Georgie asked, standing at their table, covering for Doof Doof who looked a little guilty, like they'd both been talking about him – expressing their concerns.

'Only when I'm drinking,' Declan answered, looking over to Jordan's table and making eye contact with him as he laughed at something Gary Tanser had shouted in their direction.

'Just ignore them, table of arseholes,' Georgie told Declan, looking at Doof Doof like she'd understood what he'd been talking about, that Declan wasn't himself.

'What was that?' Declan shouted over at Jordan as Gary Tanser got louder.

'Oh, watch it! There's the boyfriend!' he remarked to Jordan, who laughed again, throwing his head back this time, wiping his mouth like Gary Tanser's wit had almost caused him to spit his Coca-Cola out.

Jordan broke the eye contact with Declan, which was a small victory and one that Declan's head enjoyed, willing him on to build on it, to walk over to their table.

'Declan, fucking sit down, man,' Doof Doof snapped.

'Aye, just leave them, Declan. I'm used to insecure little men who can't handle their drink,' Georgie told him, her voice softening. 'Look, remember we were talking about The Cure? I picked up this for you.' Georgie went into her tote bag and handed Declan a vinyl of their *Greatest Hits*.

'You didn't have to do that,' Declan answered, her generosity breaking him from his trance, reseating him and turning him to look at both the warmth and the concern in her smile.

'Thank you, man, genuinely.' Declan's voice almost cracked as he wished he was sober and better company and that he could leave with her and just walk somewhere.

'What a band, man,' Doof Doof joined in, taking a hurried drink of his pint, hoping that the conversation would now change and that the remainder of their drinks could pass without incident and they could get out of here.

'I don't know what to say, man.' Declan looked at Georgie, who leaned over like she was trying to offer him a hug, pulling her bag back over her shoulder as it swung towards Declan's pint.

'Cheers, Georgie,' Declan mumbled, looking at the record,

embarrassed as he tried to stand back up to meet her arms with his own outstretched as another eruption of laughter came from Jordan's and Gary Tanser's table. He wasn't sure what exactly had been said, but he was sure he heard the word 'dyke' or something like that being used.

A look he'd never seen before from Georgie confirmed that it wasn't a drunken delusion, that her feelings had been hurt. He'd never seen her look anything other than confident. She looked vulnerable, humiliated, sad. That same sadness that he'd been looking for in the old man sat alone staring at the wall had just appeared in the smart, intelligent, confident, funny, beautiful girl in her twenties.

'Fucking idiots,' Doof Doof told her, seeing too that she looked upset.

'She canny wait to get him home to play with his big tits,' he heard Gary Tanser say, as Jordan laughed again, throwing his shoulders back and shaking around, the Keoghs joining in too as the table erupted into another intimidating-sounding laugh.

'What the fuck did you just say there, ya stupid big cunt?' Declan shouted, silencing the pub and leaping up from his chair fast enough so that Doof Doof couldn't grab him.

'Declan!' he heard Georgie screaming, confirming that he was fucking up and creating a serious problem for his sober self tomorrow morning – and beyond – confirming that he'd poured a sufficient amount of alcohol inside of him to raise this incipient anger to the surface and here it was.

'Right, that's enough,' Kenny the barman shouted as Doof Doof caught up with Declan and had his forearm under his neck.

'What the fuck did you just say?' Declan shouted, feeling his face distorting and finding the strength inside him to easily release himself from Doof Doof's restraint.

'Who the fuck are you talking to, Dolan?' Jordan was standing up now too, feeling like this was a fight he could win and an opportunity to impress.

Both of the Keoghs were nudging each other and laughing, finding the whole thing thoroughly entertaining.

'I'm talking to this smack-dealing bullying cunt, no' you, ya pathetic prick,' Declan dismissed Jordan, every ounce of the strength of his language deployed, his head encouraging him to go further, encouraging him to flip the table of drinks over them all.

Gary Tanser was no longer laughing. His face was deadly serious now, as he broke the eye contact to study Declan from top to bottom, a warning that this wasn't going to be forgotten, that no one had ever spoken to him like this.

Declan's eyes stayed fixed on Gary Tanser's, waiting for him to look at them again, to let him see that he felt dead inside but with that came a fearlessness – albeit a transient fearlessness which would soon make way for an abiding sense of dread, but, right now, that didn't matter.

'You'll get done in, ya fat poof,' Jordan warned, standing up straight but staying back, struggling to hide his shock at how out of character this explosion of anger was from Declan. Declan looked around again at the table, at Jordan's new friends, shaking his head, feeling an aggressive smirk on his face as he looked to see if there was any shame on Jordan's part, anything.

'Declan, come on to fuck, man,' Doof Doof whispered, like

the damage was done but it would still be wise to get going before it got any worse.

'Pathetic,' Declan told Jordan, waiting to make sure that he looked away first, letting twenty years of friendship – or whatever it had been – evaporate, gone for ever.

'Any more and I'm phonin' the polis,' Kenny from the bar shouted, a warning that Barry Merson waved away, putting his phone down for the first time of the night and waving to Kenny that he had it under control.

'Right, that's enough, that is,' he intervened.

'You'll get taken away, wee man, no fuckin' joke,' Gary Tanser warned, shifting on his seat uncomfortably as he took a gulp of his pint.

'I'm fucking serious. You, sit down, and you, shut the fuck up.' Barry Merson was on his feet now. Jordan sat obediently and Gary Tanser looked away from Declan, smirking to the Keoghs, who'd stopped laughing and were sat looking at Barry Merson.

'I'm sorry about him, love, out of order,' Barry Merson shouted over to Georgie, who Declan was too ashamed to look at. He felt tears in his eyes, tears of anger as Doof Doof put both of his arms around his chest, getting ready to lead him away.

'Lad, go home, right, you've had a bit much,' Barry Merson told Declan, who was breathing heavy, his legs shaking, as Doof Doof led him towards the door.

'Declan, Declan, are you ok?' he heard Georgie asking as she followed them out of the pub. She sounded like she was close to tears herself through worrying for him and from how distressing what she'd just witnessed must have been.

'FUCK!' Declan screamed into the night, seeing the BMW

X7 that Jordan had been driving his superiors around in – according to Connor – and lunging towards it, his feet aiming a boot at one of the wing mirrors as Doof Doof grabbed him, knocking him off balance and on to the floor, managing to catch his head before it hit the pavement.

'Declan, please!' Georgie ran over, grabbing him as tears poured from his eyes and the furious tension vanished from his body, leaving him limp, helpless, pathetic and fucked, absolutely fucked. His head enjoyed telling him that he'd be better off dead, that he should run out on the main road, in front of a car, but it enjoyed reminding him too that he would never go through with something like that, so what was he going to do?

It tormented him, letting him know that he was captive.

'You're ok, right, you're ok, they're just scumbags and they always will be, just calm down, right?' she told him as she felt through her bag for tissues.

'Let's do one, man, away from here, anyway,' Declan heard Doof Doof tell Georgie.

'Here, lad.' He heard Barry Merson's scouse accent.

'He's all right, man, he's just had a bit much,' Doof Doof began, presenting a case for Declan's defence.

'You all right there, lad? He gets too much at times, like, big Tanser, absolutely no need, man, here, you forgot your vinyl.' Barry Merson handed the record to Georgie as Declan lifted his head off her shoulder, sniffing so hard through his nose that his eyes bulged.

'Cheers,' he told Barry Merson, immediately wanting to ask him if he was now a wanted man and if anything was going to happen to him, immediately feeling like Declan Dolan, the 24-year-old college student and Morrisons worker who dreamed of being a writer. The voice that had sent him into battle with one of the most dangerous people in the area, the voice that had convinced him that the war was worth waging, had vanished, leaving him all alone, and his only ammunition – the buzz, the bravado, the balls from the alcohol – was beginning to run low.

'Expensive them things, man,' Barry Merson smiled, his persona totally at odds with his reputation – which was maybe a trick, the new voice in Declan's head warned him, the new, paranoid voice that would be with him for the foreseeable future.

'I'll get them all up the road like, and listen, again, that were out of order that,' he told Georgie, who offered only a laboured smile in return like she was still a little shocked and like she didn't want Barry Merson to think she saw him as any better than the rest of them. 'Safe home,' he saluted and walked back to the pub.

'We'll walk you home, Georgie, and then he can come into mine and cool himself off a bit.'

Doof Doof decided to take Declan and Georgie's silence as approval of his plan and they carried on along the main road, away from the pub, Declan wiping his eyes and trying to control his breathing whilst his head went through every single opportunity he'd had – from his class to here – to just go home.

Fuck, man.

PART 2

PART 2

Declan was woken up by his own high-pitched, whining scream – this had been happening a lot lately but it was the first time there had been a witness, other than Hector, who'd sleep at his feet and turn around as if to confront him for interrupting another thoroughly enjoyable dog dream.

'Fuckin' shat maself there, man!' Doof Doof's voice revealed where he'd spent the night. Declan started the day apologising, and trying to laugh, to make light of his nightmare. Whatever emerged from his subconscious mind had been intense, terrifying and vivid, but his prepubescent-sounding falsetto had been enough to fend it off.

'Sorry,' Declan said, acknowledging that he wasn't alone, that he wasn't home. 'I don't even know what I was dreaming about there, it's scary shit but then it just, like, vanishes and I don't remember. It's been happening a lot. Weird, man.' He tried to release a controlled cough, which turned into a prolonged fit, with each reverberation around his body making his skull feel like it was about to crack open under the pressure.

'Stress, man,' Doof Doof diagnosed, watching as Declan spun his legs round, his bed for the night instantly restored back to its default couch mode. He had no covers over him and no pillow, and he was fully clothed – aside from his hair sticking up and his fairly objectionable breath, he looked like he'd just popped round that morning.

His tongue felt dry and he knew, without needing to look in a mirror, that it would be that horrible, white, foamy colour. He coughed again, recognising the feeling in his throat – he'd been smoking cigarettes, something he only did when he was a certain kind of drunk. He didn't mind smoking a joint – at least there was a semblance of purpose to it – but cigarettes were the fucking pits, he reminded himself.

He felt around in his pockets for his phone, to check the time, but his battery had died. Doof Doof was still a few years away from discovering the iPhone so Declan settled for asking him the time, rather than for a charger.

Doof Doof paused the film he was watching and messed around with the source button on the remote, before *BBC News* appeared on the screen.

The morning's headlines were being read out, footage of protesters throwing bricks and bottles at riot police played – another country had elected a fucking lunatic or an unarmed black man had been shot somewhere in America, Declan presumed.

More high street shops were set to close and some other billionaire was getting excited about sending a rocket full of arseholes into space.

It was 9am.

Four hours until he started his shift. Twelve hours until it finished – it was daunting how distant the notion of this day being over felt, together with the problems of its own that were to be presented alongside the ones inherited from last night.

He imagined phoning in sick for work and getting drunk, like, fucking paralytic – he knew he wouldn't though, and quickly quelled his own talk of any anarchic uprising by remembering that he needed the money and that he would probably be sacked.

It was soothing, the thought, the thought of heading to the shop to buy cans or vodka, to head up the hills and to fast-forward the day or skip it completely, but then there would be the next day, with the rollover jackpot hangover and the rest of the complications that came with living in the moment, of being here for a good time and not a long time – and the rest of the vapid social media shite.

Doof Doof switched the television source back to HDMI2, back to the subtitled movie he'd been watching.

He wondered if he would ever have his own flat as he looked around Doof Doof's, aware that he was trying to distract himself from the angry mob of flashbacks – the distorted and the vivid – that were waiting to overwhelm and horrify him further.

He surveyed Doof Doof's open-plan kitchen and living room area and his bedroom and bathroom doors, which faced each other, a couple of pairs of trainers and a pair of experienced-looking Caterpillar boots forming a guard of honour in the narrow hallway that led to his front door and out into the communal hallway.

Light from the clouds had managed to creep through Doof Doof's blinds, a warning, from the day ahead, that it was waiting for Declan, whether he liked it or not.

He looked at the television, letting his eyes sting and blur to avoid having to confront his reflection whenever the screen darkened during a scene change.

The film was 'Korean' and 'a classic', Doof Doof mumbled, taking Declan's trance-like look in the television's direction as an indication that he was engrossed.

'There's only so much daytime telly you can watch, *Pawn Stars* and all that, a meth addict trying to sell his granda's harmonica.'

Declan couldn't even force himself to laugh, Doof Doof seemed to know why.

Declan wished he could remember why.

Only sociopaths could wake up from a heavy night's drinking feeling totally comfortable and at one with themselves, but he knew he couldn't write this feeling off as mere hangover-induced paranoia.

He wanted to ask Doof Doof if he had been a bit of a dick in the pub – he knew that he'd had to have been a proper dick for Doof Doof to disclose as much, but even if he could assist in tidying up the vague, disjointed details, then Declan was sure he'd be able to reach his own conclusions.

Declan was about to ask why he didn't go home last night – a broader question and a less pejorative way of asking if he'd been a dick – but before he could muster the enthusiasm to speak the words and brace himself for the answer, he felt a sharp panic that woke him up, fully, as he realised he hadn't let his parents know he wasn't coming home and it hit him how worried they'd be, his mum especially.

He was twenty-four, he could go where he wanted and to what he wanted, but, for as long as he lived at home, he owed his parents an update on whether or not he was alive, which was fair enough.

He knew his mum's imagination would never consider that he'd simply got drunk and ended up back at a mate's house, crashing out on the couch. It wasn't in her nature to conjure up a fairly mundane, uneventful outcome.

His mum would have him down as having been kidnapped, drugged or robbed, or hanging from a tree or floating in the River Clyde. She'd already be planning her 'Just come home, Declan, you're not in any trouble' address to the media and deciding what photograph she was going to use for the missing-persons appeal.

One of those photographs that always looked like it was taken with the person going missing, or dying in tragic circumstances, in mind. Declan remembered making this morbid observation after seeing a few of these news stories.

'Family appeal for help to find Scots backpacker missing in Nepal'.

'Promising footballer in tragic holiday death plunge'.

Doof Doof's house wasn't far from Declan's: he could leave just now and be home in about ten minutes, he calculated, but, being conscious of his mum's suffering, even another ten minutes felt wrong.

He thought of his mum's innocence, of how she still left voicemails, complete with an introduction and the time of the message. He thought of her panicking, vulnerable voice playing on his phone once it was charged enough to switch itself on.

She would be at work and have access to her mobile, but

Declan didn't know her number off by heart. He could ask Doof Doof to search online for the number of the school where she worked and he could phone and ask to speak to her, an idea he ruled out as quickly as it came to him, as he pictured his mum's reaction if an announcement had gone out in her work that there was someone on the phone looking to talk to her, after she hadn't heard from her son all night.

It was unlikely that he could give a message to be passed on either – the school's secretarial service probably wasn't extended out to the cleaning staff, especially the fee-paying, private school where his mum worked – so a message being put out for her to come to the headteacher's office, or wherever the school's publicly listed phone number put the caller through to, would be all he could hope for.

His mum would probably collapse in a hysterical panic before she made it to the phone.

'What a selfish bastard,' he said to himself, a denunciation that he couldn't contest.

Declan knew that his mum had noticed that he'd been quite insular recently and this made him feel even worse, as he thought of her lying awake all night, listening for him unlocking the door. He knew his dad would have been telling her to calm down and trying to mitigate her apocalyptic imagination by presenting alternative outcomes – telling her that he'd probably gone to a friend's house, or a girl's, the latter barely carrying any conviction as he'd never spoken to his parents about any romantic interests.

He realised his dad would be angry though. Declan knew his mum worried, and although he hadn't done anything wrong, he should have let her know he wasn't coming home and that he was all right, for the sake of her own health.

His dad would pick his moment to speak to him about this, no doubt.

His dad was worried about him too, and had been looking for a moment to stage one of his interventions. He wished that he could keep up the pretence that everything was going great in his life and that he was content within himself, that he could play through the pain barrier, even if only for his parents' sake.

He wished he could see his mum, to reassure her and just cuddle her – he felt like he was about to start crying.

Come on to fuck, man, he warned himself.

In ten minutes, he'd be home and he could charge his phone and text his mum and dad, to let them know he was all right and that he'd stayed at someone's house. He'd decide on the walk home whose house it was to be. Someone who could feasibly have a Wednesday off work, which ruled out Connor, or any of his other friends that they'd known long enough.

They didn't know Doof Doof, and they didn't know he knew Doof Doof, as he had never mentioned him. He'd have had to introduce him as Raymond first of all, as Raymond Buchanan, as Doreen Buchanan's son.

'Doreen Buchanan, that was so sad about her, she was such a lovely woman too,' Declan imagined the conversation going. Followed by 'Is he not a bit of a druggy?', an enquiry with its roots in the rumours that his mum would have heard at the local shops, and this would give her something new to worry about.

Her son hanging around with a 'druggy' or worse. Maybe her son was a druggy himself.

A 'druggy' was a blanket term that Declan's mum, and other parents of her generation, used for anyone who was said to have experimented with drugs – from crack heads to stoners, the one term encapsulated all.

He thought of Doof Doof's mum dying when he'd been round about Declan's age and he imagined if his own mum had died. How does anyone deal with death – this question came to him a lot lately and it was maybe the root of a lot of his fears and the nihilism that was beginning to reshape his world view.

He wondered how Doof Doof maintained his attitude towards life and he knew that he could learn from him, or maybe even talk to him about it all one night.

He wondered why everybody didn't just go fucking insane.

Declan hadn't lost anyone close; he had all that to come, as he regularly reminded himself over the years. He'd worried about people close to him dying ever since he could remember.

Right now, though, the thought of Doof Doof's mum dying was stuck in his head and he felt another intense pang of sympathy being fired at him. He felt like this was it, he was about to cry, he was about to be sitting in tears, in Doof Doof's living room on a Wednesday morning.

Thankfully, though, he forced his eyes to focus, seeing that a Korean man was eating what looked like an octopus – which was moving. *What the fuck is this?* he thought.

'You look horrified,' Doof Doof laughed. 'Have you never seen *Oldboy* before, man?'

Doof Doof was always jokingly disappointed in Declan

whenever he found out about another film that he hadn't seen, as though he'd expected better from his movie buff protégé. Declan shook his head and made a laughing sound to acknowledge Doof Doof's light-hearted tone. He was relieved that this disturbing piece of cinema had been assigned full culpability for the perturbed expression on his face.

Declan was glad to be back in the room, at least, but now he felt like he wanted to be sick. He knew there would be nothing in his stomach except that horrible, acidy, bright-yellow stuff, and that if he gave in to the urge to run to the bathroom, he would only feel worse later, at work.

He thought of how bright the lights were on the shop floor, and of the in-store radio with that same playlist of songs that could easily break a man.

He'd take some paracetamol with him and he'd be ok when he ate something, he told himself, appealing for calm, as he tried to empty his short-term memory of the images of octopus tentacles moving in a human mouth.

He looked at Doof Doof – fully absorbed in, and satisfied with, his choice of entertainment. Something about Doof Doof's contentment was infectious, Declan realised, feeling a smile land on his face, a smile that could easily have been dealt with but maybe it was worth savouring, as he considered that it could potentially be his last for a while.

Declan decided that he would leave Doof Doof to enjoy the rest of his morning. He didn't want to stay any longer as he knew Doof Doof looked forward to his day off and it wasn't fair to burden him with the pessimistic vibe that he was aware he was radiating.

He stood up, checking the couch behind him, making an effort to fix the two cushions that he'd been lying against.

'I better get going, man,' he declared, aware that this was his last chance to try and piece together the details of last night – straight from Doof Doof, face to face, as opposed to the multi-party accounts and the ambiguous text messages.

'My phone battery must have died last night and my mum will be worrying,' he told the side of Doof Doof's head, waiting for him to turn around, away from the film.

'She's a nightmare,' he added, embarrassed, making sure to downplay his mum's concerns as hyperbole.

'Cheers for letting me stay here, man.' Declan watched as Doof Doof stood up now too, letting a scene finish on the film before turning to look at him, at the vulnerability in his face, the confusion and the worrying that he'd be carrying away with him.

'I don't know why I didn't just walk home.'

Declan braced himself, deliberately dispatching his sentence on an intelligence gathering mission. Doof Doof laughed, and Declan prepared himself for the fresh revelations.

'If your old dear's worried just now, she'll be glad she never seen you last night, Begbie.'

Starting a day with a new nickname was never great.

'Begbie?' Declan repeated, in a plea for elaboration.

'Aye, man, you went fucking tonto. Ready to square go Gary Tanser, calling him a smack dealer and all that.'

Doof Doof was about to continue but he must have seen it in Declan's face that he'd said enough to bring the images back to him.

Declan felt his head bow as his shoulders sank forward. He pressed his palms into his forehead and let them descend slowly.

'What the fuck, man?' He looked to Doof Doof's ceiling, at the plastic covering that he'd kept around his lampshade like his mum had done in their house, back when she smoked, before Ciara's asthma attack.

'What the fuck!' he repeated, like he actually wanted an answer this time – unsure if he was confronting Doof Doof, or confronting himself.

He ran his hands down his cheeks again, waiting for Doof Doof to reassure him, to modulate the memories of him storming over to Gary Tanser, of Jordan jumping to Gary Tanser's defence, of the Keogh twins, Barry Merson. Fucking hell. Barry Merson trying to calm him down. It must have been fucking horrific if that was the calibre of person who was trying to restrain him. They'd be coming after him now, surely? There was no way that this was going to be forgiven or forgotten. Fuck. He sat back down. He felt a pins and needles-like feeling on the back of his neck and a jolt in his stomach as he remembered that he'd been shouting. It wasn't solely the cigarettes' fault that his throat felt like the bottom of the purple bin.

'That Barry Merson was all right about it all, he came after you to give you your record back,' Doof Doof added, bringing fresh flashbacks of Georgie screaming his name. He'd fucked it, in front of her, she'd think he was a loony now, a bampot, just another fucking bampot from around here. He'd be banned from the pub too. He'd need to apologise to the new guy, Kenny. Kenny would know Georgie was pals with him too, so he'd embarrassed her. He wondered who else had seen it all – witnessed it all – calling a smack dealer a smack dealer, in a public place. Fuck me. Fuck.

He thought of his mum worrying and of starting work in a few hours, his college course that he'd be as well putting out of its misery, his creative-writing class too, his class all staring at him as he recited *Ryzo*, his sore head, his sore throat, his dodgy stomach, his breath, Hector left at home, in his bed, their bed, all on his own, without his best pal.

His hands drummed a few beats on his chin as he leaned back in preparation to propel himself off the couch. He rose to his feet and sighed a final solitary fuck.

He put his trainers on as Doof Doof asked 'if he was sure' he didn't want to stay for breakfast. Declan didn't recall being invited to stay for breakfast initially – something that a check to confirm if you 'were sure' would imply. Fair play, he thought, trying to smile.

He wondered what they meant, these drunken rages; the exchange was blurry, but he did remember being adamant that he had a point and feeling like he was seeing what no one else could see – probably why drunk people tend to turn on whoever is trying to calm them down or hold them back in these sorts of situations.

It felt easier sometimes just to relinquish control, to concede defeat to the mind, and alcohol helped with that surrender, fast-tracking you to somewhere else you'd rather be.

The outbound journey was exhilarating, the feeling of waving farewell and fuck off to the thoughts in the head.

It was great, every time, for a while. You'd be out in front, free, you were a great guy, at least until the mind reappeared along the way, its predatorial patience stalking, ready to time its arrival with precision and expertise.

A bit of minor conflict that the rational and sober mind could probably have resolved was an ideal opportunity for the darkness and the intoxication to show their unified strength and the ease with which they could seize control of their host.

'Listen, I'm sorry, man,' Declan told Doof Doof, keen to make a start on his apologies, remembering Doof Doof grappling with him, almost pleading with him to leave it.

It hadn't even crossed his mind at the time that he was over-reacting, or at least acting irresponsibly and playing a dangerous game.

'Don't worry about it, man, and if that Barry Merson was all right with it, then it should all be fine, just stupid drunken shit, they'll have bigger fish than you, man, and anyway he was out of order to Georgie, that big wank Tanser.'

Declan felt a little better as the source of his fury was identified, remembering Georgie being called a dyke and whatever else. Fucking prick, he thought, feeling at least a little vindicated about the situation.

He didn't have Georgie's number to apologise for his behaviour – even if it was in her defence, it must have still been pretty disturbing to witness and, ultimately, it wasn't him. He shuddered as he remembered the feeling of his head willing him to make the night even worse, to walk out in front of a car.

It was a strange one, a unique form of shame, to be thinking of what you were thinking, like a hangover in itself, a hangover from your own thoughts. Something in him had managed to prevent any permanent damage – or worse – but it was a warning.

He'd always been told he was a good drunk, a good laugh, but he'd had a couple of episodes where he'd felt this way so it would be a while, he thought – he hoped – before he'd drink again.

The experience had been similar to his night terrors; the screams and the horror seemed warranted at the time and so clear, but when you woke, when you came back to yourself, after a while, there was no real terror, no fear, maybe a bit of a nothingness, if anything.

He didn't know if he'd even be allowed back in the pub or when Georgie was next working. He'd find a way, though, to apologise to Georgie and to Kenny.

He'd apologised to Doof Doof, who was already over it, and Jordan and Gary Tanser, well, fuck them, he thought, extending his arm out to thank Doof Doof again, for putting him up for the night. Their hands slapped together and Doof Doof pulled Declan in towards him, slapping him on the back and telling him that they'd speak soon.

Declan emerged from Doof Doof's flat, feeling and looking every bit like someone who belonged to a different day. His eyes struggled with the daylight and he felt intimidated by the outside world, which didn't yet seem habitable to him.

He hoped he wouldn't meet anyone, taking comfort in the rain that had only just started, slapping his face, as at least it meant that no one would want to stop and chat, at least for long.

He thought about Jordan as he crossed the road just short of the layby that led up to the farmland beside where he lived.

Jordan Langford. He thought to himself of how hearing people refer to him by his full name made him feel like they were back at school, children again.

Langford. Lang. Ford. He remembered the two syllables welded in silver letters, in perfect symmetry, on the gates of Jordan's house.

He thought back to when he went over for Jordan, and he'd have to speak into the intercom, before being buzzed up and the Lang would part with the Ford, and you'd walk between them, up the steep, grand driveway.

He felt like he didn't know Jordan Langford any more, like he was a character from his childhood. He'd known Jordan – or Jordy – one of his nicknames that never really took off. Declan remembered Jordan telling him, years ago, that he was named after Michael Jordan. His dad was a basketball fan who hated football and everything that went with it. He was as Scottish as he looked, but for whatever reason he loved basketball and he'd stay up late to watch games.

During the summer, when he was home from working abroad, he'd be seen walking around with his Chicago Bulls jersey on, his arms and shoulders bare, and no T-shirt underneath – which was a regulation for anyone not in peak physical shape who wanted to wear a basketball jersey. A courtesy acknowledgement. A nod to their lacking the muscle mass required to execute the look.

Jordan didn't take it too well, on the few occasions that he'd been slagged for his dad's spring/summer collection. His dad's name was Duncan too, which was decent ammunition for basketball-related mockery.

Declan always remembered one of the first times that he'd ever smoked weed, with Doof Doof, Connor and his brother, and Jordan. They'd been in Connor's brother's car, driving to McDonald's or somewhere, and they'd passed Duncan Langford in his Chicago Bulls regalia.

Jordan had only just finished talking about his dad – his job and wherever he had been working, usually Singapore or somewhere out that way, or a car that his dad was thinking of getting. It had been wearing thin with Declan and Connor, who had reached an age where they were realising that Jordan's dad was, possibly a bit of a prick.

Connor's brother, with the benefit of experience, had probably long since drawn this conclusion but he was unaware of just how badly Jordan hated being the butt of the joke, especially any jokes about his dad.

Connor's brother had slowed the car down and tooted the horn as they passed Jordan's dad, prompting him into a reflexive wave and they all giggled at his startled expression, as his gormless, dour face studied the car and his pale-white, freckled bingo wing flapped from side to side as his hand hung in the air.

'There he is, Wee Slam Dunc,' Connor's brother remarked, cheerful and casually, like Jordan's dad was a well-known local character, a good laugh and just a loveable daft cunt.

His car collection, his trips abroad to watch Formula One, his luxurious home and everything else that Jordan held dearly were all redundant, as the throwaway nature of the remark and the ease with which a new, beautifully ironic nickname had been bestowed upon Jordan's dad, sent Declan and Connor dissolving into an uncontrollable fit of laughter.

To them he'd always been Mr Langford – they'd never gone as far as to address him so formally, but they wouldn't feel fully comfortable with calling him Duncan, either.

They didn't know what they'd have called him, if a conversation had ever broken out. Over the years they'd offered a wide-eyed 'All right' and a nod, and that would draw a grumbled declaration of what part of the day it was, with even the word 'good' judged to be too much of an effort for him.

'Morning', 'Afternoon' and 'Evening'. In almost twenty years that was all Declan and Connor had ever got from Jordan's dad.

That 'Wee Slam Dunc' was maybe 5 foot 6, maximum, seriously overweight, and seemingly in a permanent state of disappointment and frustration made the offhand remark go down far better than Connor's brother could have expected.

The juxtaposition of this fairly flamboyant nickname and Jordan's dad's appearance – his height and physique – and then his dour personality meant that their first experience of 'the giggles' verged on the euphoric, and the more they tried to stop – seeing that Jordan was getting pissed off and not on their wavelength at all – the more they would laugh.

They'd caught their breath enough to offer a 'sorry, man' to Jordan, who was protesting that it wasn't even that funny and that they were 'wee guys' or 'gay lovers' or whatever else he could come up with. He couldn't take, or tell, a joke, so moments like this were lost on him. Declan remembered Doof Doof had intervened – sensing the tension from Jordan's end – and changed the subject whilst Connor and Declan sat, their eyes bloodshot from the joint and the tears of laughter, afraid to look at each other in case it started them off again. Declan felt himself smile, enjoying the memory, forgetting that he should be worrying. He realised too that he was already thinking of Jordan in the past tense, as someone he used to know.

He carried on past the high-rise flats that led past the local shops and then to his own estate, past the landmarks that were reminders of their childhood and their friendship.

The tiny red-ash park that they used to play football on which had seemed to shrink in recent years – this sort of thing probably happened a lot as you grew older, Declan thought.

It would usually be him, Connor, Jordan, a boy, PJ, that they hung around with at the time – who just stopped showing up one day, never to be heard from again – and a couple of other faces and names that he couldn't pair, and Connor's cousin Robert, when he was up visiting with his family.

Rob, he'd wanted to be called, Declan remembered, but a few days into his first summer holiday he was answering to the indigenous modification, Rab.

'English Rab' he was referred to whenever he wasn't present – or on the odd few occasions since that he'd popped up in conversation – and it was necessary to differentiate from the other Rabs of their childhood.

English Rab. Declan smiled, wondering what he was up to now and if he ever thought of his childhood summer holidays here. Not a holiday to Scotland as in somewhere like Loch Lomond, Loch Ness, St Andrews, Skye or Edinburgh. A holiday to here.

It must have been hard for him, Declan the adult thought as he carried out a brief retrospective analysis of Declan the child's treatment of English Rab.

They would take the piss out of his accent sometimes, and he had a bit of a nervous twitch thing in his eye that meant he kept winking and it made everything he said seem like he was only kidding.

He remembered a day Connor and Jordan had almost been fighting with each other after Jordan had been mimicking his twitch whilst talking to him. It wasn't funny and English Rab, who was naïve, not very streetwise and maybe not even all that conscious of how prominent his twitch was, didn't know that Jordan was mimicking him and was answering his questions and talking as though Jordan was having a normal conversation and simply had something in his eye, or a twitch of his own.

Declan only remembered English Rab as being someone they were landed with, through Connor, and he didn't really get to know him or ask him anything about his own area and his own friends and hobbies.

English Rab didn't volunteer much conversation either, or suggest any alternative activities, seeming content with playing football – he didn't mind going in goal which was strange, but convenient, and a civility abused by Jordan and probably Declan and Connor too.

When they got bored or lost the ball, they'd patrol the area, aimlessly. Rummaging through the nettles where the ball had landed but looking for everything except the ball. They'd look for glass bottles, and for bricks or blocks of concrete to smash them off of.

They weren't exactly best friends but Declan never joined in with the slagging of English Rab, even the slagging of his accent, which he didn't seem to mind, and to which he eventually started to give a bit back.

Every day he would have a new word or sentence he would attempt in a Scottish accent. Things like 'Curly Wurly' and 'There's been a murder.'

He must have only been about eleven or twelve at the time, so it was obvious that someone older was feeding him these lines, suggesting to Declan, now, as an adult, that maybe he did seem to mind and that he'd been going home and mentioning that he was being teased for his accent and been told to stand up for himself.

It must have been lonely for English Rab, Declan thought, as he looked down at the pitch, pausing, breathless from climbing the stairs – the 'back stairs' they were known as locally. He probably missed home and his own mates, but if he did, he kept it to himself.

Declan felt the butterfly-type feeling again in his stomach, another pang, as he thought of how far away those days were.

It was like, if you reminisced about something enough you began to think that those times could come back, you could try it all again, and everyone would go back to who they were.

He hoped English Rab was doing well and happy in his life and being addressed as 'Rob'.

Declan wondered if Jordan ever thought about English Rab or felt bad for the times when he'd blatantly bullied him. Probably not, he guessed. There were times Declan wished he could be like that, instead of letting his conscience get the better of him. It must be quite liberating, to just be a fucking prick. He felt his head nodding in agreement, as though someone had been speaking to him.

He looked around himself and then across the road, at the row of shops and the daily activity, the life that was being hosted. Errands were being run, loaves and cartons of milk were being bought, sausage rolls were being served, prescriptions were being handed over and gossip was being exchanged.

He saw an old guy he recognised, Pat, maybe, walking out of the bookie's across the road. He was always on his own, any time Declan had seen him.

Declan always made sure he said hello to him and took the time to listen, enthusiastically, to his musings on the weather or the prices of the contents of the carrier bag he always seemed to be carrying.

He knew if he pointed him out one time – or even briefly described him – to his mum or dad, then he would get his full story.

Promising start in life. Good footballer. Scouted and invited to trials. Bad injury. Alcohol. Gambling. Wife left him. Lives alone. His children are older now, with children of their own, and they don't bother with him.

It was that sort of small town, or 'community', where everyone knew everyone else and their families, their problems and their family's problems.

Declan thought of the place and how it was barely recognisable as the town that featured in the romantic recollections of the preceding generations – like his parents, his aunties and uncles, and some of his parents' aunties and uncles.

At Christmas, and any other occasion that brought an

extended family into one room, it was the tradition for the whole family to congregate and regale the children with tales of how great everything was before they were born.

He'd heard of this community that upheld the strong working-class virtues.

Everyone looked out for everyone. No one had much but what they had they shared with their neighbours. The place had a spirit, a soul, and everyone felt truly blessed to live in such a warm and unique village.

Declan didn't know whether that was ever really true or not, but the harsh reality was that time had moved on, the council houses had been bought and painted, new doors fitted, extensions built and wooden decking laid.

Declan found himself at the bottom of the hill that led up to his street. He was surprised at how fast he'd walked to cover the distance in what seemed like a short period of time. He was soaked. Miserable. Stinking of stale alcohol and feeling like he was having a mini-breakdown.

He got to his front door, relieved to feel his key in the pocket of his jeans after realising that he hadn't bothered to check for it before he left Doof Doof's, which was daft and it could have tipped him over the edge, he thought, making an admonitory note to himself whilst the fear of having to make the return journey was still fresh in his gut.

He gently navigated the key, holding it firm and turning it whilst forcing the handle upwards, applying pressure with his left shoulder, the routine that was by now a muscle memory to him, and his family.

Annoyed, he wondered when his parents would ever address

this fault in the lock barrel and arrange for a new one to be fitted, dissent he quickly shot down, asking himself why he didn't learn how to fix it and when – and how, exactly – he planned on ever moving out.

The door was pulled open, denying Declan the satisfaction that usually rewarded his perseverance, and caused him to tumble forward, balancing himself on the door frame and watching as Ciara walked back through to the kitchen.

'Cheers,' he shouted, presenting her a clearer opportunity to fully demonstrate that she was ignoring him.

He heard Hector barking, an excited bark, anticipating one of the day's many emotional homecoming reunions. Declan smiled and watched Hector skidding along the hallway, bounding towards him.

Declan kneeled himself down, to be level with Hector, who had decided the only appropriate way to greet his hero was to lie on his back – a patent indication that his belly was to be rubbed – and take playful swipes at him with his front paws whilst trying to lick his face, totally unperturbed by whatever he could taste or smell.

Declan patted and tickled Hector. 'How's my pal, how's my pal,' his hurried, whispering tone asked, sending Hector into a frenzied state of near delirium till he stood back up on all four paws and began performing a frantic routine of running through the doorway into the living room and then straight back out into the hallway, sending himself crashing into Declan, as though they were in the mosh pit at a heavy metal concert.

'How's my pal,' Declan was repeating, with Hector running

out of ways to demonstrate to him that his pal was doing fucking great.

Declan watched, laughing, a genuine hearty, wholesome laugh, and shook his head from side to side, impressed at the display that Hector rounded off by grabbing one of his mum's slippers in his mouth and collapsing back down on the floor, panting and exhausted.

Declan got up and walked to the kitchen and poured them both a much-needed water.

After all the psychological warfare he'd been engaged in with himself he welcomed this temporary ceasefire that Hector had championed. He looked out of the kitchen window to see that the rain had stopped.

He laughed again, at the satisfied sound of Hector slurping his fresh water and decided that he'd take him for a walk around the block and throw a few balls for him for a while before getting ready for work.

'What's that, *Frankenstein*?' he asked Ciara, who sat with the book opened, face down, and a page full of highlighted notes.

'Yep,' she answered, highlighting something else on the paper, further shirking a conversation. Declan finished his water and placed the glass back under the tap, looking out of the window again, trying to block any fresh memories of the previous night.

'Mary Shelley, she was only . . .' He turned to face Ciara, hoping to soften her attitude and maybe even impress her.

'. . . nineteen when she wrote *Frankenstein*. Wow! New material, please! You're getting worse than Dad,' Ciara interrupted. 'Is that just your thing to say now – about *Frankenstein*?

Have you ever even read it?' She placed her highlighter down and turned to look at Declan, at the fucking state of him. 'Her mum died after complications from her birth, did you know that? When she was seventeen, she had a daughter herself, born premature, who died – only a few weeks old – did you know that? She had two other children who died as infants too. She could probably only ever relate birth to death. Pretty fucking tragic. But yes, Dec, she was only nineteen when she wrote a book, when she did something that men were impressed by.'

Declan bowed his head, wondering if Ciara was finished.

'Jesus, sorry, man,' he coughed, not sure whether to be intimidated by or proud of his little sister and her brash dismissal of his trite remark.

'It's ok, you're just a guy.' Ciara smiled, folding her papers up and placing them into a plastic folder. 'Don't let me ever get to a stage where I only want to know the things that I already know.'

She shot a victorious smile at Declan, satisfied that she'd made her point – and an additional few after that.

'Where were you all night anyway? Out DJing?' She nodded to the record under his armpit, her face softening into a concerned semi-smile, letting him know that as well as being annoyed at him for worrying their parents, again, *she* was worried about *him*, like everyone else – maybe even more so, now that she'd demonstrated she had an insight into how his mind worked.

He'd always been the one who thought he had an insight into her mind, being the older sibling, but time was fucking whizzing by, she was becoming an adult now too, she was becoming her own person. He looked at a Harry Potter note-book that she'd been scribbling in and he thought of her last birthday – or maybe it was the birthday before that – and how delighted she'd been that he'd got her a Lego set of Hogwarts Great Hall. He knew she was impressed that he'd thought to combine her two passions – obsessions, as his mum and dad had called them, wondering when she'd 'grow up' – of Lego and Harry Potter.

He liked her quirkiness and how she did her own thing and was, quite unashamedly, a bit of a geek. He'd worried about her though and wondered if she was ok at school. He knew she was excelling academically and would definitely be the first in their family to see the inside of a university, but also that she would be an easy target for bullies.

He had no tangible evidence to support any of his concerns that she was being picked on, but he'd always made sure to talk to her and encourage her to keep studying and making sure she knew she was gifted and intelligent and that, after she left school, the world would open up and she could be whoever she wanted to be.

'I need to get going. I've got an exam. Hector's been out but he only did a pee. He's probably keeping a dump for you, a steaming pile of revenge for ditching him last night . . .' Ciara and Declan both giggled.

'I'll text Mum and let her know you're all right – did you get drunk and lose your phone?'

Declan felt her noticing the concern in his eyes, probably suspecting that she'd missed out a fair few of the facets of his evening.

'The battery died,' Declan added, like that was the only correction Ciara's succinct supposition required, like it wasn't even as bad as she'd thought, he hadn't lost his phone. 'I'll message her too,' Declan said, looking around the kitchen for a charger. 'I'll have more missed calls than Bin Laden when I turn it on,' he joked, hoping to show Ciara that he was fine.

'Ouch,' Ciara said, refusing to even pretend to laugh, cringing almost at Declan's line as she reached over the kitchen table to unplug a phone charger, handing it to him.

'Told you, you're getting worse than Dad,' she said, smiling.

'I'll take him out before I get changed for work, don't worry.' Declan walked over to the fridge to see if there was some chicken he could give Hector, feeling another wave of shame about abandoning him last night.

'Good luck with the exam, right, you'll nail it,' Declan told her.

'It's just a prelim – but, yes, I think I will.'

Their fists met and they both smiled.

He walked into his bedroom and set about himself with a towel, taking off his damp jeans and throwing them on top of his bed, changing into dry, fresh jogging bottoms. He ran his hands down the thighs, feeling the bobbles on the cotton, a reminder that their best days were behind them.

He took some shredded, solid-feeling bits of paper out from the right-hand pocket – they'd fallen victim to the washing machine, whatever they'd been, writing notes, an idea, maybe, or just something from college, hopefully – and a few sweet papers, a Milky Way and a Bounty, from a box of Celebrations he presumed.

The comfort Declan felt from putting on his veteran jogging bottoms didn't last long as he remembered that he'd soon be changing back out of them and into his work trousers. He thought of having to iron his work uniform and then of his eight-hour shift.

He kneeled down, plugging his phone charger into the power socket beside the chest of drawers in his bedroom so that it would be ready for him to continue his enquiries and issue his apologies about last night when he returned from the park.

'I'm coming, I'm coming,' he reassured Hector, who'd sensed that plans were afoot for his going for a walk and had come into Declan's bedroom to see what the hold-up was.

Declan clicked his phone, to check that it was charging, as Hector licked his face, tactically, trying to distract him from the phone, his fierce rival in the perpetual battle for Declan's attention.

'I'm coming, pal,' Declan repeated, clapping him, single-handedly, seeing that the phone had already consumed enough power to switch itself back on.

Declan was being prompted for his six-digit passcode, which his thumb entered, autonomously, freeing his eyes to watch as Hector retreated, out of Declan's room, slumping himself down on the carpeted hallway, his back to the frame of the open bedroom door.

His tail was static and he parked his head on his front left paw, letting out a sigh in a clear display of disenchantment that they hadn't managed to flee the house before his aluminium adversary had woken up.

The text messages had started around midnight, amicable enough enquiries from his mum, wondering if he had a key to get himself in as a way of prompting him for details of where he was and what his estimated arrival time home was.

Around an hour or so later the worrying had stepped up a level and the calls had started trickling in. He looked at the voicemails from his mum, three in total, each shorter than the previous one. He deleted them, sparing himself the torment of hearing the full extent of her anguish. He clicked on a WhatsApp conversation with his mum to see that she was typing, which he presumed meant that Ciara had text her already to say he was home. He quickly sent a message that contained all the buzz words, that he was safe, that his battery had run out – sparing his mum a panicked glance at a word like died – and that he'd stayed at his friend's.

He stared at the screen as his mum continued typing, knowing that there wouldn't be much return for her five minutes of effort, three or four spell-checked, grammatically flawless sentences about how she'd been beside herself with worry and how she and his dad wanted to have a talk with him. A talk that could easily be avoided.

She knew he was all right; he'd apologise in person later tonight and it was in the past now. There was a message from Connor, from this morning, asking if he was all right.

He must have heard from someone about the commotion, the fracas, the melee, whatever the fuck it could be called. Declan clicked on Connor's photo of him and Nicole, who was now, it appeared, officially his girlfriend.

They looked happy together, Declan thought, wondering

97

what the cocktails were that they were holding. Maybe he'd try a cocktail, if he ever got himself together and asked someone out on a date. Again, his stomach tensed as he thought of Georgie screaming at him to calm down. Fucked it.

Totally fucking fucked it, he told himself, typing to Connor that he was fine, that he'd had a bit of an argument with Jordan – leaving Gary Tanser's name out of it, so as not to implicate him in any sort of local gossip about him taking verbal abuse from someone like Declan, a nobody, a fat nobody, a geek or whatever – the less people who knew about their run-in, the better, even including close friends.

He felt stomach acid rise up so that it was in his throat and he felt again like he wanted to be sick, an image of one of the shots lying untouched from the forceful round of drinks he'd bought passed through his head.

He hadn't drunk that much, he considered, it was more the empty stomach and the intent behind it and the sheer speed of the consumption. He performed a controlled rift, fully expecting to have to run to the bathroom.

A quarter-bottle of vodka that had been consumed in twenty-two minutes, according to his Uber notification asking him to rate Filip.

Declan, alarmed that he could hardly recall leaving the Uber – partly the alcohol and partly his head's ability to lead him away, taking him anywhere it decided – quickly rated Filip '5 stars' and clicked on the £3 option of the tip suggestions, in belated appreciation of Filip's tolerant attitude towards alcohol consumption in the vehicle, which, he could now acknowledge, in his penitent state, had maybe been a little presumptuous and disrespectful on his part.

There was another missed call too, from this morning, from a number he didn't have saved. No one he knew would call him so early, he thought, locking his phone again to begin preparing himself for work, the fumes of expended alcohol being emitted from his pores convincing him to have a shower before taking Hector out.

He looked at his bed and thought of how it was going to feel, to be reunited with it after almost thirty-six hours apart. He lifted his jeans off the covers, conscious of the damp patch that was appearing, and went to hang them over his bedroom radiator.

He felt, in the back-pocket, a few folded sheets of paper, slightly wet round the edges and now with a blue tint, from the dye that had come off his jeans. He opened the three pages up – the back page was at the front from the way he must have folded them up after his performance.

He scanned over it all, seeing just words, spaces, commas. Only '*AAAAHHHHHHHHHH!*' drew him in, making him read the last few lines.

Ah feel numb, ah feel nuttin' bar ma own pish runnin' doon ma leg. Canny stoap greetin'. Greetin' n pishin' masel in the fuckin' boozer. This is the end. Ah'm done wae it aw.

He couldn't help but appreciate the irony that his night had ended in a similar fashion to the protagonist of his story's. Life imitates art, as someone would probably say if he'd told them all about his night, from start to finish, from his performance of *Ryzo* to the booze-fuelled commotion in his local. He put the papers on top of the drawers in his bedroom – relieved he hadn't acted on impulse and thrown them in the bin – thinking how the story could be reworked and used for something else someday.

He remembered James Cavani saying how he kept hold of every note he'd ever written.

He pulled the cord in the bathroom that turned on the immersion, to heat the shower, and looked at himself in the bathroom mirror, studying his face.

This is all people see, he thought, just a fucking person.

They don't see the intrusive thoughts, the hang-ups, the insecurities, the mistakes and the hoarded piles of insults, crit-icisms and failures. Everyone had their own shit to deal with, he really wasn't that important, he tried to tell himself – in a nice way.

Lay off yourself, he thought, looking into his own eyes, wondering if he should shave.

He may have disgraced himself in the pub but at least he hadn't gone full-on *Ryzo*, he hadn't shed any piss or any tears, and, at least, it wasn't the end, he was still here.

He heard his phone beep, from the bedroom. He looked at the shower and then at Hector, whose face looked cautionary and dejected, the phone's jingle growing synonymous to him with the mood darkening.

'A quick shower and then we're going straight out, pal.'

Declan clapped him again, brushing past, into his bedroom, to check his phone.

He looked at the time before opening the message. 'Right, give me ten minutes, pal, and I'm all yours,' he shouted to Hector, relieved that he'd still be able to take him to the park, as opposed to a strictly business only walk, up and down the street.

It wasn't a WhatsApp this time, it was a traditional text, which was strange and usually implied formality – and from a number that he didn't recognise.

'We need to talk. Where are you?' it read, making Declan feel sick again, a different kind of sick this time though – the physical symptoms of his hangover stepping back to give way to the psychological. They'd be working closely together throughout the day though.

Declan clicked the top of the screen, taking note of the last few numbers, suspecting that this was the same number that had tried to call him first thing in the morning.

'Who the fuck –' Declan snapped at his phone, seeing that the numbers matched up.

'It's ok, pal, it's ok,' Declan said, trying to reassure Hector, who'd stood up to make his way out of the bedroom, sensing the tension and no doubt feeling responsible as Declan had heard that dogs do.

'Stay here, it's ok.' Declan tried to encourage him back into the room as he settled in the hallway, unconvinced, studying Declan, too smart – too perceptive – to be deceived into thinking everything was ok. Declan read the message again as Hector sighed, his head on his paws, out of ideas – he'd had enough of watching his best friend being tormented by the little rectangular thing that was always in his hand.

'Who's this,' Declan replied.

'Jordan. Where are you?' The phone fired back instantly. Declan noticed that the text messages that he'd sent had a green background, which, he presumed, meant that Jordan now had a pay-as-you-go phone, 'a burner'. He laughed, shaking his head.

He probably still had his iPhone, Declan thought, but it was with this phone, it seemed, that they were now to communicate. Declan wasn't a personal acquaintance any more, this was business. He shook his head again.

'I'm going to work. If it's about last night . . .' Declan typed, looking around his bedroom before reading and then deleting the unsolicited second sentence.

He stared up at the Artexed patterns on his bedroom ceiling, reminding himself not to be placing the blame for the incident entirely on himself, and to hold fire on any apologies, for now. 'I'm going to work.' He read his message again, clicking send before he could doubt his blunt and strictly pertinent reply.

It was only Jordan. Even if he was doing the admin work for someone higher up the chain of command, it was only fucking Jordan. Declan felt an anger rising in him, one that would yield again to fear once he had processed the night that lay ahead – but, still, it would get him through this exchange of messages.

'What time do you finish?' asked the numbers at the top of the phone screen that Declan's phone was now to identify Jordan by.

'9pm,' Declan replied, ending the conversation, reading it back, pleased that he hadn't come over as intimidated as he now felt.

'What the fuck, man,' he whispered to his ceiling, tossing his phone on to his bed – it didn't need any further power, it was better off dead, he thought, hearing it fall off the edge, on to the floor below his bedroom window.

'Come on, pal,' he said, his gentle, high-pitched voice hoping to assure Hector that everything was ok, that he wasn't worried and daunted by the prospect of both starting and, now, finishing work.

'Come on, we're going out,' Declan announced, his voice as playful as he could make it, managing to just about convince Hector, who stood back, stretching his paws out and shaking himself around, his ears flapping and surprising Declan's face with a smile.

He leaned into the bathroom to pull the immersion cord of the shower, switching it back off. He slid his arms into an old tracksuit top that had been hanging by its hood on the corner of his door and zipped it up, ashamed at how tight it felt.

He looked back through to his bedroom, at his phone, lying face down on the floor.

He thought of phoning the number, to speak to Jordan, to try and sort out last night and establish why he wanted to talk, or to at least establish if he was definitely coming to speak to him after 9pm, after his shift, and whether he could expect him at his work or at his house.

The paranoia and the waves of anxiety had surely peaked now. It couldn't get much worse, he hoped.

Don't fucking phone him, he told himself, knowing that Jordan would love to hear him scared, that he'd get a buzz from the power of it all.

Fucking burst the cunt, he tried to laugh, reminding himself again that it was only Jordan, that he was just a wee dick.

Declan couldn't fight – he'd never tried, he'd never had to. He'd always been a pacifist, albeit involuntarily, but he'd survived high school with minimal bullying and he'd thought that his life, from then on in, would be violence-free.

He thought of phoning Connor, for advice, or to see if he'd spoken to Jordan, but he didn't want to bother him. There wasn't much that could be said or done anyway.

He'd need to face up to his actions. Deal with it himself. He was a big boy. A man, he affirmed, his eyes contradicting him as they surveyed his bedroom, his single bed and his college bag, full of untouched sociology textbooks, half-written psychology notes and, of course, his screenplay ideas and his scripts.

What are you doing, man, where are you going? he sneered at himself, relieved that a solitary bark from Hector sent the voice scarpering from his head, halting yet another attack.

He clipped Hector's leash on and opened the door. He hadn't noticed that the rain had started again until he stood on the top step, grappling with the door handle and the lock.

He thought about going back inside, for a jacket or at least something with a hood, something a little heavier than his tracksuit top, but he felt Hector glaring at him, like his patience had been tested to the limit. 'Where are we going, where are we going,' he whispered to Hector, riling him up and watching him march ahead, dragging them out to face the world.

★   ★   ★

Declan looked over to the checkout area, throwing his thumb up to say goodnight to one of his colleagues, Del, who he'd been speaking to during their break.

He carried on walking towards the main exit of the store, taking himself through another, final recap of the previous night, in preparation for the drama resuming.

He'd managed to force down and retain a chicken wrap from the staff canteen – in another hangover, he'd have gone to the KFC across the road but work offered him immunity, a sanctuary of witnesses and in-store security cameras.

For the best part of his shift, he'd been carrying out a near forensic analysis of everything that had taken place, poring over all the details, the evidence that supported his sense of dread, which, in a twisted paradox, had at least made his eight hours of shelf-stacking go by a lot quicker than usual.

He'd forgotten about the car though. The BMW X7. The one he'd swung a kick at.

The one that was now sitting with its headlights dimmed outside the twenty-four-hour gym that he passed on his way to and from the bus stop.

'Saturday, I think. Aye – see you then,' he managed to answer Sharon – one of his supervisors – as he considered his options. He could go back inside and wait for a while, he could try and run or he could carry on walking towards the bus stop, towards the car, conceding that this wasn't a problem that was going away and at least the worrying was about to be over – one way or another. It was merciful of them, in that respect, he joked to himself.

He carried on towards the car, humming a nervous melody as he watched it out of the side of his eyes. Fuck, man. Fuck.

He wished the Declan from last night were here, to deal with his debris. He wondered what the punishment would be or what he'd be forced into doing in order to avoid it.

Fuck them. Fuck them. He remembered he'd had a point. He looked at the car Jordan was driving his immediate superior around in, and thought of the lifestyle that pricks like Gary Tanser lived. He thought of the eight mundane hours that had just passed and the hourly rate that would barely pay for two driving lessons.

People like Gary Tanser loved finding a new goon like Jordan, to run around for them, selling their shite and collecting their money so that they could keep the mothers of their children satisfied with a steady cashflow – which, Declan imagined, was probably used to fund breast enlargements, arse implants, lip filler and Botox injections as they spent their vapid afternoons taking selfies of themselves in gym clothing, looking for an Instagram filter that concealed the fact your boyfriend was a heroin dealer and that you were tormented with trying to compete with your own mental images of the two or three younger girlfriends that you were aware existed but who were never seen, or to be spoken of.

Declan knew Gary Tanser and the rest of them would have seen plenty of Jordans and that they were always scouting for new ones: naïve, impressionable guys in their late teens to mid-twenties, lost in their personal quest for virility, and enjoying the initial streams of income and the local clout, and then craving further power, of being someone, a name that people were scared of. And that was when they'd pounce, dishing out to them the jobs that the rest had outgrown, that they'd tell them were essential for their evolution, for their career progress: the driving people around, wherever and whenever they wanted to go, the Friday nights going round collecting money, and next being made to look after all sorts of contraband – cannabis, ecstasy, cocaine and then fuck knows what.

You'd be recompensed for the risk and the paranoia, but the eye-opening down payments would diminish if you had the sense to equate them to the potential years spent in prison or the years spent in exile if you didn't fancy the jail time and chose to name your superiors. Your own complaisance would eat away at you as the undesirable workload piled up. You couldn't say a word to anyone above you, so you'd take out the fear and the frustration of the claustrophobic, subservient world – that you'd voluntarily entered – on anyone you deemed to be beneath you, and this was where Jordan and Declan were at. Last night in the pub had seen to it that Declan was fast-tracked to the front of a queue that he otherwise wouldn't have joined.

He felt himself getting worked up, angry – which was probably better than panicking, he thought, watching as the driver's side door opened and Jordan walked round to meet him.

'Awright – this yous here to give me a lift home?' Declan opened the exchange, relieved that he'd had a line, relieved that his voice hadn't quivered, that he hadn't attempted to run, to hide.

He looked at the passenger seat, at Gary Tanser and the

same smug expression on his face that brought back further vivid images of last night, encouraging Declan to stand his ground – being in the right was as strong a self-defence as any, he tried to tell himself.

'You're lucky you've not been fucking leathered for all that shite in the pub. I had to talk them out of taking you away. You fucking owe me,' Jordan started, keen to get the meeting underway. 'Look at me,' he followed up, turning round to Gary Tanser. The lack of conviction in his voice heartened Declan, calming him almost, and alarming him – in a comical way – that Jordan seriously considered he had a future in this sort of world.

'I owe you fuck all, Jordan,' Declan dismissed him, taking a step beyond him, to begin walking away.

He felt his knees shaking. He had no idea what their plan for him was and he knew his act would disintegrate as soon as he let it.

He knew Jordan would be feeling the same, somewhere within him.

'Listen to me, man.' Jordan grabbed Declan's arm, turning him round and looking back to the car, to make sure Gary Tanser was watching before butting his head into Declan's.

'He's no' happy about last night and your life won't be worth living if you don't play ball here,' Jordan started.

'Play ball,' Declan repeated, shaking his head, grateful to now have a condescending smirk masking his fear.

'I don't want anything to happen to you – to happen between us – but they won't listen,' Jordan carried on, seeing that Declan was looking right through him, at all the years they'd known each other. They'd grown up near each other, their mums had been friends for years, but true friendship required stronger qualifications than just geography and history, as Declan was beginning to learn.

'I need you to look after something – and there's a grand in it for you, a thousand pound – that's a lot of trolley pushing.' Jordan nodded at the Morrisons sign.

'What do I need to look after?' Declan said, curious as to how deep Jordan had got himself in, an enquiry that Jordan took as a sign of his interest, as a sign that negotiations were advancing.

'It's a shooter.' Jordan looked back to the car, back to Gary Tanser, who was messing about on his phone. 'A grand – two weeks, four tops,' Jordan added, his gullibility already stretching the terms, like Declan was almost convinced.

'A shooter,' Declan repeated, making sure to laugh, right into Jordan's face, making him look away, embarrassed, humiliated, angry.

'Get to fuck, man,' Declan told him, attempting to walk away again, looking back through the window of the silver BMW that Jordan had been driving about in to make sure Gary Tanser could see that Jordan hadn't secured a deal – that he was getting nowhere.

'I'm fucking serious,' Jordan shouted, looking around himself again and grabbing Declan. 'You're lucky he's not cut you up, ya fat ugly cunt' – his voice got louder, shooting spittle into Declan's face.

Declan felt his heart pounding and a lump in his throat, his bottom lip was quivering and he pleaded with himself not to break down, not to show any weakness – he pleaded with himself to get angry, to throw a punch, fucking anything, just don't cry.

Gary Tanser opened his car door – laughing, entertained. He looked like he could see that Declan looked rattled and close to tears. 'Ladies, ladies, come on,' he addressed them both.

Declan saw that Jordan was getting agitated too, and panicking, running out of ideas. He was clearly acting under duress and Gary Tanser – or whoever it was – probably didn't give a fuck who looked after a gun, or whatever, as long as someone did.

That Declan had said no meant that this was back on Jordan. It was up to him to take care of the 'shooter' – to take it home to Slam Dunc's mansion.

'Please, man, I'm sorry, right, come on, man, you'd be doing us both a favour, you'll make a grand – and last night's forgotten.' Jordan had lowered his voice, making sure that Gary Tanser hadn't heard him pleading.

Declan had never seen this side of Jordan before – a vulnerable, humble side – because it didn't exist. He knew it was an act. Manipulation. It seemed a horrible situation that he had managed to end up in, for whatever reason, but Declan spared himself the futile search for sympathy. 'I'm not playing ball, mate. No chance. It's your problem,' Declan said, making sure to be heard by Gary Tanser, hoping to mask his fear, to at least deny them the satisfaction of seeing how terrified he felt, and to show that he wasn't about to be bullied, that he'd take his punishment, that he'd be choosing a potential few nights in hospital over a potential few years in jail.

'I'll need more than a G to hold a shooter,' he told Jordan, a final effort at making him realise how ridiculous the whole situation was and how his new patois and his new demeanour were fucking embarrassing. He tried to smile, to make himself laugh even, trying to get into the character of someone who didn't give a fuck whilst hoping there was someone watching, someone who would deter them from at least bundling him into the boot of the car.

Fuck that, he thought, studying Gary Tanser, watching for a cue for any violence to start – he sold shitloads of drugs and he made a fortune so he wouldn't want to be up on an assault charge if the store cameras caught anything, and under Scots law Declan wouldn't be able to have any charges against him dropped, as Doof Doof always mentioned whenever a victim or someone was being intimidated in a film or a series. Pathetic pricks, Declan thought, and then said aloud, doubling down, fully resigned to the fact that something bad was about to happen and that he'd be as well speeding the whole thing along.

'Looks like your wee plan's not working then,' Gary Tanser told Jordan, looking at Declan, who kept his stare, just like the night before, breaking it only to watch as Gary Tanser slid something down his sleeve, moving towards Jordan, brushing against him as Jordan took whatever it was off him.

'Go! Get it fucking done!'

Declan moved his head towards Jordan. 'Get it fucking done, Jordan, do what you're told,' Declan said, patronising Jordan, before being knocked to the floor, feeling his head crunching off the concrete, bouncing back up to see Gary Tanser appear behind Jordan.

'Think you're a fucking hard man, a fuckin' wideo in front of every cunt in the pub. Fucking fat mongo – and this is going to happen every time we fucking see you.' He shouted into Declan's face as the blood poured from what felt like his eyeball.

'Get intae him,' he barked at Jordan, who kicked him in the ribs. 'Fucking hit him,' Gary Tanser screamed as Jordan booted Declan again and again.

'Fucking go, hit me!' Declan screamed into the sky, hoping to both keep his dignity and to attract some attention to halt the attack.

'Ha!' He forced himself to laugh through the impact of each boot landing stronger than the previous one before Jordan finally staggered back, putting his hands on the back of his head and slumping against the car, shaking with anger, or fear, or whatever it was that he felt upon realising that, despite his offer of money, his emotional blackmail, his use of a weapon, his repeated booting of someone he'd known his entire life, whilst he lay on the floor – the gun was still his problem and he'd been laughed at.

'Harder, go, harder, harder, ya prick,' Declan spluttered, proud of himself that he wasn't pleading with them.

He'd managed to bait Gary Tanser into kicking him himself now, a serious boot that felt like it came right through his kidneys. Declan closed his eyes and tried to think of Hector, of Georgie, of his bed, of the hills, of a life away from all of this, hoping the excruciating pain could somehow pass in silence.

'See if you're still laughing next time – ya fucking fat freak,' Gary Tanser warned, his voice one of total hatred.

'Fucking pathetic,' Declan whimpered, seeing through one

112

eye that Jordan looked close to tears as Gary Tanser pushed him into the passenger side of the car, deeming him unfit to drive.

'What's going on, what have you done?' a voice shouted at Gary Tanser as he got into the car.

'You just tell your wee passer-by here that this was a hit from the Sainsbury's mafia,' Gary Tanser told Declan as he tried to get to his feet, his eye totally fucked and his ribs definitely broken.

Declan heard Gary Tanser drive the car towards him, rolling the window down as the older, educated-sounding man who'd witnessed him booting Declan told him that he'd be calling the police and taking note of his vehicle registration number.

Declan watched as Gary Tanser threw a pile of paper napkins out of the car window, confirming the amount of blood that was pouring from his eye, from whatever Jordan had struck him to the floor with. 'There you go, fatty, every little helps,' he laughed, accelerating away, the laugh hanging around for a few seconds, making sure Declan recognised it. It was the same laugh as in the pub the night before, when he'd been insulting Georgie, the same laugh that started it all, the laugh that required a victim.

Only the blurred shape and the translucence of the moon managed to make it through the blood and the swelling as Declan tried to open his badly injured eye.

He listened as the car sped off, screeching to a halt at the roundabout beside the gym and then off again, into the night. The terror, the hurt, the sadness, the exhaustion began pouring the tears out of him, now that they'd been cleared to do so.

Declan wiped his face with the sleeves of his work fleece as the tears diluted with blood from his injury – telling the man that he was fine and just needed left alone.

'Please, man, just let me go, please. I'm begging you, mate, it's done, I'll be fine.' Declan made it on to his knees and then his feet, coughing and wiping his nose as he staggered away, hopefully in the direction of his bus stop, like his journey home from work was to simply continue.

'Declan, Declan. Oh my god!'

He heard a car slowing and a female voice screaming. It was Sharon, his supervisor.

'Declan, stop!' she shouted.

The pain and the concern in her voice had been like Georgie's last night. He stopped, turning to let her look at him.

'You need to go to hospital, Declan. Oh my god, what happened?'

Declan looked back across the car park to see that the man who'd witnessed the end of the attack was walking towards the store, probably to let someone – someone like Sharon – know that one of their colleagues had been attacked.

'I'm fine. I need to go home. I need to let my mum know I'm all right and I can't leave my dog alone again.' Declan felt his voice crackling, his head reminding him how pathetic he looked and sounded as Sharon got out of her car to try and help him.

'I'm sorry, man,' he told her, staggering away, leaning against a bin to avoid collapsing in agony. He knew he wouldn't make it to the bus stop, he knew he couldn't get on a bus in the state he was in, and he knew it was a bad idea to go for a walk around, like this, with just his head for company, especially with the fresh feelings of degradation and helplessness that would all be fighting for their say. And then there was Gary Tanser's threat, that there would be more to come, which his head would enjoy reminding him of.

'Declan!' Sharon snapped, like she seemed to know that he was listening to voices other than hers. 'Please! You need to get to hospital, now get in the *fucking* car . . .'

PART 3

The flight to London Heathrow hadn't yet been assigned a gate so he'd stationed himself in the JFK airport departure lounge's neutrally positioned Dunkin' Donuts.

His Americano scorched his taste buds – he estimated it to be at least a quarter of an hour away from attaining any sort of drinkable status. Lisa, his wife, always laughed at his infantile habit of never allowing hot beverages the sufficient time needed in which to cool down.

The metallic-like feeling on the tip of his tongue always made him think of his dad and of them going to the football together and his disregarding his dad's warnings – like he now did with Lisa's – to let his Bovril cool first. He had the impatience and the folly of youth to blame back then, but he was now in his forties.

He blew into his coffee cup, glancing back over at the Dunkin' Donuts counter, thinking of the effort it would take to walk back over to the front of the queue, off to the side, as though forming a breakaway queue of his own.

He'd have to hold up his full, steaming-hot plastic cup to the wary eyes, to demonstrate that he'd already made his purchase and it was the after-sales department he required.

He'd ask for a drop of cold water – or even milk – but he

knew he'd have to repeat himself a couple of times with either request. His accent would consolidate the two syllables of the word water into one; a flat, incoherent grunt whose registering with American ears would all depend on whether or not the letter T put in a shift.

Milk came with its own linguistic obstacles and it also had potential to open up an enquiry – there was no such thing as just milk any more, in the age of lactose-free, soya, almond and organic, and all the other words that started to bother you after you turned forty.

He considered using his generic American accent, which, as well as serving him well professionally, often proved to be a convenience in situations like this.

By the time it took to gather up his passport, he countered, and his boarding pass, both of which he'd laid out in front of him, at the small wooden ledge against the Dunkin' Donuts window, which faced the Hudson's newsagent's store with its multitude of self-help titles on display in the window – everyone who passed through an airport wanted to improve it seemed – and by the time he'd lifted up his rucksack, which wouldn't survive long, unattended, in an American airport . . . and by the time he got a staff member's attention . . . and, and if he took his belongings and left the seat, then someone would probably take it . . . He felt like he still had more points to make in favour of remaining seated and simply waiting for his coffee to cool but he'd already stopped listening to himself, the verdict was unanimous. Fuck it.

He didn't even know if he wanted a coffee – it was late and he hoped to sleep on the plane, to make a start on catching up with the UK, but he wanted somewhere to sit and the coffee was the proof that he'd paid his dig money.

He blew again into his coffee, considering the efficacy: was it ever the air you blew that cooled the contents or was it just time itself?

He wondered why airports instantly made him feel tired.

He sent a text to Lisa telling her that he was taking off. It was late in Glasgow – he couldn't be fucked trying to figure out how late, but he knew Lisa would be in her bed and she wouldn't go to sleep until she'd heard he was on his way back across the Atlantic.

He'd been spared the full details of Lisa's day at his old family home, keeping an eye on Siobhan, who'd been re-adjusting back into the real world, back into society, after another three-month stint in treatment. He knew the first few weeks were crucial and that the boredom, the job-searching process – to try and add some stability and structure to her days – and the judgemental staring and gossiping in their home town had the potential to send her spiralling again, back off the radar.

Lisa had probably known he would have too much time on the flight over with which to overthink and blame himself for things that he'd been told he couldn't control, and that it was best to wait until he'd got back to Glasgow, or at least London, before she confirmed if any new lows had been hit.

He noticed she'd begun writing her reply as soon as his message had sent – presumably she'd been lying with her phone in her hand, struggling to keep her eyes open, awaiting the cue to clock off for the night and to enjoy the freedom of their king-size bed.

Their *super* king-size bed, he said to himself, in a comical exaggeration of the superior voice of their noble neighbours in Glasgow's 'salubrious' West End.

He hadn't known that there was a size bigger than king size until a few months before, when they'd treated themselves to a complete bedroom overhaul, Lisa's way of telling him that she wanted them to spend more time at home, in Glasgow.

Super king was still a term he associated with cigarettes though, not sleep.

He felt an excited jolt go through him as his eyes lifted ninety degrees from his phone and performed a rapid, covert inspection of the immediate vicinity. He familiarised himself with the location of the nearest toilet. He looked back at his phone to see his wife was still typing: he knew her message and he knew his reply. He'd spent a sizeable chunk of their marriage in airports. His mind was now consumed with the thought of sneaking a few draws of his electronic cigarette.

He wasn't sure if vapour could set off a smoke alarm, but when he was in airports and he felt powerless and at the mercy of his nicotine addiction – and the formidable alliance it formed with boredom – he was always careful to try and guide his exhale, aiming it down towards the toilet bowl and then flapping a free arm around, attempting to restrain the splinter groups of mist that had fragmented from the original flavoured cloud and were sauntering to their freedom, on the other side of the cubicle door, drawing suspicious glances from the urinals.

He always unlocked the door apprehensively, fully expecting a member of the airport security team to be waiting to lead him away, but when he'd safely reached the sink, and the residue from his permanently leaking vape tank had been washed off his hands and the nicotine had bullied his endorphin receptors into easing his tension and restoring his energy levels, he'd feel a sense of bravado, his swagger returning, and he'd smile at himself in the mirror, thinking of how he should be commended for his efforts – it was a monumental feat, to leave the men's toilet of an airport smelling like a home economics class.

The ammonia, the sulphur – the excess coffee and sugary drinks and the violent aftermaths of KFC meal deals – would all be temporarily masked with vanilla, rhubarb or strawberry custard pie.

Unfortunately, these scents seemed to arouse suspicion in gentlemen's restrooms.

He quickly searched on his phone to see if JFK Airport had a designated smoking area, which were harsh places to go to, for a reformed smoker, turned vaper.

To have to share a confined space with those who chose to inhale tar and tobacco when he didn't want anything stronger than propylene glycol or glycerol gracing his lungs. *John F. Kennedy International (JFK) is a completely smoke-free . . .*

He put his phone back down.

A nicotine craving only lasts six minutes, he had read or overheard somewhere.

Was it six minutes? Doubting himself, he picked the phone back up.

How long does a nicotine craving last? he asked Google, typing as quickly as he lost interest in the answer.

Twenty million results. Fuck me, he sighed at his phone, looking back at his coffee, shaking his head as the steam was still rising from the cup.

He looked back over at Hudson's window, at the self-help books. He wondered how much income that 'quitting smoking' literature generated and tried to make out a few of the books' complete titles. He could only read the emboldened buzz words. Think. Overcome. Clarity. Secret. Control. Responsibility. Habit. Routine. Morning. Success. Emotional intelligence.

All the shit that sales executives, investment advisers, hedge fund managers and budding young future CEOs and internet start-up entrepreneurs got a buzz out of reading and recommending.

Self-help books or prostitutes – if you want to lure in business travellers just stick either in your window, he summarised.

He considered writing this sentence down, thinking it could work as dialogue some day for a character, but his pen was in his bag and his bag was on the floor and unreachable from his elevated seated position on the narrow metal bar stool that had started to give him pins and needles in his left leg.

He didn't put up any resistance to the evening flight, airport departure lounge inertia and let it convince him that it wasn't that good of a line anyway. He was a big-time movie star now, not a lowly writer, he told himself, feeling his own words sting before trying to distract himself from cogitating on the matter, examining the twenty-dollar hardback solutions to life's problems.

Americans fucking love a solution, he declared, smiling and

widening his eyes, not entirely sure of what he meant. Take this if you're tired and take this if you can't sleep, he explained to himself, feeling his eyebrows moving in sync with the rhythm of the examples as they came to him.

Take these before you work out, take those after you work out. Take these if you end up addicted to those and those if you end up addicted to these, but you shouldn't, but you could, so take that after you take it.

'Fucking nutters.' He shook his head, looking over at the Dunkin' Donuts queue, at America, smiling wider, in a playful 'what are you like' type of way, as though America was just the world's big daft pal – a strong and dangerous, often volatile pal, but daft, all the same.

The word 'fuck' featured quite a lot in the titles of self-help books, he noticed, squinting. He could make out things like 'not giving a fuck' and 'fuck it': the sort of thing that gave these books a quirkiness – like they wanted to give you good advice, to steer you away from any pitfalls, but they didn't want to seem like a teacher or a parent, more like your youngest uncle or your older brother's cool friend.

His phone vibrated, confirming delivery of the 'have a safe flight' text from Lisa.

His phone told him that she loved him and that she couldn't wait to see him, along with a rapid thumb's worth of kisses – everything that could serve as consolatory final words to look over should a loved one die in a tragic plane crash. 'Love you too,' he replied. 'I'll phone you when I arrive.'

He remembered he'd need to actually go into Hudson's, to buy Lisa a Milky Way – every time he'd been in America without her he'd brought her one back, it was a tradition based on one of their many private jokes, stemming from years ago, when she hadn't believed him that in America a Milky Way was what they knew as a Mars bar.

He smiled, thinking of cuddling her when he got back to Glasgow in a few days and of her being genuinely delighted that he'd remembered the Milky Way. She had a way of making silly things like this seem like they were the true essence of what life was all about. He thought of how much he missed her too.

His phone had no meaningful use now until he landed in the UK. He knew he should turn it to airplane mode and put it in his bag and maybe buy a newspaper, or a magazine, or even a book – something which he could apply some linear focus to, as opposed to the infinite, chaotic, limitless, ADHD abyss of the Wi-Fi-enabled smartphone.

He took another painful sip of his coffee and caressed and studied his phone again. It was nearly one o'clock in the morning in the UK and he knew all the football scores from earlier and there would be little else happening.

He looked at all his applications – he couldn't remember the last time he'd listened to an episode of one of the twenty-odd podcasts that he'd subscribed to or the last time he'd achieved his daily goal of Spanish or French practice and made the little guilt-tripping green owl thing happy.

He remembered being in Cannes. A film he'd written and co-directed had been nominated for two awards. It won neither, but he'd taken Lisa with him and they'd travelled north to Nice for a few days' holiday and his French hadn't been as good as the needy, sycophantic green owl had told him.

He considered getting a beer. Getting drunk was tempting – it had fast-forwarded many a journey. It had been nearly five months since he'd drunk, he calculated, a personal record. He'd stay fresh though; if he was promoting something that he was passionate about, then maybe he would enjoy it and view the upcoming release as a celebration.

Next time, he thought, his thumb still hovering over his phone.

He'd had to lose two stone for this latest role and the studio had their own dieticians and personal trainers, so his health and fitness apps had stagnated too, and they would remain that way for the foreseeable future as he'd granted himself at least a stone and a half to be spent on takeaways. He'd never had to do anything like this – he'd grown a beard and shaved his head before, but this was the first time there had been any real aesthetic requirements in the contract.

He thought of the press tour being over and the film, hopefully, being forgotten and of receiving his final payment for it and then moving on.

He thought of spending time with Lisa and maybe going on a holiday and then he thought of Siobhan – which had become a form of self-harm.

He found the feelings that came to him when he pulled back from the undeniable success of his own life – the productive, creative hours spent in writers' rooms, the film sets, the chat shows, the luxury hotels, the transatlantic flights – hard to explain, but he'd thought about it that much that he'd begun forming analogies to try and make it easier when he'd spoken about the situation, to Lisa or Dr Nikouladis, a cognitive behavioural therapist that Lisa had found for him in London.

He'd been thinking about his childhood a lot throughout the week in New York, it was that kind of city, the epicentre of 'look at me now' and 'who would have thought . . .' moments of reflection.

It made you feel like you'd lived your whole life in a sleepy, backwater ghost town, bereft of opportunities, but now you'd made it, you'd reached the pinnacle of the world, he remembered thinking, the first time he'd ever visited.

He'd thought of his third or fourth year at high school. He'd got into an argument at the end of lunchtime with Michael Taylor, a reputed hard man, who'd told him he was 'dead' or 'getting it' or whatever, after school.

The threat had been issued in front of enough witnesses to ensure that there was pressure on the aggressor to follow through with it, or else he'd be seen as being 'all talk', thus denigrating his status as one of the school's mentalist cunts.

He had a double period of English that afternoon and the teacher had spent the entire first half of the class focused on a homework assignment that he'd handed in.

Mr Higgins had heralded James Cavani's work as an example to the rest of the class on the use of great descriptive text and of forming narrative structure. He should have felt like a geek, like a teacher's pet, he should have been embarrassed, but he loved the subject and he knew, even then, that his future lay in writing and creating stories.

He admired Mr Higgins too, so he was delighted and remembered feeling goosebumps and wanting to head home, there and then, to tell his mum and dad.

The elation that went through him only lasted as long as it

took him to remind himself that the clock was rapidly ticking towards half past three.

His fear wouldn't let him enjoy the acclaim or let him concentrate for the rest of the lesson. An hour after Mr Higgins had proclaimed James Cavani as the golden boy of the standard grade English class, Michael Taylor punched fuck out of him.

When he got home, he knew that his mum, and later his dad, were too concerned with his cut lip and black eyes to listen to the news of his moment of glory, so he kept it to himself. It was a life lesson that had manifested itself several times since.

The gratification of the top marks, gold-star homework assignments were all too often mitigated by the Michael Taylor jab, cross, uppercut, left hook, right hook combinations.

Only Lisa knew how much it ate away at him, how much he loved Siobhan and how hard he'd tried to fix things, to fix her.

He felt a bad mood coming on.

He knew he couldn't do anything about Siobhan right here, in this present time, and he tried to focus on something else before it consumed him. He tried to switch his mind to thoughts of anything else, quickly, like grabbing a dish towel in the kitchen before the flame from the pan engulfed the whole house.

Be in the moment, control the now, he told himself, looking again at the books in Hudson's window.

He knew he was up to no good with his phone, and the longer he carried on flicking, the more inevitable it would be that the part of the brain responsible for making shockingly bad decisions would have its way.

He'd known since he first saw the script and who was

directing that the film wasn't his kind of thing, and that he'd hate everything about it.

It was a big role though, 'the next level' as his agent had said, when telling him the original fee offer, before vowing that he would tell the producers to 'have a look down the back of the sofa' and come back with an even better figure.

Agents loved this, that was how they got their buzz, he knew.

They'd receive as reasonable enough an offer as could be expected for a role, or a script, but they'd take a little bit off the fee when telling the artist about it, promising to work their magic, to have it increased.

They'd seek assurance from the artist that if the producer, or commissioners, agree to the amount that agent was going to fight for – the amount that had been offered in the begin-ning – then the artist was in. The artist agrees, appreciating the hustle as well as the work, and the fee.

He'd never let on to his agent that he knew this went on, and he never would, he played along with the game. His industry was full of bullshitters and there was a charm to it, sometimes. It *was* the world of entertainment, he supposed.

He began typing the name of his latest film into the Google news section, stopping before clicking 'go' like a relapsing alcoholic holding a can of cider against their lips and con-templating the risks, pleading with themselves not to take a sip, or a recovering gambling addict, deliberating over whether or not to stick some loose change into the fruit machine, just to see what happens.

He thought of the press and what they'd be saying. 'You should never betray your artistic principles' – this, he would accept – 'no matter the size of the cheque' – but this he would dispute. What would they fucking know? It's easy to turn down something that you'll never be offered, he thought, responding to something that hadn't actually been said.

He'd heard that the early critics had been scathing, especially the British press, who had singled him out, taking the condescending 'We thought he was better than this' angle and the predictable narrative of the 'homegrown talent' who'd had his 'head turned' by 'Hollywood' in a 'complete departure' from what had made him successful.

These same critics had loved his early work, describing it as gritty, edgy, dark and all the other adjectives that didn't pay very well.

He'd been praised for the 'cutting-edge' writing of his three award-winning series and other critically acclaimed shows and 'arthouse' films which he'd written and also starred in. The production company had sold the rights for his first television show, a dark comedy, initially set in a young offenders' institution but which followed the adolescent inmates after their release back into society and the contrasting paths they chose to follow.

The American remake, set somewhere in Massachusetts, had been a success. It was now in its sixth series – or season – which was one more than he had written so it was no longer his work.

It infuriated him at the time that his agent neglected to put in place some sort of clause in the contract that said he'd have an input in the script and the direction.

Still, though, the new custodians had created a part for him and it had gone down well.

He'd landed gradually more prominent roles and his profile in America had built steadily, to the point that he'd been invited on to a couple of late-night talk shows, where he'd managed to charm with his strong accent and his dry, and at times scathing, sense of humour. He hadn't exactly cracked America, or been trying to, as the British press would have it. He didn't know what he'd been trying to do. What is anyone trying to do?

He knew the remainder of his time in Dunkin' Donuts would be more productively spent looking through the press schedule that had been forwarded on to him, his agent had told him earlier in the afternoon, when wrapping up a phone call that he couldn't remember much else about.

There was to be a Zoom meeting with someone that he'd pretended to have heard of, a producer, someone who'd worked on something . . .

'He's hot just now,' his agent – thrilled about the new realms that they were operating in – had told him over the phone, as he'd been lifting a sock up from his hotel room floor with his foot, flicking it on to the bed, disappointed at missing his suitcase by mere centimetres.

'No, thanks,' he'd shouted, appreciating the hotel's housekeeping staff announcing their arrival and gently knocking on his door. He'd held the phone away to listen for an 'Ok' or a few seconds of sustained silence that would indicate that they'd moved on to the next room.

'Sorry, carry on,' he'd said, his agent laughing, and the subject of who was hot and who was not was stopped in its tracks, as his agent asked how the hotel was.

'No, thanks. No, thank you. I'm checking out later today,' he'd shouted again, louder this time, enunciating every word and sounding like a Scottish expat, like the ones he'd met the afternoon before, when he'd walked downtown to an Irish bar to catch the second half of the Celtic game.

'Aye, it's nice. Ideal.'

He'd run out of words to describe hotels. In the early days, in his twenties, when he'd acted in a few small touring productions and the cast had stayed in depleted, horror-movie-vibe bed and breakfasts, he'd had more entertaining reports for anyone calling him from home. In the early days of his success too, when he'd first stayed in four- and then five-star hotels, and then luxury suites, like this week, courtesy of the production company's dollar.

He always tried to remain grateful but the novelty had worn off and he tried to spend as little of his time away in hotel rooms, especially in New York, where he and Lisa had lived for a year. He knew the place well but he could still get lost and spend entire days walking, stopping for a coffee, writing, reading and doing nothing.

Taking in people, taking in life.

He knew that there was nothing to be gained from searching the internet for feedback on your work, or on yourself, but when he began typing, he felt like he was yielding to an urge that had been with him since the film's North American release.

He felt present and in the centre of himself for the first time in hours, since a yellow taxi had almost collided with the Mercedes people carrier that had brought him to the airport, sending him diving into one of the three seats that had been facing him and then back again as he impulsively attempted to counter the g-force.

The driver had rolled down the window and shouted 'Asshole' and afterwards apologised, several times, for the outburst, for the language and for having made his passenger feel uncomfortable, or in danger, or offended.

The driver's repeated apologies began to grate on him, more than the initial fright of being fired up and down the back of the vehicle had bothered him. He was probably used to chauffeuring the worst fucking people in the world though, the type who'd want him sacked for less.

He considered shouting from the back that the driver of the yellow taxi was a wanker, to show his own proclivity for profanity, before remembering American's didn't use this term, or the hand gesture. 'Cunt' was a bit much for Americans – it shocked them and tended to sour the ambience.

'What a prick. Forget about it, mate,' he'd declared from the back.

'Totally,' the driver replied, sounding more natural. He glanced at his interior mirror for eye contact, and Cavani nodded, confirming the end of any drama.

He began browsing over the first page of articles related to the film. A few interviews from the main cast members were already online and a couple of lukewarm headlines from indifferent reviews begged to be clicked.

'Visually stunning' seemed to be the closest thing to praise that the film had received. A quote that would no doubt be pounced on by the press team and be emblazoned below the film's title – and the names of the lead cast – across billboards and on the sides of buses, and wherever else that they felt they could let people who wanted to be stunned by visuals know that their employers had made just the thing for them.

At least his name wouldn't make the bus, he consoled himself, as he typed it into the Google search bar, craving more of a hit, looking to confirm some personal accountability for the film's lukewarm-to-poor early write-ups and the undoubted flop that it was to become.

Searching his name was something he only did when he knew a project had been a failure. He'd never set out in search of positive reviews; he knew within himself when something was good. He knew when something was bad too, but he always wanted to explore and discover exactly how bad. He'd put a ceiling on positivity but negativity was infinite.

He remembered advice he'd given when speaking at an event at the Edinburgh International Film Festival, where he'd spoken about his concerns at how creativity being hindered by self-consciousness was a particular problem, now, in the age of instant, impulsive feedback, like the kind found on the internet, where everyone had access to hundreds of platforms from which to voice their opinions, even people who didn't have anything meaningful to say.

Looking at comments on social media was like being offered, say, 100 pills and told that approximately 70 of them would give you an instant, but very short-lived, Dopamine hit. About 20 could ruin your day, 5 could ruin your week and 5 could do significant long-term damage. Would it not be better to simply carry on, without the pills?

He'd put it to the crowd, presuming that the majority of them agreed.

There were no benefits to reading criticism, or praise, provided you were of a reasonably rational mind and weren't deluded enough not to know when something had been substandard, or shite, he'd continued; shite was a simple yet effective term.

You knew what you were getting. Most people didn't review anything, they simply told others that it was good or shite. Sometimes brilliant, sometimes utter shite.

James Cavani knew he had a human touch and a reasonable grasp, still, on what people liked. He understood people and, despite his past decade of success, he hadn't changed as much as his comfortable life suggested.

He knew there was no end, that no one ever 'made it'.

Even if you produced a masterpiece, the trophies would simply stare at you from your new shelf in your new office, taunting you about being unable to follow your own work and how the glory days were behind you.

The more successful you became, the harder the work got, and once you accepted that, then trivial things like reviews or online comments were an unnecessary impediment.

He knew all of this. The learning process had started after he'd followed up his debut short play – which had been given a short but favourable review in one of the Scottish Sunday papers' culture supplements – with a contrived dud in which he'd almost tried to tailor the story and the characters to placate Scottish Sunday Paper Culture Critics.

He remembered a review being dismissive, rather than overly critical, which was probably worse.

The respectable-sized audiences, considerably larger than his first run – a consequence of its success – had shuffled out in silence, a little disappointed after his promising first effort.

He'd read the script back a few weeks after the week-long lunchtime residency had finished, and he didn't recognise his own characters or his own storyline. He felt bad for the audience members and ashamed that they'd taken a chance on him and he'd let them down.

He'd made a rule – there and then – of always asking himself if he would pay to watch whatever he was making. If he would, it was a success, and if he wouldn't, then it needed work or put out of its misery. Everything else was irrelevant.

He thought of that afternoon in Edinburgh, of dispensing life advice to a few hundred people in a tent. He winced at himself now, the worst version of himself ignoring every danger that the best version of himself had warned of.

He hoped that at least someone would have taken heed of the advice that had been dispensed, with so much authenticity and conviction, even if it wasn't to be him.

His eyes moved from the screen to the side, to his passport with his boarding pass tucked inside – just over halfway, like a bookmark. He looked at his coffee and then up and around at the airport in general.

It had got considerably busier – the gulf separating him from the self-help books was now packed with passengers walking with purpose, too busy concentrating on getting to their own gate, to start their own journeys, to their own destinations.

It was just a film, he was just an actor, so fuck, he thought, relieved he'd managed to pull his head above water before his obstinate refusal to let any positive feedback register had him drown in a self-flagellating sea of negativity.

He watched a parent pull a plastic, cartoon-tiger-designed mini-suitcase on wheels, with a delighted-looking toddler on the back. The little girl looked as curious as you would expect a child in a crowded airport to be and he watched as she placed her foot out, halting the tiger, whenever something new took her interest.

She slammed her brakes on right in front of him and her face turned stern, as though his smiling at her had killed her buzz.

He tried a wave but she'd looked away. The dad nodded at him, offering a defeated but polite enough 'Hi' and then said something to his daughter in what sounded like Dutch, or a Scandinavian language, before picking her up, along with the tiger. The little girl let out a piercing scream, intent on making the whole airport aware of her perceived injustice.

He thought of how many times he'd have lost the plot trying to navigate a busy airport with a toddler on the back of one of these, if he and Lisa had ever had kids.

He always felt a little melancholic when he contemplated what his children would have been like and what kind of father he would have been. It wasn't too late though, but it had been a while since it had been mentioned. They'd gone through – well, Lisa had gone through – the IVF process three times now and they were both beginning to accept that it wasn't to be.

He reached to take a sip from his cup, feeling his entire face crease as he swallowed the bitter-tasting, cold liquid, looking around to see if anyone had been watching him.

The entire coffee had passed him by. He pressed for his

phone to light up, to check the time, looked at his boarding time and then his flight time. 'Fuck,' he announced, the word landing with a thump and halting any conversation within a twenty-metre radius. He grabbed everything in front of him, crushing it into the front pouch of his hooded jumper.

He felt the glare of the older couple beside him but he felt like he didn't have time to even offer a hurried smile at them, in apology for his sudden, coarse outburst.

He took the 50/50 gamble and turned right out of Dunkin' Donuts, power-walking over to the nearest screen to check the status of the flight and from which gate it was to be leaving. The red 'Gate Closing' notice beside London Heathrow revved up his heart rate, filling in for the coffee that he never drank.

He looked at the ascending order of the gate numbers and set off through the terminal, weaving in and out of bodies, like a tricky winger dancing round defenders, being roared on by the thoughts of having to waste another few hours in an airport, of having to go and collect his bag and get rebooked on a new flight to London, subject to availability, of course. He thought of having to fly to Dublin, or Amsterdam, and having to connect and how tired he would be, all day tomorrow, doing the interviews for this film, this fucking film. He'd have to pay for it himself too. Would he go business class if it was coming out of his own money? At the last minute? He knew his working-class upbringing wouldn't let him. He'd be listing all the things he could have bought – but wouldn't have bought – with the money instead. If he'd only fucking paid attention, instead of sitting in a Dunkin' Donuts, googling himself.

'Fucking pathetic.' His angry reprimanding of himself

played like an audiobook in his ears as he managed to sustain a steady 'Gate Closing' pace, making it to the gate as his name was being read out.

He handed his crumpled boarding pass and his passport over to the gate stewards, with a smile that conceded he was at their mercy.

He began thinking of how his narrowly missing a flight, in an American airport, had been like a scene from a 1990s romantic comedy, before he heard the words '*Milky Way. Fuck!*' fire out from his mouth.

It was so impulsive that he didn't even have time to adjust the volume – to remind himself of where he was. Getting yourself arrested in an American airport was an extremely straightforward task, and even catching a taser, or a bullet, wouldn't be overly challenging.

'Excuse me, sir?' the woman behind the young guy who held his boarding pass and passport said, walking over, studying him.

'Sorry,' he replied, realising he was a lot more breathless than he thought and forcing out a noise that he'd intended to sound like a laugh but which only added to the manic, tense vibe that he'd brought to the gate.

'Ah-meant-tae-get-ma-wife-a-Milky-Way, ah fuck,' he heard himself say, in a voice he felt like he hadn't used in weeks. He looked around the departure lounge, his legs dancing – moving from side to side – like a child pleading to be allowed to go to the toilet.

The two gate stewards now stared at him, taking a moment, rummaging through the debris of his sentence, probably only managing to salvage 'fuck', and, maybe, 'wife'.

'I promised my wife I'd buy her a Milky Way,' he said, taking on an entirely different persona, speaking in perfect English, translating for himself.

His words being understood only added to the confusion, however.

'When does the flight leave exactly? How long do I have,' he asked, as though speaking to Alexa and Siri.

'The gate closes in exactly three minutes, sir.'

He looked around again, unsure whether or not to run to the other, smaller, Hudson's that his eyes had located on their frantic reconnaissance mission.

Lisa would think it ridiculous, if he'd missed his flight for the sake of a private joke, but it had been almost fifteen years that it had been going on and the daftness of these little things was sacred.

He pictured her laughing, like she did every time, and then laughing even more when he told her of the high stakes involved in procuring this particular bar.

He'd heard enough from himself and ran, knowing he'd be unable to stop until he saw a Milky Way.

He felt the two members of airport staff's eyes on him the entire way, not sure what they should be doing about this behaviour, that could very much be labelled as suspicious.

They still had his boarding pass and they'd see he was a business class passenger, so that should ease their concerns, he thought, as though you only got nutters in economy. The 9/11 hijackers flew business class, his head reminded him. 'Shut the fuck up,' he whispered, out loud, to show his head he was serious and this wasn't the time to try and wind him up. He got to Hudson's and began rapidly examining every chocolate wrapper on their shelves, their names firing through his head before he'd read them.

'Fucking yes,' he whispered, grabbing the Milky Way and surveying the queue as he bounded towards it with purpose.

There were two people in front of him and he saw that the older, white-haired man who was being served – dressed in double denim, Stetson boots and a red baseball hat – was only just inserting a card into the reader as the bored-looking guy serving looked to the floor.

'Fuck. Come on. Come on to fuck.' He willed both parties to speed up the transaction

'Come on to fuu-uuck,' his breath sang, adding some harmony now to his impatient muttering.

He glared through the exposed semi-circle of the back of the old man's head as he was carefully entering his pin number. 'Use the contactless, man. Jesus.' He felt his words just about escaping from his barely open mouth, as he tried to count the number of items in the hands of the guy immediately in front of him.

He side-stepped out to the left of the queue, checking first that there was no one behind him, and then looked back at his gate to see the young guy who had been holding his passport and boarding pass speaking into a handset before placing it back behind the desk.

'Fuck,' he opened his wallet. He had a hundred-dollar bill and a fifty. 'Fuck it.'

He slid the Milky Way into the pouch of his hoody and walked to the front of the queue, his eyes hurriedly searching around the old man's in-flight provisions for a charity tin. He slid the fifty inside, unsure of what needy cause that he had alleviated the guilt and the shame of shoplifting, in support of.

'Wow, very kind. May the good Lord bless you, sir,' announced the man as he waited for his 'payment processing'.

He sprinted back to the gate.

'There,' he said, proudly, showing his Milky Way to the two baffled staff members as though the whole situation would now make sense to them.

He exaggerated his breathing and made a satisfied, exerted, puffing noise – to break the silence of the wary confusion – and collected his passport and boarding pass with a cheerful 'Thank-a-you' and made his way into the air bridge.

He heard the gate staff telephone through to the onboard crew, their routine call to let them know that boarding was complete and he laughed as he wondered if they'd mentioned that there was a potential lunatic on the flight.

He looked around him, at the business class cabin of the plane, looking at the expressions on the faces of his fellow business classmates as they hammered away at their laptops and sipped at their Merlots or their Malbecs, or Riojas – he hadn't checked the wine list. The novelty of flying business class wore off when you weren't drinking, but the food was always all right and the feeling of lying flat on your back on an aeroplane, with your legs fully extended and your head on a pillow, made the world seem more accessible.

He passed some of the time between meals browsing through the entertainment menu on the flight, but it had only reminded him, again, of how bad the film he was travelling to London to continue promoting had been.

He'd looked below the film titles, at the star ratings that had been assigned by previous passengers of this airbus A380, and thought of flying in a few months' time and seeing his past four months' work sitting on top of a solitary star out of a possible five or maybe two, at the very best three – the idiots of the world sometimes came to the rescue of films like this.

There had been some decent-looking explosions, granted, and the effects team would no doubt be nominated for some awards, so at least the film would have something in return for its obscene budget.

He hadn't seen the final cut, or any cut, of the film. He'd been invited to sit in on some of the editing days but he'd declined. He only had a supporting role and he'd had no creative input to the script, so the film's inevitable flop wasn't exactly all on him.

He knew he'd been drawn to the money though, the most he'd ever been paid for anything, and it wasn't work that he could be proud of.

'Work', that's what it was, he thought, feeling like he'd just been pulled aside by a wise voice, a voice of reason. Very few people actually enjoy their work. He was one of life's rare exceptions. Not every job, however, could be expected to be fulfilling, or gratifying or whatever other feelings that 'artists' were supposed to strive for.

He thought of being back home and of the few friends from his childhood he was still in touch with, and of their jobs. Some of them worked on building sites, early-morning starts in brutal weather, working for hours – real work – where your whole body ached and you collapsed over your front door at the end of the day, wishing it was a Friday and you could go to the pub and blow a hole in your wages.

Going to the football on the Saturday, or Sunday, with an Indian takeaway and time with their children weaved in between.

It was a life where fulfilment and gratification only showed up as and when they saw fit.

Your team scoring a last-minute winning goal, a winning football coupon, your child cycling for the first time without stabilisers, the Indian takeaway throwing in a complimentary portion of chicken chaat as a spontaneous thank you for your loyal custom.

Fulfilment and gratification weren't things you could demand from life seemed to be the point he was making to himself, or whatever – he was bored of reminding himself how he had it better than most and how he should be grateful and had nothing to complain about.

He looked down at the outlines of his feet as they protruded from under the airline's branded blanket as a member of the cabin crew appeared at his right-hand side, holding a tray towards him and addressing him by his choice of evening meal. 'Beef tenderloin?' she said, smiling. 'That's me, thanks very much,' he answered, accepting that the point the assertive voice in his head was trying to make had just manifested itself in physical form.

He looked for the button to revert his bed to a reclined-seating position and unwrapped his napkin, gently tipping his knife and fork on to his tray table, beside his two miniature cans of Diet Coke.

'So, James, I know you can't give away too much but what can we expect from the film . . .?'

He played out some variations of the questions that he knew he'd be asked over the next two days in London, accepting that he had to fulfil his promotional duties, professionally, and then it would be over with.

'It must have been a great laugh on set, we saw this clip, on Instagram . . .'

He tried to shift away from the generic, to be prepared, knowing that they loved to ask about all this sort of stuff, especially if there had been clips and photos uploaded from the set, granting the public a sneak – thoroughly vetted by agents and press officers – peek at what goes on behind the scenes.

His blunt, airline-secure knife struggled to make an incision in the flesh of the late cow that lay before him, as he felt his lips moving: 'James, big role, what was it like working with . . .?' He mimicked the dead-behind-the-eyes, robotic, early-evening magazine show hosts and their vacant, mid-distant stares as he'd answer, knowing that their focus was on their earpieces and their producer's voice, telling them how to react to the answers and what to ask next.

Aw, who gives a fuck? he'd be thinking, willing himself to say, for the cathartic value rather than the shock, but, of course, he'd smile and answer like a true celebrity – upbeat, enthusiastic, selling the fuck out of something and delighting the publicity team as they sat in the green room, eating wasabi peas and talking about how exhausting it was, working in their industry of double-barrel surnames, where emails and phone calls are considered units of energy.

He managed to cut himself a couple of mouthfuls of flesh and then messed around with his dauphinoise potatoes, his shallot onion, the flat-cap mushroom and some vine-ripened tomatoes, deploying a childlike tactic, hoping that his re-arrangement of the tray would disguise how little he'd eaten.

He pressed at the beef with the back of his fork and watched the blood as it seeped through the gaps between the tines, knowing that this was one of those moments when he'd tell himself that, one day, he'd go vegetarian.

He lifted the airline's headphones off his head and placed them round his neck; he hadn't been listening to anything but they served well as a do not disturb sign – the last thing anyone wanted on an evening flight, sober, was to meet a new friend.

He'd shunned the entertainment options in favour of observing the aeroplane's progress over Nova Scotia and Newfoundland and then across the water, as an elementary-looking graphic of a small aircraft crawled, from left to right, along the northern hemisphere.

The outside air temperature was displayed on the screen too, along with the altitude that the airliner had reached and the speed at which it was firing him through the air.

It was everything that reminded you of your insignificance, that it could be all over in minutes. He'd started to feel a bit claustrophobic and panicky, like he wanted to get off the plane, as though it were a bus. He told himself, futilely, that some fresh air was what he needed.

He looked at the screen again and tried to breathe deep,

conscious breaths, alerting himself to the fact that they'd flown just south of the Labrador Sea, hoping that this would prompt wholesome, happy thoughts – a sea full of dogs, retrieving tennis balls and bringing them back to the shore.

He was aware how hard he was trying to force a laugh or a smile, speaking to himself like an overwhelmed new parent speaks to a crying baby.

He tried to think of Lisa and if she were here, and how she'd probably take the piss out of him for this, which would genuinely make him laugh and smile and calm down.

He knew from experience that only he could talk himself out of these anxiety attacks and that if he alerted any other passengers or any of the crew, then it would make him worse. They'd try to calm him, but it would have the opposite effect. Once people were aware you were panicking, it was too late.

They'd assume that horrible-sounding tone which was intended to soothe and to reassure, but that to the person freaking out just sounded so disingenuous, like it belonged with members of a religious cult – and all you could picture were the sets of eyes above your head, looking at each other, bemused, wondering what the fuck your problem was.

He held the button that controlled his chair, straightening himself up, as though preparing for a landing. He searched up and down the aisle until he spotted one of the cabin crew, walking with purpose, carrying a fresh tray towards someone seated behind him, who'd presumably complained about something, or amended their meal choice at the last minute. 'Hi, sorry, I'm done with that, if it's ok,' he informed her, knowing his words weren't important, that the unfastening of his seatbelt and his sweating, grey-coloured face would see that his tray was removed without any polite resistance centred on how little he'd eaten or his perceived lack of satisfaction, followed by the insistent offers of a replacement beef dish or a fish or vegan alternative.

He lifted his tray table and led it to its fall into its compartment, on his left-hand side, above his remote control and his complimentary vanity pack.

He threw himself out of his seat, noticing how fast his heart was beating, his legs feeling like it was the first time they'd ever carried him.

Going to the onboard toilet was the only acceptable reason for a passenger to be wandering the aircraft during the in-flight dinner service, but the thought of entering the cramped restroom and feeling even more confined worsened his anxiety and he felt like he was actually willing himself to panic, telling himself that of course he should be freaking out, it *was* terrifying, there *was* nowhere to go, he *was* stranded.

He wanted off, he wanted down, but, obviously, it wasn't an option.

He began moving towards the front of the plane, using the back edges of the other business class passengers' seats to propel himself forward.

All around him were screens playing in silence and food being chewed semi-consciously, supplementing the dystopian theme that his mind had been going for.

He didn't want to turn back, for fear that anyone had been watching him, curious as to what he was up to, wary even.

He approached a curtained-off area, simply because he

wanted to keep moving forward, abruptly finding himself apologising to another member of cabin crew, who'd burst through, into Cavani's side of the curtain, narrowly managing to avoid colliding straight into him, almost dropping a full tray of drinks.

'Can I help you, sir,' the man challenged Cavani – his name badge introduced him as Alejandro, a senior flight attendant, who, according to the national flags beside his name, spoke Spanish and Italian, as well as English.

This unexpected, mid-course trespassing into the service area had clearly irritated Alejandro, and his eyes scanned the quartet of effervescing glasses, trying to gauge whether or not top-ups would be necessary, once the fizz had settled.

His uniform had overruled his instincts and he'd just about managed to cut off what would have been a fully justified 'Fuck sake!' – or a Latin equivalent – and he forced his face into a professional smile, to compensate for any of the initial hostility in his tone, remembering that he was there for the passengers' comfort and well-being.

'Sorry, mate, sorry,' Cavani apologised, pressing his back against the partition that separated the business class area from the first class. He felt the colour racing back to his face – he was grateful for the embarrassment, it had brought him back to himself, it had centred his mind and presented him with something tangible and trivial to be concerned about.

'Are you looking for the restrooms?' Alejandro asked, presuming Cavani had simply got himself lost, which was pretty hard to do, but, then, he was a senior member of the team, so he'd probably dealt with all sorts of morons over the years.

'Aye. Yes. Back there, are they?' Cavani said, pouncing on

the offer of an explanation for his aimless wandering around the cabin.

'Straight back down and they're on the left, and the right,' Alejandro said, offering a more sincere smile, a smile that apologised for having snapped at his passenger but that also questioned how anyone could struggle to locate one of the plane's many toilets.

Alejandro took a step back and, with a cheerful nod of his head, invited Cavani to lead the way, seemingly satisfied that his four flutes contained sufficient champagne to avoid any grumbling from the onboard revellers.

Cavani's senses were returning and a new, relieved calmness had come over him. He looked over the heads of the passengers, towards another curtain – the one that separated business class from economy – he mouthed a silent 'Ah' and threw his head back and accelerated himself towards the toilet sign, as though suddenly enlightened; a charade for anyone who had maybe recognised him and been curious as to what he was up to, if they'd observed his sudden meander in the direction of the flight deck.

He noticed a few subtle double takes from the, presumably, British passengers as he made his way past them. He opened the toilet door and stepped in. He hesitated – acknowledging that he'd only narrowly averted a panic attack – and then locked the door. His eyes struggled with the sudden brightness that the swipe of the door latch had brought.

He looked himself in the mirror, took a few deep breaths, and then splashed his face and the pulse points of his wrists with cold water. He wished he'd brought his vape from the front pouch of his bag, but he hadn't known that his fear-induced saunter would lead him to the toilet.

If he were to set off the aeroplane's smoke alarm it would mean serious fucking bother, he reminded himself, paraphrasing the sign above the toilet seat, cautioning his instincts. The nicotine would be great though, even if just to blast away any last remnants of anxiety, the reckless part of his brain contested.

Alejandro hadn't been entirely convinced that he was just another gormless passenger, lost in search of a toilet. He imagined Alejandro's reaction if the toilet's alarm had gone off and he saw who emerged from the scented fog. Fuck it, he thought, regaining control of his mind.

He dried himself with a paper towel and flushed it down the bowl, watching as it paused before being hauled into its chasmic black hole. He unlocked the toilet and walked back to his seat, smiling as he made eye contact with the flight attendant who'd removed his meal for him. She smiled back, as though she'd been concerned about him and was glad to see he looked a bit calmer and healthier.

He put his headphones in and messed about with the remote control until the screen switched off. He reclined his seat and tried to disembark his head from the plane: he filled it with thoughts of being done with the film in a few days, of seeing Lisa and of the rest of their stuff being packed up from their flat in North London, their home for the past twelve years, and of the big move back to Glasgow.

He thought of Siobhan and hoped maybe this was the time that she'd given her treatment and rehabilitation programmes a real chance, again, and of her getting her life back. He thought of his own life, and of regaining some control of who he was.

He was making more money than he'd ever made and it was only going to keep going that way – there were offers on the table, big offers, big films, big piles of fucking shite. He was comfortable, financially, but not within himself. He thought of getting back to writing, to where it all started. It was escapism to him, until he got good at it, and successful, and then it trapped him and left him needing an escape from his escape, which was usually where drink, drugs and gambling came in, but that had been done, and done better, by bigger and better 'celebrities' than him. He felt himself grin – he'd forgotten where he was. He tried to open his eyes but they were too heavy.

Cavani woke up to Alejandro smiling and apologising – this time for interrupting what had felt like and must have looked like a deep, peaceful sleep – informing him that they were well into their descent towards Heathrow and that he'd need to return his seat to its upright position and fasten his seatbelt. 'Ok, mate,' he yawned, checking for the vanity kit, his stale breath hanging in the air in front of him.

'Do you have much planned for your trip to London,' Alejandro asked, waking him up fully, as he tried to formulate an answer, whilst feeling for the seat's recline button.

'Just working, sadly,' he laughed, insincerely, wishing he was back asleep.

'They tell me you are an actor, a very famous actor? Maybe I can have a picture with you, when we land?' Alejandro was saying, whilst leaning over to adjust the seat for him.

'Thank you,' Cavani said, smiling in acknowledgement of his own struggle with the seat. 'I've done some acting, yes,' he said, feeling the awkwardness in his stomach.

He'd never quite mastered the answering of questions like this, from people who didn't know him or any of his work, but who'd been tipped off that he was famous.

It had happened a lot. People were obsessed with fame, it was a modern thing, he thought, just about managing to restrain the old man inside him.

'I'm a writer mainly though,' Cavani said, for his own benefit, aware that Alejandro didn't give a fuck. Fame was fame. 'We'll get a picture, no problem,' he followed up with and Alejandro smiled.

'Amazing, I'll be at the front of the aircraft when we land.'

'Nice one, mate.' Cavani nodded, reaching for the vanity kit, telling himself, 'Two more days of being a celebrity and then back to work.'

The distance to the hotel and the expected time of arrival were displayed on the oversized tablet in the middle of the dashboard, to the driver's left, along with the in-car temperature, the outside temperature and the day's weather forecast in general, and some other details that he didn't study enough to figure out. The early-morning news and sports headlines passed across the bottom of the screen, swiftly, as though aware of the viewers' indifference and knowing that the smartphone app notifications would be the first to divulge the information, if anything major were to happen.

He didn't recognise the artist's name or the name of the

track that had been playing for a minute and twenty-four seconds before, presumably, being paused by the driver, when he'd left the car to enter the terminal building with 'Mr Cavani' on his company display card.

It was a comfortable car, quiet, and it looked expensive. An electric, he presumed.

He didn't know a lot about cars. He was forty-two and he couldn't drive. It had held him back a couple of times, for driving scenes, but only in the early days, when the production's budget couldn't stretch to a low-loader and it was more practical to cast someone else if the driving scenes were essential.

He pressed himself further into the back seat, enjoying the leg room and the armrest.

He had his own touch-screen device in front of him too, at the back of the passenger seat, which controlled the temperature and had a heated-seat option. He could also choose what he wanted to watch as the driver had explained, in the swift in-car briefing, when welcoming him onboard.

There was a selection of charging cables too, if his iPhone, Samsung, iPad, laptop, Kindle, Nintendo Switch, headphones, vape and all the rest of it were in need of power.

The executive car company knew that the last thing any of their passengers wanted was to be alone with themselves, with their thoughts.

He still hadn't taken a proper read of the press schedule, he reminded himself. There was no point now though, as the print interviews would probably be starting as soon as he arrived at the hotel. He was headed for a series of exams that he hadn't studied for.

He'd wing it though, and try and divert the conversation on to anything other than the actual film. He realised he hadn't yet switched his phone back on. He'd do it in the hotel. He should probably have let his Lisa know, by now, that he'd arrived safely, but arriving was subjective, he justified.

He'd call her from the hotel. You were, however, many more times likely to die on the commute to and from the airport than on the flight itself, or whatever it was that parents told their kids on planes when they were young and kids told their parents on planes when they were old.

He hoped the film could maybe creep under the radar, which was unlikely given the lead cast and the delays in production which had built anticipation, and then frustration, from fans of the franchise and from the movie press.

A new royal scandal, that would bail him out and take the heat off the film, he thought, shooting a laugh through his nose, as the car crept along the M4, passing a billboard with a picture of Buckingham Palace and all the other Visit London attractions.

'Advertising London to people who've just arrived in London?!' He heard the intonations of every stand-up comedian he'd seen at the open-mic nights in the New York comedy clubs screech round his head.

The big-budget action film had had its day and the cinema experience was a thing of the past, with viewers preferring to stream content into their own homes, he considered.

A valid, if obvious, hypothesis and the type that he'd probably need to keep to himself over the next few days.

The superficial thrill of a helicopter crashing, a skyscraper burning or a gorilla firing a bazooka at a spaceship was negated by personal devices and humble-sized living room televisions with their speaker's limited capabilities being pushed to the limit.

Film was a writer's game again and this should be his time to step up: it was the time for real, truthful storytelling, something with some substance and most importantly something that he would actually watch.

He thought of how liberating it would feel to be truly honest and to fire off some of these soliloquys – that were heard only by his wife and, on several, recent, heated occasions, his agent – on a prime-time chat show and on the four or five radio shows and whatever other contractual obligations he had to fulfil for the next few days in London.

It would be cowardly though, and pretty transparent – deride your own work before everyone else can. He'd taken the money, he'd finish the job, which included the shameless promotion.

He thought of the chat shows, the radio shows and podcasts, newspaper interviews, magazines, cookery shows. It would be nothing he hadn't done before, just maybe not to the same extent; and at least, previously, there had been an element of pride and of genuinely wanting to let the public know when and where they could see your new project.

Fuck it. He unzipped the front pouch of his bag, to get his phone and to declare himself available and ready for whatever was lined up over the next couple of days.

As he reached into the bag, he quickly realised that the cabin pressure – or whatever it was that happened on aeroplanes –

had caused his vape pen to leak and the liquid had spilled all over his phone, its charger and a few notes that he'd scribbled on a Marriott-branded notepad. 'Bastard,' he whispered, looking at his hand, parting his fingers.

'Is everything ok, Mr Cavani?' the driver asked his mirror, slowing the car down.

'Yes, sorry, just something has burst in my bag,' he answered, wishing the driver hadn't got involved and anticipating that the word burst had been lost in his accent.

'My, eh, electronic cigarette,' he pronounced, 'it's leaking, on my phone.'

He shook his head, to show he was annoyed at himself and held up the phone and the vape, so that they were in line with the driver's view from his interior mirror. He began looking around the back seat, in search of something with which to wipe his hands.

The driver turned to face him and then looked quickly back to the road, torn between providing comfort or safety. The car indicated and moved out of the middle lane, towards the hard shoulder. The driver looked round again, alarmed at the thick, sweet smelling liquid as it settled on a gleaming model of the latest iPhone.

'Oi, oi, oi,' he said, indicating again and pulling off to the side of the road, slowing the car to a halt and putting his hazard lights on. He reached over to the passenger seat, his head disappearing as he let out an exerted groan – signifying that he was over-stretching his obliques – before reappearing, fixing his hat and tailored jacket, and handing back a packet of fresh hand wipes.

'Aw, what a man!' Cavani thanked him, still unsure if his

phone had suffered permanent damage but relieved that at least his hands wouldn't be marinating in a sticky, nicotine-laced residue for the remainder of the journey.

'No problem! No problem!' the driver said, pleased with his rapid-response rescue effort, his personality bursting through his work suit.

'The phone, it is ok?' the driver asked, in an accent that more or less confirmed Cavani's initial supposition that he was Spanish.

'*Yo no se*,' Cavani announced, looking at the driver, waiting for his laugh. He sat the phone carefully on his lap and wiped his hands, his vape now back inside the pouch of his bag, wrapped up in Marriott-sponsored, half-baked plot and character ideas.

'Ah, *muy bien tu español*,' the driver said, laughing, and then, in perfect English – as though this was too serious a situation for a language exchange – he encouraged Cavani to try and switch it on.

The driver looked up at him, then back at the phone, as if to state that the car would not be moving until this critical situation was resolved.

Cavani cradled the phone, held the button on its side and waited for the Apple logo to imprint itself in the centre of his double-chinned, fatigued-looking reflection.

'Vamos!' the driver greeted the emblem, followed by a cartoon 'Phew!' using the back of his right hand to wipe the imaginary beads of sweat from his tanned forehead.

The driver turned himself round and looked out of his right-hand-side window and then over his shoulder at the traffic as it whizzed past them. The pace at which the cars, buses and lorries were headed for London made the car feel like it was rocking from side to side.

'Apple! They charge me the full price for a new phone, two months ago. *Qué cabrones . . .*' he announced to Cavani, setting out to explain why he was so personally invested in the phone's survival – that it was too late for his phone, but he could try and salvage somebody else's, seemed to be his angle . . .

The driver checked the interior mirror again, halting his anecdote, to take a glance at Cavani, fearing that he'd crossed the executive driver/VIP passenger line with his swearing, albeit in Spanish.

Cavani was silent. Staring at his phone as it vibrated and pinged. Text messages and WhatsApp messages, which had been loitering in the firmament – in the cellular doorways, awaiting confirmation of his arrival in the UK – flooded in.

There were four missed calls, from Lisa.

He felt weak and ashamed of his internal whining about having to assume a persona, answer a few questions and tell a few light-hearted stories, to promote a film. Now, life was about to present him with some real problems.

His eyes scanned the text previews – *Call me as soon as you land. It's about Siobhan.* His stomach reacted as though the car had just accelerated over a hump on the road. He looked ahead, holding his phone to his left ear and then out, in front of his face, checking to see if his call to Lisa was dialling.

The car hadn't moved, as the driver, feeling the tension that had appeared upon the phone's awakening, edged it forward, slightly, waiting for a safe enough opportunity to rejoin the motorway and race towards the destination, assuming that whatever vicissitude that had just revealed itself to his passenger was unlikely to be resolved from the back seat of his car.

The sound of the car's right indicator played like a rapid countdown to Cavani, ticking off the seconds to another moment at which his life would never be the same again.

She's dead. She's dead. Your little sister is dead. He struggled to restrain his head as the blows rained down on his heart. He imagined Lisa having to say these words to him, after everything.

'Fuck! Come on, come on, answer,' he told his phone, as though it had been ringing for a length of time – but the call hadn't even connected yet – the permutations playing out in his head darkening.

This could be it. The day that he'd spent years worrying about. His little sister. Found dead in the street. Washed up in the Clyde. She'd be breaking their mum and dad's hearts one last time, by reuniting with them, in the grave, far, far too early.

'Come on to fuck,' he shouted at the roof of the car as it re-entered the left-hand lane of the motorway, the driver unsure whether this meant for him to hit the accelerator or the brake.

His phone let out a couple of defeated beeps, telling him, bluntly, that the call had failed. He restrained himself from smacking it off the car door. His leg was shaking now, his heel relentless in its banging on the floor of the car.

'I need you to turn back, mate. Back to the airport,' he ordered, his thumb setting about the phone again, as he stooped himself forward, through the gap between the driver and front passenger seat, to see through the front windscreen.

He looked through the right-hand-side windows too, and then the back, looking for the next exit that they could cut off at, checking the traffic flow in the opposite direction, trying to calculate how far they'd come from Heathrow and trying to work out, from experience, when the next flight to Glasgow would be.

He'd overwhelmed his brain with this sudden influx of enquiries and, at the same time, he was trying to process the rumour that it itself had created.

'But they tell me, the hotel, Royal . . .' The driver looked down at his display screen, to check for the full name of the hotel that the production team were putting Cavani up in, for the next two nights, before quickly realising that semantics wouldn't be well received in this moment.

'Fuck them,' Cavani snapped, feeling like he was in a car-jacking scene of a movie, an action movie, before he quickly pulled back and took the time to steady himself and calmly check the settings of his phone, to make sure it definitely knew he was back in the UK. He switched it to airplane mode and back again, as Lisa had taught him to do anytime it was being a useless piece of shite or whatever else he'd branded it.

'Sorry, pal, sorry,' he said to the interior mirror, with precision aim, direct into the driver's concerned and intimidated-looking eyes.

He reminded himself that he hadn't been told that Siobhan was dead, that he'd raced to the worst possible outcome from the concerning amount of missed calls and, admittedly, ominous messages.

Becoming aggressive to an innocent party though, especially a good-natured, cheery guy who was only doing his job, wouldn't help any situation.

'Not your fault, sorry. I need to go back, back to Heathrow. I'll sort it with them, I'll explain,' Cavani asserted, his accent unfiltered, but only the word Heathrow was necessary, given the sudden change of atmosphere.

'*Mi hermana,*' he told the driver, an apologetic nod to any rapport that they'd built up before the phone had been switched on and the outside world had permeated what could have been a pleasant enough car journey.

The sound of Lisa's phone number dialling made him straighten his shoulders. He passed the phone on to his right hand, checking the windows again as he sat up, fully focused.

'Ok, sir. As you wish,' the driver replied, in a calm but tentative voice.

'Lisa,' Cavani announced, confirming the call had connected, that he was present, and alarmed, and that he'd appreciate it if Lisa could get straight to the point. He listened in silence, staring at his knuckles as his hand clung to the car's interior door handle.

'She's ok, she's in hospital. She'd told me she was going to her work and then I didn't hear from her all night. I didn't want to worry you – I didn't know what to do, James.' Lisa sounded like she'd been crying and that she was about to, again, like she'd been dreading this call for hours.

Cavani knew his Catholic upbringing still lurked around

somewhere inside him as he tipped his head back, breathing in through his nose as he closed his eyes, thanking God that Siobhan was alive.

'It's ok, it's ok, there's nothing you could have done,' Cavani reassured Lisa, realising that he needed to pretend to be calm.

'She's in intensive care, James, I'm so sorry.' Lisa began sobbing. 'I'm so sorry. She told me that she was fine and even starting to enjoy her job, James. I thought this was it.' Lisa sounded truly heartbroken for both Siobhan and for him.

His eyes closed again, hearing Siobhan was in intensive care, aware that his gratitude to the Lord had been a little premature.

'Please, God, please,' he said, closing his eyes tighter, hoping to feel something in and around his chest, where he imagined the soul to be – like he'd done as a child, in mass, when he'd first started receiving communion and he'd kneel and pray to God to please never let his parents die.

'Right, keep me updated if you hear anything – I'm going to try and get a flight home as soon as I can,' Cavani said, leaning forward again, to see if the car was approaching any exits or service stations, aware that he was travelling at seventy miles per hour away from where he needed to be.

'We need to try and stay positive. She's in the best possible place and all of that, James,' Lisa said, words she probably didn't have much faith in, but she was trying to compose herself and stay strong, like she always did, for his sake.

'I'm heading straight back to the airport. I'll be on the next flight,' Cavani told her, looking at the side of the driver's face to check that his tone had emphasised the importance of his over-ruling of the destination on the car's display screen.

'What about the press, James, they're expecting you, your name's in all the listings. I didn't want to tell you but I couldn't not have. I'm so sorry.' Lisa sounded like she was about to break down in tears again.

'It's just a daft film, it's just work. This is family. It's going to be ok, right? We're a team.' Cavani softened his voice, hoping to calm Lisa down.

'I know. I know, but won't everyone be angry at you for just cancelling at the last minute?' Lisa asked, concerned, apologising as she blew her nose.

'It doesn't matter. Probably. Fuck them,' Cavani answered, making sure the driver heard how firm his decision was.

'I better get off the phone so I can book the flight. Keep me updated, right. I love you and I'll see you soon.'

He held his phone tightly and with his free hand took his wallet from his pocket, placing a credit card on his lap. He looked at the driver again, he hadn't turned around or looked in his mirror and was silent, nervous probably.

Cavani hoped that a generous tip could help offset any hesitation the driver might show about going against the executive car company's pre-booked system, which probably had a tracker. He probably had another job too, picking up in central London. He put a gentle hand on the driver's left shoulder.

'I'm very sorry. Family problems. My sister is in hospital, very serious.'

He articulated, parting the back compartment of his wallet, 'Take this, mate, for you, for the inconvenience,' he said, forgetting he hadn't gone to an ATM since he'd landed.

'Fuck,' he whispered. 'Here, a hundred dollars. You can

exchange it, maybe about . . . seventy-five pounds.' His attempt at generosity now just seemed tacky and disrespectful. 'Sorry,' he said again, carefully placing the hundred-dollar bill on top of the little compartment which had supported the driver's left elbow earlier on in the journey, when his demeanour was relaxed and he looked like he enjoyed his job and providing a personable service to his passengers.

Cavani rolled his eyes, embarrassed at himself, but he knew he wasn't thinking straight.

I just want home, he thought, feeling like he was going to be sick.

He thought of how he'd need to let his agent know – to let the film's producers know, to let the press team know, to let the television and radio producers and journalists know – that he was cancelling, that he was heading home, that his sister was in intensive care.

He thought of how any compassion, or concern for Siobhan's well-being, would struggle to even make it beyond the first link in the chain.

He looked at his right hand, noticing how tight he'd gripped his phone, as though it was a weapon, which, in a way, it was, he supposed. A weapon that had caused this pain and misery.

A few other messages pinged in but he was busy, trying to process his thoughts, staring through the car's back-right window at the steady flow of traffic as it made its way towards Heathrow, whilst he was being whizzed further and further from where he needed to be.

He wasn't sure who else had heard the news but he would be able to guess just by reading the names of who had text him. He had friends and family who were only there in the good times – a precious couple during the good and bad times – and some who were only there in the bad times. He hadn't heard from the first group, and he wouldn't, until the film's release, and maybe not, if it had bombed as badly as he expected.

He felt nostalgic for barely a quarter of an hour ago, when promoting this film was his sole concern for the day.

The middle group, he would see, no doubt, in person, later today, and the latter group had already begun getting in touch, judging by a couple of the names inscribed across his phone's home screen, across the photo of Lisa and him on the great wall of China.

They were a strange bunch, the ones who sent their thoughts to your sick and their prayers to your dead before disappearing back off the radar.

The meerkats of misery, he'd referred to them as, after his mum's funeral, when whispering for Lisa to rescue him and pull him away to the other end of the function room of the local pub where he grew up. He remembered laughing at Lisa laughing at this, and then both of them crying – the sadness and the grief recovering from its momentary lapse and returning, twice as strong.

He checked only the names of who had text him, which was enough to deduce the gist of their messages. His agent, checking to see he'd landed and making sure he was all set for the day. Allan, his accountant, fuck knows, something mind-numbing – it was halfway between January and June so he was up to date with end-of-year and mid-year taxes, a VAT return due, maybe, fuck knows, he'd find out another time. Claudia, the head press officer, confirming he'd received the schedule for the days ahead and with some pointers on what to avoid talking about, and, of course, reminding him to hammer home the cinema release date, as well as the streaming release date and to talk about how exciting and fun it had been on set, how the film had blown him away when he saw it . . . Again, he reminded himself of his own privilege, wishing he could go back to his old problems, prior to switching his phone on, when the superficial banality of the showbiz world was all that had been getting him down.

His cousin, Peter, had text too, possibly Siobhan-related: he'd be on a scouting mission for further details, on behalf of his parents, who'd long since cut Siobhan off, she'd told him.

They'd been ashamed to speak to her, even though she'd got herself back together and was managing to hold down a part-time job working in a café in the middle of the local shopping centre.

He clicked on the message from Peter; it was a screenshot from Derek Carruthers' Facebook page. *Who the fuck is Derek Carruthers?* he thought, before seeing his own name – James Cavani, but with two 'n's – in the middle of an early-morning rant, which had been shared and liked and commented on, related to Siobhan being seen wandering around the area, in a heroin-induced, zombie-like state, whilst her brother was living it up in London and appearing on chat shows, only concerned with promoting his new film.

He felt the car slowing down and the indicator ticking. He looked down and out of the front window to see they were pulling off the M4, to rejoin it and commence his homeward journey.

He'd long since learned though not to give heed to the Derek Carruthers of the world and their Facebook pages with their opinions on him and his little sister, their faux outrage and pity, their jealousy or resentment of him, or whatever it was – concern for Siobhan being something that could definitely be ruled out.

He felt angry, and then sad that his cousin had ensured that he'd seen this though.

He read Peter's message, below the photo, that said he knew someone who worked with Derek Carruthers, and that he could ask him to delete the post, if he wanted?

Who gives a fuck? he thought, scrolling up to see the last message Peter had sent. *Saw the paper. Are you ok?* it read, four months before, December.

December? The paper? he asked himself, as if trying to solve an equation, before remembering a tabloid paper had printed a front-page story on him being arrested following a 'brawl' in a hotel bar in Cardiff.

It had alleged he'd been the aggressor, which a police statement and subsequent lack of charges later confirmed hadn't been true, that he'd acted in self-defence against a man who had been charged with assaulting his girlfriend and a member of the hotel's staff and then Cavani himself, when he'd intervened.

He'd pressed his agent to ensure the newspaper printed an apology. They had done but Peter hadn't read it, or chose to ignore it, scarpering at the sight of a positive outcome.

He realised that he hadn't asked Lisa for the exact details of how Siobhan had been hospitalised this time. That she hadn't volunteered any though meant he could whittle it down to the standard, multiple-choice selections: she'd overdosed on heroin, there was another dodgy batch of heroin going around, or she'd branched out and tried the latest, brutal, synthetic street drug.

He looked ahead to see that they'd rejoined the M4, heading to Heathrow, his back to central London, to the film. He still hadn't let his agent know, a phone call that was certain to turn ugly.

He searched for Heathrow to Glasgow flights, distracting himself from the doubts that crept in as he anticipated his agent's barrage of persuasion, followed by threats, legal, financial, and about the damage this would do to his future, especially in America.

He thought of Siobhan, lying wired up to monitors, a burden to him, a burden to 'James Cavani' – that was how they'd seen her, the couple of times the papers had printed a story about her: an arrest for shoplifting and a photograph of her when she was younger and dreamed of being an actor herself, compared to how she ended up.

He saw the driver check his mirror for the first time in a while. He realised he'd been getting agitated again, rocking back and forward in his seat. He let out a sharp puff of breath, which he noticed had fought off the airline mouthwash and turned sour again.

This was a good time to make the contentious call to his agent, he thought, retreating from the comparison website pop-ups and their special offers and dialling his management office, his agent's direct line.

'Hi, is that you, Ray? It's James – is Curtis there? Or Christina? Thanks, mate.' He played out in his head what he was going to say, turning to look out the window as a car came racing past them, well over the speed limit, making him wish that his driver would rise to the challenge.

'Curtis, it's James,' Cavani went on: firm, authoritative, with the foresight to cut out the pleasantries about how his flight had been and if the driver had met him ok, if the car was comfortable, the London traffic, the press schedule – everything that would be even more hollow once the purpose of the call had been established and the anticipated reaction had manifested itself. It was the easiest way to do it – just getting to the point.

'Listen, Curtis, I'm heading home – to Glasgow – my sister is in hospital and I need to see her.' Cavani held the phone away from his ears, like he'd just thrown a grenade and he was protecting his hearing from the blast.

'Jim, this can't happen. Believe me,' his agent began, 'Jim, mate, come on, think man,' he backtracked, stuttering at his false start, unable to decide which tone to take.

Unable to decide whether to threaten or to plead, settling instead for a heavily caveated form of concern.

'That's terrible news, Jim – really, sending her big love, big strength, but come on, man, this is huge.'

The insincerity cemented Cavani's instincts – he'd been considering leaving his agent anyway, or firing him, whatever it was. Maybe this was the time.

'I won't be appearing on anything or talking to anyone. I'm done with the film and I'm heading home to make sure she's all right, right?' Cavani interrupted, his own tone growing threatening.

They'd had run-ins before, over his refusal to do an advert, despite the hefty fee involved, and – a few times – over comments Cavani had made in interviews. At least this wouldn't be a concern now.

'The studio will be livid, Jim, you'll never land a movie again – you're nowhere near big enough over there to survive a reputation for being unpredictable. Over here too, the chat shows, everything, fuck. Come on, Jim.'

Cavani could already feel the threats bouncing off of him. He was impervious to them, for now anyway.

'They won't have you on again, cancelling at the last minute like this . . .'

He could hear his agent's mind working, clambering for more examples to further substantiate his nigh-on apocalyptic premonitions.

'What about if you ever make something of your own again and you need to promote it . . .' his agent began, going for Cavani's weak points. '. . . and the networks too, they won't commission it to begin with . . . Fuck, Jim, come on, man. This is insanity.'

Every point his agent made about how reckless he was being only solidified his position, and the fact that the reason for his cancellations had been merely brushed over, the human cost forgotten. He considered telling his agent that the only way he'd be turning back to London would be to come into his office and put his head through a wall.

'And the money.' His agent's voice softened, like he was

going for the big one now. 'The studio wouldn't pay the final instalment of your fee, which specifically relates to your carrying out of the agreed amount of press and promotion.'

Cavani asked how much this was, an enquiry that his agent took as a lifeline. He didn't know why he'd asked though – his mind was made up and his heart was set. It was nothing but a morbid curiosity, or maybe his head wanted to store the figure for later, when it could taunt him about how everything was going to dry up some day.

'Close to 100,000 dollars,' his agent estimated.

That's how much his concern for his little sister would be setting him back, about £75,000, according to the exchange rate he'd used when trying to tip – or bribe – the driver.

'Well, I'm done with it and I'm done with you, all right. Game over. Fuck this.'

Cavani finished, doubling down in a pre-emptive strike on the inclinations of doubt that were already beginning to build in his head.

'You're a lunatic, an idiot, you're scared, scared of this, of real success.' Cavani placed the phone face down beside him, eavesdropping on his agent's voice as it whined to the car seat.

He turned his phone round to see that his agent had hung up, checking the length of the call to see that in just under three minutes he'd potentially lost a film career in America, a TV career in the UK, seventy grand and his agent.

He reached for his bag and, unzipping the front pouch again, took out his vape, before looking for a paper towel that he'd used before, to give it one more wipe. He clicked it a few times, making sure that it still had power and he checked the tank to see that some of the flavoured oil had survived the flight.

'Is it ok if I take a little smoke of this, it's an electronic?' he asked the driver, inspecting the advanced-looking control panel on the armrest of the door, for the button to slide the window down.

'*Cigarillo electronico,*' he affirmed, smiling at his hazarded guess in Spanish.

'Yes, sir, no problem,' the driver said, his tone one of understanding. His passenger was having quite the morning, and he could at least spare him the feelings of nicotine withdrawal.

His thumb pressed for the element to blast the heated chemicals into his lungs, as he released the clouds from the moving vehicle, to mix with the CO_2 emissions of the motorway air.

It was, by far, the highlight of the day.

His other thumb had discovered that there was a flight to Glasgow just after mid-day, which seemed achievable.

He entered his card details and waited for confirmation of his payment, and then the email arrived, innocent in its ignorance of the purpose of his trip.

Mr Cavani, you are going to Glasgow!

A low-flying plane roared overhead, indicating that they were approaching the end of their round trip. He wondered when he'd be in London again as he clicked his vape pen back off, sliding the window closed.

There was no action movie like life itself, he thought, cringing, as though he was concluding a scene. That he could never switch off, entirely, from work mode – from seeing everything as potential inspiration – made him feel ashamed.

Your little sister is in intensive care, he reminded himself, feeling dams of sweat bursting under each of his armpits and a stream running down his spine.

You can't control your thoughts, don't feel ashamed of them, they aren't you. He quoted Dr Nikouladis, from their first ever session, as a way of excusing himself.

He reached forward to take a can of water, like the ones that he noticed that were always on film sets now – eco-friendly, sustainable or something: he rolled his eyes – from the back pouch of the driver's seat. He'd been told, at the beginning of their outbound journey, that there were some under the armrest that separated him from the other passenger seat, where his rucksack was sitting, but he'd anticipated struggling to fathom how the thing opened, convincing himself instead that he wasn't thirsty.

He hadn't noticed how warm, dizzy and dehydrated he felt, until now, and the slight reach over to his right was less of a challenge than grappling with one of the fancy car's fancy storage compartments.

The can of water wouldn't open. He pulled the ring pull, like it was a can of lager, but it required him to slide it back and then pull it, or something. He placed it back in the pouch, frustrated.

Who decided to put water into cans and who decided to redesign the ring pull of the fucking can? He halted his internal tirade, seeing that the car had pulled off at the roundabout beside the airport, exiting towards Terminal 5. Siobhan and Lisa needed his energy today – the contemporary world was evolving and would continue to evolve regardless of his remonstrating from the sidelines.

'I hope everything is going to be ok, Mr Cavani,' the driver told him, pressing a button to close the car's boot and placing his suitcase on the kerb.

'Thank you. *Gracias*, pal,' Cavani said, distracted, but aware of how Scottish a thing to say '*Gracias*, pal' was, like he'd just been handed a *cerveza grande* at the poolside bar of a holiday resort in Tenerife.

The clock on his phone confirmed that he would indeed have made the half past ten flight. Typical, he thought, vindicating his own cynicism with a nasal laugh. He slid the phone back inside his pocket, aware that he owed the driver a final apology and an attentive and sincere thank you.

'Again, I'm sorry about all of that. One of those things, and thank you.'

The driver smiled. '*No pasa nada, mi camarada.*'

Cavani nodded, confused, his *Duolingo* Spanish being pushed beyond its threshold.

'Take care, mate. Cheers,' he said, taken aback by the strength of his own accent.

A puff of vape smoke caught his eye, reminding him that he'd be going another couple of hours without nicotine. He walked towards it, swinging his bag round from his back, feeling inside the front pouch for his own.

The little light around the power button was flashing, signalling that the battery was running low, that it was last orders. He hurried, rather than savoured, the last few puffs, extracting as much mist as he could until it was only fresh air hitting the back of his throat.

He placed the vape back in his bag, making a note to

remember and place it inside one of the little plastic bags that they hand out at security, or to at least keep it separate from his phone, as he entered the terminal building.

The screen informed him of his check-in desk number and that his flight was on time. He stood still, scanning the airport's vast, bright forecourt, plotting his route to the check-in desk and then to security, and stressing to himself, now, the importance of paying attention to the departure information screen.

Content with his journey plan, he set off, pulling his suitcase to the baggage drop-off, next to the less busy of the two security queues. Spotting and seizing upon an unobstructed opening, amidst the throng of tourists, couples, families and business people, he picked up momentum, advancing on his target without having to stop, change direction, or issue an excuse me.

He touched the 'confirm' icon on the screen, sending his suitcase on its way to Glasgow, feeling pleasantly surprised at himself, for being patient and managing to successfully operate an automated machine that had been performing what, 'in his day' as the old man who lurked inside him had been shouting from the distance, was a human's job.

'*No pasa nada, mi camarada*,' he said out loud, as his case set off on its journey, satisfied at how suave it sounded.

He walked towards the far side of the terminal, to the 'A gates', where his flight would be departing from, according to the information screen. He messaged Lisa as he walked through the corridor of designer fashion stores and jewellery outlets, telling her the time of his flight and his expected arrival time into Glasgow and asking for any updates.

Ninety days, Cavani thought to himself, putting his phone back in his pocket and searching for a seat that would give him a clear visual on his potential departure gates and a screen to update him on which specific one he'd be boarding through.

Ninety days she'd been clean and in treatment – what an effort, and for nothing.

He felt angry at Siobhan and then devastated for her, and then angry at the treatment programme itself. It had been a waste of time, a waste of money, like the rest of them.

He felt angry at whoever she must have run into when she'd returned home from her stay at the centre, which had been somewhere near the Scottish borders this time.

The peace and the isolation of being cut off from the local 'scene' and from all of her nameless, lost-cause acquaintances, had been his and Lisa's, and, eventually, Siobhan herself's, thinking behind the choice of location.

He felt angry at the tan-injected, veneer-toothed sociopaths who sold the shite and angry at the politicians whose criminalising of the drugs enabled them to make vast, untaxable profits from their unregulated products. Every time he read of a massive drug haul seized, he feared the subsequent dry-ups, the inevitable rise in street prices and what new, innovative cutting agents would be used to best utilise the stuff that had made it all the way through to the end of the supply chain. The less drugs on the streets the better, of course, but he'd yet to hear of anyone who'd gone clean as a result of financial constraints or obtainability issues.

You'd simply have to find new ways to generate an income

once you'd exhausted all of your start-up capital and then completed the pawn shop scene. The next stage would be shoplifting followed by burglary and prostitution, or else you'd have to find a more economically sustainable buzz, of which there was now an abundance.

Siobhan had never been charged with any sort of crime so didn't have a criminal record, that he knew of, and funding her addiction wasn't a problem, as yet.

He felt angry at himself.

With one of his first big pay cheques, he'd bought and renovated their parents' old council house, where he and Siobhan had grown up.

When their dad and then their mum, shortly after, passed away, Siobhan, after separating from her boyfriend at the time – their relationship crumbling under the pressures of her drug addiction, as it united against her with the trauma of her parents' dying in quick succession – had moved into it, promising that this was it, she was determined to sort herself out, once and for all.

As he thought back now, it had been the perfect recipe for another bout of self-destruction and he'd been too immersed in his own life, his own career, to foresee such a predictable outcome as this.

Siobhan had been funny, intelligent, thoughtful and, by all accounts, very attractive. She would have done well in film herself, he'd always thought, smiling as he remembered how embarrassed she used to get when he'd encouraged her to think about taking on some small roles in his productions over the years, to see how she enjoyed it.

He'd worried about her for as long as she'd been old enough to make her own decisions and live her own life, for as long as she'd started going out and attracting interest from men. There had been a young guy called Dominic, who'd thought he was going to be a professional footballer. Siobhan had been delighted for him when he'd landed a professional contract, but, panicking at the first sign of success, he chose to turn his focus on going out to pubs and clubs.

His income from football had been too humble to support the lifestyle that he'd craved, and, sensing the effort and the sacrifices that would be required from him to earn a wage increase and any additional bonuses, he got himself involved in the supply of ecstasy pills in the area's local nightclub.

He was eventually arrested and his house was raided, and he was charged and sentenced to five years in prison. Siobhan had stood by him though, despite her brother's and their mum and dad's pleas to forget about him and to move on with her life.

It was only when Dominic slipped up with his carefully synchronised prison visits that Siobhan realised that he'd had several Siobhans on the go – she arrived one afternoon at the same time as another girl, who'd aggressively introduced herself to Siobhan as Dominic's girlfriend and demanded he tell her who Siobhan was.

She'd just been a component in his archetype of the perfect life, the good-looking girlfriend to go with his football career and hopefully his car and his house. Siobhan meant no more to him than his Burberry shirts, his Armani jeans and the gold bracelet on his wrist.

There was no doubt that it had hurt and humiliated her, finding out, in the visitors' room of a prison, that she was being cheated on. It seemed obvious that she deserved better, but maybe, looking back now, to Siobhan it hadn't been.

After Dominic there had been Eddie Reynolds, who was older than Siobhan and had been in Cavani's year at school. Eddie Reynolds was another drug dealer, albeit on a much smaller scale, at that time, than he was now.

He didn't drink or take anything and he was besotted with Siobhan. Their parents didn't know much about him other than that he seemed polite and charming and thought the world of Siobhan. It had been Cavani himself who'd had a word with her, about where the money for her birthday, Christmas and random presents had come from.

She had broken it off with him after a year and he'd been heartbroken, Siobhan had said, but he'd wished her well, admired her honesty and been understanding that a relationship with someone in his line of work wasn't for everyone.

He'd always got on all right with Cavani too – they weren't exactly childhood friends, but they'd known each other all through school and they'd always been on civil terms as adults. Cavani couldn't help but concede that Eddie Reynolds was a nice enough guy, or, at least, a nice enough guy for someone who'd break every limb in your body and throw you into the Clyde if you owed him money or crossed him in any way.

James Cavani and Eddie Reynolds were the area's two success stories, which was quite sad, but he smiled, thinking of how they were both acclaimed figures in their respective industries of film and crime.

Cavani considered that if Siobhan had stayed with Eddie then he probably wouldn't be sitting here, waiting to fly home, to go to the hospital, again. She'd probably never have tried drugs and, if she had, at least they'd have been complimentary and strictly recreational.

That she'd have been a beaten-down, paranoid, guilt-ridden gangster's wife assuaged any guilt he felt about intervening in his little sister's personal life.

He'd been relieved that she'd left Eddie, and their parents had been too, when they'd found out who he was and then witnessed, through newspaper articles and regional news stories, who he became. Maybe he'd have straightened himself out and turned away from crime if Siobhan had stayed with him, and, in turn, Siobhan could have stayed away from drugs. It would have been mutually beneficial, but he'd got involved and ruined it. Aware that he was tormenting himself, Cavani calmly picked apart his hypothesis, acknowledging, again, that his head had been in screenwriter mode, that the Reynolds family were career criminals, that's simply what they did, it was their thing. Their dad had been a crook and Eddie and his younger brother had naturally followed suit. Siobhan, as beautiful as she was and as sweet-natured as she was, was unlikely to reverse the trend and whisk Eddie away, to start a new life in Paris or something.

Cavani doubted that they would have lasted anyway. He could tell Siobhan hadn't truly loved Eddie, at least nowhere near as much as he had loved her, so it probably wasn't entirely down to his cautionary intrusion that she'd ended it.

A few years after Eddie though was Euan.

Euan was well spoken and studied music at university.

Their mum and dad had been pleased that Siobhan had found someone well-to-do, and Cavani himself managed to get on, well enough, with him, despite the very little that they had in common and the fact that Euan was tight as fuck and never seemed to buy a drink on any occasion over the years that they were together.

He'd gone to a private school, his parents were both academics and the clock was ticking on his dreams of being a famous musician before his dad would intervene and demand that he change universities and enrol in a 'real' course with a view to getting a 'real' job. Siobhan had sensed that Euan's parents saw her as being beneath their son, and they especially weren't happy that she was a couple of years older than him and that she hadn't gone to university.

Again, like with Dominic, Siobhan was an accessory to Euan and it made him feel like a rock'n'roll star when she'd accompany him to the sweaty, sequestered basement venues where his band took part in competitions and appeared at unsigned, upcoming-talent nights, auditioning for stage time at festival tents and whatever else.

Lisa had convinced Cavani to accept one of Siobhan's invitations for them to join her and they'd gone along once to see them play. He remembered being genuinely taken aback by how shite they were and Lisa having to nudge him in the pub after the gig, sensing that he'd sunk too many plastic pints of Red Stripe during their set and had got the kind of drunk way where he was likely to give Euan some constructive criticism, which would probably have crushed him.

Siobhan must have loved him, he'd thought, her motives

KEVIN BRIDGES

altruistic, as there was no way Euan and his band were headed anywhere.

It was through Euan and the band scene that Siobhan entered the domain of soft and, eventually, hard drugs. She'd started smoking so much cannabis that she probably hadn't noticed the years pass by, speeding ahead of her, and how long she'd been with Euan, whose parents had been appalled and ready to disown him after he'd abandoned his degree, telling them that he had no intention of returning to any sort of university.

His dad had transferred a large sum of money to his bank account, a trust fund that had been saved for him, presumably in the hope that it could change his mind and clear any student debt he was in, enabling him to start over afresh and apply to study law or accounting at Edinburgh or Glasgow.

Euan and Siobhan went backpacking to Thailand together with some of the money, spending six weeks experimenting with whatever they came across.

Euan had needed creative inspiration, he'd convinced Siobhan, who'd noticed that his doses were getting stronger and his cravings more intense. He hadn't given up on the rock star dream, even if his bandmates had, accepting that they weren't very good and finding new hobbies and getting married and having children.

Siobhan and Euan moved into a flat in the Partick area of Glasgow that Euan's father rented to them, at a favourable rate, throwing another lifeline to his only child. The move amplified Euan's struggle with the real world and he'd spend the days claiming to be meditating, and strumming his guitar

184

and smoking whatever the powerful, ground-breaking, mind-altering lyrics needed in order for them to appear before him.

Only Siobhan had been working, returning to her work at a travel agent's, where she'd pass the days helping couples put together romantic breaks, assisting hard-working mums and dads with payment plans and special offers for their family holidays, and taking deposits from groups of young people, confirming the bookings of their first holiday together. Childhood friends, going abroad as young adults, celebrating their freedom and their youth, like she'd never done.

She'd quickly banish these thoughts though, condemning them as envy or self-pity, and she'd pass her shifts dreaming of getting married abroad or of using her staff discount one summer to go with her husband, Euan, and their children to Majorca and the Algarve and wherever else her workmates, her friends and her cousins had been with their families.

Not long after the move to Partick, Euan had begun smoking heroin. If he couldn't replicate the lives of his musical heroes with talent, then he could at least conform to a few clichés. Smoking heroin was a lot more commonplace than she'd thought, he'd tell Siobhan, when she'd expressed her concerns about his rapid progression from recreational to hard, class A drugs.

They stopped going out together, to gigs and to pubs, and Siobhan stopped seeing their parents and her phone calls to Lisa and him grew less and less frequent. She'd said she'd been exhausted at having to pretend that her new life with Euan, in the West End of Glasgow, was going great and of always having to fabricate alibis to excuse Euan's absence, telling her family that he was away somewhere performing or recording something and that his big breakthrough was on the horizon.

Siobhan eventually tried heroin too, accepting one of Euan's offers one night and his reasoning that it was perfectly sociable, unless you were consuming it intravenously.

It was boredom, perhaps, or despair, a feeling, again, that this was the only life she deserved. Or it was her final attempt at trying to reconnect with Euan, who she'd genuinely loved, as she'd told her brother one night, when he'd tried to convince her to leave him and to stop trying to save him, warning her that she was destined to be collateral damage in his eventual implosion. You can only do so much for someone before you eventually need to respect their right to fuck their life up. His stomach turned and he felt his sweat glands burst open again as he remembered this advice that he'd given her and how heartless it must have sounded. He now knew exactly what she'd been going through.

Siobhan had come home from work one day, to find Euan lying on their kitchen floor, with a vodka bottle and pill containers all around him and a note, which didn't mention Siobhan, his parents or any of his family, only the struggle he felt, to find the meaning of life and of the world that he hadn't asked to be brought into.

Siobhan had said that there were poems too, and lyrics and quotes from books he had been reading. He'd written of how it was his time and that twenty-seven was the right age for him to die and of how he would be joining the likes of Jimmy Hendrix, Brian Jones and Kurt Cobain in the infamous '27 Club'.

Siobhan had made the emergency call and the paramedics had arrived in minutes, Euan was rushed to hospital, treated, briefly assessed by a psychologist, and discharged the following morning.

The doctor had told Siobhan that the pills Euan had taken hadn't been in his system long enough to do any long-term damage and that it had sounded like a classic cry for help. She wondered when exactly he'd made this cry for help, as it seemed like it had been timed for her arrival home from work.

She'd wanted to doubt her suspicions but remembered that he'd text her at her work, when usually she wouldn't hear from him all day – the day was his creative time – to confirm that she was, like every other day, heading straight home when she'd finished and that she didn't have plans.

It was a message she'd thought strange at the time and she'd hurried out of the travel agent's, almost excited, thinking that maybe he had a surprise for her – he'd cooked something or done something to the flat, to begin making it feel like more of a home, as she'd always wished, or maybe they were going out somewhere.

She'd felt terrified and humiliated once it had all made sense – he'd wanted her to rush home, to save him, again.

Siobhan barely slept the whole night and when she'd gone over to the hospital in the morning, she was told Euan's parents had collected him. He didn't answer his phone, and when she'd managed to get hold of his mum, she'd told Siobhan, in no uncertain terms, that she and Euan were finished. It was as though Euan's hard-drug abuse and suicide attempt had been down to her and it had vindicated his parents' belief that she wasn't good enough for their son.

Euan had messaged a few days later to say that he'd come

home to live with his parents, who were going to pay for his stay at a private rehabilitation centre, like the one Siobhan had just returned from. He told Siobhan that his dad had given her two weeks to be out of the flat, as though this was thoroughly decent of the old prick, and it was to be taken as some sort of consolation.

Siobhan arrived at Lisa's and his house that same night and broke down in tears as soon as Lisa opened the door. She'd told them everything, about Euan's parents, about the hospital, the 'suicide note' and the text. She'd pleaded with him, hysterically, not to go over to Euan's parents' house, to confront them all and to extract a real cry for help from the selfish, narcissistic, manipulative, spoiled little cunt.

He had never felt a fury like it. He remembered being intimidated by his own anger when he'd seen how distraught and traumatised Siobhan was, and he'd thought of the note and the 27 club, and all of that shite.

Time had passed though, and he'd spoken about it all to his therapist, who'd educated him and helped him to form a greater understanding of mental illness and especially drug-induced mental illness and addiction. He'd even gone into a chapel, early one Saturday night, not long after, to speak to a priest about the thoughts he'd had that night, but he felt like he'd disturbed the old man, and quickly threw in a few more mainstream, generic sins to wrap it up: blasphemy, swearing, not keeping the sabbath day holy and whatever else he'd remembered from his childhood, before asking for his penance, the way he'd ask for the bill after an unsatisfactory meal.

He felt his eyes begin to water, unsure if he was getting emotional from recounting Siobhan's man-made downfall, from Dominic to Euan, via Eddie, with his own interference thrown in, or simply that his eyes had been fixed at the exact same sign on the exact same chair for so long that they'd gone blurry and started to sting.

He forced his eyes into a blink and read the words 'Priority seat, please keep free for people who are disabled, elderly or less able to stand'.

He thought of the hospital, and of Siobhan being wired up to monitors, her pinpoint pupils, her shallow breathing and her pale-blue skin, and then, when she'd regained full consciousness, the mental and the emotional ramifications that would be waiting for her, detailing the journey that lay ahead, now that she'd landed all the way back at the start of the recovery process. It would be even more difficult this time, she'd know.

That was, of course, if she wanted to try again.

He concentrated, again, on inhaling deeply and exhaling slowly before standing up and walking over to the screen to see that his flight had been assigned to the gate directly opposite where he'd been sitting. He sat back down, satisfied that the flight was unmissable, even for a wandering mind like his.

Less than a year after Euan had set Siobhan on her road to ruin and abandoned her, for his parents and the disposable income that they could throw at his latest problem, he and Lisa had been home in Glasgow – for something that he couldn't remember, filming, presumably – and Euan had appeared on the Scottish evening news, discussing the work he'd been doing for a charity that helped recovering addicts rebuild their lives through 'the power of music', as an immaculate-looking Euan had put it, his smiling face and his white teeth glowing through the camera as he told of overcoming his own demons, his addictions and mental health problems, before they cut to a shot of him strumming his guitar and then pausing to adjust someone's finger positions on the fretboard of theirs.

Lisa had recognised Euan's face first and had tried to find the remote control, before seeing it was too late and she'd turned to watch as Cavani's shoulders rose and his head protruded, in confrontation, like a dog watching a cat food advert.

He'd taken the time to think it through though, and process how he felt, discovering that progress had been made with his emotions, that it hadn't bothered him. It was the past and at least Euan had moved on, he'd fucked off out of Siobhan's life, which was all that could really be asked of him.

After Euan, Siobhan had stayed back home with their parents for a few months, but her drug use gradually worsened, resulting in her being fired from the travel agent's, following a series of incidents, which they'd acknowledged had been uncharacteristic from a regular employee of the month. Siobhan began neglecting her – usually immaculate – appearance, falling asleep at her desk, showing up late and, eventually, not showing up at all.

She'd found her own drug contacts now, and the money she'd saved from working full time, from her commission bonuses and from the low living costs of being back home with their parents was now financing her addiction.

After hearing – from one of the meerkats of misery – that Siobhan had been seen wandering the local shopping centre, in a trance-like state, as she'd done most days, when they'd thought that she'd been working at the travel agent's, their parents had intervened. She'd come clean to them about being sacked and about her drug use, which she'd downplayed but admitted had got a little bit out of control.

It had hurt their parents, who couldn't believe that their daughter, who'd had everything going for her, as they'd told her, her whole life, had turned to drugs. She'd succumbed to peer pressure and fallen in with a bad crowd, her parents had explained to him, as though it ran no deeper, like it was just a silly phase she was going through. It had hurt him too to hear how distraught his parents were and to hear them speaking about Siobhan like she was still a child, like it was their fault and that there was something they should have done or should be doing.

Siobhan, realising the emotional toll that her continued drug abuse would take on their parents, managed to get herself together, consulting her GP, who placed her on a home detox programme, referred her to a counsellor and prescribed a heroin substitute along with a detailed timeline of what she was about to go through and when she should eventually begin weaning herself off that too.

Progress was made, and after the twelve-week programme she looked healthy and, above all, happy again. She'd tried to get her old job back but it was too soon, and as much as she'd been popular and a great worker, she knew that she'd have been under constant surveillance and that the rest of the office would have been speculating as to what had gone on with her. She accepted her counsellor's advice, agreeing that she needed a completely fresh start, and she began applying for other jobs.

After getting herself back into full-time employment, Siobhan met a new man, Michael, who she'd been totally honest with, about her past, her recovery and her ongoing battle with addiction.

Michael was supportive and understanding, and proved to be the first guy she'd met who'd had Siobhan's interests at heart. After a while, they moved in together and Siobhan's drug issues were beginning to look like a silly phase she'd gone through after all and she'd ditched the bad crowds that she'd fallen in with.

Cavani's own career had been taking off and he'd amassed a fairly prolific list of writing and then directing credits, and he'd acted in some decent enough films. He'd won awards and he was spending more time in America, making some gradual inroads there too.

He'd married Lisa and they'd finally managed to buy a house in London, after renting for years, their living standards steadily increasing as he gained ground on the dreams he'd been chasing since his early twenties.

He'd been in the financially rewarding yet mentally forgiving sweet spot of being a household name, but one that could walk around in relative anonymity. There wasn't much media interest in his private life, only his work, at least outside of Scotland. Siobhan was working in her new job and living with Michael, and they'd come down, a couple of times, to London, to visit him and Lisa. They'd gone to shows, they'd eaten in nice restaurants and there was no doubting that Siobhan, somehow, had scrapped and battled and managed to stumble upon happiness.

It was when their dad passed away after a short battle with cancer and then their mum, less than a year after, that Siobhan reached for the self-destruct button, embarking on the road back to where she now lay, unconscious and connected to machines.

The overwhelming grief at their parents' dying had teamed up with the guilt at all the years that she'd wasted – the years that she wished she could give back, in exchange for moments spent with her parents – and at all the distress and heartbreak she'd caused them.

She'd let them down: she had been their princess, their pride and joy, and all of that. They'd had high hopes and dreams for her, and as she grew up, she'd shattered them, one by one.

He'd tried to tell her how much their parents had loved her and how unconditional their love was, and of how proud they'd been, that she'd pulled back from the brink, that she'd turned her life around and that she was still here, moving forward despite everything that had gone on.

All they wanted was for her to be happy, and to never go back to her old ways, he'd remembered saying to her, as she'd been crying harder than he'd ever seen anyone cry. He could have been more subtle but he wanted her to know that he knew what sort of coping mechanisms the dark forces of her mind would be suggesting.

She'd lost both parents in barely a year – it was the perfect excuse to go into standby mode for days and weeks, months maybe, even shut down completely.

He'd spoken to Michael too, telling him about his concerns and he'd agreed to be on high alert, but ultimately, they both knew, it was down to Siobhan herself to decide whether or not to hit the button. He and Michael were merely protestors whose voices no longer registered, once her decision to go to war had been made.

'James Cavani, ha, ha! No fuckin' way, man.' A voice brought him from deep down in the basement of his head, back up to ground floor. He looked away from the chair, where his eyes had been idling, to see that his flight had commenced boarding.

The voice had made his heart jump and he tried to laugh as it fluttered in panic like it had done, just before the point of impact, when he'd had dreams that he was falling.

A man who looked to be in his late twenties, holding a bottle of beer, was walking towards him, catching up with his words, which had slapped Cavani awake and turned the heads of almost the entire queue for the flight to Glasgow. He glanced across to see a collection of mumbling heads turning around, and then back again, satisfied that he was, indeed, James Cavani.

Another man with a bottle of beer was walking over too, messing about with his phone before joining his friend, who'd carefully placed his beer bottle at Cavani's feet, sitting down beside him. His friend sat on the other side so that they flanked Cavani, and they both leaned in so that their heads were touching his.

They posed and pointed their index fingers just beneath his chin. Cavani was surprised by how impulsively he'd smiled for the camera but he could see the worry in his tired-looking eyes as the man clicked away at his phone.

'Cheer up, ya cunt,' the second man laughed, standing back up, studying his photo.

He then nodded at Cavani, realising that he might have misjudged the mood, that this was maybe a bad time. Cavani saw that his face looked unsure and apologetic, for the sudden change of energy that they'd brought to him.

The man had only been trying to bait a genuine smile from him and he laughed as best he could and nodded back, acknowledging that he knew the men were in high spirits and well-meaning, and that despite being a big-time-movie-star-showbiz-celebrity, he was still familiar with his home city's amicable use of the word cunt and he wouldn't be going all precious on them.

'Thanks for that, mate. Appreciated!' the man said, his thumb clicking in and around the photo of the three of them. He slid his phone back into the pocket of his designer jogging bottoms and took a sip of his beer, studying Cavani.

'You flying home to Glasgow?' his mate asked, picking his bottle back up from the floor, glancing quickly around the airport and then back at Cavani, uninterested in the answer to his question as his mind tried to process better ones.

'Were you down filming something?' his friend interrupted, his tone now calm and contemplative.

'Aye, well, I was over in New York, just doing some promotional stuff for a new film, it's out in a couple of weeks,' Cavani answered, feeling himself getting nervous as he properly considered, for the first time, the ramifications of his phone call to his agent. Fuck it, it's done, he reminded himself, as though he wouldn't be warned again, that there was not to be another mention of it.

'Aye, that looks brilliant, man. I loved the first two. Fucking mental that you're just sitting there.' Cavani heard the tension in the laugh he forced as a response to the more manic of the two guys, who hadn't followed his friend's lead and adjusted his volume.

He picked his bag from the floor and unzipped it, placing his right hand inside, listing items as he felt them. Pens, scrap bits of paper, a travel adaptor, Lisa's Milky Way.

He looked over to the gate, wondering what the hold-up was. Maybe he was due a delay, he reasoned with himself, karma for cutting it so fine in New York that morning, or last night – whenever the fuck it was.

He zipped his bag back up, unsure of what he could do next, to distract himself from the discomfort of his new company.

It was almost Thursday afternoon his phone told him. He glanced over a few of the other messages he'd been sent, compiling a list of the names of the people he'd reply to later, after he'd tried to deal with the situation at hand.

There was a missed call from his agent's office too, and a voicemail, almost two minutes long. *Who the fuck still leaves a voicemail?* he said to himself, shaking his head, aware that he was seizing upon even the tenuous evidence now, as a means of further justification for his rash decision to part company with the management team he'd been with for over a decade. He remembered he hadn't text Johnny yet, his oldest friend and former – very much unofficial – agent in the early days before he began taking his work seriously. Cavani pounced on the opportunity to occupy himself and began texting, asking to be picked up at the airport – looking at the departure time on his boarding pass, he calculated roughly when he'd be landing, adding an extra bit on, remembering that he had checked a bag in.

He sent the message to Johnny and then went back to click delete on the unplayed voicemail from his agent's office. With his spare hand he tried to halt a yawn.

He felt a sharp ache below his ear, like his jaw was about to lock. It hit him how tired he was and that he must have been yawning all through his internal inquest into Siobhan's latest disaster.

He cautiously opened and closed his mouth, massaging his left cheek in a circular motion as the two men stood over him, discussing their favourite James Cavani films, as though they'd said their goodbyes and walked away.

He thought of how he could change the subject away from the film and his work in general, looking again at the gate, to see the screen above it had changed from 'boarding' to 'final call' despite there being no progress made by anyone in the lengthy queue.

He thought of the Q&A with the two guys, the whole way through the airbridge and on to the plane, and then of them being sat near him onboard.

It was a difficult one, a fine line: if he projected a stand-offish vibe, they'd leave him alone but consider him a bit of a prick, and if he carried on pretending that he didn't mind their company and was happy to answer their questions, then they'd stay and consider him their best mate.

My little sister's in intensive care after a heroin overdose. I've just blown 100,000 dollars. Sacked my agent. And the new film is fucking abysmal. I need some time on my own, to sit and worry, he thought of himself saying, but knowing that he would never be this honest, as liberating as it would feel.

He heard laughter and looked up to see both of the men were looking down at him, smiling, it was his cue to talk, a question had been asked. 'Sorry, mate, what was that?' Cavani said, clicking his phone to lock it, showing that he was all theirs and that he hadn't mean to come across as ignorant. He felt like he could feel the daring, honest voice in his head roll its eyes, turning away smugly, like it had won a bet.

'He was sayin' jump on the plane to Vegas, with us,' the more sensible of the two repeated, finishing his beer and looking around for a bin, as his friend looked on suspenseful, waiting for Cavani to take him up on the suggestion. 'For the fight,' he added, hoping to seal the proposal.

'I wish!' Cavani said, hearing the relief in his voice at this new information, that the two guys, as harmless as they were, weren't going to be on the Glasgow flight.

'We better make a move and find oot the gate. Finish that,' the man said to his disappointed friend, who asked Cavani for one more picture, of just the two of them.

As the men walked away, he checked his bag was fully zipped before standing up, throwing it round his right shoulder and meandering over to join the rest of the patient, muted queue.

He turned around to watch as the two men stopped at another screen, the daft one was grinning at whatever his thumbs were telling his phone and the sensible one examined their surroundings, studied the information on the screen and then looked to his boarding pass, as though seeking a second opinion.

He felt guilty that he'd perhaps been a bit distant with the guys, or snide, as they would have put it. They were fans, after all, and they had probably expected more from him.

Fame meant that you waived the right to be in a bad mood, in public anyway, regardless of what was going on in your life and in your mind. You always had to be alert and ready to play the version of yourself that was expected or else you'd 'disappeared up your own arse' and 'lost touch with reality', 'lost touch with real people'. The image of Derek Carruthers' Facebook page came flashing into his head. He felt annoyed at himself for remembering his full name.

It had been his choice, nobody had forced it all on him. Celebrity was simply another role that he'd auditioned for and got and it had been clearly stated in the contract.

When he'd have these moments of uncertainty, self-doubt or even self-pity, he always reminded himself, that in his chosen industry, if a job was a success, people would know who you are and your privacy, should you wish to continue living a life of relative normality, would be at their discretion.

He'd had several jobs that could be deemed a success, as subjective as the term was in the world of art and entertainment, so this was how it was going to be. It was admirable that he'd put Siobhan first, ahead of his career, but ultimately, she was part of it now too, and his career had been complicit in her becoming a tabloid story, a Facebook rant, and the topic of conversation in the area's pub, its café, its post office, chemist, convenience store and its living rooms.

Lisa had told him that Siobhan had mentioned to her that she'd struggled with her job as a barista in the local shopping centre. Her confidence had plummeted and she'd developed all sorts of social anxieties and a feeling of general paranoia, which was only intensified on the occasions that she'd seen tables of people whispering to each other and then looking over at her, as a phone was passed around, before they all took their second turn, to look at her again, a pale, gaunt, Google image of her fresh in their heads, before collectively nodding in agreement that it was, indeed, James Cavani's junkie sister.

They'd then sit and preach away their pots of tea, their cheese and ham toasties, and their cinnamon swirls, a playlist of opinions, waiting for the previous one to finish. They'd pontificate on her and her drug problems, in accordance with the red-top scriptures and the prophet Derek Carruthers and the like, and on her brother and his films, his money, and his homes in London and the West End of Glasgow – how could he sleep at night, knowing that his little sister was rotting away?

Siobhan knew it wasn't her mind playing tricks on her and that she had been the focus of discussion at several tables like this and it made her dread going into the job. Lisa knew she wasn't imagining it too.

Siobhan had made Lisa promise not to tell him anything like this, so as not to burden him with any further feelings of culpability. Siobhan had always been quick to exculpate her brother whenever anyone had tried to weave his success in with her own struggles. He'd done everything he could, and the two situations – his rise and her fall – were entirely exclusive of each other, she'd told him and Lisa. He knew this too, but he had no doubt that he'd heightened her problems and brought a superfluous attention to them, especially in their home town. He was also aware of how Siobhan was only capable of self-reproach – even Euan had been pardoned for his part in the mess she'd found herself in. It was all on her, she'd fucked her life up and she'd let everyone down, as she'd told him and Lisa a few times. They now took this as a heads up that a relapse wasn't too far away. He spotted the pattern.

She'd break down in tears, they'd embrace her, she'd apologise, saying she was just 'being silly', and then she'd go back through the routine of pretending that that was all she'd needed – 'a good greet' – and to let it all out. 'Look at the state of me,' she'd remark, indicating that she'd shown enough emotion for one day. Her smile as natural as a politician's, she'd wipe her eyes, looking in the mirror, her face a reminder of how much time had been wasted.

They'd try and talk to her but their words of compassion, reassurance and optimism sounded pathetic as they bounced back off her. Everything else was futile, once she'd decided that she needed something stronger to mitigate the misery that had trapped her.

Lisa had only broken her promise of confidentiality to Siobhan when she'd been presenting a case for her defence, after he'd found out that she'd quit the job in the coffee shop, having only started it a few weeks after her return from the first ninety-day treatment programme.

He knew he couldn't control how she'd handled the grief of losing both of their parents and afterwards her break-up from Michael – who'd tried his best by her, she knew, they all knew – but the rest was down to him, and as much as he meant well, he should have foreseen the perils of boredom Siobhan would experience from living on her own and not working.

She was living rent- and mortgage-free, with some disposable income that he'd transferred to her, with the intention of funding her enrolment in college, like she'd said she'd wanted, to study veterinary nursing, or with a view to setting up a dog-walking business, as she'd said she'd have loved to do, a few of the times when she'd been recovering, feeling positive and going on long walks with Lisa, through Kelvingrove Park.

He shook his head as it told him how fucking naïve he had been.

'Of course, we shouldn't give them money; they'll just spend it all on drink and drugs!'

His head mimicked a caller on a radio phone-in show, but it was quickly cut off by an announcement which apologised for the slight delay to his flight and was pleased to inform him that boarding was now commencing. He looked at the screen, which told him his flight was closing. He looked too for the Las Vegas flight, which was at final call. He hoped the two guys had made it.

He looked over his phone again and saw there had been a missed call from Dr Nikouladis during the drama, and now a message, asking if he was running late. The message above it – sent the day before – was a confirmation text for today's session at 12pm. He looked at the day on his phone again, still not entirely convinced that it was a Thursday, and then at the date. It was a Thursday, and the second Thursday of the month. Fuck.

Even before the news of Siobhan, when he'd been bound for London, he wouldn't have been able to go, because of the press schedule. He felt annoyed at himself for not cancelling, for letting Dr Nikouladis down. The last session, four weeks ago – before he'd flown back out to New York – was to be their last together, then, if the move back to Glasgow was to be permanent.

The queue to the plane was shortening now and boarding had picked up momentum. The gate staff had probably been briefed to try and help the airline claw back some of the time that had been missed, for whatever reason.

If he called Dr Nikouladis now, he could get his apologies in but it wouldn't leave a lot of time to let him know that he'd finally decided on leaving London – to move back home – and to thank him for everything. Dr Nikouladis would probably have a lot to say to him, advice to dispense, as a professional, and then online Skype or Zoom therapy sessions to promote, as a self-employed private healthcare worker.

He knew he would have to cut in and excuse himself and abruptly end the call, if the pace at which he was approaching the turn on to the home straight – towards the boarding pass check and the eye retina scanner and whatever – was maintained.

A text was too flippant and even if he used Siobhan – who the therapist would surely feel like he was acquainted with – as an excuse, a perfectly valid excuse given that she was in intensive care, he would feel guilty. Siobhan wasn't strictly the reason for his absence: he'd simply got lost in everything else and forgotten.

He'd been more honest and candid with Dr Nikouladis than he had been with anyone in his entire life, perhaps even including Lisa, so he wouldn't feel right lying after all this time, and also the Catholic in him warned that Siobhan's situation was far too precarious to be used as a convenient vindication of a simple scheduling oversight.

He hoped Dr Nikouladis wouldn't have taken his un-explained absence the wrong way, especially after their last session, which had been a little stilted. He'd shown up feeling all right and his only immediate, pressing concern had been thinking of how he was going to fill his allocated time.

He had his problems but who didn't? – and at least he had money, he'd told himself, thinking of the money he was paying Dr Nikouladis, 'his therapist', he'd sneered, accepting that his upbringing would be engaged in perpetual conflict with his new life. What does he have to be miserable about? Give me his money, he figured his 24-year-old self would have said of his 42-year-old self.

He'd considered cancelling that day, but as it was less than forty-eight hours' notice, he'd be charged in full, and if paying to discuss his hang-ups with a North London therapist evoked scorn from his younger self – along with the unified voice his head had formed of his hard-grafting adolescent friends, his shipbuilding dad and uncles, and his war veteran and immigrant grandparents – then paying and not attending was unforgivable.

'More money than sense.' He felt a pang of sadness as he tried to imagine his dad's voice. He checked his boarding pass to distract his head from his heart, and looked up to see that he was approaching the electronic scanner.

He stood back, nodding for a younger couple to go ahead of him, a tactic that he hoped would have him pulled to the side, to present his boarding pass to a human, instead of a machine.

'This way, sir.' It had worked. He walked towards the smiling face that was politely telling him to hurry the fuck up.

'17E,' his lips mimed whilst he rattled through the first six letters of the alphabet with the image of a standard Airbus 319 in his head. 'A middle seat, fuck.'

He should have paid the extra money, he told himself, before bowing his head slightly, in contrition, reminding himself of the purpose of the journey.

The sole objective had been not to leave Dr Nikouladis's surgery in a worse mood than when he'd gone in, so he'd opted not to speak about Siobhan or his parents or anything else that had the potential to trigger him off. Instead, he'd gone through the motions, telling Dr Nikouladis about the last decade of his own life, and how it still felt new, fragile, a novelty.

His success was temporary and he felt like someone was going to end it all at any minute, someone who knew – as well as he knew – that he was out of his depth and not good enough. He'd spoken more like a podcast guest than a patient.

This was known as imposter syndrome, Dr Nikouladis had told him, seemingly going through the motions himself.

He remembered this had annoyed him, especially as he'd only just keyed in the four digits of his debit card, to pay him his hourly rate of £130. £130 for a diagnosis that the pseudonyms of Reddit could have made for free.

He wished he had cancelled as he'd felt himself casting doubt on the entire concept of therapy, feeling himself siding with the voice from the macho patriarchal control tower stationed in his head and the heads of men, for generations, centuries – real men, like he should be – that navigated them through life and all the turbulence that was to be encountered.

All the good work he and Dr Nikouladis had done together had almost been invalidated. All of the breakthroughs that had helped him unburden himself from some of the potentially harmful thoughts that he'd been carrying around.

Together they'd raided the packed drawers and the crowded cupboards of his head, and he'd watched as the fears, the worries, the regrets, the shame, the grief had all piled up on the floor.

They'd decided what to throw away – what was done with, useless – and then what couldn't be thrown away but could be mended a little and maybe used for some purpose in the future.

It had felt good, to place all these things neatly back into their own separate compartments, and he'd left the practice with a sense that his head had been converted into a minimalist, decluttered living space from the chaotic, dingy, barely habitable basement that it had been allowed to turn into.

But this day – which was to be his last day – he'd struggled to fill the rest of the time, excusing himself to go to the bathroom shortly after the commencement of the monthly hour that he'd allocated for the maintenance of his mental and emotional well-being.

He'd sneaked a few puffs of his vape and then stared in the mirror, convincing himself that he felt fine and that maybe he just hadn't seen his pals in a while, that he should try and arrange to go out for a couple of pints soon.

£130 could get you into a decent state, he'd thought, even in London.

He remembered hearing words come out of both Dr Nikouladis's and his mouths, but the rest of the session he'd spent imploring himself to pace his glancing at the clock on the wall behind Dr Nikouladis, to avoid further disappointment, after diving in too early and seeing it had only just left quarter past the hour.

The minute hand had to hit the very bottom before it could begin its rise back to the top, he'd thought, impressed at the metaphor that had presented itself to him in his pensive daydream. He'd nodded along to whatever Dr Nikouladis was saying, managing to block a self-satisfied smile that had tried to hit his face.

As he walked through the airbridge, he text Dr Nikouladis, apologising that he wouldn't be making it today and that he would call him later that afternoon to explain everything; he then set a reminder on his phone, like Lisa had shown him how to.

Lisa – he looked at her name on his phone. She was calling him. What now? Fuck.

'Hiya, sorry, I know you're probably on the plane, it's just to let you know that Siobhan is stable,' Lisa began.

'Brilliant, well . . . good,' Cavani replied, hoping for Lisa to keep going, to relay as much detail as she could before he was told to switch his phone off, conscious too that he was being stared at and recognised.

'A non-fatal overdose, the wee doctor called it – he wants to keep her in for maybe a day or two, for observation, just to make sure there's no complications. Phone me when you land, ok? I'm here just now so try not to worry and I'll see you soon,' Lisa told him, hurrying to the specifics.

'Ok, right, thanks for letting me know and thanks, for everything – and sorry, man, what a mess,' Cavani replied, his self-consciousness lowering his volume and taking precautions to keep his side of the conversation generic and not to reveal any particulars.

'Can't wait to see you. Right, safe flight. Love you and don't worry – we'll sort it out,' Lisa finished off, the intent in her voice and her positivity coming straight through to him. He thought of how he missed her and of how frustrating a one-hour flight could be, when you just wanted home.

'We will. Love you too,' Cavani said, hanging up, relieved that Siobhan was all right but thinking of how this had to be it, for her own sake, but for Lisa's too, and, well, his own – that he'd put everything else to one side to travel home to the hospital could only help strengthen his appeals.

He went to switch his phone to 'airplane' mode and place it back in his pocket, but the memory of switching it back on, in the car, to the ambiguous, ominous news about Siobhan, was still raw. He kept it connected, hoping that if anything further developed over the next hour or so, he'd receive the update as soon as the aircraft came within range of a network signal.

'Good afternoon, Mr Cavani,' a member of the crew greeted him as he walked onboard the plane. He smiled, and a combination of hi, hey, and aye left his mouth in response. Another yawn threatened his jaw as he watched the last of the passengers engage in passive-aggressive battles for the vestiges of overhead storage space and rushing into decisions on which luxury item to choose – iPad, laptop, Kindle – to help in speeding up the next hour.

He noticed that the cabin crew member who'd recognised him was studying the first few rows of the plane, no doubt presuming that Cavani would be sitting in one of the larger, comfortable seats. He looked to be anticipating a bit of a problem, seeing that they were all occupied, just as the aisle cleared enough to allow Cavani to pass through the curtain, to the last-minute, panic-booking seats.

Cavani hadn't made much progress before coming to a standstill again. Seeing that the plane was nearing full capacity, he looked ahead, towards row 17, trying to eye up who he'd be sandwiched between for the next while.

The sound of a phone camera clicking turned his head to the left, to a girl in her late twenties, sitting motionless, staring ahead at the back of the seat in front of her, the crimson glow of shame appearing through her sharply con-toured make-up.

He tilted his head to see past the woman in front of him, willing the balding head of a man around his own age to hurry up, to take his seat, so that he could advance, away from the awkward tension.

The girl's friend, realising what had happened, began laughing, which at least broke the uncomfortable silence. 'Sorry about her, she's a fuckin' riot!' she proudly declared.

He laughed and said, 'No problem', convinced that he'd sounded like a prick, as though he'd enjoyed the attention or he got it all the time, or it was part of the job, or something. A few sets of eyes had turned towards him and then the whispers and the nudges began multiplying.

'Giesa wee picture, James,' an older woman said, grabbing the seat in front of her for support as she shuffled out from her window seat, across the laps of two confused-looking men, to meet him in the aisle. 'I need you to take your seat, madam.' The member of crew who'd greeted him had appeared from behind, sensing a commotion.

He rolled his eyes at Cavani, acknowledging the price of fame.

'Ach, al no be a minute, you! Here, how dae ye work this?'

Cavani couldn't help but laugh at her audacity as she ignored the caution and handed her phone to the member of staff who'd issued it, as though he was to make himself useful, seeing as he was here.

She reminded him of someone, one of his mum's old aunties, maybe, or someone's old auntie. Not wishing to draw the episode out any longer – for Cavani's sake and for the sake of the take-off slot of the already delayed flight – the man obliged, clicking a few photos of the woman's smiling face as it leaned into Cavani and his professional smile.

'Right, now back to your seat, you,' he said, handing back her phone, his good nature proving effective as she slid in front of the man in the aisle seat, who tried to accommodate her by angling his lower body so that his knees almost touched Cavani, and the man in the middle, who slid himself up the back of his seat, slouching his neck as his head touched the reading light at the top of the cabin; it was a stance that looked to have grown rapidly uncomfortable as the woman turned back to tell Cavani that she was just back from visiting her son in Boston and that they'd watched one of his talk show appearances.

'Ye were brilliant, son, and ye dae Glesga proud.'

The genuine warmth of her compliment made him smile and he thanked her and nodded at the man, an apology, for his part in the discomfort he was experiencing. 'Watch your back there,' he said to the woman, through a playful laugh.

'It's ok, it's ok, I'm just about managing,' the man said, his English Home Counties accent – somewhere upon somewhere – was exactly like his agent's.

'Oh, right ya'r, sorry about that, son.'

The man behind her shook his head and rubbed his kneecap, unable to see the funny side, turning to glare at the woman as she sent herself crash landing back into her seat.

'Thanks, James, god bless ye,' he heard her shout, noticing the aisle had cleared and he was the last man standing on the plane.

'Ha! James Cavani, no way, man!' he heard another voice shout as he took his seat.

He made a note not to go to the bathroom for the duration of the flight – the middle seat was maybe the hiding place he needed.

'Changed days, eh,' the voice at the window said. A powerful scent drifted towards him as he felt the presence studying the side of his face, awaiting a reaction.

His head ran through the names of the first few aftershaves that he could remember. Creed, that was it, fucking expensive as well. Lisa had bought him it for their tenth wedding anniversary.

'Aye,' he said, with a single laugh so false that he'd have been as well just saying 'Ha' – or 'LOL' – the prospect of an hour of conversation looming over him.

He wondered what the voice was getting at, changed days from what? It's just something people say, he reminded himself, rags to riches sort of thing, working class, done well, all of that. It was rare that his head didn't wish to overthink something so he wasn't going to argue, appreciating the break.

Who the fuck would still go to Venice? he thought, looking at the leather pouch on the seat in front of him – that his knees were pressed against – and the cover of the airline's in-flight magazine.

He remembered lying awake in a hotel room recently, jet-lagged, watching a BBC World News documentary about the damage that mass tourism and cruise ships had done to the place, and he'd read articles too about anti-tourist protests from the locals.

Advertising the place was a borderline hate crime, he thought, noticing the face of the man's watch reflecting off the gloss of the well-browsed and mistreated magazine.

He couldn't see what brand it was; it wasn't a Rolex but it looked fucking expensive anyway. 'Changed days, eh,' he repeated to himself, annoyed that he hadn't let it go.

To spare further analysis of the comment, he turned to look at the man, thinking that, maybe it *was* someone who knew him, someone who knew that his days *had* changed.

Fuck. He felt himself break sweat again, that horrible sweat.

Of all the fucking people. The last fucking guy I need to be stuck beside. Fuck me, man.

He begged his face not to relay his thoughts.

'Eddie, no way. How's it going, mate?' Cavani wanted to look away in embarrassment at his – or his character's – opening line. Being an experienced, half-decent actor was useful in these incidences. Eddie Reynolds. Fucking hell. Fuck this. The words that he wished he had someone to whisper to pounded round his head as he tried to settle into the role. An hour. A whole fucking hour. The whole fucking walk through the airport too, all the way towards the baggage reclaim area, at least.

'Thought ye would be too big now to remember us little people,' the gruff voice laughed, the thick arms folded on top of the proud-looking belly and the shoulders turned further round. They made eye contact, proper eye contact, which seemed to go on far too long. Feeling awkward or uncomfortable got you nowhere in Eddie Reynolds's industry, so it was up to Cavani to look away first. He felt his left hand poised to pull the in-flight magazine out from its pouch, before accepting that it would have been too obvious an indication of his intimidation.

He didn't know why he felt intimidated, why he felt like he was an adolescent or something. He wondered if there was a term for it – a variation on the term starstruck – like when he'd met movie stars – proper movie stars – and he'd been trying to think of what to say to them whilst his head played a montage of all their iconic scenes, or of the few times that he'd met legendary footballers and he'd been replaying all of their greatest goals as his nerves pleaded with him not to say something stupid, settling, instead, for the damage limitation tactic of saying nothing and letting the moment fizzle.

He wondered what the word was for running into people like Eddie Reynolds and trying to think of an appropriate conversation whilst wondering if they'd ever murdered people, or what sort of methods of torture they'd deployed over the years in the interests of business.

All of the success of his career, the young girl who'd stolen a photo of him, the older woman who'd posed for one, all of the fans asking for photos – all of it – it just seemed pathetic following a few milliseconds of prolonged eye contact with a possible psychopath.

There was no question that Eddie Reynolds had found his calling in organised crime. Even his laugh had a hostility to it – it was hearty, though, and his smile seemed genuine enough, it was like he didn't have a care in the world. Or, at least, he didn't have any cares that couldn't be resolved and turned into someone else's.

'This you headin' home then?' he heard himself ask, the director in his head yelling 'CUT' at the stupid question. It broke the tension though and gave him the chance to at least try and laugh: sometimes these laughs, in moments of tension, could turn into sincere laughter.

'Naw. Ah'm gettin' aff at Carlisle,' Eddie Reynolds answered, elbowing Cavani in the ribs as they both chuckled and the plane began picking up speed along the runway.

'Ye look stressed oot yer gourd, Jimmy, working too hard?' Eddie added, aware that his joke had taken advantage of Cavani's distant and congested mind and that there was something bothering him.

'Aye, just life, eh?' Cavani leaned forward, joining Eddie in staring out of the window, watching London grow smaller and smaller before fading away.

He thought of Siobhan – and all the rest of them – who'd contributed to the financing of Eddie Reynolds's aftershave, his watch, his designer jacket and his expensive-looking jeans and shoes.

'How is Siobhan?' Eddie asked, still staring out of the window.

An enquiry that almost startled Cavani, making him feel like he'd been speaking his thoughts out loud.

'Aye, she's fine,' Cavani composed himself to answer. A full stop audible as he studied Eddie Reynolds's profile, his double chins, the fat of his neck and a scar on the back of his head.

He fantasised about the version of himself he wished he could be at these sorts of times. *She's in intensive care helping to keep you and cunts like you in business.*

Cavani's engineered silence made Eddie Reynolds turn to face him and, noticing that his eyes were squinting in the sunlight, Eddie pulled the window blind down before facing him again.

The thought of Siobhan, in hospital, encouraged Cavani not to break the stare this time, to stand his ground. It wasn't him who had anything to hide, it should be Eddie feeling uncomfortable, ashamed. Fuck him.

'Aye, well, tell her I was askin' for her,' Eddie said, fixing himself upright in his chair and reaching for his own designated in-flight magazine.

Cavani felt himself standing down, snapping him out of his stare. It had worked.

'I'll tell her you were asking for her, your best customer. I heard Colonel Sanders was asking for you.' Cavani was unsure if he'd said this or thought it. It certainly hadn't been deliberated over – if it had, then surely his agreeable, rational self with its aversion to conflict wouldn't have signed off on it.

The man on the aisle seat beside them leaned himself forward, peering over his magazine – the *Economist* or the *Spectator* or one like that, Cavani thought, judging by his brown cord trousers, the elbow patches on his suit jacket and the general 'supply teacher' look that he'd gone for – to look at Eddie, whose laugh seemed to be filling the plane.

Fuck. He had said it. He felt shocked at himself – but impressed – and unsure if Eddie's laugh was genuine or if he was about to abruptly halt the hilarity and turn deadly serious and confrontational, like a scene from a movie.

There was no way he was that good an actor, Cavani thought, and, after a wary few seconds, began to laugh himself, both at his own joke and at the reaction to it, the relief hitting him that it had been taken in good humour.

'Cheeky cunt,' Eddie said, coughing and spluttering through his fit of laughter.

The man on the aisle turned again, glaring at the side of Eddie's bright-red head as it sat atop his shaking shoulders. Seeing that he couldn't communicate his disgruntlement direct to its source, the man settled instead for making eye contact with Cavani, who gave a semi-apologetic roll of his eyes, an acknowledgement of the coarse language and the chuckle that had taken control of Eddie's sizeable figure and was reverberating through all three of their conjoined seats.

The conversation grew more natural after Cavani's fat-shaming, ice-breaking gamble, and the plane's engine noise and poor audibility lent a certain discretion and a freedom to their in-flight catch-up.

'What brought ye to London then, Jimmy? Filming?' Eddie asked, folding his arms as though he was waiting to be entertained with some showbusiness anecdotes.

'Filming, aye, and then just some press stuff, interviews and whatever . . .' Cavani answered, trailing off, rinsing his answer of all enthusiasm and excitement in the hope that he'd be shielded from any further work-related questions.

'What about you?' he asked Eddie. 'Working?' Cavani smiled, almost laughing at how determined he'd been in making sure the subject was changed.

Eddie wouldn't be keen on disclosing too much about his 'work', and Cavani would be allowed to be equally equivocal about his.

'Aye, just a few work things, Jimmy,' Eddie confirmed, smiling that he'd understood and agreed to Cavani's unspoken proposal.

What a fucking day, Cavani thought, or two days. He tried again to work out at what time in the UK he'd left New York and at what time he'd woken up the day before, the jet lag and the exhaustion clouding his calculations. He felt himself getting frustrated.

He tried to think of anyone else who called him Jimmy – Siobhan sometimes, or Jimbo, she'd address him as sometimes, usually when everything was fine and she was on good form.

He thought of how quick-witted and funny she could be, sighing to himself as he made another silent prayer-like appeal that, as well as her health, her personality could be salvaged from the wreckage too.

Aside from Siobhan the odd time, the name Jimmy had been pretty much confined to his schooldays, and maybe Eddie's use of it had been deliberate, like this was a time before their lives were complicated, before they both darted off in different directions, with only Siobhan seeing that they ran into one another again somewhere along the way.

'I'm just fucking exhausted, man, with it all.' Cavani heard his voice return, his real voice, the one that didn't factor in occasions, situations or who he was speaking to, his default, his factory settings.

'Siobhan took another overdose. I've fucked this latest film off. I was supposed to be doing press, telly, all of that, but I've just left. It was shite, the film, anyway . . .'

He felt the tension leave his bones and aches that he'd forgotten were there seemed to disappear. He felt loose, relaxed, fearless as he went on.

'Sacked my agent. Sacked London. Fucking . . . just fed up, man.' He realised, now the frustration and the anger were pouring out of him, that he'd been in an almost permanent state of acting since fuck knows how long ago.

'I'll take a tea, please, sweetheart,' Eddie shouted past Cavani, beating the crew member to ask Cavani if he wanted anything himself.

'A black coffee, please.' Cavani smiled at the crew member as he answered Eddie, hearing the jaded familiarity in his voice, his eyes turning to focus on a marketing photo of a couple holding hands on a gondola as he unhatched his tray table.

'Will yer agent and the executives – or whatever ye call them – be sound with that? Their main man, just fucking off?' Eddie enquired, surprising Cavani with the concern in his voice and the complimentary presumption that he was the film's lead.

'It wasn't a huge role I had, but aye, I guess they'll have to be, but it's done now, eh?'

Cavani leaned back to let Eddie collect his tea from his eyeline and waited to receive his own coffee.

'Silly, ye've worked too hard to be where ye are.'

Cavani turned his eyes to see Eddie shakin' his head, emptying a sugar sachet into his paper cup and ripping the top off another.

'It might be an age thing, eh – we're gettin' on a bit,' Eddie began, stirring his tea and opening the packet of shortbread that had accompanied it.

Cavani lifted the lid of his coffee to let it cool on the table before attempting a sip.

'An age thing, aye? Maybe. I don't know. It's been coming for a while, maybe I'm just fed up, maybe it's not for me any more, I don't know.' Cavani reminded himself who he was talking to, that this was a conversation to be had with Lisa.

'Aye, ye start contemplatin' yer own mortality – well, I've probably done that for longer than you, Jimmy, longer than most,' Eddie laughed, elbowing Cavani in the side again, making him even more wary of lifting his coffee cup to his mouth.

'But, aye, forty-two, whatever we are, ye feel like yer re-emergin' for the second half worryin' that ye've played all of yer best stuff in the first and that maybe it's no' been good enough – and ye will struggle to make up fur it before full-time. All the while yer beginnin' to question what the fuckin' point of the game is anyway and if there's anythin' – at full time, at the end – that separates the winners and the losers, or if that was it, it was simply game over, no trophy, no points, nothin', it's all just been a fuckin' kickaboot.'

Eddie smiled, turning to look to see if Cavani was impressed by his metaphorical side, his figurative speech that had brought existentialist philosophy all the way down to meet with football.

Cavani wondered if Eddie had said all this before, but to who? There couldn't be too many people in his life that he could concede any weakness to.

He remembered a time when Eddie had suggested that he write a script based on Eddie's life and that he'd have helped out and contributed with stories 'that Cavani wouldn't believe' and characters 'Cavani couldn't make up', even offering to help him direct it – so that it was authentic – and to play a cameo role. Someone else was to play him though, he'd forgotten who, but he remembered Eddie had given him a few names, which he'd found funny at first and then alarming when he'd realised the levels of conceit that Eddie was operating at and that he was deadly serious.

Maybe this explained why he was trying a retrospective, almost confessional approach, maybe he'd been working on adding some depth to himself, some layers.

'Ah think aboot Siobhan, Jimmy, and if it had worked out between us. Ah know her life would have been different – mine as well – well, ah don't think ah'd have gone doon the same roads – as far doon them anyway, if she'd been there . . .'

Cavani turned to look at Eddie again, interrupting him without saying a word.

He didn't know if it was anger that he felt, or hurt, or like he was betraying Siobhan by even speaking about her – as she lay in a hospital bed – to someone who was simply an ex-boyfriend of hers, Eddie Reynolds or not.

It had frightened him to hear her being referred to in the past tense, but then, she was in Eddie's past, he reminded himself, which was something he was relieved about.

'Her life will be different. She's stronger than the two of us anyway. She'll sort it for good. I know she will,' Cavani said, closing off the conversation, forming a protective barrier around his little sister.

Cavani looked to the man on the aisle, reassured that he had fallen asleep and hadn't been listening in to their conversation. He looked at the article in the magazine which lay folded open on his lap, something about Bitcoin. He wondered how many more articles he'd need to read before he'd begin to grasp how crypto-currencies worked. He thought of asking Eddie for his take on it: it was a subject that he'd probably get excited about and was probably capable of talking confidently on – they loved all of that shit, any sort of new scam, any sort of new way of tricking the system. Cavani nodded again, wondering why he saw an innocence or something childlike in a feared gangster, a man who ran a criminal empire and who'd probably carried out horrendous crimes.

'Ah didn't mean anything by that, Jimmy – she's none of ma business. But just know ah truly wish her well, ok? And she'll be in ma thoughts during all of this.'

Eddie's voice lowered into a conclusion and his hand tapped Cavani's kneecap, like a father comforting his son during a sombre moment.

'Ah don't think Colonel Sanders set oot with the intention of causing heart disease, obesity and strokes and whatever . . . ah don't blame him for this.'

Eddie smiled, his hand patting his belly, waiting for Cavani to laugh.

'Ah feel the same way about ma game as you're feeling with yours. Ah probably always have done, Jimmy,' Eddie went on, attempting to pick up on what they'd been talking about prior to him letting out his feelings about Siobhan. Cavani blew into his coffee cup, deliberately sparing himself having to think of something to say that would seem too inquisitive. He knew Eddie would fill in the silence, and whether he was about to talk a pile of shite or not, it was decent enough entertainment for a domestic flight, Cavani thought, relaxing, smiling.

'It's like someone else's life was handed to me, and don't get me wrong, we always had money, nice things, respect – or what ah thought was respect but, really, everyone was fuckin' scared of us. There was a map there for me and ma brother – from ma old man, from ma uncles, a map covered in fuckin' blood, guilt, shame, a map that half of these wee pricks nowadays would slit their own maws' throats to keep followin'.' Eddie looked across Cavani, seeming to be aware that he was getting worked up, checking to see if any apologetic nods or smiles were needed. No one had heard anything though, so he went on, his voice calmer.

'Ah looked at you, Jimmy – same age, same class – and at

what you built up, from fuck all. Remember, ah was round fur dinner a few times.' He nudged Cavani with his elbow, making sure his reference to his time with Siobhan and his humble family home would be cleared to pass as an innocent joke. Cavani smiled.

'Ah watched yer telly shows, films, and it was like you sold the opposite of me. Ah sold fuckin' misery and you took that misery and turned it into entertainment, and powerful entertainment at that. It made me feel like a prick, every bit of the prick ah should have felt like – it's me who should be chuckin' jobs and stormin' away, Jimmy, is the point ah guess ah'm makin', but ye'll figure it oot. We both will.'

Cavani wondered if he should thank Eddie or agree with him or at least be saying something, but Eddie was off again, like he was intrigued to be tip-toeing through his conscience.

'Ye watch that YouTube, it's rife with these cunts . . .'

Cavani heard the man on the aisle seat groan in his light sleep, like he didn't have to be fully conscious to be offended by Eddie's language. He looked to check the man's eyes were still closed and then looked back to Eddie, who'd taken the check as a cue to lower his voice.

'They're the new reality TV stars, *ex-gang members*, *ex-drug bosses*,' Eddie went on, his emphasis making it clear that these were other people's labels, journalists, the police, whoever . . . 'Grasses are in high demand – it used to be a faux pas, the ultimate faux pas but now it's how ye land a book deal, a wee pension, and get yersel' on these daft podcasts to plug the fuck oot eh it. Some arselicker presenter askin' ye yer favourite questions so ye can tell yer favourite stories. That's not remorse, that's not someone ashamed, that's not an ex-anything, that's just some workshy bullyin' bastard that's found a new income source and a new market.'

Cavani felt Eddie assessing him, satisfied that he'd been drawn in by this new side of Eddie that was being revealed.

'It's an occupational hazard in ma line of work, delusion, fantasy, believing the shite that ye need tae believe in order tae get a sleep at night. If ye truly faced up tae the truth, if ye faced up tae things ye've done then it's fuckin' . . . fuck knows.'

Eddie coughed, leaning in – Cavani's cue to do the same – which lent some added suspense, a conspirative edge to the conversation despite the poor acoustics of the plane and the fact that Eddie wasn't actually saying anything incriminating. It was for Cavani's benefit then, maybe, he thought, feeling the man on the aisle seat playing around with his seatbelt and tray table, awake.

Cavani wasn't sure whether or not to respect Eddie's honesty, his apparent sense of remorse – to try and empathise with him – or to halt the conversation entirely, for fear of hearing things that he didn't want to hear, things he didn't want to know, things that Eddie would forever know he knew.

'Ah see it aw the time, people, bad people – deeply unhappy people, shaped by too much time in the company of – what's the word? – sycophants?'

Cavani nodded, sensing that Eddie was sure he'd used the correct word but that he wanted some sort of explicit acknowledgement that he wasn't an idiot, that he wasn't a thug – or whatever. Cavani knew this, so it hadn't been necessary. He waited for Eddie to continue, intrigued.

'Ah know it was you who first got in Siobhan's ear aboot stayin' away from me, to end it, about what ah done, who ah am – well, who ah was, hopefully – and ah respected that, Jimmy. Ah did. Ah respected the balls that maybe took and ah respect that she wasn't daft and she'd have got oot in her own time, probably. Ah respect that ah'm an ugly bastard as well and she could have done better.'

Eddie laughed, coughing, and then gulping his tea to wash away the wheezing before continuing.

'Ah see people who've been left to stray intae the abyss of their own bullshit, abandoned, with no one brave enough – or who gives a fuck aboot them enough – to try and rescue them. Ye must see it in yer game too.'

Eddie placed the empty sugar sachets and shortbread wrapper into his teacup and closed the lid as Cavani thought of how he had indeed seen this in a lot of people in his own industry and that maybe it had been about to happen to him. Or maybe it already had but no one wanted to tell him – fuck knows.

He felt taken aback by how insightful some of Eddie's musings were, like he was beginning to forget who he was. Who was anyone, really? Behind the writer – the actor, the director, the celebrity – there's a human, and behind the gangster maybe there's one too. It's just that perhaps it's a safer and an easier life to keep the two as segregated as possible, for as long as possible, in the gangster's case. In Eddie's case.

'At the end of the day, we've aw got a fuckin' past, Jimmy, and even in ma prime years, or whatever, ah never enjoyed any of it, the years ah was supposed to be caught up in the thrill from the power of it aw, from bein' Eddie Reynolds junior, the financial rewards – everythin' in the films, the box sets and the rest of it.'

Eddie nodded to Cavani, seeing that he was following.

'Ah just fast-forwarded all of that, straight to the paranoid years, the hideout years, the safe house, the lockdown – always waitin', always waitin' on someone comin' through the door. The polis, some bam, armed polis, armed bams, anythin', anyone. Wakin' up durin' the night, sweatin', terrified . . .'

Eddie trailed off, shaking his head. It had caught Cavani off guard – it was his turn to cover for the silence.

What the fuck is going on, man? Cavani thought, like he'd finally pulled himself in to take a look back at the last twelve or so hours. Flying from New York to London, sitting in business class, a fucking movie star, to here, the middle seat at the back of the plane back to Glasgow with Eddie Reynolds confiding in him about his nightmares.

The jet lag. Everything. It felt fucking trippy.

'Do you ever wet the bed,' he heard himself asking Eddie, from nowhere.

He felt more shocked at himself than he had for the Colonel Sanders remark, reminding himself who he was talking to – that Eddie was still a dangerous dude – but he felt himself giggling and tears beginning to well up in his eyes as he saw that Eddie was laughing too at his unexpected enquiry and its abrupt altering of the tone, from penitent to farcical.

'Sorry, man, sorry,' Cavani attempted to say, surrendering to a second, wheezing quake of laughter, letting it shoot up from what felt like his feet and fire out of what felt like every orifice in his body. He felt powerless, unable to stop himself shaking; he thought of when his parents took him to chapel and he'd make eye contact with someone from school, as the priest was singing a hymn that had had its lyrics altered in a blasphemous playground remix.

Something simple like the word 'shine' being changed to 'shite' could make it borderline impossible for a twelve-year-old to repress a fit of the giggles during a clergyman's chorus of 'Shine Jesus Shine'.

These moments that grew progressively less frequent as you grew older.

Cavani noticed that Eddie looked confused and curious but that he was laughing heartily, like the way his parents had done when he'd tried to tell them a story about something that had happened at school, but he couldn't fight through the hysterical giggling to get it out, but knowing anyway that the story wouldn't be able to top the entertainment of his attempts to tell it and wanting the moment to last for ever.

Cavani put his fist to his mouth, feeling the air of his nose fanning his knuckles, hoping to suppress whatever had taken him over and waiting for the laughter to dissipate completely.

It was like a side effect of the travelling, the tiredness, the pressure, the worrying and then the anxious, claustrophobic feeling when he'd considered that maybe Eddie had mastered a glib charm that was now serving to exonerate him from the way he'd lived his life and Cavani had fallen for it. He'd been away from home for too long.

Cavani felt the rest of the mirth being shuddered out of him as he repeated Eddie's almost comically understated, loveable rogue, 'we've all got a past' summary of the undoubtedly horrific crimes he'd committed. Or maybe he was being honest, who the fuck knows and who the fuck cares, the flight would soon be over with and they'd both be back on their way.

'Ye ok, Jimmy?' Eddie asked, his tone a fusion of amusement, intrigue and embarrassment, like he was waiting for order to be fully restored so that he could categorically state that no, he didn't wet the bed.

'Here,' he said, bursting open a plastic wrapper from the pouch in front of him and handing Cavani a napkin for his eyes, smiling but still looking a little wary, like he'd been freaked out by Cavani's erratic outburst.

'Sorry, mate. My head's all over the place,' Cavani said, wiping his eyes and turning to smile at the man on the aisle, who looked unsure of *him* now, as well as Eddie.

'It's sound, mate, good to let it aw oot, and naw, ah don't wet the bed,' Eddie joked.

Cavani felt Eddie's elbow in his ribs again and saw that he was checking for his seatbelt as an announcement was being made. A member of the cabin crew asked Eddie to open his window blind. 'Aye, aye, sorry, sweetheart,' he said, handing over his empty teacup.

'Are you finished with that, sir?' the woman asked Cavani, who smiled, thinking back to JFK Airport, like this was now a private joke with himself, ordering a scalding-hot coffee and leaving it untouched. 'Aye, yes, thanks.' He handed it over, turning to look out of the window at the grey sky. At least it wasn't sunny, at least it was hospital weather.

Cavani felt his phone vibrate in his pocket and instinctively went to pull it out, welcoming the distraction from having to recover his and Eddie's conversation, before feeling his heart jolt – this could be anything, he warned, pulling it out and reading the text message before his head had a chance to run away with him.

'Siobhan is mortified that you've cancelled everything, they want to keep her in for observations and a few tests but she's adamant that she's fine and that you go to London and finish the interviews.' He slowly closed his eyes in an attempt to extend gratitude to whoever he'd tried to pray to as he text Lisa back to say that he was still in the sky but that he'd call as soon as he could.

He looked out over Clydeside. He didn't have the energy for another flight – and the vacancies he'd left on the television and radio shows and whatever else would be filled by now.

What's done is done, as his dad would say. He smiled, a sad smile, thinking of his mum and her range of quotations too; everything happens for a reason.

'Stick yer number in there, Jimmy, we'll need to get a proper catch-up one time.'

Eddie had pounced and caught him off guard, caught him daydreaming.

He'd struck at a moment of weakness. It was impressive and that was why he was at the top of his 'game'. Cavani wanted to say that he didn't give his phone number out, but he'd used up all his credits and he felt like he couldn't speak his mind for a third time.

This was the bill then, the reparations for the Colonel Sanders and the bed-wetting quips. He typed his number into Eddie's phone, surprised that it was a smartphone too.

'Don't worry, it's no' ma business phone. Just family and old friends.' Eddie smiled.

He was back in Glasgow now and he couldn't afford to be the vulnerable Eddie – the almost likeable, almost harmless Eddie. The airborne existentialist concerns were to be forgotten, never to be mentioned to anyone. Strictly confidential.

'No bother,' Cavani said, despondent, dreading the texts and calls and the favours he'd be asked.

'Don't be a stranger,' Eddie replied, taking his phone out of Cavani's hands. Their eyes made contact again. Cavani went to look away first, to concede any stare, but the plane scudding off the tarmac beat him to it, giving his heart a jolt and throwing his arse off his seat.

The landing had been as harsh as the journey from New York to here, he thought to himself.

This was it then. Home.

PART 4

'Was there something in the water down your way last night then?' the doctor said, smiling at his clipboard as Declan confirmed his address.

His mum turned to study the doctor. Declan watched her eyes begin at his faded Converse trainers, working their way up his fragile-looking legs and slender body, and on to his energetic, gleaming face; unhospitable to stubble.

Declan could tell she was taken aback by how young the doctor looked; he probably wasn't that much older than Declan. It could have been him, his teachers had told her, he could have gone to university – medical school – he could have been a junior doctor by now.

Declan knew this too but so fuck, he thought, feeling himself getting frustrated at what he thought his mum was thinking.

His mum turned to study Declan's reaction, to see if he'd understood what the doctor had meant by his opening line, worried that something else had happened that she didn't know about.

Declan passed his mum's quizzical look back to the doctor, with a confused smile, indicating that the remark had been lost on him too.

He didn't feel like talking but he had to try and be polite, especially to a doctor, especially to a doctor who was about to decide whether or not he could go home.

He reckoned his eye was bad, by the pain on his mum's face every time he caught her looking at it. 'Is he blind, Doctor,' his mum said, sounding like she had already resigned herself to the fact that he was. 'In that eye, I mean,' she clarified, realising that Declan would have mentioned that he couldn't see her when she'd arrived.

She seemed overwhelmed by everything else she wanted to ask – both the doctor and Declan – and she sounded like she was going to cry again.

'Mum, fuck sake,' Declan shot her down, apologising to her immediately and apologising to the doctor too. The doctor reassured his mum that his vision was fine, but warned that it could have been different if they hadn't acted in time, which was probably part true and part the doctor feeling sympathetic for his mum, justifying her concerns and assuring her she hadn't been as hyperbolic as her son had thought.

'Thank you, Lord,' Declan's mum announced, tilting her head back to address the polystyrene ceiling tiles before looking back down to face the doctor – who didn't seem bothered by, or was used to, this type of misplaced gratitude.

'What else happened?' she asked, kissing the miraculous medal around her neck, quickly adding, 'Doctor'.

She forced her eyes to blink and rubbed her hand over her forehead as though her hair was in her eyes. Her hair had been short for years now, but Declan knew this was just part of the routine for when her mind had bundled her into a boot and driven her off somewhere at high speed, but her physical self had to appear focused and attentive.

She looked old. Fucking hell, he thought, wondering why he hadn't noticed this before, wondering if it was temporary. He hadn't come home on Tuesday night; he hadn't come home on Wednesday night. The consecutive sleepless nights, that was probably what it was. They had taken their toll on her. Fuck. He felt the shame momentarily numbing his aching body.

'No, nothing remarkable. Just when I saw the address: James Cavani's home town. He's along the ward, visiting a relative who had a wee, eh, incident herself.'

'Declan loves him, don't you, Declan. He'd love to meet him,' Declan's mum interrupted, looking at the doctor, as though he could make this happen.

'Mum, get a grip,' Declan said, trying to laugh to show the doctor that he wasn't being short with his mum again.

'Sorry.' His mum put her hand over her mouth before taking a sip from a plastic cup of water that a nurse had handed her – during the initial battle to calm her down when she'd first seen Declan – and said 'Sorry' again, to the doctor.

He looked embarrassed, like he regretted mentioning James Cavani's presence. 'I probably shouldn't have said that. It didn't come from me, ok!' he appealed to them both, acknowledging that he'd breached a confidentiality rule.

'We won't say a word, son . . . Doctor, I mean,' Declan's mum assured him.

His relative youth and inexperience were no doubt a factor in his excited, starstruck disclosure. 'Don't worry about it,

Doctor,' Declan said, embarrassed too at the thought of someone like James Cavani being asked to come in and see him.

He wasn't a terminally ill child. He was an adult. An adult who'd been beaten up on his way home from work. It was a bit of a bastard but hardly a story that was likely to touch James Cavani's heart and have him come by the ward to try and boost morale and offer support.

The doctor nodded at Declan's mum, both accepting and dismissing her apology. His face looked sympathetic to her shattered nerves.

Reading from his clipboard he told Declan that his CT scan had returned showing a blowout eye socket fracture – his mum gasped and rattled off a few biblical names – but there would be no permanent damage, the doctor emphasised, pausing to make sure this had registered with her.

He'd cracked a couple of ribs too, the doctor told them both, and once the nurses had strapped them up again, they'd get him some painkillers and he'd be on his way.

'A blowout eye socket fracture,' Declan repeated, prompting the doctor into elaborating on different types of fractures and the force that each one usually required.

He didn't want to interrupt the doctor but he regretted speaking his thoughts aloud, now that the images in his mum's head would be growing more graphic as the doctor mentioned the potential use of a blunt instrument.

He'd only been considering the irony of being able to trace his 'blowout' fracture back to a drunken argument, two nights ago in the pub.

There was a lot more to it though, as he now knew. His

drunken argument with Gary Tanser and Jordan had been a convenient excuse. If he'd agreed to Jordan's demands – that he looked after something for a few weeks – he'd have a lot more to worry about.

He was proud that he'd stuck to his guns, an expression that made his eyes roll as it passed through his head.

He thought of how he always cringed when anyone said 'pardon the pun'. It reminded him of his old Modern Studies teacher at school who'd thought he was hilarious, and that no one could tell that he'd deliberately shoehorned in a double meaning so he could say this.

Declan remembered his horrid, slippery laugh and his narrow eyes checking round the class, hoping for the day that they'd join him in hysterics, before forcing out a disappointed cough and resuming the lesson. Declan would curl his toes and fantasise about one of the nutters in his year throwing a chair at him and laugh to himself.

Pardon the pun though, he maintained, seeing that the doctor had turned to answer his mum's questions about treatments and follow-up appointments and all the other shit he'd have to deal with.

He felt proud that he hadn't backed down. He hadn't fought back or defended himself – at least in a traditional sense – but something inside him had almost enjoyed the feeling of being alive, of being comfortable in his own skin, of having a clear conscience.

Lying in the hospital bed last night he'd felt relaxed – at least until his mum had shown up and he'd seen how distressed she was.

They'd given him strong painkillers, which no doubt contributed to his feeling, but he was convinced that part of his new-found serenity had been self-propagated too. He'd realised how much power his mind had had over him and how anxious he'd been – constantly worried, constantly braced for some sort of devastating impact – and this had been calming, to have a pain caused by something outside the self, to be reminded of your own fragile animal body. For all the torment the conscience and the mind could bring, it was refreshing and humbling – a relief – to be restored to mammal status. Blood, bones, ligaments, tendons, nerves.

This wasn't normal, he knew, and it made him think of a girl in his college class and the scars on her arms, which he'd presumed were from self-harm. He hadn't self-harmed but he certainly hadn't done much to avoid being harmed.

Very few people enjoyed being struck with a pole – or a bat, or whatever it was that Gary Tanser had handed Jordan. Declan hadn't had much time to study the choice of weapon, but it had been dark grey and it felt like it was made of titanium or aluminium.

Very few people enjoyed lying on the deck and being booted the fuck out of, but Declan remembered trying to laugh.

'Every little helps,' he remembered Gary Tanser had shouted, forgetting that he'd said they were the Sainsbury's mafia, not Tesco.

He was probably delighted with his closing line too. Pablo Tescobar would have been more obvious, Declan thought, laughing and feeling the true extent of the pain in his ribs.

'Righty-o, then, you see and take care of yourself, Declan,

don't be getting into any more scrapes and make sure to rest up for a couple of weeks.'

'Thanks, Doctor,' Declan said, like he'd been listening the whole time. He knew his mum would be able to repeat the aftercare instructions verbatim though.

His mum helped him swing his legs round to climb out of the hospital bed. He tried to suppress every groan his body squeezed out of him, aware that it was compounding his mum's own pain and trauma.

He'd miss college for a week, maybe longer, probably longer, but he had fucked it anyway, so this could put it out of its misery and he could go full-time in his work, if they'd allow him.

He pictured Sharon, his supervisor who'd seen him staggering towards the bus stop and picked him up, insisting that he let her drive him here.

He'd only got in the car after they'd arrived at a deal: she wouldn't call the police or ask the store to check their CCTV – or report this in any way – if he'd let her bring him to the hospital.

It was a deal she accepted with a few disapproving grumbles before accepting that the most important thing was getting Declan the medical attention he needed.

He'd been able to workshop his alibi with Sharon before his mum had wanted to know what had happened.

He'd told Sharon he'd been jumped and she'd gone on to tell him about how it was happening more and more, lecturing him about his generation and how they don't pay attention, that they were always too busy on their phones and before you know it, they were swiped straight out of their hands. She'd seen documentaries on this sort of thing, she'd gone on and on, telling him about moped gangs in London and clips on Facebook she'd seen. He'd be more careful next time, Declan assured her, trying to think of a way of changing the subject but aware that there wasn't much else that could be said.

Just as Sharon was continuing on about her son and how he had a thing on his phone that helped him track it, so that he could locate it if it was ever stolen or lost, Declan heard his phone slide out of the left-hand pocket of his work trousers, wedging itself in the gap between the passenger seat and door of Sharon's car.

He glanced to Sharon, seeing it register on her face that he hadn't been jumped – why wouldn't they have taken his phone then? He hardly looked like he'd fought them off. *Why else did they jump him?* she'd been asking herself, aware that any further interrogation could see her lose Declan at the next traffic lights.

'Look, I'm so sorry, Sharon, it's just a mess, right. I'd rather not talk about anything. I can get out here and just go home. I don't know what happened. I'm just . . . sorry, right.'

He remembered how supplicating he'd sounded in trying to intimate to Sharon that the police being involved would ignite a whole load of new problems for him, whereas his eye – and whatever else was damaged – could be sorted and that would be the end of it. Well, maybe, if he didn't leave the house ever again.

He'd apologised for getting blood on her car seat and grabbed the door handle to prompt her to slow down and to stop, to release him back on to the street, where he'd been quite content to deal with his problems on his own.

She'd told him it was ok, that she accepted his privacy terms and conditions, she'd take him to the hospital and she wouldn't say another word. 'I just want to make sure you get that eye seen to,' she'd told him, her face even more concerned as she took advantage of a red light to have a thorough inspection of it.

Declan had thanked her, appreciating that was the end of the matter, that one emergency service was all that the situation required. He'd pulled down the passenger seat vanity mirror to see the rapid progress of the swelling, aware that he'd need to think of a better story.

Leaving the hospital ward, he'd gone over what he'd told his mum when he'd messaged her to say that he wouldn't be coming home again – that her worries from the previous night had come to fruition, albeit twenty-four hours later. Getting his story straight for his dad coming home from work. A guy, two guys – two guys, he'd decided, which had technically added an element of truth to his account.

Two junkies, he'd thought of saying before considering it too unrealistic; he was by no means a skilled pugilist but his dad would have doubted that junkies could have left him in this state – and they'd have used a knife or a needle or something and, of course, they'd have robbed him.

Two guys who'd been trying to shoplift, that's what he'd told her, he'd caught them, stopped them and then they'd been waiting for him after his shift. Just two young guys, wee guys, two wee bams but they were all into going to the gym these days, wee guys, so they could all fight like fuck, he'd tell his dad and add that his work had reported it to the police and that they were dealing with it. That was all. He didn't want to talk about it. He felt a little shaken up and just wanted to forget about it. That should surely be enough, he reasoned.

His mum hadn't asked any further questions so either she'd believed him – that he'd stepped up, taking a zero-tolerance stance on stealing, making himself counted, for the Morrisons cause – or, more likely, she just wanted him treated and home before she could start her real interrogation.

If he'd told her it had been Jordan, he'd be terminating another friendship which went all the way back to when their mums had been at school.

His mum would march up and drag Jordan's mum out of her Porcelanosa kitchen by the hair, demanding to know where Jordan was. He felt himself laugh in admiration at his mum as he turned to look at her, smiling at the reception staff, asking if any of them knew if their bus stopped at this side of the hospital, and still smiling at them when they'd all told her they didn't have a clue.

They didn't have a car and they lived in a recently bought council house, but he'd never wanted anything that his parents hadn't provided. He'd never wanted much though, and nor had Ciara, aside from books, Lego and a couple of limited-edition comic books that Declan had helped to source.

Maybe that had been a deliberate parental tactic of theirs, to try and manage their children's material expectations by encouraging them towards more economically viable and sustainable interests. In a way it was a shame for Jordan: he only understood love in the form of things, stuff – brands, names, logos – love that expired every few months, love that came in and out of season.

He wanted to thank his mum and cuddle her but he knew he wouldn't. He tried to promise himself that this was the last time he put her through anything, but he didn't know what was next.

They walked towards the door, to leave the hospital. His mum halted them and they stood aside to let an old woman push a gaunt, terminally-ill-looking man in a wheelchair back inside.

The old woman thanked them both and they smiled at her and carried on out of the automatic door in a contemplative silence, Declan feeling ashamed of all of his problems and any complaints he had about his life.

The smell of second-hand smoke hit the back of Declan's throat and the sound of a sudden burst of laughter from a crowd of nurses interrupted his coughing. He looked over to see them all huddled round someone with one of them taking a picture.

The doctor hadn't been bullshitting. James Cavani was at the hospital. Fuck sake, Declan smiled, studying the man who he'd read so much about and had so much to say to but he felt himself getting nervous. 'Mum,' he whispered, interrupting her as she was about to quiz an ambulance driver on his bus route knowledge.

Declan nodded his head, signalling for his mum to look over his right shoulder.

'Oh, that wee doctor was right enough, James Cavani,' his mum said, walking into his path as the nurses behind him giggled and played with their phones.

Declan hobbled over to try and grab his mum's arm – to

lead her back towards the direction of the hospital's bus stops – feeling instantly sorry for James Cavani and regretting having alerted his mum to his presence.

He felt like he knew him, like he got him, but now they were just another two fans annoying him outside of the hospital where he was visiting a family member.

'Mum, leave him. Give him peace,' Declan whispered, defeated. It hadn't registered with his mum yet that she was being insensitive, given the location and the information that the doctor had leaked to them, that a member of his family was ill or had been in an accident.

As much as Declan wanted to meet him, there was a time and a place and he could separate the celebrity from the human being – he was here as a concerned family member, not as a movie star.

'James, excuse me, sorry to bother you but my son . . .'

'Mum,' Declan objected again, grabbing his side as he felt another shooting pain go through him. He turned away, humiliated as his mum had changed direction and was walking back over, in conversation with James Cavani. What the fuck, Declan thought to himself. Embarrassed, nervous, excited, he didn't know what the feeling was, but he smiled, and it grew wider as he saw James Cavani laughing at something his mum had said. He seemed sound. Thank fuck, Declan thought.

'What happened to you then?'

Declan felt like he was in a film. What the fuck. He tried to stop his face going red. What the fuck had happened again? He tried to recite the story he'd told his mum but all he could think of was the truth. Fuck. He looked at his mum and then at James Cavani again, who broke the silence by commenting on his eye.

'That looks a right bad one.'

'Aye, he could have gone blind. Two shoplifters, apparently.' His mum's sarcastic tone her first explicit acknowledgement that she knew he'd been lying.

'Aye? Where do you work?' Cavani asked, sounding genuinely intrigued, expecting Declan to say he worked in an art gallery, or a jeweller's, judging by the extent of the injuries he'd received in the struggle.

'Morrisons,' Declan answered, looking down at a menthol cigarette dout on the pavement, ashamed at how ridiculous his story sounded now that he was actually paying attention to it himself, ashamed too that he'd written his mum off as being out of touch and susceptible to believing any old shite.

Cavani looked like he could tell that Declan felt uncomfortable and that there was a lot more to the situation that he'd rather not discuss just now – he needed time to form a better lie or privacy to unburden himself and divulge to his mum the full details of what had happened.

'Well, hopefully it heals up soon, pal,' Cavani said, smiling and turning to Declan's mum as though to check if he was free to go.

'Thanks,' Declan replied, aware that his moment with his idol was fizzling out and trying to think of other times his face had felt this red. School trip to Alton Towers. Trying to piss in the toilet of a moving bus. Splashes on his light-grey jogging bottoms. What a fucking slagging.

'He's a bit of a writer himself, you know,' he heard his mum say, his face about to detonate.

'Mum, man.' He turned to look at her, pleading to be spared at least this, he'd been through enough.

'Oh, aye?' Cavani said, looking to Declan for more information rather than shutting the conversation down, which would have been well within his rights.

Sensing Declan's discomfort had just about peaked, Cavani turned to Declan's mum instead, prompting her to elaborate and allowing Declan time to compose himself, which was appreciated.

'I'm not a writer,' Declan mumbled, torn between wanting his mum to hurry up so they could leave and wanting to talk to James Cavani for ever, about everything.

'Well, what do you call someone that writes all the time and goes to a class every week to learn to write better?' his mum shot him down.

Declan laughed, taken aback at how encouraging but confrontational she sounded; the smile from his laugh stayed on his face as he imagined his mum jabbing him in front of James Cavani.

He could tell him that it was his mum who'd put him in hospital in the first place. He laughed again – there wasn't much else to do, it was fucking surreal, Declan told himself.

'Sounds like a writer to me,' Cavani said, laughing himself as he looked back to Declan, relieved for him that his nerves seemed to be settling.

'Well, I'm trying to do little bits. I carry a notepad and all that, like you said in your book, and just take down some notes for scripts and characters . . . ideas and things.'

Declan felt like there was an echo or something, it was like his words weren't his, like he'd no idea what he was saying, he was talking without thinking, the words that came out were new to him too.

'Ideas and things,' he mimicked himself saying. He felt the sweat on his back, the horrible sweat. He was starstruck. That's all it was. He breathed in, smiling, calmly accepting his diagnosis.

He remembered this was how Doof Doof had said he'd felt that day on the golf course. Ask him if he remembers, Declan thought, as if daring himself. Ask him if he remembers Doof Doof? Fuck sake, he jumped in, trying to restore some order to his thoughts, trying to take control of the situation.

Cavani seemed normal, sound, brand new. Relax, ask him if it's his sister he's visiting, Siobhan. Don't. Don't. It's none of your business. Fuck.

It hit Declan that he didn't know what to say.

'That's good, that's it, write everything, there's a story everywhere. The Morrisons worker with the zero tolerance approach to shoplifting, willing to put his life on the line. There's a comedy drama in that.'

Declan laughed. He wanted to say something funny to riff along with Cavani, but he couldn't trust that he wouldn't say something incoherent – something cringeworthy that would make the situation uncomfortable again, so he just continued his laugh, hoping for someone else to pick up the conversation.

He felt his mum studying him again, probably wondering what could be done about him, probably looking at the fucking state of him. He turned to look at her. His laugh stopped, his smile faded and his eyes apologised for everything she was processing.

'We're sorry for troubling you, James. Can I call you James?' his mum went on, not waiting for a reply. 'I hope everything is ok in there, is it a relative you're visiting?'

Declan took his opportunity to shoot his own accusatory look back at his mum – they knew why he was here, what did she want, gossip?

They both turned to Cavani as he answered, 'Aye, my sister, but she's doing ok. Hopefully she'll get out later today. What a mess. Family, eh. I'm just down for a wee smoke of this thing before the battery chucks it. Better off with the fags, less hassle.'

Cavani held his vape pen out for Declan to see, indicating that it was his turn to wrap up or rescue the conversation.

'My pal used to smoke one of them and he said that too, that the batteries were shite,' Declan said, ashamed to look at Cavani, fearing that he sounded like a wee guy, a wee prick. Your pal used to smoke a vape too, did he? Who gives a fuck, wee man?

Declan would have forgiven James Cavani for such a response and then making him flinch with a dummy punch before walking away from them and back inside the hospital.

Declan felt himself getting flustered again and then angry as he realised the 'pal' that he was talking about was Jordan, he remembered he'd started vaping. He hadn't ever smoked cigarettes though, he'd just gone straight to vaping, fucking idiot.

He felt his mum looking at him to hurry up and say his final words, so as not to hold Cavani up any longer, to let him get on his way – seeming to have forgotten that it was her who had interrupted him and brought him over in the first place.

'Your prescription!' she announced, like she'd finally worked out what the next thing was that she could worry about. 'We forgot to collect it.' She unzipped her bag, snatching a bit of paper out of it.

'I'll run in and get it for you, Declan – and meet you back here, ok?' his mum instructed.

'Aye, aye, thanks.' Declan nodded and watched as she turned, smiling at Cavani, impressed with his patience and his charm.

'It was lovely meeting you, James, son – and I'll say a wee prayer and light a candle for your sister.' His mum looked towards the hospital, her face showing she was already daunted by the thought of navigating her way back around it.

'Thank you, lovely to meet you too,' Cavani replied, clicking his vape pen on, like he was finally free to do what he came outside to do.

'. . . And good luck with the new film – here, come here, are you not supposed to be on the telly tonight? I hope you're not dogging it!' His mum winked at Declan.

'Mum, give the guy a break, man,' Declan added, not as embarrassed as he'd pretended to be, impressed more at his mum's confidence.

'I'm only joking, son, take care of yourself,' she told Cavani, who laughed and wished her well as she walked back towards the hospital.

'So, what actually happened to you then?' Cavani asked Declan, who'd begun to feel a bit more like himself now. He'd been too trapped in his own self-conscious state to notice how tired Cavani had looked, which made Declan feel ashamed again that they'd hassled him, but impressed and grateful at how sound he'd been, especially to his mum, who he'd genuinely seemed to warm to.

Declan saw that Cavani was looking at him, studying him, almost, as he thought of whether or not to tell him the truth about what happened or to stick to the shoplifter nonsense.

He felt like he hadn't started coming to terms with the reality of last night, that Jordan had hospitalised him. Hospitalised him for not agreeing to look after a gun.

'My pal, well, an old pal, attacked me, outside of work,' Declan began, the burden of bullshit lifting off his shoulders, the relief of it all. Of telling everything from the start, for the first time and, to James Cavani, it was like one of his fucking scripts. Fuck sake. Declan carried on.

'I go to a writing class every Tuesday in this arts centre on the Southside, after college. I had to perform a spoken-word piece. The class, they fucking hated it.' Declan smiled, watching as Cavani blew a vape cloud away from them both.

'They all sit, deconstruct it, analyse it, the usual sort of thing, it wasn't for them, so I think, well, they're writers, I'm not. It hits me. I go and get drunk, like, fucking . . . on a mission drunk. Staggering about. Embarrassing.' Declan held his ribs to let a cough escape.

'In the pub there's a girl I know, well – fancy – or whatever, but she's too good for me, man.' Declan waved his hand, swatting away this part of the story.

'Anyway, there's these local gangster guys in who my pal cuts about with now. He looks up to them – the way I look up to you,' Declan looked at Cavani for a reaction. 'I don't mean that to sound, like, whatever, but aye, I'm a big fan and when I read your book I was genuinely fascinated by your work and the craft of it all. Anyway . . .' Declan coughed again. 'They're all drunk too, and giving her a bit of a hard time and I try and defend her. Like a fucking idiot.' Declan paused to let Cavani take a look at him.

Cavani looked absorbed in the story, which encouraged Declan to keep going, to hold nothing back. It felt cathartic too, to tell someone every detail. It didn't seem like a superstar he was talking to now, it felt like an old pal, someone who knew him.

'We end up arguing, me and my old pal and his, well, his boss or whatever . . .'

Declan saw a couple walking towards them, whispering to each other, the woman smiled at Declan and he smiled back, hurrying his story, hurrying his time with Cavani, like he was holding up the queue.

'They threaten me, we get chucked out of the pub. I'm drunk, crying, going mental. Humiliating myself. The next night I come out of work, in Morrisons – that bit is true.' Declan laughed, checking over to the hospital to make sure his mum wasn't on her way back or anything. The couple had stopped, keeping a respectful distance, seeing that Cavani was deep in a conversation.

'They're waiting for me, my pal and his boss. They want me to look after something, like, fuck knows, man . . .' Declan trailed off, looking to his feet, realising he'd only just met Cavani and maybe it wasn't wise to be sharing too much of the specifics.

'Look after what? Drugs or something, cash? A gun?' Cavani volunteered, checking over both of their shoulders, letting Declan see that their conversation was in confidence.

'Aye, the last one.' Declan checked over his own shoulders too, lowering his voice again to emphasise further how sensitive this information was, at least to him, as he had to go back there, back home.

He looked up at a bus that had pulled in to the bus stop closest to the hospital, but he couldn't see the number or the destination. He looked back to Cavani, watching as he clicked his vape pen and placed it back in the pocket of his jeans.

'So, I said no, they threaten me, offer me money to do it – a grand to look after it, for a while – or I get leathered for the carry on in the pub.'

Declan stopped, watching as the story finished in Cavani's head.

'So, you never took the grand, eh?' Cavani said and they both laughed. 'Sorry,' he added, watching as Declan clutched his side. 'Same old fucking shite, eh? Sounds a bit like where I grew up,' he began.

'Aye, because it is,' Declan shot back, interrupting, an excited smile on his face. 'We went to the same school; my house is two minutes from where you grew up. Montclair Street, you grew up in Garrison Avenue.' Declan heard a high-pitched enthusiasm in his voice, reminding him that he was just a fan talking to his idol, realising that he'd just told him where he'd grown up too, like this was news to him. Fans did this, he guessed, clung on to a detail that connected them to their idol and Cavani would have been used to it. Declan managed to let himself off the hook.

'It's a small world, man. Fuck sake.' Cavani seemed to step back, adjusting his view of Declan and seeming genuinely surprised.

'Anyway, I should just have gone home after my writing class, simple as that, then there would have been no drunken arguments, no fractured eye sockets, no broken ribs and I wouldn't be on the radar of any shady bastards.' He summarised: 'I wouldn't have met you though, so it was worth it, man.'

Declan laughed, his fully operational eye widening in an approving acknowledgement of the counter-argument that he'd said aloud as soon as it had come to him.

He saw the couple approaching now and nodded to Cavani, interrupting whatever he was about to say.

Declan watched as Cavani turned round and smiled to the couple, asking them to give him a minute before turning back to Declan. 'Listen, what's your name?'

'Me?' Declan said. Obviously, you! Fucking idiot, his head answered on Cavani's behalf, prompting Declan into a nervous laugh, composing himself as his face started to turn red again. 'Declan, mate. Declan Dolan.'

'Wait there. Two minutes, mate.' Cavani turned, nodding to the couple to pull a phone out and guide him into a pose for a photo. 'Who's taking it?' the man asked his partner, turning to look at Declan. 'I'll take it, mate' Declan said, as though it had been his idea. 'Aw, brilliant, thanks, pal,' the man said, appreciating his charade being embraced.

The couple walked away, thanking Declan – his photos deemed acceptable – and telling Cavani they were looking forward to his new film.

Declan enjoyed seeing how happy they looked and thought of how it must be annoying at times, being constantly stopped, but also satisfying, to make people's day like that.

He wanted to say something like this to Cavani, to ask him if it did his head in or if he didn't mind it, but what was the point? Let the man go.

'Have you got a phone or a pen and paper or something,' Cavani asked

'Aye, I've got a phone. Naw. Bastard. It died,' Declan said, wondering what Cavani needed a phone or a pen and paper for, but his excitement overruled his curiosity.

'There's my mum coming back, she'll have a pen,' Declan announced, relieved as they watched her walking past a group of smokers, looking around the hospital grounds, disorientated.

Declan considered shouting on her but he didn't want to burden Cavani with any added attention. 'What kind of stuff do you write then?' Cavani pulled his vape out again, for a final few puffs before Declan's mum joined them – this was a question Declan had never been asked before. None of his friends knew of his ambitions and his family sort of left him to it, he realised, struggling for an answer.

'Just sort of, this.' Declan widened his shoulders and looked down to his feet and back to Cavani, letting him study his injuries along with the story behind them. 'Real life shit.' Declan laughed. 'Guys getting put in hospital for not carrying a gun for their childhood pal who's ditched them for gangsters.' He gave a defeated half-laugh at his abridged version of events before nodding in the direction of the hospital entrance, conscious that his mum was now walking towards them.

Cavani smiled, clicking his vape pen off and nodding that he understood the real story behind his hospitalisation was to be kept between them.

'Like the stuff you done at the beginning, before the movies,' Declan added, immediately scolding himself for his unnecessary remark, for saying something that could be construed as a dig and definitely interpreted as delusional.

'I love the movies; I don't mean it like that. Just the stuff that you wrote yourself, it was, powerful, man, real, I don't know, and I'm not saying anything I've wrote is anywhere near that level, like nowhere near it, man . . .' Declan looked at his mum to offer a distraction as his face burned bright red yet again. Fuck.

'I get you, man.' Cavani laughed, like this wasn't the first time someone had said something like that to him. He nodded and turned to look at Declan's mum too.

'I'm looking for a pen and a bit of paper, to write my e-mail address and he can send some of his work over, I'll take a wee look at it, see if I can give any pointers.'

Declan's face pleaded with her to pull out a phone with sufficient battery life or a pen and paper – he felt like a child again, watching his mum unzip her handbag like he was waiting to be given money to go to the shop.

'Hold on a wee minute, James,' she said, looting her handbag as Declan and Cavani exchanged a smile, listening to her whispered commentary on the raid.

'Here we go,' she announced, opening a Wordsearch puzzle book and scribbling across the inside cover of it with a blue-lidded Bic pen before handing both over to Cavani.

'I've not seen a Wordsearch in years,' Cavani told them both, laughing at the nostalgia.

'She's addicted to them,' Declan replied, checking for Cavani's reaction.

'My mum loved them too.' Cavani smiled.

'Fifty grand jackpot they say, my arse. Oh, sorry, James.' Declan's mum covered her mouth as though she was shocked at herself. She looked at Declan, embarrassed. It was his turn to bail her out too.

'Arse is hardly swearing, Mum.' Declan laughed, watching as Cavani scribbled away.

Declan shook his head, indicating to his mum to get over it. She hardly ever swore, he realised, feeling bad about his own regular cursing in her company and finding it strange to have realised something new about his mum.

Her over-the-top apology had been partly for show though, he knew, it had been out of respect for Cavani and she didn't want him thinking they were a family of ruffians, or undesirables, or however she would jokingly put it.

'You can send me some of your stuff. I don't have much on over the next few weeks so I'll take a look. That's my e-mail address. I'd give you my phone number but I don't know if you're a nutter,' Cavani said, smiling and handing Declan his mum's Wordsearch book. Declan looked at his mum, who nodded at him with a smile on her face as if to say he owed her a thank you for providing the writing implements, but most importantly for approaching Cavani in the first place and then informing him about Declan's passion for writing.

Declan felt the hairs on the back of his neck rise. No fucking way, he thought to himself, relieved that he'd stayed quiet, stayed cool. What the fuck. Fucking amazing.

'Aye, that's fair enough,' he said, talking without processing what he wanted to say; his head was allowing him to enjoy the moment. His voice boomed with confidence as he heard himself continue: 'Ye canny heavy breathe doon an e-mail anyway.'

Cavani let out a cackle. It sounded different from his previous laughs, it sounded real. Declan laughed too, taken aback that he'd said aloud the first thing that came to him as opposed to saving it to the drafts and opting for something safer.

'What are you talking about?' his mum asked Declan, laughing too – she looked happy to see him happy.

'Heavy breathers!' Cavani repeated, laughing again. 'You're too young to remember them. A blast from the past. That was before all the creeps had the internet,' he continued, shaking his head, like it was a subject that he'd totally forgotten but was glad to be reminded of, like it had intrigued him and he wanted to discuss the matter further. Declan was delighted, enjoying being enjoyed. He couldn't decide what to say next, but he'd only ruin it if he tried to be funny again.

Declan felt Cavani looking at his eye as his laughter fizzled out. It felt like he was wondering about the people who'd done this to him and what Declan was like, who he was, what he was all about, that sort of thing.

'Remember and send your stuff over,' he said, perhaps aware that he'd been caught examining Declan and trying to perform a background check on him.

'I will, I definitely will,' Declan said, mindful that his cool persona was dissipating and he was about to sound nervous and starstruck again.

Cavani smiled at Declan's mum and looked over towards the hospital doors, no doubt checking if his route was clear or if he was likely to be stopped again.

Declan, unsure whether or not to walk away or say something, watched as Cavani went to take a smoke of his vape before rolling his eyes, shaking his head and looking at Declan, a look that suggested the battery had died.

'What's your name again, sorry, mate . . .?' he asked Declan, slipping the vape back in his pocket and holding his hand out.

'Declan, mate, Declan Dolan,' Declan replied, delighted to have earned a 'what's your name again' from James Cavani.

'Look after yourself, Declan, and get in touch, right?'

Declan smiled and nodded. He wanted to tell James Cavani that he'd have taken an even bigger tanking last night if he knew this was going to happen.

Fucking yes, he breathed to himself, feeling his fist clench.

He walked towards his mum, seeing that she was looking around for someone else to ask about their bus stop.

'Cheers, mate. Great to meet you!' he shouted back at Cavani, realising that he'd let him walk away without saying anything. Declan watched Cavani stick a thumb in the air and walk back inside the hospital, his head down, studying his phone, so as to look inconspicuous.

Declan couldn't remember the last time he'd smiled like this. He felt himself ready to start laughing again. Fucking yes, he repeated. Yes!

What if he thinks your stuff is shite? He won't, a confident Declan butted in, aware that it was only his head, trying to ruin the moment, and if he does think the stuff shite, at least his feedback will help to make it less shite, Declan nodded.

'We learn from failure not from success,' he said to himself, smiling, thinking of Big Rugby Ross from his class and of the Tuesday night that he could walk in and tell them all that he was working with James fucking Cavani. He smiled again before cutting himself off, realising that he had got ahead of himself and was thinking like a prick.

He wasn't working with James Cavani and was unlikely ever to be – he'd met him, and Cavani had offered to take a look at his work. Whatever it led to, it was fucking exciting and the happiest Declan had felt in years. He wished he could walk home, with his headphones in, listening to music, thinking of the future and of something great happening.

'Right, thank you,' he heard his mum say, walking back towards him, nodding to the direction they were headed in.

'We need to walk to the other side of the building to get this prescription, but that's where the bus leaves from,' she said, marching ahead with intent.

He let his head drift off as they walked, already planning on when to e-mail Cavani, what to e-mail him, what sort of stuff that he had that was Cavani's thing.

'What's your name again, wee man,' he repeated to himself, smiling, laughing and then holding his side in pain.

'There's a guy called Raymond at the door,' Declan heard his mum shouting from the hallway, making her way towards his room. Why did she have to shout that if she was coming into his room anyway, Declan thought, pushing the back of his head into his pillow and sighing at his bedroom ceiling, listening to her approach.

He felt like he could tell each individual floorboard his mum walked over and exactly how many steps away she was from opening his bedroom door.

He'd lived at home far too long, he reminded himself, resigned, embarrassed that Doof Doof would have heard the wariness in her voice, embarrassed too at all the bits of paper which were lying around him, short stories, scripts, fucking nonsense, all of it, he snapped at them as he grabbed a couple of fistfuls and forced them into the centre of his notepad, placing it under his pillow; the only hiding place that was quickly accessible to him in his debilitated state.

He managed to sit up so that his lower back pressed against his headboard and he watched as his bedroom door opened and his mum's voice led her inside.

'It's an older-looking guy, I've never seen him before,' she warned as she reached the foot of his bed. Declan watched her turning back round to face the bedroom door, her head warning her that she'd left an unsavoury character unattended.

She looked back to Declan for instruction – he just needed

to give the nod and she'd see that the police would be on their way.

It was going to be like this for a while, he'd accepted, after telling his parents a version of the story that verged on the truth, albeit with any names they'd have recognised omitted, most notably Jordan's.

He'd got into a bad argument with some dodgy people and they'd came to get him for it and that was that. The conflict had been resolved in their favour and life was to move on, Declan had said, hoping his parents would accept his simplistic breakdown and the lessons that were to be learned. His mistake. He was drunk. These things happen.

He'd lay off the booze for a while. Lie low. Focus on college. He'd thrown everything at avoiding their lectures, their interventions, the appraisal period where the big questions would be asked. Where was his life headed? What were his plans?

There were only so many times you could be asked questions that you didn't know the answers to before snapping. He'd avoided falling out with them, that was a consolation, but the house was a tense place and he felt suffocated at times by his mum's anxiety and his dad's disappointment.

'Aye. It's Raymond, Raymond Buchanan, my pal, well, Connor and his brother's pal but my pal now too,' Declan said, getting flustered, frustrated at the length of his own answer. It was his parents' house though, and he knew they had a right to perform any background checks they deemed necessary on whoever graced their top step and chapped their door. 'He messaged me to say he was coming to pick me up after his work, we're going to go around to his house for a bit.'

This was the first Declan had heard of the plan. Doof Doof finished early on a Friday and had only said that he'd visit Declan on his way home, but there had been no mention of going to his house until Declan had said it out loud, suggesting it to himself.

It sounded a great idea, exactly what he needed.

'There's football on,' he added, trying to pacify his mum by adding a semblance of meaning to the evening, rebranding it as an event. If she had asked who was playing, he wouldn't have known what to say.

It was an option for her to at least consider and it was better than leaving the purpose of his visit to this unknown guy's house open to her imagination, which would no doubt lead her down the usual dark alleys, some darker ones now too, after everything that had happened.

'Connor's coming over too,' he told her, hoping that the presence of a familiar name, a trusted ally, would relieve the waves of trepidation that had already slumped her shoulders and would dominate her head all night as she wondered what was coming next.

She said nothing as she walked out of his bedroom, heading back to the front door to inform Doof Doof that he'd been given clearance to enter.

He patted Hector, who'd been ready to jump off the bed, sensing that Declan's mood was about to sour.

He'd been in his bedroom all day. A couple of hours would do him good. Plus a few smokes of a joint would maybe help with the pain. Doof Doof wouldn't mind too, and he'd probably suggest it himself once the initial pleasantries were exchanged, the concerns expressed and Declan's parents' strict no-smoking policy adhered to.

There wasn't even anywhere for someone to sit other than the edge of the bed, which lent a death bed vibe or something. Fuck that. Doof Doof had five minutes to suggest that they go to his or else Declan would, he decided.

Connor had said he was going to visit Declan after he finished his shift but he could just as easily make his way to Doof Doof's, so that wasn't necessarily a lie he'd told his mum, just a truth that hadn't yet been formed. A truth that hadn't yet been formed – Declan repeated his thought, impressed by the sentence. He wanted to scribble it down, but he could hear Doof Doof talking to his mum. He was inside the house now and he'd wonder what Declan was writing if he walked into the bedroom and caught him with a pen and paper.

He didn't know if it was original or if he'd heard it somewhere. There had been an abundance of new synonyms for lying over the last few years, so it had probably been said before. Still, he was pleased his brain was working like this, thinking, writing, creating. He felt himself calming down and Hector looked convinced too, enjoying his chin being tickled.

He could hear a warmth return to his mum's voice as she spoke about Gayle Buchanan, Doof Doof's mum. He'd been given the all clear. Maybe his mum would relax now and not worry about him going out, over to his. He was driving too, and Connor would give him a lift home as long as he left at the same time, which would be early. Even better then, for his mum's sake.

Connor might be able to provide some further information

as well, anything that he'd have picked up about Jordan and what was going on with him, and, of course – Declan felt a knot in his stomach – Connor might have any intelligence that would suggest if there was to be anything else for him to worry about or if it, whatever 'it' was, was over and done with. Surely, Declan pleaded to his ceiling.

'Fucking hell, man,' Doof Doof whispered as he entered, walking towards Declan, studying him and then looking away to compose himself before apologising for his blunt assessment of Declan's injuries, apologising for being taken aback.

'Jesus Christ, sorry . . . that fucking eye . . . scumbags, man.' Doof Doof turned away from Declan, interrupted by the sound of Hector jumping off the bed and walking towards the door, to leave the room, feeling the anger in Doof Doof's voice when he'd referred to Jordan and Gary Tanser. Doof Doof turned to Declan again, surprised at Hector's reaction; he'd never had dogs before, so their empathy and their acute ability to read and react to any changes in the atmosphere were new to him.

'It's ok, Hector, come here,' Declan called, but Hector, unconvinced, refused to turn back . They both watched as he took advantage of Doof Doof having left the bedroom door open, listening as his paws made their way through to the living room, where he was greeted by Declan's mum.

'Ah, shit, sorry, was that me?' Doof Doof asked, lifting himself off the edge of the bed in a physical offer to go and bring Hector back.

'He'll come back, it's cool, Ciara's due home from school and she'll take him out.'

Doof Doof nodded, turning to examine Declan's eye again. Declan could see in his face the amount of questions he wanted to ask, every one of them being restrained as he no doubt considered if they were appropriate or insensitive, unsure whether or not Declan was ready to talk about what had happened yet.

'I'll tell you everything later,' Declan said to placate him, acknowledging the shock in Doof Doof's uncomfortable silence, aware he was only processing things *not* to say.

It was also a strong hint, he'd hoped, that Declan didn't intend to spend the evening stationed in his own bed, with just Freeview television and the diluting juice or the crisps that his mum shouted in to offer, which they both declined.

Declan was pleased at this clear indication that her mood had lightened though. She'd thought highly of Doof Doof's mother, it seemed, and if there had been any snippets of talk about her son's cannabis, or 'drug', use, then she'd chosen to ignore them. He liked that his mum took people as she found them, which was a lot easier to preach than practise, especially in a small town.

'We can head round to mine if you want,' Doof Doof volunteered, adding, 'I've got the van. The cooncil-mobile. Cruisin' in the whip!'

'Fuck, man,' Declan yelped as he laughed, prompting Doof Doof to apologise through his own warm laughter, turning away to let Declan's pain dissipate, studying his bedroom.

'What's this, a script?' Doof Doof asked, picking up a bit of paper from the foot of the bed. Declan wanted to grab the sheet of paper back but the pain of lunging forward wouldn't have been worth it.

'Alisdair: You've to call her a he and him a she and them a binary or sumhin, they and them. If ah cannae keep up then whit chance huv the weans got. Changin' their pronouns? Fuckin' pronouns? They didnae huv pro-nouns when ah was at school . . .'

Declan watched the curious smile on Doof Doof's face as he dictated Declan's own words back to him.

'They didnae huv pro-nouns when ah was at school,' Doof repeated, laughing. 'That's a belter. That is something a cunt called Alisdair would say, man.' His laugh grew heartier. 'Are you writing a play or something?' he asked, impressed.

Declan felt his face go red – bright red – to the point he felt it was an injustice, that his face had overreacted. He was convinced he wasn't that embarrassed until he'd blushed, and now he was embarrassed at how embarrassed he looked.

'Sorry, man. Sorry,' Doof Doof said, forcing his face to look serious, to acknowledge that he might have been intrusive and to apologise – he'd seen how mortified Declan looked.

'Naw, it's cool. I've been doing a wee bit of, well, I'm trying some writing.'

Declan looked to the floor as he spoke, noticing another few bits of paper that he hadn't seen and managed to get cleared away in time. He could feel how interested Doof Doof was though, intrigued. He'd known he'd be supportive, but, still, he felt like a dick. *Ideas and things*, his head repeated, reminding him of the nervous wreck he'd been the day before, talking to James Cavani. 'James Cavani, he's asked me to e-mail him some of my stuff,' Declan said, surprising himself by how far he'd fast-forwarded his answer.

'Eh?' Doof Doof responded, a confused smile on his face

as he looked at Declan, who began smiling too. Declan didn't know what to say next.

'I've been going to this mad class, right,' Declan continued, attempting to strip the pretence from his admission. 'That's where I was the other night, before the pub,' he laughed.

Doof Doof laughed too. 'Whit is it, a cocktail-making class?' Doof Doof said, reminding Declan of the nick he'd shown up to the pub in. 'Sorry, sorry,' he said, holding his hand up, acknowledging that it was hurting Declan to laugh. It had been a good one though, fair play, Declan thought, holding his side, coughing, shaking his hand in front of his face to let Doof Doof know it was no big deal and he just needed a minute to get himself together.

'What kind of mad class? Like a writing class? With James Cavani? Whit?! Does he teach it or something? That's brilliant, man.' It heartened Declan how intrigued Doof Doof was, his curiosity and enthusiasm were appreciated but doing nothing for Declan's cabin fever.

'Aye, it's a writing class, some guy who worked at the BBC and all that teaches it. I don't think I'll go back but I'm finishing up writing some things to send over to James Cavani.' Declan laughed along with Doof Doof, it was quite a surreal thing to be saying.

'His sister was in hospital. I think she's ok though, he said, but we ended up speaking to him outside and I told him we were from here and that I done some writing and whatever . . . and he gave me his e-mail address, to send some of it over.'

Declan shook his head, thinking back to the conversation the day before with Cavani, finally convinced that it had happened.

'That's fucking brilliant, man. Remember I told you, he's brand-new, man, sound as fuck.' Doof Doof shook Declan's shoulder. 'Shit, sorry,' he said, a pre-emptive apology for any pain that was about to shoot through Declan's body.

'I'll tell you everything later,' Declan asserted, moving his legs round to the side, pushing himself across the bed. Doof Doof stood up and turned to take his arm, helping him to his feet. 'Fucking hell, man.' Declan forced a laugh through his groaning, in recognition of the state he was in just trying to get out of bed. It should start to ease off in a few days, he told Doof Doof, noticing he was holding another bit of paper, smiling as he recited: '". . . a few other cunts shoutin' me back but it's done noo. It's aw over wae. Ave made ma mind up. Goodbye ya cunts and fuck yees. Everywan eh yees." What's this one, a suicide note?' he asked, looking at Declan, who looked at the paper, seeing that it was his *Ryzo* story from the other night.

'Sorry, man, that was a stupid thing to say. Genuinely, sorry.' Declan heard the sombre change in Doof Doof's voice and turned to see him place the paper on top of the bed, holding his hand out, waiting to see if Declan needed any help walking across the room.

Declan hadn't fully processed what Doof Doof had said, but he'd never seen him embarrassed before, ashamed, even.

Declan felt embarrassed at how embarrassed Doof Doof was and at how immediate and profuse his apologies had been, like this was a tasteless comment, a touchy subject around Declan, like this was how people who knew him now viewed him, what they thought – that he was on the edge of killing himself or something and it was at the point they didn't even want to joke about it.

It had been like when Declan had first found out that Doof Doof's mum was dead, after Connor's brother had made a generic 'yer maw' type joke in response to something Doof Doof had said one night that they were all sat in his house.

Declan remembered that Doof Doof hadn't seemed to mind whatever the joke was, but the change in the atmosphere had been palpable. And Connor and his brother's excruciating looks to each other, and then Declan's look to them and then to Doof Doof, his mum's presumed death registering on his face, made more of the comment than there needed to be.

Connor's brother had tried to change the subject, but it had been too obvious that that was what he'd been trying to do and it had only added to the rigidity, the tension. Connor's brother had looked as uncomfortable then as Doof Doof himself looked now.

You can't make a 'yer maw' joke to someone who's lost their maw, in the same way that you can't make a suicide joke to Declan, given how he'd been behaving of late, it now seemed.

It had just been a throwaway remark, the first thing that had come to Doof Doof's head. Declan knew this and felt sorry for him, knowing that he'd never have meant to cause any upset or offence.

'It's cool, man, don't be stupid,' he said, hoping something else would follow, a joke of his own maybe, to meet the issue head on, like Doof Doof's suicide note joke had some ambiguity but hadn't been taken personally.

The silence only worsened the situation and made the remark a bigger issue than Declan wanted it to seem.

Declan wanted to make it clear that he hadn't been taken aback at Doof Doof's line in itself, more his reaction: the immediacy and sincerity of his apology and how telling that it had been.

Declan looked back over to the piece of paper that lay on his bed as his head emerged through the neck of his jumper, the significance of Doof Doof's remark growing as he helped him pull the jumper down over his waist, fixing his hood so it sat right.

Declan walked the few steps to reach over his bed, grabbing the piece of paper and placing it in his notepad underneath his pillow.

'You've been busy, eh, well done, man!' Doof Doof said, his tone upbeat but unnatural, relieved to have stumbled upon something to say, nodding towards the thickness of the pile of paper from which pages of dialogue, characters and ideas spilled out, the contents of Declan's mind.

'Aye,' Declan replied, distracted, forcing a laugh of his own, almost leaving it too long to reply, which probably exacerbated the guilt Doof Doof felt because of his remark.

'Probably all shite though,' Declan added, deliberately laughing again, to halt any disputing of his negative comment.

'You never know,' Doof Doof said, aware that Declan just wanted the subject of his writing dropped and to be out of the bedroom, to be out of the house.

Declan heard Doof Doof turn away, stepping over to the far side of his bedroom, turning around to look like he was studying some of the books on Declan's shelf, to give him the privacy to stash his writing, his work, somewhere that no one else had a right to see.

Declan thought of his mum reading something like the *Ryzo* story and jumping to the same conclusions as Doof Doof had, albeit in part jest. His mum's conclusions would be serious though.

He wanted to be clear to Doof Doof and everyone else now that he'd never thought of harming himself, let alone killing himself. He'd never thought of it seriously anyway.

He would never do that to his mum and dad, Ciara, Doof Doof and everyone else, he always concluded, but it was a soothing thought, it shut his head up, that he had the nuclear codes, that it could just all be over. *But then what?* he'd always thought, imagining if there was an afterlife, imagining hell, imagining hell being having to watch your family at your funeral, ripped apart, destroyed, having to watch them trying to move on without you. Fuck that, he'd think, and then his head would seize its opportunity to remind him of how selfish he was, to even be thinking like that, and on and on the battle would rage.

This was a sign though, Doof Doof had done him an inadvertent favour. It had been a warning, that people close to him were concerned for his well-being. They had a point too, Declan acknowledged; he knew that he'd begin obsessing about this now as well, and feeling bad for how bad he'd been feeling.

Fuck sake, he thought to himself again, as he struggled through the hallway, stopping as he felt his face turning pale.

'Two minutes,' Declan turned to tell Doof Doof.

'You ok, man?' Doof Doof asked, walking towards him with his two hands poised to be of assistance when called upon, confirming the lack of colour in Declan's face, his own face still warm from the regret of his remark.

'All good,' Declan answered, walking into the living room.

A gameshow was on the television that his mum wasn't watching.

Declan patted Hector who didn't respond, aware of the difference between a nervous, fidgeting pat and the excited, good-natured contact he was used to; it was like he could detect when his coat was being used as a stress relief tool, like he knew that, if he wasn't there, then Declan would be playing with the netting inside the pockets of his tracksuit bottoms or twisting the toggles on his hooded jumper as he spoke to his mum.

Declan mumbled through his full evening's itinerary, complete with travel arrangements, assuring his mum that he wouldn't be late and that he was only going to be indoors, watching whatever game was on and getting a takeaway, probably – he'd be getting a lift there and Connor would give him a lift back.

'Ok?' he said, attempting a disarming nod, looking to her eyes for an indication that she was at least trying to believe him, that there was nothing to worry about, that nothing bad was going to happen, that this was a turning point.

If Doof Doof wasn't already here he'd have cancelled the plans and stayed in. He wanted more than ever just to be with his mum, to comfort her. She looked exhausted. He wondered if she ever really slept that well.

He looked around the living room, looking at his and Ciara's first holy communion photos. He thought again about his concern for Ciara and if she'd been getting bullied at school.

His only evidence was from his own years at high school, where children like her tended to get a hard time, but now he considered that this was probably the dark cloud in his own head affecting how he saw her.

Ciara was probably fine. She had her own hobbies and she'd do well. She was introverted – different, maybe – but there was nothing wrong with how she was and it definitely wasn't up to him to try and mould her into something she wasn't. She was probably a lot more comfortable within herself than him. He was the one being bullied too. That was still the term for what Jordan and Gary Tanser had done to him. Even if he was an adult, seven years older than Ciara, he was the one being picked on.

He was the one causing the distress to their parents, not Ciara.

Projecting, it was called, or transference – something like that – he remembered from an article or a podcast, or something Doof Doof had been on about, fuck knows.

He hadn't intentionally looked for his own failings and mis-givings – weaknesses or whatever – in her, it had come from a good place, he went on, realising he'd leaped to his own defence before his head had started on him, calling him a narcissist, a megalomaniac, controlling. Was everyone to be an extension of him? To be moulded in his image?

What the fuck was he talking about? These terms, these expressions – he realised he couldn't stop thinking, thinking about what he was thinking.

He could only see dark-coloured shapes and the little patterns they were forming. It made him think of when he was a child, and his dad had bought him a packet of marbles. They were boring, there were better toys, but he enjoyed looking inside them, at the patterns.

He wanted to get out of the living room before his mum noticed that he was sweating, and his fully visible eye felt like it was moving, flickering. He closed it, hoping it would reset itself, opening it again only to see more coloured patterns, circles and then one massive, lighter, orange shape appear, like it was shooting towards him.

'Declan,' he heard his mum say as she stood up, walking towards him. He heard Doof Doof bounding in now. 'All good, man,' he tried to say, noticing that Doof Doof was lunging towards him and Hector had started barking.

'Drink this, Declan, big sips,' his mum told him as he put his hand to his forehead, feeling the end of the cold, wet cloth that his mum was holding as she instructed Doof Doof on how to open the living room window.

Declan took a sip of water and heard his mum asking Doof Doof to go into their cupboard, that there were some biscuits in there, some sugar would help get his blood levels back to normal.

Declan felt himself ready to cry. 'I'm sorry, man' – he looked at his knees, telling whoever was listening.

'Just take it easy, Declan, breathe,' his mum instructed him. They needed to talk, there was no avoiding that now but this wasn't the time.

'Here, eat some of these, man,' Doof Doof said, tearing

the top off a packet of ginger nuts, using his thumb to free the top couple from the pack.

'Thanks, mate, thank you . . . two minutes,' Declan mumbled. The vulnerability in his own voice alarmed him. He asked himself who he'd been trying to be this whole time? Was this him? Now that he'd been stripped back to the core, was this really him?

He felt scared to lift his head back up in case he had another dizzy episode and passed out again. 'I'm sorry, mum.' His voice crackled as he noticed a tear had splashed on to the top of his black trainer. He studied it as it settled. Teardrops on your trainers, good title for something, he half thought, exhausted with himself.

'It's ok, Declan, just relax,' his mum told him. He could feel her miming more instructions to Doof Doof.

'What time is it?' Declan asked, feeling the warmth of Hector's breath blowing against his face and his wet tongue frantically clearing his cheeks from the tears that had formed, causing him to smile and move his head back. He pulled the sleeve of his jumper between his fingers and his palm to wipe away both the tears and the affection.

He made a note to himself to brush Hector's teeth when everything settled – the smell of his breath was appalling but comforting, and it had forced Declan to lift his head.

'Slowly, Declan, slowly. Hector, sit back down, sit!' he heard his mum reacting.

Hector's direct, no-nonsense approach to nursing had done him a favour though – he was up, he was there, back, looking around, fuck sake, he thought, realising what had happened. 'I

feel like Dorothy,' he said, expecting his mum and Doof Doof
to laugh, at least out of sympathy, or out of relief – like when
someone makes a joke after being in an accident or hurting
themselves and everyone is reassured that it wasn't that bad.

Confused at the silence, he lifted his head up further and
turned to face his mum. 'You feel like what?' she asked.

'Dorothy,' he repeated. 'Was that not her name. *The Wizard
of Oz*?' He turned to ask Doof Doof, who laughed this time.

'Aye, aye, Dorothy . . . When she wakes up from the dream,'
he answered, explaining the joke on behalf of Declan whilst
trying to acknowledge that it was a good one but he'd been
too distracted to laugh.

Declan could tell they hadn't been convinced that he was
fully cognisant or if he'd been delirious and unsure of what
he was saying.

He must still have sounded and looked terrible, he gathered,
pulling the cloth off his head to wipe his face.

'It's just after four, mate,' Doof Doof told him, answering
the question now he was certain it was a fully conscious Declan
who'd asked it.

'You were only away with it for half a minute or something.
I think you fainted,' he added, his head turning, along with
Declan's, to his mum to see if she had a better term for what
had just happened. She let out a concerned but loving sigh,
picking the cloth off Declan's leg and wiping his face again,
his head moving back slightly, to indicate that he didn't need
to be nursed, that he'd sort himself out.

'I think you should stay in here, rest up and eat something.
I'll come back round later, if you want? Or else tomorrow. Any

time you want, we need to get you better.' Declan could see his mum's trust of Doof Doof growing as he dispensed the advice that she wanted to but that she'd have had easily dismissed, her reputation as a worrier, an over-protective parent, a nag perhaps, preceding her, even in circumstances as serious as this.

'Aye, probably for the best,' Declan accepted, his mum's hand arriving on his shoulder, relieved at his decision. 'I'm sorry,' he heard his voice repeat as his elbows sat on his thighs, forming stanchions for his head to come back to rest on his palms.

'It's ok, it's ok,' his mum told him again. He could feel her head turning to Doof Doof, this time looking for him to say something, aware now that Declan listened to him and that he sounded sensible enough.

Declan felt his eyes filling again. He was present enough this time for the embarrassment to register, and his head made sure that it did. It made sure it let him know that he was crying. Full on fucking tears. Full on fucking crying. His mum comforting him as he cried. Crying in front of his pal. His mum comforting him as he cried in front of his pal. His pal who didn't have a mum. He's the one who should be crying. Pathetic.

Declan wiped his palms down his face and then his palms on his tracksuit bottoms. His mum handed him a tissue for his nose.

'Look at the state you're in, man. Because of these pricks. That wee prick. Fuck him, he'll get his, they all will. Sorry for the language, Mrs Dolan, it's just . . . infuriating, man.'

Declan had tuned in now. He looked down at the floor, waiting for his mum to say something in response to Doof

Doof, her silence leaving Declan to presume she must have nodded to him, excusing his language and encouraging him to continue.

She'd have been curious now, and not prepared to allow her own dislike of strong language to intercept a delivery of specific details on what happened to her son and especially who Doof Doof meant when he'd said, 'That wee prick'.

Declan lifted his head up. It was past the point of hiding his face anyway, past the point of hiding the streaks from the tears that had flowed from both his good eye and his swollen eye. He looked at Doof Doof, frowning, his head forward, trying to balance an appreciation of his words with the issuing of a direct order to him to slow down, to back up; to communicate to him that he'd said enough, that he'd got carried away.

Hector jumped up out of his bed, his tail wagging as he made his way across the living room. Declan, his mum and Doof Doof turned as the front door opened and Ciara walked in.

'Who do you mean by them, Raymond? Who's that wee prick?' Declan's mum asked, in the hope she could hurry more information out of Doof Doof, aware that time was running out on this rare opportunity, aware that Ciara was home and she'd want to know why Declan was crying and who the stranger in their house was.

Declan looked at Doof Doof again, for confirmation that he'd read the signal.

'Just . . . them . . . the people who done that to Declan and the wee prick that hit him,' Doof Doof answered, running his eyes over their living room, taking in nothing, as he hoped

278

he'd done a convincing enough job for her to cease her line of questioning.

Declan could tell the vagueness had pained him, like he'd felt he was being deceitful to his mum. He waited for Doof Doof, now staring at their muted television, to turn back to him so that he could give him a nod, an apologetic and appreciative nod acknowledging his withholding of information. It wasn't nice but it was necessary, they both knew.

Declan wiped his eyes again, preparing for Ciara's interrogation.

'I better be off, Declan, I'll give you a wee shout later on and see how you're doing and I'll pop back over if you want,' Doof Doof announced, looking at Declan's mum, his face diffident now, aware that he'd broken away from the united front they'd begun to form, with the purpose of helping Declan.

It wasn't an easy situation for Doof Doof. Declan's mum would know he was Declan's pal and only acting under instructions. It was up to Declan to fill his mum in with whatever information he deemed appropriate.

'How was the exam?' Declan's mum asked Ciara as Doof Doof zipped up his fleece and patted his pockets, checking for his phone or keys or whatever. He looked like he just wanted something to do, to try and look less awkward than he felt.

'What's going on,' she answered, as though she was offended at the naïve little sister that she'd been taken for, as though she'd been expected just to tell her mum how school had been, paying no notice to the peculiar set-up that she'd walked into and the clear tautness in the room.

'Declan, why are you crying? And, eh, hiya, who are you?'

Declan was taken aback at how confident Ciara had been in addressing the situation and he'd felt a smile come back to him, impressed at her storming in, spraying the living room with questions.

Declan was realising that he hadn't known her as well as he'd thought, like he hadn't been paying attention to her evolution into a young adult.

He hadn't let Ciara grow up in his mind, he realised, he'd reached his conclusions on her and her character as though she were an adult, like she was who she was always going to be. It was part of being an older sibling, he realised, that your little sister would always be that: little, wee, a child, dependent.

Ciara's face was alarmed, angry almost, as her eyes shot from Declan's teared-up eyes and the scrunched-up paper handkerchief in his hand, to the wet handcloth, the glass of water free from any colouring at his feet – *When was Declan drinking water?* she would be wondering. She looked with concern at her mum's exhausted-seeming face, with its own tears pending, and at Doof Doof – who the fuck was this guy, had he caused this?

Declan saw a protective, accusatory expression on her face as she examined Doof Doof, causing him to look away, uncomfortable, and turn to Declan, his face still sympathetic but willing him to at least say something.

Declan watched as Ciara's eyes settled at the badge on Doof Doof's fleece before shooting straight back to her mum. 'The council? What? Are we being evicted or something?'

Declan felt himself laugh. It hadn't been that funny but it had relieved the tension. His laughter continued as he thought of how reasonable a conclusion Ciara had come to, given that she'd just arrived and could only assess the situation at face value. His mum laughed as well, looking like she was about to reach out and cuddle her.

'I'm serious,' Ciara declared, annoyed at the type of laughter she'd elicited, annoyed that she'd inadvertently said something innocent, something childlike. She felt like she was being laughed at in a patronising way.

She'd simply alleviated the tension of the last half-hour, Declan wanted to tell her, but Doof Doof took over, feeling it his duty, as the stranger in the house.

'I'm Raymond, Declan's pal. I just came over to see if he was all right after the other night,' he said, pausing before he had to venture into deceitful territory.

It was up to Declan or his mum to explain the tears and the rest of it. 'My hay fever,' Declan said, looking to Ciara, hoping she'd pick up that his lie had been so bad that it was his way of telling her that he'd tell her later, when their mum wasn't there.

'Very good,' she said, sighing, fed up with the constant drama.

Declan looked back to his trainers, acknowledging that he understood Ciara's frustration, that he was fed up with himself as well. 'Nice to meet you, Raymond,' he heard her say as she left the room. Declan's head lifted itself back up to face his mum at the sound of her bedroom door closing – it wasn't quite a slam but she'd definitely used enough force to issue a clear do not disturb notice.

'I'll go and speak to her, she's at that emotional age,' Declan's mum told him, like she'd have had an attitude anyway, even if the last couple of nights hadn't happened, which probably wasn't true, Declan knew. He smiled at his mum to let her see that he appreciated her attempt to spare him any further guilt, to let her see that he knew that she just wanted him better, that she wanted him happy.

'I'll tell her everything's all right, that we're not getting evicted!' his mum said, forcing a shot of cheer into her voice as she rolled her eyes. 'This is a bought house, the cheeky wee madam,' she added, her words escorted by a hyperbolic laugh. She'd sounded like she was delivering a line in a pantomime Declan had thought, or a Scottish soap opera. He watched as his mum nodded to Doof Doof that it was ok for him to laugh too.

Declan wouldn't have been surprised if she'd broken down in tears herself – she seemed on edge. He smiled and looked down again, noticing a few crumbs from the bite of the ginger nut he'd taken lying on the floor.

Doof Doof smiled at her as she also told him that it had been nice to meet him and that she'd see him another time, no doubt.

Declan was glad that she'd seemed to like him, at least that was something.

'Sorry, man.' Declan lifted his head to begin trying to form a conclusion from Doof Doof's botched visit, trying to make some sense of his breakdown, his fainting. Fainting, man, he thought to himself – he'd never fainted before, was this a new thing? He'd worry about it later, he told himself, intercepting his head before it could draw up a fresh list of conditions for Declan to diagnose himself with.

He wiped his eyes with the sleeves of his jumper and again stuffed the paper handkerchief into his pocket – out of sight – beginning his masculine cover-up.

His crying was to be forgotten, it wouldn't happen again – in fact, it hadn't happened at all, he decided, letting his nose temporarily clear itself with a deep, unsatisfying phlegmy inhale before he looked to Doof Doof and got ready to speak, unsure of what he was going to say. Doof Doof saved him the bother – saved him the struggle, the further apologies, the explanations – by seizing control of the moment with his own summary of events.

'Listen, man,' he started, sitting himself down beside Declan so that his volume could be adjusted and an air of confidentiality could be created, a trust.

Declan sniffed again – managing to stop himself from wiping his nose with his sleeve – taking Doof Doof's cue to look at him, to really listen, to switch his head off and hear what he needed to hear.

'I don't want to sound like yer da or something, but take it easy, Declan, man.'

Declan nodded, looking back to the floor. 'I know,' he said, clearing his throat to repeat it with more conviction, hoping for this bit to be over with, but accepting that Doof Doof had a right to reply after everything he'd witnessed. He had a right to offer his take, to offer his advice.

'Get your head straight, man, however long it takes, you're not in a good way, you know that, man.' Declan felt the toggle of his jumper twisting tight round his finger as Doof Doof put a hand on his shoulder. 'Right, man?' he repeated, lowering his voice again to make sure his words were as compassionate as he'd intended them to be. 'Yer goin' aff yer heed,' he said, his hand gently shaking Declan's shoulder, to make sure he laughed.

'Aye, man, aye,' Declan heard himself say, sniffing again, using his sleeve to wipe his eyes and then his nose. 'Sorry, that's disgusting, man,' he said, hearing the whimper in his voice as it was beginning to crackle again.

Doof Doof had noticed that Declan was on the verge of fresh tears and kept on talking. Declan was grateful at being granted the time to get himself together before feeling any obligation to respond.

'I'll give you a phone later and see how you're doing but you should get a rest, let your body get back together and your head.' Declan nodded, looking to the side, using his other sleeve to try to rub the tears and whatever else from the one he'd used as a hankie, watching as the fabrics rubbed together and the tears and the catarrh and whatever else that had poured out of him thinned and hardened on his jumper.

'Fucking disgusting. Sorry, man, sorry.' Declan let out another cough.

Doof Doof's hand shook his shoulder again, hoping to force a smile or some sort of reaction anyway, to bring him back into the moment.

'Crack on with the writing, that's brilliant, man, mental, James Cavani, mental, I don't mean mental – just brilliant, just mental that you met him and he said that, to send your stuff.' Declan's smile turned genuine now, at Doof Doof speaking so fast that his sentences were spiralling out of control.

'Write what happened to you,' Doof Doof announced, his excitement at his own idea almost giving Declan a fright as he shook his shoulder about with more energy, letting his hand rest for a bit, giving Declan the time to emerge from his own thoughts, to process what he'd meant. *What had happened, man?* Declan asked himself, confused, before quickly realising the stupidity of his own question. His eye, his ribs, fucking fainting, his tears, his sleeves, his fucking everything.

He felt Doof Doof lifting his hand off his shoulder, aware, like Declan, that he was approaching the stage where it could be classed as a cuddle.

'All this shite. It's real. It's life. Write it and make it happen to someone else, fuck knows, man. You're the artist.' He laughed. 'They're all nutjobs, man, geniuses,' he concluded. Declan laughed, pleased at how freely Doof Doof had implied he was a nutjob. He made sure to keep laughing before Doof Doof realised that it could have been taken as tactless or hurtful.

Declan couldn't handle the atmosphere changing again, he knew, and he didn't want for Doof Doof to feel ashamed again, to feel that he'd said the wrong thing, that he'd been insensitive.

It was still just new to Declan, that his struggles – his demons or whatever – were no longer a secret. If they'd ever been one.

At least he didn't have to pretend everything was cool any more, he consoled himself, thinking of the energy that this would help to free up, whilst making sure that he kept laughing until the conversation had reached a safe distance from Doof Doof's nutjob remark.

He wasn't an artist, mental, a nutjob or a genius, especially. He was just a guy, man, a wee guy, he was at the crossroads between guy and wee guy – that was it, he decided, relieved at the tenderness of his verdict.

'You'll be good at it. I know you will,' Doof Doof said, his voice rising along with his comically skinny legs and slender frame. 'Right?' He looked down to Declan, placing his hand on his shoulder again, checking to see if he'd collected himself enough to offer any closing remarks of his own.

'Cheers, mate, I will try,' Declan said, the notion of switching off from everything except his writing for a few weeks distracting him from the pain of standing up.

He wouldn't go out, only to walk Hector, and he'd make sure he took him over the hills rather than anywhere residential where he could bump into Jordan or anyone else like that.

He felt the anger in him again, the same anger, but he'd anticipate it now, he told himself. It was reasonable, it was understandable, maybe he was in shock about being attacked or something like that, and it hadn't hit him until now, until today.

He should have explained this to his mum and Doof Doof, that he was suffering from shock, mild PTSD or something, but maybe he wasn't, maybe the anger and the rest of it would just come and go for a while, and as long as he knew this, he could stay on top of it and not let it control him. He could write about it too, Doof Doof was right.

Focusing on writing definitely appealed to him, he could lock himself away and force it all out of him. All the frustration, the anger, the confusion, whatever it was – it was life, it was human, like James Cavani's earlier stuff, his best stuff, it was authentic, propelled by real-life energy, real experiences.

He could borrow Ciara's computer and type everything up properly and send it to the e-mail address James Cavani had given him, and then who knows?

Maybe he'd ignore it. Maybe he would dismiss it, tell him to keep on working hard and that it was nice to meet him. Maybe he would like some of it though, or help him with some of it.

Use some of it. Declan smiled again, a smile that felt like it was warming his whole head.

Doof Doof and Connor could come around and keep him company some evenings. His work would understand if he took a couple of weeks off – Sharon would vouch for the state he'd been in when she'd picked him up and taken him to the hospital, plus they'd maybe feel partly responsible that the attack was on their premises. College was gone anyway. He'd reassess the situation in a few months, in the summer, maybe he'd find a new course, maybe not, fuck it, a few weeks as a writer, see what happens, that's it, that's the plan.

He couldn't go back to his writing class, not with his eye. They'd already thought he was a wee guy. A ned, a chav or whatever they said these days. Performing another *Ryzo*-like story, this time with his injuries, would hardly shatter their stereotypes.

Declan followed as Doof Doof led them both out of the living room and through to the hallway, forcing his feet back into his work boots and stepping aside to allow Declan to open the front door.

Declan cautiously placed his shoulder against the frame of the front door, trying to look natural, comfortable. His house, his front door. Relax, all good, he calmed himself, noticing that

Doof Doof was stood with his back to him, on the top step, looking over at the buildings in the distance and out across the skyline of the city of Glasgow.

He looked like he was posing for an album cover or something. Declan smiled to himself. He looked like he was dreaming of a better tomorrow, of the future, tomorrow and all that it held in store, all that shite. He laughed again, a laugh that continued as it appeared Doof Doof's mind had gone no deeper, no further, than the new Chinese takeaway that had opened across the road from the row of local shops, as his dinner plans for the evening were being dictated in detail to Declan.

Declan still didn't have an appetite, but he tuned in as Doof Doof was putting together his order, working it out aloud in the hope that Declan would volunteer some suggestions, offering a second opinion; some advice of his own.

It wasn't easy getting a Chinese order right when you lived alone, Doof Doof stressed, like he'd taken the opportunity to do every other time the subject arose.

'Aw!' he announced, his face seeming to light up as he turned to Declan to explain the agreement he'd reached with the guy from the Chinese, on the phone, the previous Friday night. 'I explained that their starter portions were too large for single-occupant households – like, I told him I could eat them, not a problem, but say, like, I want to try a couple of different starters before my main course, then it's too much, man, beyond my appetite and definitely beyond my budget – so maybe an idea would be to offer some smaller portions of a select couple of starters . . . I don't mean a combination starter, or a mixed platter, or that,' Doof Doof asserted, as though he'd already faced dissenters, probing his idea's originality.

'They usually come for two to four people and *they* decide what's included. I mean *you* decide, like, say, two spare ribs, two chicken wings, two spring rolls, two bits of sesame prawn toast and then they charge you the price of one starter.'

Declan lifted his head back, forcing his good eye to widen, beginning to nod, to look impressed, in anticipation of Doof Doof turning to check for this exact reaction.

'Like a pick'n'mix,' Declan added, indicating both his understanding and his approval.

'Aye, aye! Exactly, a pick'n'mix.' Doof Doof laughed, studying Declan's face, convinced that he was all right, that some weight had been lifted from him, delighted that he'd done his job as a pal – as a friend. Delighted too that his idea had been embraced and that Declan had given him a new terse way of explaining it.

'He agreed it was a crackin' idea, the guy,' Doof Doof went on, turning back around to let Declan enjoy the fresh air and the view of the distance – of further away, of wherever he wanted to go – without feeling like he was being observed.

'I'm gonny say to him to stick it on the menu, people will go mad for it.'

Declan smiled again as the conversation reached its natural conclusion.

'Tranquilise oneself with the trivial,' Doof Doof announced, which was quite the segue.

Declan felt his head lift as he repeated the words to himself, struggling to attribute them to a film or a book that they'd spoken about. 'Aye?' he responded, letting his confusion hang between them, skipping his turn to speak, passing it back to Doof Doof, who stood in a silence of his own.

'Who said that?' Declan asked, noticing how Doof Doof's taciturn, contemplative profile, staring into the distance, added to the intrigue and brought an extra gravitas to his quote.

'Kierkegaard or someone, a Danish guy, fuck knows how you say his name,' Doof Doof answered, deeming sufficient time to have passed for his quote to have been digested and looking like he was staring further into the distance as he went on.

It suited him, this, theorising, philosophising; the existential dilemma of man solved, from your doorstep, courtesy of the council.

What the fuck sort of leap was this that had been made, from takeaways to philosophy? The bizarre but profound proclamation and the posturing and then the emotion and tension of the last hour fused together, daring him to hit the giggles.

'I think he meant it as a dig, about people like us, well, people like me. "The immediate men", I think he called us, like, Philistines.' Doof Doof turned, checking Declan's face to see if he was laughing or confused, or a bit of both.

Declan managed to indicate that he was close to laughing, a little confused, but definitely interested, and Doof Doof turned around to look back out to the distance, encouraged to continue.

Declan had enjoyed Doof Doof's seminars in the past when he was comfortable – in Declan's company anyway, it seemed – tackling weightier subjects, and his unique terminology, his idioms, his elucidations were funny, insightful, undoubtedly flawed, but disarming and, above all, quite helpful.

He'd been speaking for Declan's benefit, then, it registered, now that he'd made it clear that he'd worried about him, that he'd recognised the appeals for help amidst the drunken mayhem.

'Like, people who don't want to question anything, because they're scared of the answers, so they work, eat, drink, go to the football, buy a car, pay a mortgage, Chinese on a Friday, all of that, right?'

Declan nodded, indicating that he was sort of following.

'It's easier to blend in. To follow the manual. To do what's been done before. To follow the well-trodden path, as they say.'

Doof Doof was never too far away from making a semi-coherent point, Declan knew, and he wondered why his greenskeeper friend had never pursued a different career path, why he'd never been tempted into further education – at least a college course like Declan's.

Declan had never directly asked him these sorts of things, why he'd settled for a life of labouring on building sites and working on the golf course – not that there was anything wrong with that, he acknowledged. But he could surely have been a candidate for going into a more cerebral line of work, teaching, man, Mr Buchanan – Mr Doof. Declan let out a short breath of laughter, catching himself studying the back of Doof Doof's head, examining a scar that he'd never noticed before.

His own head seemed to be flooding with questions, feeling like he was getting back to how he usually felt in Doof Doof's company, like they could have spoken for hours.

His dad had been a prick, Declan knew that much. He'd been physically abusive and a heavy drinker, so that was maybe something to do with it. His house hadn't been a happy place, which was probably why he just wanted to be out all the time during his teenage years, hence his ecstasy- and whatever else fuelled party phase, from which he now seemed an entirely different person, with his nickname the only remnant of the period and maybe, Declan now considered, his brain's unfulfilled potential.

The drugs and the books must have clashed at some point, Declan thought, but now they seemed to operate as a team, a team that usually made Doof Doof's parables and sermons a captivating listen.

'To not want much from life and hope that life won't want much from them and then they show up somewhere on a Sunday to thank a higher being for it all and hope that they'll get to do it all again sometime, somewhere,' Doof Doof declared, his voice sounding satisfied with his efforts at paraphrasing whatever books he'd been reading.

'I think that's what Kierkegaard, the Danish guy, meant anyway, like, the meaning of life and death is only known to God, only God knows the meaning of it all, and all that, and that in order to avoid neurosis, as he put it, or, like, going full on fucking mental, you should believe or else distract yourself with the day-to-day stuff, leaving less time for thinking, less time for fear.'

Doof Doof waited for Declan's nod before continuing.

'God daft, I think, but that was the nineteenth century he was hitting oot with all of that.'

Declan laughed, as did Doof Doof. When he felt he was

getting out of his depth or running out of steam, or whatever, he'd drop in a term like 'hitting oot wi'' to bring his discourse back down to earth, to make it more accessible.

What a teacher Mr Doof would have been, Declan thought, taking advantage of the designated chuckle break.

'Too much time thinking isn't good for you, basically, so either get believing or get busy. I think that's what he was getting at, fuck knows. A pick'n'mix from the Chinese and a beef satay. Friday night. Shit like that. Just take the pleasure when it presents itself.' Doof Doof turned to Declan, who looked unsure if he'd listened to Kierkegaard's advice or Doof Doof's, or a hybrid of the two.

Between them, they'd made sense though, fair enough.

'Everycunt calm doon, I think he meant, right? If he didn't, then that's what I mean, right?' Doof Doof concluded, signing his counsel off with his own stamp.

Declan laughed. 'Aye, sound advice.'

Doof Doof put his hand out and Declan grabbed it, hiding the pain as Doof Doof pulled him in and patted his back as his voice lowered and turned serious again.

'There's fear and insecurity inside everyone, man, it's normal, of course it is, especially now, especially younger people, but it's dangerous if you don't find your way to manage it.' Doof Doof whispered, like he didn't want anyone other than Declan hearing his solutions, his game plan.

'All we have is distractions, now, it's a huge market, maybe we've ended up *too* immersed in the trivial and not left any time for sadness.' Doof Doof laughed, a sad laugh, like he was talking for his own benefit now too. 'Like, we were never designed to be as happy as the modern world, the internet – Facebook and all that – is trying to make us. I think anyway. Maybe we'll evolve over time, to catch up, but just now we're the first ones to take the hit.'

Doof Doof stepped up so that he was on to the same step as Declan, his voice getting lower and intensifying Declan's concentration.

'You'd be surprised how fucked up some people feel, Declan. Embrace the sadness sometimes, man, get to know it, it's normal, man, its human.' Doof Doof raised his head, turning to look into the distance for further inspiration.

'There's too much pressure on folk nowadays to try and fully eradicate any form of sadness – any fear, anxiety, depression or whatever ye want to call it, or they want ye to call it – it's probably always going to come and go and it's daft to try and hide from it, because then it just builds and builds the longer you ignore it, and then, first thing in the morning, last thing at night, after a mad night oot, after an argument – whenever – it's back, stronger, tooled up, back with a bang . . .

'Boo! Ya cunt, remember me?'

'Sorry, man.' Doof Doof laughed, realising that he'd caused Declan to flinch, realising that his emotions were still all over the place. 'Remember it's *your heed*, it's *your* home, *your* home game, don't let it be an away game, man, a tough place to go, fucking Tynecastle or somewhere.'

Doof Doof laughed, aware that football wasn't his strong point and that his reference was maybe flawed or outdated.

'Aye, good way of putting it' – Declan spoke and coughed, his voice reminding him of his fragility.

Doof Doof must have been reminded too, as Declan felt him pushing his shoulder back with his right hand before grabbing the other one with his left, checking his face, like a boxing trainer examining his fighter after a punishing round.

Declan forced another embarrassed laugh, hoping that his face would settle into the smile that Doof Doof was inspecting it for.

'I don't mean to sound like one of these cunts but speak about it, man, these are just my thoughts – about shit – but everyone you speak to will have different ones and then together we all agree we're all fucked and it's not so big of a deal.'

Doof Doof shook Declan and they both laughed, proper laughs.

'We're all fucked but fuck it,' Doof Doof announced, turning to face the distance again, impressed at his own proverb, which made Declan laugh and smile out of admiration.

'You get writing, right? Send me some of it, if you want, before Cavani, but – whatever, and if he dingies you, or says it's all shite, then we'll go and fucking leather him, right?'

Doof Doof laughed, looking to Declan, who held his side in pain again as his laughter and his coughing battled for control.

'Aye, see you soon and thanks, man, thanks, it means a lot,' Declan said, making sure Doof Doof could see that he'd done his job as a pal, that Declan felt cool, calm, all good.

'. . . And look after your mum, she's worried about you,' Doof Doof whispered, turning before the mood turned sombre again and Declan felt compelled to say something or to apologise yet again.

'I will, mate, I will,' Declan assured him, thinking how he

was in the mood for a Chinese himself now. He'd treat them all, his mum, Ciara – unless she had plans, maybe she went out on Friday nights now, who knows – and his dad when he came home.

He'd phone for it and ask the guy about the pick'n'mix starter and tell him that he'd heard everyone talking about it and that he thought it was a great idea. It was the least he could do for Doof Doof. He smiled, watching him as he used the parallel railings at the front step to lift himself into the air, clearing the five steps in one manoeuvre, signalling the resumption of his Friday afternoon.

A nineties-sounding indie song resumed blaring from Doof Doof's van as the engine started. Cast or some band that he'd introduced to Declan – the age gap between them came in handy with regard to decent tunes. Declan smiled, appreciative of this and of everything. He hoped that Doof Doof's Chinese and his Friday night were everything that he wanted them to be. Trivial or not, it was life, it was contentment.

'Fuck,' Declan groaned, at the pain that shot through his side as he raised his hand in Pavlovian response to Doof Doof's van tooting as it turned out of the street.

Wee prick, he whispered through his teeth, hurrying to rush the latest image of Jordan attacking him out of his head.

He hobbled back inside, releasing a quick puff of frustrated air, the last of it, he vowed, warning his head that he was in charge, that there was a revolution, a new regime was starting and it was starting now.

No one else would be hungry yet, he decided, looking at the clock, estimating that he had an hour or so to himself.

Holding his side securely – still wary that another shot of pain could release fresh anger, and fresh frustration, and threaten to undermine the barely inaugurated administration – he reached under the pillow for his notes, his years of documenting what made him laugh, what made him sad. It was a fucking mess but surely there was something that could pique Cavani's interest.

He plugged his headphones into his phone, scanning the playlists of songs that he'd overplayed, stripping them of their meaning, at least temporarily anyway.

It was a fresh start. New tunes. He looked at the record player he'd got two Christmases ago. 'Fuck.' He looked around his room, surprised and excited, remembering the record that Georgie had given him. He saw it sitting on the top of his chest of drawers and carefully climbed off the bed to collect it, sliding the vinyl out of its sleeve and making sure the record player was switched on.

He looked over at the piles of paper that were to be assessed and put into some sort of order, right now, as Doof Doof's words and Georgie's tunes wandered his head, assessing the damage and then commencing the recovery operation.

The Cure – 'Friday I'm in Love'. That was the tune, Declan thought, delighted that it was all coming together as he made his way back to the bed in time for the door swinging open as Hector bounded in, jumping straight up, almost flying through the air to beat Declan on to the bed, sending papers flying everywhere.

'Daft bastard,' Declan whispered as he patted him, rewarding his anarchic arrival and ignoring the pain as he laughed at the mess that had been made.

'Boys Don't Cry', that's another tune of theirs, he said to himself, before smiling to concede both the irony and the significance of his head's recommended listening.

Fair enough, touché. He turned to check the sleeve notes and skipped the track on, watching Hector chew a piece of paper, his laugh making way for the opening guitar strums as he thought of how he could get in touch with Georgie, to apologise for everything, without having to go into the pub.

He thought back to Doof Doof too, and his doorstep discourse. What a man. He shook his head in admiration, keeping it shaking from side to side as the music kicked in, scribbling to check that his pen was working.

'We're all fucked but fuck it,' he wrote, checking too that his head was working and that it knew who it was working for, that he was – or at least he would soon be – back in charge.

He paused his thoughts to look at Hector, who'd instantly calmed down and got himself settled, his head lying on top of his front paws. 'What is it?' Declan whispered, wondering if he was going to break his stare. 'I'm here, pal, I'm in, in for the night.' He comforted him, patting his head, reassuring him, turning back to his notes only to feel Hector's stare grow more intense.

'Whit?' Declan laughed, the sort of laugh only Hector could elicit from him. 'Why are you being a wee weirdo?' he teased, rubbing his head with more enthusiasm, hoping he'd snap out of his trance and relax, but still he stared.

Declan put his pen down, to give Hector more focus. He tried to listen over the music, for any unfamiliar sounds, or anyone shouting on him, wondering if he was being paranoid –

wondering if another fainting-like episode was coming on – if Hector had sensed something bad was about to happen. Was Hector trying to psych him out, or trying to remind him that there was something to worry about? Aw, shut the fuck up, he told his head, feeling the smile shooting straight back to his face.

Here, that's a show, that's the one, he almost said out loud. Delighted with himself. Delighted with Hector, he wrote 'The Black Dog' at the top of a sheet of paper, the first page of a script that he'd attempted a few weeks ago, for his class, that he could tidy up and send to Cavani.

Hector turned himself round now, resting his head on to his left paw, releasing a calm exhale as his eyes closed as if to say, 'Aye, you're welcome . . .'

Declan laughed again. Fuck sake, he said, lunging his torso further down the bed to fully reach out and rub Hector's head with even more vigour.

The pain shot through his side and he caught the first glimpse of his eye in a while, through his black mirrored reflection on his television.

So fuck. He stared at the papers that he was ready to set about.

'Eccccctorrrrrr,' he shouted, silencing the H and rolling the R, like he was in a Spanish soap opera, stopping only to cough the pain away.

'Fucking yes, man. Yes, Hector. You're the man, Hector. You da man!'

He walked back over to the record player, to skip the track back to 'Friday I'm in Love'.

His head nodded. His shoulders moved. Hector's tail let out a solitary wag, confirming that yes, he was the man, and that he was delighted that Declan was home, and safe, and singing to him as he drifted off into his pre-dinner nap.

Declan couldn't remember the last time he'd sung; he knew he was awful but so fuck. Hector loved it and the words resonated. Tuesday had indeed been grey, as had Wednesday, Thursday he didn't care about but it was Friday and it felt good, the feeling. It felt like a Friday, like the first Friday in a long time.

PART 5

PART 5

'My name is Otto. I love to get Blotto.' Cavani looked up to see Siobhan glancing over the cover of a book that she'd lifted out of one of the translucent containers that were filled with shite that should never have been cleared to make the journey from London.

Her American accent was impressive. He laughed, the quote from *The Simpsons* registering with him and evoking happy memories.

He watched as she placed the book on the floor and carried on looking through more of their old stuff, following Lisa's brief to be ruthless except for books or anything that could survive a trip to the dump and make it to a charity shop instead.

Cavani walked over to pick the book up, studying the cover, trying to remember if he'd bought it or if it had been a gift. *Art and Artist: Creative Urge and Personality Development* by Otto Rank.

He'd started reading it – he was sure. He'd definitely never finished it though.

The artist, or something about the artist's lived experience, means that they view the world – and existence itself – as a problem, or something like that, that was his thing, Otto Rank; that the artist's work was their own way of trying to achieve personal immortality, to live on through their work, their creativity was their private religion. Fuck sake. He smiled to himself, imagining relaying some of these theories to his childhood mates, appreciative that Siobhan hadn't gone any further than taking the piss out of the author's first name.

He must have ordered it during some sort of epiphany or something – to impress himself, or maybe it had been a present from someone, an actor probably. It looked a thick fucker too.

'It was a good one to be seen with – in America and London anyway,' Cavani summarised, cringing at whatever phase he'd been going through, placing the book into the separate charity-shop-bound container.

'A good one to get yourself slapped about in Glasgow though,' Siobhan countered, making them both laugh.

'Aye, fair play,' Cavani conceded, checking the time.

'Thanks for helping with all this, pal,' he told Siobhan as she stood up, stretching her shoulders. 'Sorry it's a bit of a riot,' he added.

'Sorry I've been a bit of a riot.' Siobhan smiled, walking to the table Cavani had been sat at and pulling herself a chair out, nodding for him to join her, like this was an opportunity she'd been waiting on.

'I mean it, I'm sorry – you know I am, right?' He felt both of her hands clasp his left, prompting him to add his right, to complete the pile.

'Lisa told me about your plans, about selling the house.' Siobhan squeezed his hands, seeing that he'd looked away, seeing that he was uncomfortable, that he wanted to have this conversation another time, or never.

'I don't want the money. I don't want any of it.'

She held his hands as he tried to break free, to tell her she was being silly, to insist that she needed at least some of it, to help her with her latest fresh start.

'It's your money, you bought Mum and Dad the house, you worked for it,' Siobhan went on, like she'd honed her script, even factoring in the reactions and her responses.

'I just want you to get your life back and I want to help,' Cavani started.

'Listen to me,' Siobhan cut him off, shaking the pile of hands. 'You've helped enough, you've helped me more than anyone's ever helped me.' Siobhan broke a hand free, rubbing her eyes with her palm. Cavani noticed that her face had filled out and a glow was returning to her skin. He took his turn to squeeze her hand, encouraging her to continue, accepting that it was his turn to listen to her, to listen to *her* solutions to *her* life.

'I need to help myself now. I want my life back but what is life, James? Life is problems.' Siobhan's voice cracked as she dropped her bottom lip as she exhaled, guiding some air over her face, flicking her fringe with her right hand. Cavani looked around to see if there was anything for her to drink or some tissues.

'I don't mean overdosing, taking whatever shite that's going. I mean normal problems – paying rent or a mortgage, finding work, going to work. You removed all those problems for me – with the best possible intentions – but it wasn't what I needed. I know that sounds terrible, James, and ungrateful . . .' Cavani jumped off his seat to embrace her as tears began to trickle down her face.

'I'm fine. I'm sorry. I'm grateful, oh my god I'm like, so grateful. I'm so proud of everything you've achieved. I'm proud that you're my big brother, that James Cavani is my big brother, but for as long as I live down there, I'm always going to be James Cavani's sister, James Cavani's junkie fucking sister.' Cavani pulled Siobhan in closer to him, shielding her from her own words, listening as Lisa walked towards the room.

'Like, I come back from these fucking treatment programmes, I reward myself for the first few days, and then weeks, maybe months, everyone tells me how well I'm doing – but what am I really doing? Not taking drugs? Not doing something you're not supposed to be fucking doing anyway.'

Siobhan laughed, the kind of laugh you release to chase tears away, a selfless laugh, the type of laugh that gives whoever is listening a cue to laugh themselves, to release the tension, like a family member giving a eulogy at a funeral, that sort of thing, Cavani thought to himself.

'Come on, you,' he told Siobhan, shaking her gently, smiling at Lisa as she entered the room, noticing her face looked almost relieved to see that Siobhan had finally managed to open up to him. Cavani realised that they must have already spoken about what she wanted to do, what she needed to do, and that Lisa had agreed.

'To really quit something, you need to just forget it, I think. Anyway, you need to introduce replacements, new . . . whatever . . . new things. You can't be defined by what you don't do any more. Siobhan the junkie or Siobhan the ex-junkie. I need to move away; I need to build a new life.' Siobhan lifted her head and began fidgeting with a necklace that Cavani recognised as one their mum had left her.

'I need some goals, a purpose, whatever they're calling it. I need to stop being co-dependent, all that shite that you read about . . .' Siobhan laughed, seeing too that Lisa was in the room, and that this was something they'd laughed about before.

'Come here, you.' Lisa grabbed Siobhan from Cavani. 'This is it, we're all in it, you've come through it all. It's done, right?' Lisa lifted Siobhan's head up to look into her eyes.

'I know. My new fucking eyelashes.' Siobhan laughed. 'Sixty quid pished away.' Lisa laughed as well, pulling her back in towards her.

'There's your first problem,' Cavani joked with full commitment to releasing the tension, relieved to hear Siobhan snort with laughter, prompting Lisa to reach her hand round to her bag to find her a packet of tissues.

'Right, it's all going to be good – not going to be, it *is* all good, right?' Lisa turned to Cavani for his reaction on everything that Siobhan had said, for a positive declaration of his own.

'It's all good, baby, baby,' Cavani laughed, watching the Biggie Smalls reference register with Siobhan and Lisa as he embraced them both.

'Right, get yourself squared up and we'll get out and at it,' Lisa told Siobhan, winking to Cavani that she hadn't forgotten he needed the house to himself, that he had an online therapy session, a farewell and an apology to Dr Nikouladis for his no-show weeks ago, when Siobhan had been hospitalised.

'I need to go to the chemist too, but only after we've dished these CVs out!' Lisa told Siobhan, helping her to wipe her eyes, her smile beaming into Lisa's.

'Is that the PlayStation? I forgot we still had that.' Lisa nodded towards a container, seeing a black controller squashed against the side.

'Aw aye,' Cavani said, his voice cheery, his memory syncing with Lisa's as they remembered when Lisa's sister and her two children had been down visiting them in London and they'd played a go-karting game, and then they'd stumbled on to a game where you controlled a bit of bread and you had to wander round a kitchen trying to get toasted.

They both smiled at each other, remembering how fucking daft it had been but how funny and how brilliant a time it was. Cavani thought of how happy Lisa was in her niece and nephew's company, and how much too that they loved being with her.

He braced himself to let the customary pang of sadness that they'd never had children pass through, greeted with the – by now involuntary – reminder to himself that there was still time.

'Right, let's get going, I'm fine, all good. Let's do it.' Siobhan stood up. 'Give me five minutes, tops,' she told them, walking into the hallway down towards the room that was hers for as long as she needed, they'd assured her.

'I think this is it, eh?' Lisa walked towards Cavani, kissing him and wishing him good luck with Dr Nikouladis.

'You better get the laptop and all of that set up,' she laughed, relieved to be leaving the house, escaping outburst after outburst of technophobic bile.

'Enjoy yourselves.' Cavani winked, pulling Lisa in for a cuddle before turning to look around at the containers that narrowed the room, arching his back and listening to it crackle in satisfaction.

'When I'm finished speaking, I'll stick my thumb up, right . . . for you to speak. It's not a great signal, ok?' Cavani felt the impatience of his smile pulling at the sides of his face as he tried to resist being drawn to look at himself on the top of his laptop screen.

'Ok. No problem,' Dr Nikouladis agreed, pausing to allow for the delay.

'Sorry, I should have put my thumb up there . . .' Cavani mumbled, giving in and looking at himself as his forced and fake laugh was dispatched on its journey from their flat in the West End of Glasgow to Dr Nikouladis's North London practice.

'What was that, sorry?' Cavani asked – Dr Nikouladis's enquiry as to how he was finding being back home in Glasgow registering in his head just as he'd requested him to repeat himself.

'Good, really good' – which was true, he was enjoying being back home. Life was good, considering, and this session was a farewell, if anything. A rescheduled farewell, an apology for his no-show a fortnight before and a thank you – for everything – for all the good work they'd done.

Dr Nikouladis was smiling, his subtle smile that had been a consistent through all their hours of work. The subtle smile of someone who had so often managed to bait the biggest answers with the smallest questions, the subtle smile that willed you to keep on talking to the point that you didn't know where you were going and then, from nowhere, you'd reveal something and he would swoop down, pecking away for more details and the hour would be gone.

'Really good,' Cavani repeated, his eyes lifting over the laptop, taking in the room that was to be his office, his creative space.

So much shite. Stuff. Stuff that he'd bought. Stuff that he'd been bought. Just fucking stuff. CDs, DVDs, chargers, cables, documents, ornaments, pictures, books.

'So how have you been, James,' Dr Nikouladis asked, keen to get to work, prompting Cavani for an update on everything since their last session, all those weeks ago.

'Aye, well, good – sorry, first of all, for the last time. It was . . . it was crazy,' Cavani began, getting his introductory apology out of the way, the apology which was probably the main purpose of accepting Dr Nikouladis's offer of an online rescheduled appointment. He tried to think back to what had already been covered in the text that he'd sent to explain his absence. He looked at the Marriott-branded notepad that he'd lain beside the laptop, with the bullet points of everything he'd wanted to discuss that he'd managed to scribble in the short window of preparation between remembering he had the session and clicking on the Zoom link that Dr Nikouladis had e-mailed through to him.

Siobhan, and then abandoning the film and his agent, the flight home with Eddie and his existential crisis, and then Declan.

Cavani felt a smile eclipse his concentrated face, thinking of how much Siobhan had been laughing at one of Declan's characters and at how impressed he'd been at some of his work, writing that took him back to places he'd forgotten – geographically but also emotionally, socially, financially. He looked up at the cornerstone patterns on the ceiling of what was soon to be his office, panicking about all the times he'd taken his success for granted.

He shut himself down in time to concentrate on Dr Nikouladis, who'd been passing on his wishes for Siobhan's speedy recovery.

'She'd overdosed – like I think I'd said, in the text that day . . .' Cavani realised he was waiting on Dr Nikouladis confirming this, carrying on before the signal frustrated him again. 'She'd come home from her treatment programme and boredom, guilt, familiarity or whatever it was – or whatever else it was – led to her going to meet up with a couple of her "friends" – or whatever you call people who take heroin with you.' Cavani shook his head. 'I doubt she has much else in common with them,' he explained. 'Like they're never going to quit heroin together and take up playing badminton through the week instead.' Cavani looked to the screen, waiting to see if Dr Nikouladis would laugh, or at least smile.

'It's hard to make new friends – I suppose – all of that sort of stuff that you don't think about when it isn't your life.' Cavani paused, trying to relax himself into the session and the connection, he had time.

'Everything is focused on quitting, but somewhere there needs to be a positive element,' he added, realising that

Siobhan's words were growing stronger the more he contemplated them. He smiled, placing his thumb towards the camera, reaching out to take a drink from his coffee cup whilst he waited on Dr Nikouladis to return a comment or a question, but realising the coffee cup was empty.

'May I ask how she is doing now and how are things with the two of you?' Dr Nikouladis enquired, his own thumb pointed to the camera as Cavani turned back to face the screen, smiling in acknowledgement that Dr Nikouladis was implementing his means of mitigating any technical issues.

'Aye, she's good. Really good, I think.' Cavani felt his voice warming up, realising the magnitude of his belief in Siobhan and her statements of intent, of purpose, of the future and her determination to give life another shot.

'We spoke, well, we always speak, but we've been speaking, a lot . . . She's living with us. Just for a while.'

Cavani looked away from the screen again, aware that he'd left himself wide open for an enquiry about how Lisa felt about this, about how they had their own life – and their own lives – and about setting clear boundaries, all of that.

He could love her, care about her, worry about her, but she wasn't his responsibility, he knew this. Dr Nikouladis had reminded him of all of this, but the sentiment only felt convincing now that it had come from Siobhan herself.

Was it a compulsive behaviour, constantly trying to save someone? Saviour complex or whatever it was that he'd read, or maybe Dr Nikouladis had said. Fuck knows.

He warned himself to keep speaking, in case Dr Nikouladis seized upon the opportunity to ask a question like this.

Cavani's thumb was down though, and he was in charge, they were there for him, he reminded himself.

Compulsions. Complexes. These fucking words. Trying to save your little sister's life. Care. Compassion. That's what it used to be called until the fucking internet, man. He felt himself sighing, turning it into a deep breath, filling his lungs and calming himself before speaking again.

'I think this is it with her, really, I think she's going to be all right.' Cavani leaned back on his chair, looking over the laptop at another container full of fuck knows what before continuing, telling Dr Nikouladis of the plan that had been put in place, releasing the words of intent before any doubt could detain them.

'She's out just now, looking for a job around here, and she's going to apply for a college course. We're selling the house, her house, well, my mum and dad's old house. She doesn't want to live in the area we grew up in any more, which is a crackin' shout . . .'

Cavani stopped to wait on his words reaching North London, smiling as he watched Dr Nikouladis's eyes narrowing and a few extra lines on his forehead appearing, drafted in to assist him with his concentration efforts.

'A wise move. A good idea,' Cavani clarified, laughing, waiting for Dr Nikouladis, who smiled and nodded for him to carry on – indicating that he'd understood both the translation and the understatement – his hands resting on his notepad, reminding Cavani that he had time. 'It's true, she has the right to have her own problems.' Cavani looked away again, nodding, impressed still at Siobhan's assessment of her situation, of life, really.

'It's fucking life, man – problems, distractions, it stops you going fucking mad. Stops you realising you're going to die, that we're all going to die.' Cavani wasn't sure if he was joking but he made sure to laugh again, at his own bleak brutality.

Dr Nikouladis knew him well enough by now to know his humour and he'd seen some of his work, he'd admitted, so he knew that he wasn't a nihilist, that he always left a message of hope somewhere in his writing – he wouldn't be coming here if he was a nihilist, either, he reminded himself, breathing, realising that he was doing that thing again, putting forward a defence against an accusation that no one had made, only himself.

'She's right though, it's true,' Cavani mumbled, trailing off, the full weight of Siobhan's conclusions, her problems – and her solutions – registering with him.

Cavani looked at the vague expression on Dr Nikouladis's face on the screen, realising that he hadn't actually told him anything that Siobhan had said and realising that he wouldn't. It was over to her now, he was there for her, to support her in her plans, her solutions, not to make plans and solutions for her. He felt like he'd let her down, breached their relationship by speaking at length about her struggles with someone like Dr Nikouladis. 'She'll be fine, I believe that,' Cavani affirmed. Sliding his Marriott notepad over towards him, the logo reminding him of all the days, nights, weeks, years that had passed – reminding him of all the time that he'd forgotten – he scribbled over Siobhan's name. She wasn't Dr Nikouladis's and his' problem, that was true, in a good way though – in a great way, he hoped, smiling.

Cavani watched as his thumbnail checked the depth of a

scratch on his office table, prompting him to search for more, his thoughts aligning, centring themselves in the moment – aghast at the state the table was in and that it had gone unnoticed.

He needed a new one, then, that was it. He'd look online, after this, after saying farewell to Dr Nikouladis. A brand-new table.

Or he could learn to fix the table, learn to perform a bit of restoration work. It probably only needed sanded down a little and a coat of varnish or whatever – he could learn how to do it rather than fucking Amazon bringing him a fresh table, first thing the next morning, the transient burst of consumeristic excitement dissipating at the speed of a pinged cigarette. Packaging to get rid of, the old table to get rid of. More stuff. More shite. He thought of how he could enjoy the distraction and then, ultimately, the rewarding feeling of having sorted it. He could admire his efforts, his new skills, and feel his confidence growing as a problem was ticked off his list, and no matter how trivial, it was one less, and it would probably drive him on to fix something else.

There was no point hiding from shit, putting it off, hiding from it because it was too big, too overwhelming – or too small, too trivial – you just had to fucking battle through, as Lisa had always tried to tell him.

Here was a problem, presenting itself to him. He smiled, realising he was listening to Siobhan now too, that *he* was taking *her* advice, rather than trying to guide her, instruct her, watch over her.

He felt a feeling in his stomach, a good feeling though. He wanted to look at the clock, but he wasn't sure if he wanted the session to hurry up or to savour it. If anything it was an excuse to think in safety, enjoy the positive thoughts and know that any negative thought at any point could be said aloud, could be dragged out of his head, and he and Dr Nikouladis could decide whether or not it was to be allowed back in or if they were to slap it about a bit, booting its arse as it staggered down the street.

Yer barred, ya cunt.

He considered sticking his thumb up – aware that the silence was lingering on. Dr Nikouladis's expression hadn't changed, with only his blinking showing that the connection was holding up and that he'd heard every word and watched every thought.

'Sorry,' Cavani said, allowing another quick glance over the table that he was going to fix. His afternoon was sorted. He'd walk to a hardware shop or somewhere to buy sandpaper, varnish, a paintbrush, whatever else he needed.

'I got a bit lost in everything there, just . . . thinking . . . but it's all good,' he told Dr Nikouladis, snapping back into the session, his eyes shooting back to the screen, ricocheting off the clock – that told him they still had a substantial stretch of time to fill – and back to the table before landing on his notes.

What a few weeks, man, he thought, sticking his thumb to the camera as he glanced over what remained of Siobhan's name and the other bullet points, his agent, Eddie, Declan, a modest assembly of nouns but each carrying considerable significance.

Declan, he read again, wondering how he was getting on and how someone like Dr Nikouladis would deal with him.

'I met a young guy,' Cavani declared, forgetting that he'd

cleared Dr Nikouladis to speak. Covering his mouth, he used his free hand to convey his apologies to the camera, anticipating his words arriving in London just as Dr Nikouladis was about to say something.

I met a young guy, he repeated to himself, accepting that he needed to laugh, that it was funny, having to remain silent, paused on an announcement like that.

The smile from his laugh pointed towards the camera, waiting for Dr Nikouladis's reaction when the sentence landed, along with the connotations, the double entendre, and all of that.

Dr Nikouladis smiled before building to a laugh himself, a real laugh, the only type of laugh he seemed to have.

He only ever laughed when something was genuinely funny, a trait which Cavani had found awkward initially, but then admirable, and one he wished he could adopt. But it wouldn't be worth having a reputation as a prick with everyone who'd ever shouted a line from one of his films or television shows at him.

'That's quite the development, James – and how is Lisa with this?' Dr Nikouladis smiled, taking a sip of his water as his joke travelled north. Cavani made sure to laugh generously, like the way you laugh when someone you don't associate with humour makes a joke.

Cavani's smile stayed in place as he watched Dr Nikouladis adjust himself on his seat.

'Give me two minutes.' Cavani put his hand up to the camera, unsure of whether Dr Nikouladis was about to talk or if he'd handed back to him. They'd pick it up in a minute,

Cavani told himself, confused as to why he could hear his phone ringing, but he didn't know where it was. His laptop seemed to be ringing too. He looked around the cluttered office space, confirming that he was right, that his phone wasn't even in the room. What the fuck. Someone was phoning his laptop. 'Sorry,' he said again to Dr Nikouladis, whose face was composed, neutral still and patient, but keen to get back to work.

Cavani remembered that Lisa had synced his phone with his other devices or something like that, so when he received a call it would come through his laptop, so that was it, that's what was happening.

'How the fuck do I stop this ringing?' Cavani demanded, every note of the ringtone shooting through him.

'Why the fuck is this ringing so loud?' He swung back in his chair, an accusatory look fixed on the laptop, as though it had autonomy over its sound settings, like he'd devolved the volume adjustment powers to it and now it was abusing them.

'Nightmare, man. Sorry,' he laughed, glad that the ringing had stopped and the computer screen had settled down.

'Sorry,' Cavani repeated, fixing himself on his seat, aware that he'd looked angry, frustrated, aware that his face, his voice – his accent, his cadence, whatever – had changed and that he'd almost gone fucking mental.

But he hadn't, so leave it, he told himself, it was still too early to analyse and criticise the unconvincing performances, just accept the victories.

A single beep came through the speakers again, prompting Cavani to issue yet another apology. He saw Dr Nikouladis give a solitary nod, a nod of confirmation that the apology had been received and accepted, a nod in recognition of Cavani's helplessness and that this was one of the moments when he was to focus on his breathing, to take his time.

Cavani smiled, breathing in to read the opening lines of the text message that appeared on the top of the screen from the unknown number.

Good to see you the other week, Jimmy. Hope Siobhan is doing well. I'm up your way this week.

'Sorry, one minute, one minute.' Cavani stood up and shot out of the room, feeling his socks sliding him off the wooden hallway and into the kitchen, remembering where he'd left his phone, remembering Eddie Reynolds was one of the few people who still called him Jimmy, remembering he'd given Eddie Reynolds his number.

He picked his phone up to read the rest of the text message.

I have a couple of books for you that you might like, I'm about this afternoon so I can drop them off and we could get a coffee if you're free.

Books, fuck me, Eddie Reynolds' books. He smiled to himself, shaking his head, trying to remember how long it was that Eddie had done in jail – long enough to take up reading anyway, it seemed. He's probably good at chess too. Cavani smiled, thinking that it would be all right, in that respect, a bit of jail time. Cavani glanced away from his phone to consider how he'd reply to the message. Then fearing any further distractions and any further threats to Dr Nikouladis's stoicism, Cavani switched his phone to flight mode and shot back through to the office, back into his seat, back into therapy.

'That's my phone switched off,' Cavani confirmed, nodding his assurances that there would be no further distractions, sticking his thumb up too, and waiting for Dr Nikouladis to get them back underway, the clock on the top of the screen tempting him over, telling him they had thirty minutes left. Thirty minutes left of the session, of the last session. Thirty minutes left of all the sessions.

Again Cavani felt embarrassed to be leaving it like this, an online session, a disrupted online session.

'So, you met a young guy, James?' Dr Nikouladis resumed.

'Declan, aye,' Cavani rushed back in, apologetic, hoping to hide that he was still distracted, thinking of Eddie, of returning his call or his message, of his books, of how to get out of meeting him that afternoon.

'When I got to the hospital, with Siobhan . . .' Cavani rotated his wrist, like he was fast-forwarding away from anything to do with Siobhan.

'He was in the hospital at the same time, the wee guy, the young guy, Declan.' Cavani tried to think back to the hospital without thinking of Siobhan. He looked at his notes, at Eddie's name. Fuck me, man.

'Right, there's a lot.' Cavani leaned forward towards the screen, like he was trying to regain control of his story, of the events that had unfolded.

'When I flew home, from London, well, New York, I was sitting beside an old school pal, well, an old school acquaintance.' Cavani felt like he needed some guidance from somewhere on how to explain his relationship with Eddie Reynolds.

It wasn't a courtroom or a police station, so the relationship could be whatever he wanted it to be, a business associate or a former lover for all Dr Nikouladis cared. Cavani smiled at his own advice, making sure to take another breath before going on.

'On the flight home I ended up sitting beside a guy I went to school with. A serious guy. A gangster, right? Dodgy. Dodgy as fuck.' Cavani noticed his voice had lowered and he'd leaned in so close that his face took up the entire square that the screen had allocated it. He shrugged to the camera as he leaned himself back, communicating that he didn't know how else to explain Eddie Reynolds and acknowledging – almost apologising – that he'd brought this sort of world to Dr Nikouladis, an academic. Cavani knew Dr Nikouladis would know it wasn't his world, either, but that he'd grown up close to it, close to bad people who'd done bad things, bad people who'd done good things and good people who'd done bad things, like Eddie, possibly.

'He used to go out with Siobhan. Treated her well, treated me well, a nice guy, I suppose.' Cavani laughed, permitting himself a glance to the screen to confirm that his face had gone red before urging himself to carry on.

'Sitting beside a drug dealer on the flight home to see my sister, who'd taken a drug overdose, and outside the hospital I met a wee guy . . .' Cavani paused, tripping over a misplaced thought. 'A young guy, I mean, when I say wee guy. I met a young guy who'd been attacked by his pal, well, an old pal, a pal who'd started selling drugs and taking them too, like, taking a lot, to the point he ended up owing a load of money to real drug dealers, money he couldn't pay back unless he ran around doing jobs for them, and one of the jobs ended up being that he had to look after something.' Cavani looked around the room, like someone could be listening in, looking back to the laptop, reminding himself that he was connected to a wireless network and talking into an Apple device, and that that's where any fear of incrimination should stem from. Reminding himself that he wasn't talking about anything he'd done, or speaking any names of anyone who'd done anything. Reminding himself that he was thinking too much again. Reminding himself to get on with it.

'He got asked to carry a gun and he shit himself, realising what he'd got into. The wee guy, Declan, he got drunk one night, after fucking up at a writing class that he goes to.' Cavani laughed, thinking of Declan's writing and of him performing any of it to a creative-writing class in an arts centre.

'One thing leads to another and he ends up in a pub brawl or whatever, with his old pal, in front of all these dodgy people. The next night the old pal comes looking for him, insisting *he* takes the gun, threatening him, but the wee guy, Declan, stands his ground, stands up for himself and there it goes. Battered, beat up, hospitalised, scared to leave the house.

'His mum asked me to come over and say hello to him outside the hospital and then I told him to send me some of his work over, he sends me maybe a hundred pages – like, a shitload – of funny stuff, heavy stuff, original-like stuff I wouldn't feel comfortable showing a lot of people, but that's it, that's what it's all about. If it's made its way out of your head and on to the paper, then there's a chance it's going to connect with at least someone . . . To me that's writing. To me

that's what I used to be, what I hope I still am, somewhere.'
Cavani leaned back in his chair, like he was settling into the
idea of his new office, where something was going to be created again, something he cared about.

'He's got something, definitely, it's raw, rough, but there's
an honesty in it. Siobhan, she was in tears laughing at some
parts.' Cavani paused to enjoy the thought of Siobhan, sober
and laughing, something he'd seriously considered that he
might never see again.

'It's really good and I think we can work on something
together. We met last week, we went to a wee café up here,
so I could give him some feedback, sound him out properly
and all of that, but I've never met anyone as nervous, like, he
could hardly fucking talk, maybe it was too soon, he was still
too paranoid, worried that he was going to get attacked again,
even up here.' Cavani nodded to his window. 'Up here, like,
in a nice neighbourhood,' he added, knowing that it probably
hadn't been necessary.

'We're supposed to be meeting again tomorrow afternoon . . .' Cavani looked around his office, realising he'd need
to get it decluttered before having anyone in to begin working.

'Going back to the start, working on something. It's exciting,
really.' Cavani wiped his palms on the front of his jeans, turning
to watch Dr Nikouladis offer an impressed smile in receipt of
yet another positive declaration from Cavani.

'I don't know what to do or say, but he has something, I'm
sure of it. He just needs to try and sort himself out,' Cavani
dropped in, hoping that his appeal for professional advice to
hand down to Declan, second hand, was disguised enough.

Not everyone could afford private therapy – well, hardly anyone, and the NHS, well, fuck knows what's going on there, Cavani thought, aware that he was in a privileged position to be able to afford Dr Nikouladis's hefty hourly fee. £130. Cavani smiled, thinking of anyone from Declan's area – from his area, essentially – being handed that sort of budget and given an hour in which to cheer themselves up and the fucking state they'd be in.

It was more complicated than that though, more nuanced, a voice – that didn't feel like his – reminded him, a conditioned voice, jumping on his thought and smothering the humour out of it, smothering the truth out of it.

He wasn't a celebrity any more, that had been decided, so he was free now, to think what he wanted to think. Maybe he *was* scared, scared of where he'd been headed as his agent had accused – scared of success – scared of failure too, but that was fine, both things were subjective. He was scared of losing himself, or, of having lost himself – that was the objective truth.

Whether he succeeded or failed now, it would be as himself, it would be in his name and he'd be there, paying attention, overseeing the journey and there would be a pride attached to that.

He'd made enough money to live a comfortable life – for a good while – so it wasn't that much of a renunciation, that much of a rebellion, but, still, it felt liberating, and Declan's work – as rough as it was – had brought out something in him, it had reminded him of who he was. Something like that, but not quite. It had reminded him of who he could have been, if he hadn't achieved his success – success being that he'd made a living with his mind, with his thoughts, like Declan hoped to – or maybe it reminded him of who he was, right now.

'This young guy, James – Declan, you said his name was? It sounds like maybe you think you can save him?' Dr Nikouladis interrupted, bringing Cavani back to the session.

'Or maybe he can save me,' Cavani shot back, impressed at his own reflexes. It wasn't something he'd considered before – that this might be true – but his thoughts retreated, giving way to see what was coming next. Dr Nikouladis lifted his chin, intrigued.

'It's like, people ask – well, people ask me – people have asked me . . .' Cavani stumbled around before ordering himself to drag the words out. 'In interviews and shit like that, what would you say to your younger self? Like, presuming that we all see our younger selves as naïve, clueless, worried, lost, whatever. I was nervous. I wasn't all that popular. I didn't take to childhood and adolescence as naturally as everyone else seemed to, but now I see the skills I was honing back then, the survival skills. I got comfortable being on my own. I got to know myself. I got to like myself and I got my own thing going on with my writing, to the point that I wanted to be alone. I thrived on it. I made my own world. I could pay attention to the physical world – going to school, going to work – and then take it home with me and reshape it, rework it, varnish it, sand it down.' Cavani smiled, noticing that his eyes were fixed on the table, appreciating the assistance and the encouragement to keep going, to keep talking, to let it all out.

'I could take a fucking drill and sledgehammer to it too. I mean, that is life, it's not all smoothing and polishing. I learned to get good at it and the confidence that everyone found from other things – from being good at school, from having loads of friends, girlfriends, being good at football or good at fighting – I found that through writing, and that's a confidence that grew and grew and branched out into other aspects of my life. The success came – success as in someone is willing to write you a cheque in exchange for your thoughts and daydreams, your mind becomes a commodity – and then you're popular, you're invited everywhere, you've got a surplus of best friends, you're suddenly attractive.' Cavani paused to laugh to make sure he hadn't sounded arrogant or anything, looking to Dr Nikouladis, who smiled for him to keep going.

'The confidence scales heights you never imagined to be possible, before taking a step back, letting a bit of fear in, but just the right amount, so that your dream becomes your job – and a high pressure job – one where you know you need to deliver and every time you do deliver, the fear advances and you need to deliver again – and better – on it goes until the point it's just a job, a well-paid job but the self-doubt, the insecurity – whatever you want to call it – is stronger than anything you've ever felt.

'It's got you by the fucking balls, it owns you, other people's opinions own you, to the extent that you wished you'd kept your head down and just embraced life in the background – the signs were there, man, you were supposed to be quiet, nervous, scared, a passenger. What the fuck were you thinking? You'd laugh at yourself; you'd turn on yourself, and once that happens . . . then . . . fuck me . . .' Cavani trailed off, staring into his empty coffee cup.

'The problem is you've committed, you've got money,

you've become popular, you head off on journeys you never wanted to go on – acting in films you'd never watch.' Cavani looked up, the coffee cup between his hands like a crystal ball, a crystal ball that was stuck in reverse, he told himself, continuing his retrospective analysis.

'Your fulfilment and happiness and general – fucking, general, just, fuck knows, man . . .' Cavani coughed again, sliding the coffee cup out of sight.

'The feeling of what life is about, it goes – you run out of shit to buy, you realise you don't need to be up on Monday morning and then everything that comes with that. You miss your old self. You know he's in there somewhere but he couldn't survive in this new world, so you keep him buried, drown him in booze, or whatever your thing is. You're embarrassed by him. You're surrounded by people who don't know you and it's sad, man. It's a fucking scary, scary place to be. You need a new escape, a new way of finding meaning, you realise that you're no different from anyone else, maybe we all want to attach ourselves to something bigger than us, something beyond us. If it's not a god, then it's a band, a football team, whatever, a drug, a gang, conspiracy theories.' Cavani looked over Siobhan's name again.

There was something about her self-destructive past that he understood, and as well as giving him a strong sense of empathy towards her, it also scared him. 'Maybe we're all looking for our own heroin,' Cavani declared. 'My sister's problem was that she actually went for fucking heroin.' Cavani leaned back in his chair, halting himself, conceding that he couldn't keep up with the pace of his own mind.

He felt caught somewhere between a laughing fit and a

flood of tears. Whatever it was, it felt vivid and intense, like he was too big for his own body or something. It felt fucking powerful. He considered trying to explain it to Dr Nikouladis, but some things didn't need to be explained.

'Maybe I lost my soul, man,' Cavani offered, releasing a reluctant laugh of acceptance. 'Some things need an interpretation, not an explanation,' he announced, running his hands down his face, over his smile, letting them meet at his chest as though joined in prayer. Maybe his soul was returning, Cavani told himself, making sure the thought stood its ground in the face of the ridiculing voices that had come out in force to pounce on his moment.

'When I read Declan's work, it took me back to who I was. Who I am, really, if that makes sense . . .' Cavani put his thumb up, fearing that he'd been rambling on.

What would he have done with himself if it hadn't worked out, if he wasn't famous, a celebrity, if he hadn't 'made it', as they'd put it?

Cavani drifted, playing back all the chat show research chats, all the newspapers and the magazines who'd asked him these sorts of questions. Maybe he'd still be in his parents' house, writing in his bedroom, listening to music, sitting in his stoner mate's house, dreaming, maybe he'd be worrying. It was easy – when you'd made it – to dream back and be nostalgic for the days before you'd made it, he supposed. It could have been him, he could have been Declan, working in a supermarket, dropping out of college courses, going to a midweek creative-writing class, getting attacked by drug dealers, bullied, scared to leave the house.

He thought of all the times he'd even struggled to come up with a witty answer or anything like that, the question was so terrifying, like his head processed it as 'So, James, what will you do when all of this comes to an end, when you get found out?'

Maybe he had been found out, then, but he'd found himself out and, rather than being terrifying, it was powerful.

'You seem to have done some soul searching, James – for want of a better expression.' Dr Nikouladis smiled, surprising Cavani by using an expression like soul searching as opposed to a more clinical – a more scientific – equivalent.

'I'm glad that Siobhan is ok and it sounds like you've all been through a lot. I hope you'll continue to be kind to her and that she'll be kind to herself and as for Lisa, well, she sounds like she truly loves you, James. She loves you for who you are, good, bad, sad, happy. I hope you both remember to leave some room for yourselves, in everything, away from work, away from everything else that you do.

'You're just a human, James, and you don't have to take so much onboard. Let yourself breathe, ok? Let yourself make the mistakes, but let other people make their mistakes too.

'It isn't always on you, James, it's all part of being human.

'Some things require an interpretation, not an explanation, as you said, and I hope that you will write that down and refer back to it from time to time.'

Cavani laughed, accepting the compliment by smiling to the camera, waiting for Dr Nikouladis to continue.

'The school friend of yours, the man you said was a criminal, maybe he wants something from you, but you don't have to give it, and the young writer you met, maybe you want to give something to him, but he doesn't want that either, do you understand?'

Dr Nikouladis paused, seeming to wait until Cavani began to look uncomfortable with the contemplative silence before carrying on.

'You can help people, sure, but you can never save people unless they want to be saved – as you know. In the end the decision lies with them.' He went on as Cavani listened for any movement at the front door, dreading the idea of Siobhan walking in as she was clearly being referenced, clearly being spoken about on a laptop by a therapist that only Lisa knew about.

'The mistakes you've made and the people you've hurt, the people who've hurt you, you can't change that, you can't go back, they have a right to remember you however they want, and you them. But you also have a right to change and not to be the same person, as do they – or, as it seems in your case, to go back to the person you believe you used to be before feeling like you got lost, like life overtook you as you tried to pursue something that was never coming – because it was something that you hadn't actually identified. Instead, you let other people identify something for you, if I'm correct?' Cavani nodded, confirming that Dr Nikouladis had a sound grasp on everything that had been spoken about over their hours together.

'The people you hurt and the friends you lost, they're human beings too and not merely characters in your life, and you're not merely a character in theirs. It's life, James. People change, people do good, people do bad. You do good, you do bad. It can be very, very difficult but it can be beautiful if you let it, which I know you want to.'

Cavani nodded again, adding 'Definitely', coughing another warning to his voice not to crack, thinking of Lisa and Siobhan coming home to see him sitting crying at his laptop, an image that he was grateful for, as it brought a smile to his face.

'Take your time and work slowly, and if you feel that what you want from life lies away from all of your success and your acclaim and from being "James Cavani", then that's what you need to do. If you feel the need to go back to the start in relation to work, to write something with the "young guy" who you met' – Dr Nikouladis smiled, in reference to the earlier hilarity: the hour was almost up so it was fine for some informality seemed to be his thinking – 'then that's what to do. Take the time to listen to yourself and to be honest with yourself.' Dr Nikouladis nodded, looking away from his camera for what seemed like the first time in the entire hour.

'"You should never bullshit yourself", as you once put it, James. That was a crackin' shout,' Dr Nikouladis said, holding his laugh to try and release it alongside Cavani's. 'I'm always here whenever you feel you need to come back. I'm proud of the work we've done and I wish you well, James.'

Dr Nikouladis fixed his tie and smiled – a far goofier smile, sticking his thumb up and moving it towards the camera.

'I'll send you a message in a week and let you know how everything is going and thank you, thanks, Doctor, genuinely.'

Cavani closed the laptop over and clasped his hands behind his head, pulling them back down again as he caught the sweat patch on his left and then right armpit, realising that he'd been sweating through his jumper during the session.

He lifted his coffee cup and stood up to walk through to the kitchen, turning to look at the computer table, thinking that surely there was something more important he could do with his afternoon than fixing the table, remembering that this was how it started: he'd put off the small things so that he could free up time to think of something bigger, and then worry and do nothing about either – big or small – and then he'd be left with another day wasted.

He thought of how he could go back over some of the film script that he was helping Declan with, but maybe he'd go back to it with a fresher approach. It had potential but it needed a lot of work, he knew, so maybe the distraction of the table would be a good thing. He could read it over and let his mind take aim at the plot holes and the dialogue, and think of what bits of his own writing and his own ideas to incorporate. He had containers full of paper that had never been seen by anyone, work that he'd abandoned because of something more important.

Fix the fucking table, he ordered himself, promising that it would help him switch off and view Declan's writing, and his, from a distance, rather than from point blank range. It always worked better that way, as he knew and as he'd told Declan.

The office was only for typing, the writing was done outside, in the real world, in real life, Cavani reminded himself, walking into Lisa's and his' still cluttered bedroom to spray himself with some deodorant and find a fresh jumper before he headed out to find a hardware store. He was sure he'd passed one loads of times, though he couldn't picture where exactly it was yet, but the walk would help him, and if he got lost, then who cares, he'd enjoy his own company.

He listened to the front door open and took a step back out to the hallway to watch as Lisa and Siobhan returned home from their walk, anticipating being told how many steps they'd managed or who they'd met, or given a full breakdown from Siobhan of every dog that they'd passed in the park. He smiled.

'What?' Cavani said, his smile not sure whether to stick around or not, whether something serious had happened or a joke was coming, a wind-up.

Cavani was surprised and then alarmed at how edgy their arrival had made him feel, alarmed too by the way Lisa was looking to the floor and at the way Siobhan had stopped – stood at the door – looking straight at him, and then joining him in staring at Lisa, who'd continued walking towards him, her eyes fixed on the floor, her hair covering her face. His smile was replaced by what he could feel was a look of genuine panic. Siobhan had been doing great, but it was no time to be complacent, no time to be messing around or pretending that something had happened. His nerves were shattered, Lisa knew, so she wouldn't be playing a joke on him.

'What is it?' he asked, his voice louder than he'd intended, but it had shown how serious he was, how concerned, and how quickly he needed one of them to start talking.

He could feel a fresh outpouring of sweat trickle through the armpits of his jumper as Lisa's arms grabbed him towards her. Three of his fingers slid through the handle of the coffee cup to try and secure it, receiving the embrace that was really beginning to frighten him, that had brought all the dark forces of his head out, every one of them with its own morbid theory.

'What? What's happened? Tell me?' Cavani softened his voice as he looked over Lisa's shoulder, hoping that Siobhan would give some sort of clue to explain what was going on, but she turned away, her back to him as he tried to release Lisa's head off his shoulder. Feeling her shaking, hearing her sniffling, he released himself away far enough to confirm that Lisa was crying. He pulled her back in whilst looking to Siobhan as she turned round to look at the back of Lisa's head and then to Cavani. She was crying too, but smiling.

'What the fuck is it?' Cavani managed to laugh and snap at the same time, the relief he'd felt from Siobhan's smile clearing the way for Lisa's words to get through to him.

'I'm pregnant, James, I'm pregnant,' Lisa announced, trying to shout through her tears.

'Eh?' Cavani wanted to push her back to look at her face, to be sure that she hadn't made a mistake, to be sure that she was serious, but his instincts wouldn't let him. Instead his arms grew tighter and stronger around her whilst Siobhan began jumping up and down, letting out a scream.

'Fuck sake. Fuck, man. Fuck sake.' Cavani watched tears of his own landing on the wooden floor behind Lisa's light-green gym trainers as she'd tried to tell him through her tears and coughing and smiling and shaking – and her staggered breathing – that she'd been feeling sick for the last few mornings and that she'd told Siobhan, who'd gone into the chemist to buy a pregnancy test for her and they'd stayed for a coffee and she'd used the toilet in one of the cafés that Siobhan had handed her CV in to.

Cavani closed his eyes and laughed as the tears were now running down his face, landing a kiss on the top of Lisa's ear as he encouraged her to make sure that she was breathing properly, aware that it was all a bit overwhelming and that she didn't need to rush the whole story out.

He thought of the very first day they'd been told it was unlikely that they'd ever be able to have children. How they'd tried and failed with IVF and they hadn't gone for any more, so how had it happened? What the fuck. His head was pouring over with questions, but one by one they backed down, with Cavani realising that his head wasn't needed, just his heart.

He lifted his eyes to look as Lisa's right hand released itself from the embrace and watched as it reached out from behind her. He nodded to Siobhan that this was her cue to join them. Their heads bowed into each other, and Siobhan's tears sent Lisa off again, and then Cavani again, the happiest tears he'd ever cried and the happiest he'd ever seen Lisa and Siobhan.

It was that feeling again, like he was expanding from inside himself, like his mum and dad were there too, surrounded by his racing heart and Lisa's and Siobhan's, surrounded by their souls.

'A miracle baby,' Lisa managed before shaking with tears again. That was it. Cavani couldn't think of any better way of putting it; nor did he want to. Some things needed an interpretation, not an explanation, he reminded himself, pulling Lisa closer to him.

'I'll be the best auntie of all time, an auntie the child can be proud of. I'll get a job, get to college, get a flat, get it nice, and my wee niece or nephew can stay at their auntie Siobhan's,' Siobhan announced. 'Sorry,' she halted herself. 'I'm pure taking over the moment,' laughing at how fast she'd been talking and apologising, mentioning that it wasn't all about her.

Cavani grabbed her shoulder with his left hand, confirming that he knew she was going to be a great auntie.

'That's the best trip to a chemist I've made in a while anyway,' Siobhan joked, prompting the three of them into a burst of genuine laughter as they all broke free, wiping their faces.

'We need to celebrate,' Cavani announced, wiping his eyes with the sleeve of his jumper and encouraging Lisa and Siobhan to follow him into the kitchen, listening as they both pulled out stools from under the marble breakfast bar at the window side of the kitchen, which was their way of telling him to sort them out with a coffee.

Cavani poured himself a half-glass of water, which he gulped down in one, handed them both some kitchen roll for their eyes and waited to take their orders. 'Is there any decaffeinated coffee?' Siobhan asked, turning to Lisa, waiting for what she'd meant to register on her face.

'Aw, aye!' Lisa laughed, her face glowing.

'That's you as sober as me now,' Siobhan added, pulling Lisa towards her for another cuddle. 'Just a black coffee for me, same as you.' Siobhan winked. 'How are we going to celebrate then, big Poppa?' Her face beamed, alive, fresh from the walk, fresh from the freedom. It was like a new person, Cavani thought, or at least someone he'd forgotten existed.

'We could get burgers from that place, what's it called again?' Lisa asked, immediately answering her own question. 'El Perro

Negro, is that right?' She looked to Cavani, giving him his moment to show off his Spanish.

'Perrrrro,' Siobhan declared, exaggerating a Spanish accent and her rolling of the double 'r'. 'The Black Dog it means, Jimmy, is that right?'

Cavani nodded, his stomach tensed and his head began to drift off.

'The one we walked past earlier?' he heard Siobhan ask as he turned to set up the coffee maker, feeling himself leaving the room.

'El Perro Negro,' he repeated to himself. 'The Black Dog.'

He thought of Declan and the film script, of writing with a young guy who he hardly knew, who he'd only met by chance outside of the hospital. Maybe he'd felt sorry for him, maybe he hadn't been thinking straight because of Siobhan, because of everything, maybe he *had* been trying to save him. Maybe he'd been so caught up in himself that he was acting with the story in mind – with the chat shows in mind, the articles, the headlines: James Cavani and his new project with a young apprentice who he plucked from obscurity, from his home town. 'I saw a lot of myself in the kid.' He cringed at the image of himself in jeans and trainers, talking to some radio presenter or a talk show host, trying to sell an image of himself, that he was still cool, that he was taking risks, that he was real, authentic, that he'd never forgotten his roots as they'd say.

Maybe his rebellion had been too harsh, too indulgent, and now he had the future to consider. A pregnant wife and then a child to think of – maybe he should phone his agent, arrange a meeting and see if the damage could be repaired. He thought of the money he'd walked away from and the opportunities. He could apologise, grovel, see what could be done, go to the meetings, explain he'd been in a bad place and all of that.

Or, he thought, he could stick to the fucking plan. He thought of Dr Nikouladis telling him to relinquish trying to control every aspect of life – and beyond – and instead to wrest back control of himself and be who he really was. He could only develop the good in himself and work on the bad once he'd accepted that they were both a part of him, a part of everybody.

He didn't have to be who his agent wanted him to be, who the public wanted him to be, who his upbringing wanted him to be, who the pay cheques wanted him to be.

He could keep working on this renewed confidence that he was instilling in himself, the confidence that – when he allowed it – made him believe that he could make something great again, great in the sense that he'd watch it, he'd promote it, with pride, financially rewarding or not. He could end up making good money again, of course, and he could get a new agent – he could write a box office hit and he could do his parents and his background proud, but it would be for himself this time, and if that meant collaborating with a young guy from his home town, who he felt like he knew inside out through his writing but who he'd only met twice, then that's how it was going to be.

He thought of Eddie Reynolds, of returning his call, of meeting him, in public. It was another problem that wouldn't be going away unless he faced it head on. A moment of weakness and he'd ended up in contact with him. He could be honest with Eddie, that they had to stay out of each other's worlds, and he'd understand probably. He thought of meeting him. Face to face. Accept his books and his coffee and that would be it, another potential problem dealt with.

He thought of Declan, who'd landed himself in Eddie's world of crime when he'd wanted into Cavani's world of creativity. He thought of how he could return Eddie to his own world and release Declan.

Cavani thought of Declan and his friend who'd turned to crime – his friend who'd wanted to be a gangster – of how Declan wanted to be like Cavani and his friend wanted to be like Eddie.

Declan had a far better chance of reaching his goal than the friend though. To be fair to Eddie Reynolds, he'd never been a bully, and he didn't choose the life, he was born into it, that was the difference, Cavani supposed, feeling like he was already trying to justify meeting a career criminal in public, like he was working on his explanation, to himself and his own conscience first of all, but also imagining what if they'd been photographed together, if anyone – a tabloid journalist or whatever – saw them and did a little research and found out who Eddie Reynolds was?

Again he realised he was still thinking like a celebrity. He was going to meet an old school friend for a coffee and whatever the old school friend did with his life was entirely independent of their friendship, if that's what it could be called.

Maybe crime was Eddie's own personal religion, his own immortality project, which at face value was the pursuit of money and power but which could have stemmed from the same place as everyone else's neuroses. Maybe he was just a bad bastard and Cavani had lived in leafy suburbs for too long, had too many doors held open for him and been called 'sir' too many times and he'd forgotten where he'd grown up, he reminded himself as he thought of how Eddie could make sure the people who'd attacked Declan would leave him alone now. Being petrified to leave your own house to go to work was a dangerous, dangerous place for your head to drag you.

He thought of how he'd go about telling Eddie this though and it made him shudder. What, was he organising a fucking gangland hit now? He could plead with Eddie not to use violence, just to make sure Declan was left alone, left out of that world altogether. But diplomacy wasn't exactly Eddie Reynolds's speciality. They could give him a small part in the film, if Declan was left alone and no one was hurt in the process. Fuck knows what to do. He shook his head, grateful to be interrupted.

'Hawl! Are you listening?' Lisa was laughing and Siobhan was waving her hand from side to side. 'We'll get burgers and watch your new film?' Lisa repeated.

'Come on, let me see my brother in a blockbuster,' Siobhan pleaded, anticipating Cavani's categorical refusal.

'I know you hated it but we want to see it. Come on. I bet you're brilliant in it,' Lisa added, her face showing that she was asking for more than a film to be downloaded. That she was asking for him to see the occasion, the moment, the magic of the news and the three of them together, after everything.

'Aw, man, it'll be shite,' Cavani laughed, aware that he was agreeing, that he needed to get over it. It was out now. 'Please,' Lisa and Siobhan seemed to say at the same time. 'Or we'll just watch it and you can go into the room,' Lisa added, laughing.

'Well, I need to fix my office table, it needs sanded down and varnished,' Cavani announced.

'Eh?' Lisa answered, laughing.

'My office table, it's all chipped and bashed in looking and I don't want to just buy another one. I've wrote some good stuff on it. There's memories there.' Cavani laughed before his face could go red – it didn't suit him, self-praise, or pride in his work, but there, he'd said it. He noticed Lisa nodding, impressed that he'd turned some sort of corner. He hurried on before she made him repeat his admission.

'It needs a bit of work done to it and that's all life is, solving problems,' Cavani stated, smiling at Siobhan.

The atmosphere in the kitchen felt great. Warm, excited – it felt like they were going somewhere and it was like the conversation could never dry up. There was overwhelming emotion – reflection, shock, joy, relief – all sorts of positivity, all fusing together.

Cavani held his smile and his eye contact as Lisa looked right into him, thousands of memories of their relationship playing out in their hearts, the good and the bad, the large and the small, the vivid and the vague.

Lisa knew he'd been putting the work in on himself and that his office table was a tangible, objective means to try and show that he was progressing.

'Speaking of problems, what about they sweat patches?' Siobhan said, slagging him and letting him know how much she loved him at the same time. Lisa laughed and watched as Cavani looked to both his armpits.

'I'm heading out to meet someone for a coffee but ...' Cavani coughed to clear his throat, laughing along with Lisa and Siobhan, who were giggling and mimicking his frog-like voice.

'Chocolate throat,' Siobhan declared. Cavani laughed at how hyper they both were, like schoolchildren in the last class before the summer holidays.

Cavani turned to pour Siobhan her coffee and a water for Lisa.

'Have you got any chocolate?' Siobhan asked.

'Aw fuck!' Cavani threw his head back, walking out of the kitchen, down to the bedroom to find his rucksack, returning with the American Milky Way that he remembered he still hadn't given to Lisa.

'What is that? A fake Milky Way?' Siobhan laughed, looking at the two of them, missing but enjoying the joke.

'Aye, man, a Milky Way is a Mars bar in America,' Cavani enjoyed informing Siobhan.

'Is it?' she asked, shocked.

'Aye, it's true,' Lisa added, laughing. 'I thought you'd forgotten,' she told Cavani.

'I nearly did, nearly missed the flight because of it!' he admitted.

'Weirdos,' Siobhan laughed, asking to see it and try it for herself.

'Just packaged different but the exact same on the inside.' Cavani smiled, thinking of Declan as he watched them both study the chocolate and break it in half. It was daft, it was innocent, funny, life. He smiled at how he'd never thought he'd see the day Lisa would come in and tell him that they were going to be parents and that Siobhan would look so calm, so happy, so comfortable within herself.

'I'll be back in an hour or whatever. Coffee and then a hardware shop for my table.' He smiled, designating a pause for some more confused laughter.

'. . . And we'll order burgers and all that and we'll watch this shite . . .' Cavani listened to the cheers as he turned to pour Lisa a water. 'I'll bring some decaff coffee in too.' He winked at her, leaning over the worktop to kiss her head before walking out of the kitchen to the bedroom, to change his jumper.

'You'll need to phone and book the scan then. I'll finish this college form and phone this letting agent,' he heard Siobhan, as he left the room.

'Fuck me, man,' he said to himself in the bedroom mirror, his own face beaming too, like he'd risen up from inside himself. He sat on the edge of the bed to take a few minutes to process everything that was happening and everything that was going to happen, before reaching into his pocket to switch his phone back on, forgetting that he'd turned it off during the therapy session.

There was a text from Eddie telling him he was free for the next hour or so but that it was no problem if he was busy. He appreciated the out, but there would just be further texts suggesting a meet up and Cavani knew he was only delaying the inevitable now that Eddie had his number.

Everything happens for a reason, he reminded himself, thinking of *The Black Dog* and how it wouldn't have happened if Declan hadn't been attacked and if Siobhan hadn't taken her last overdose.

What if it's shite, The Black Dog – a disaster? his head enjoyed interrupting to enquire.

What if it's fucking brilliant? He stood up, impressed at the ease he was swatting away the voices with now, his head was his again. He opened the wardrobe to find a fresh jumper, unlocking his phone as he scanned his options.

'Where do you want to meet?' he typed, looking at the digits of Eddie's unsaved phone number and then at his last text, considering – one final time – what he was doing. He thought of Declan and of himself at that age and the fear, the insecurity, of it all. He'd found his escape in time but it could have been him. It could have been him. He wasn't asking for anyone to be hurt – the opposite in fact: he was asking for someone never to be hurt again.

He was confident Eddie would give him his word that there would be no violence, he was confident that a warning from Eddie would be enough for Declan to get on with his life without worrying, scared to go to the pub, to walk his dog. He thought of Declan's mum and the confident front she'd put on outside the hospital, but he could see she'd looked heartbroken, shocked, terrified that this was just the start of it. She'd reminded him of his own mum when Siobhan's problems had started.

Fuck it. It was the right thing to do – well, the rightest. He hit send and closed his phone, placing it back in his jeans.

'Right,' he announced – through a purposeful breath – to his reflection in the mirror, watching himself considering the three problems he was about to face up to.

Eddie Reynolds, the neglected table and the shite movie.

Take them on. One by one. It's life, man. He smiled to himself, pulling his new jumper down at the waist, satisfied with how it fitted. Satisfied that he was good to go.

Cavani wondered if Eddie realised how many of his stories began with either 'what about that time?' or 'do you remember when?' Rhetorical prompts, cues for a nod or a laugh; Eddie was the kind of guy who liked to make sure his audience knew the story before telling it.

Cavani thought of how many people he'd met like this over the years and wondered if he did this himself, or maybe it came at a certain point in your life, when you'd settled for a greatest hits tour rather than trying out anything from the new album.

The past was easier though, it was comfortable, it helped delude you into believing you knew someone and that someone knew you, that *you* knew you.

The clarity of Cavani's thoughts reminded him that it had been a while since he'd updated himself on how long it had been since he'd last drunk alcohol. He tried to work it out quickly whilst Eddie went on – about an old science teacher of theirs or something – but he'd lost count of the weeks. It wasn't something he thought about any more, so maybe that was it, he'd quit.

Cavani had mastered the use of his semi-automatic smile, which was by now working in tandem with the fluctuations of Eddie's speech patterns, his rhythms and his cadence, and it could change to a laugh when a pause confirmed that a punchline had been delivered.

Cavani nodded at the names he remembered and the ones he pretended to remember – old classmates, old teachers – and at the stories that he doubted but didn't dispute.

In Eddie's case, Cavani assumed, not many of his recent anecdotes would go down well in a West End coffee shop.

He thought of how Eddie had spent time in the editing suite, deleting whatever he didn't like and reworking it all so that he was the star, the hero; never the villain. He'd even added a few extra lines and scenes where Cavani came out all right too, no doubt to seal his complicity in the delusions.

Cavani felt like he was putting a lot more work into humouring Eddie than the guy he'd brought along with him as he watched him typing on his phone, a scouse guy whose name Cavani had forgotten. Or it hadn't properly registered when he was initially taken aback at realising he was meeting with two dodgy bastards – this one who he didn't know, who he didn't trust.

Not that he truly knew Eddie Reynolds, or trusted him, but at least there was something there, Cavani thought, trying both to pick up on Eddie's story and conclude his own train of thought.

He coughed to allow himself a look to the side, to break the intensity of having to pretend to concentrate on Eddie's stories whilst his head narrated its own.

Eddie's skill was in letting you believe he'd taken over – that you weren't getting a word in – but every derisive thought that Cavani had felt that his face was managing to hide seemed to be picked up on. It was a powerful tool, and despite the brash, loudest guy in the room character that he played, beneath it were an astute mind and, there was no getting away from it, a fucking scary guy.

The past, his head insisted, that's what he had with Eddie Reynolds, bullshit or not – embellished, romanticised even, given the paths that both of their lives had raced off on. Whatever it was, it was there, and if he was serious about working with Declan, to help make something out of his screenplay, to find his own passion again, then he should help him with at least this problem of being harassed, of living in fear. Again he tried to summon the memories, the worries, the insecurities, the fear of his own younger self as justification for who he was meeting with, who he was talking to.

He thought of what he'd have to do in return for Eddie – something related to film. They'd probably need to think seriously about writing a character based on him or to cast him. Fuck knows. Cavani felt the armpits of his fresh jumper now being soaked in sweat.

It wasn't revenge that was needed, just a warning. A non-violent warning, Cavani repeated to himself, aware that he was practising in his head for how he was going to ask Eddie for a favour. He looked again at Eddie's mate, wondering who he was messaging and wondering what he was messaging about.

Stop trying to solve other people's problems, that's what Lisa would tell him here. Again his stomach tensed as he thought of what he was doing, given the news they'd just received. Cavani looked to the table, at the bag of books which Eddie had brought along – the supposed purpose of their meeting. Eddie would know he hadn't agreed to meet him just to start a book club though, so at least he'd be aware there was something that had brought Cavani along.

A few emboldened words from the book's titles stood out through the white plastic bag to Cavani's eyes, taking his head back to being sat in Dunkin' Donuts, his eyes fixed on the window of Hudson's book store in New York's JFK Airport and how much had changed since then. There were no manuals for life, man, they were only distractions, more semblances of control. That was Eddie's private religion. Total control. He probably knew that too, but if he was in it for life, and gave in, he'd be shot or be jailed or be back in the real world, back to the daily struggle that they'd both escaped, Cavani through his writing and Eddie through his surname.

Maybe they had been closer than Cavani had remembered at high school. They'd sat beside each other in a couple of classes, but they hadn't spoken much outside of them, which was in part – well, largely – down to Cavani being intimidated by Eddie, who had a reputation even at thirteen or fourteen years old and not a reputation that he seemed to have had to work for. He was never in a fight or anything else and he never disrupted the class or bothered the teachers, he left that to the nutters. He must have known though, even back then, that he'd be the king of the nutters one day, and sure enough he'd fulfilled his destiny. Cavani thought, there and then, what Eddie would have done if it had been different, if he'd started life with a blank canvas, a clean slate. He noticed a scar beneath his eye, remembering that they'd been sat side by side on the plane and he'd marched off with his head down to avoid being stopped for pictures when they'd landed.

He didn't have a choice, Cavani supposed, as justification for Eddie or as justification for being sat with Eddie. Stop seeing the best in everyone and the worst in yourself, his head quoted Lisa, or was it Dr Nikouladis? – someone had said it to him though – and it was true, he admitted, putting a stop to his hunt for empathy towards Eddie.

He thought of their conversation on the plane that day, a conversation that wouldn't have been possible in the presence of Eddie's pal. That probably explained why the pal was brought along then. Eddie's way of letting Cavani know that their conversation that day was never to be mentioned, that today was a different Eddie.

'Ah told them aw that he was a good cunt and that debate wis healthy.' Eddie leaned back into his chair, laughing and coughing, delighted with his story, looking at Cavani, seemingly oblivious to everything else in the café except his reaction.

The laughter and the coughing – and the strength and the volume of the word 'cunt' – dragged Cavani back into the room, attempting to balance the release of a laugh to appease Eddie with a scan of the surrounding tables, to commence the issuing of apologies.

Cavani remembered that he lived here now, the West End of Glasgow, not a natural habitat for the word 'cunt'. Which was ironic. Cavani smiled to himself as his apologetic nod was met with a condescending disdain by a man who looked only a couple of years older than Eddie and him.

'Sorry about that, lad,' Eddie's mate added, turning to look at Cavani, his teeth gritted and his cheek bones raised in an exaggerated comic acknowledgement that he'd seen too that the man was furious.

'There could be kids around, Ed,' the pal said, looking at Cavani to show that he shared his embarrassment. 'Ridiculous, man. What's he like?' the pal added, seeming relieved that at least Eddie's story had finished. He slid his phone back into his pocket and looked around for a member of staff.

'I give up with that, man,' the pal said to Eddie, pausing to give him his cue to explain what he'd been doing on his phone, aware that he'd only be interrupted if he'd begun to tell Cavani himself.

'He buys and restores old furniture, this yin. Any old shite lyin' aboot the hoose, let him know,' Eddie explained. Watchin' as Cavani smiled, his first natural smile of the meeting, a smile of relief that he wasn't in the presence of invoices being sent out or hits being ordered. 'There's some skilled men in this industry. It's not all thuggery and mindless violence.' A smile appeared on Eddie's face as Cavani's disappeared. He felt taken aback, like Eddie had read his mind.

He seemed all right, the mate, Cavani thought. Thinking of his office table and of how one favour was enough for the day, for a lifetime, and the table was his problem and his problem to enjoy.

'Sorry, what's your name again, mate?' Cavani asked – trying to force himself to relax or at least to act relaxed – adding that his head was all over the place.

'Barry, mate. Barry Merson.' He smiled. 'I'm a big fan of your work, like.' Cavani nodded his head a few times, his eyes closed, hoping to demonstrate that he'd known his name was

Barry but he just needed a reminder – alarmed at how far off he'd drifted during the initial introductions. He stuck his thumb up, presuming that they'd already shook hands.

'Some accent that, Jimmy, is it no'? Ye should get disability benefit fur that,' Eddie Reynolds laughed.

'You'll be getting disability benefit soon, eat any more of them pineapple cakes.' Barry Merson nodded to the crumbs on the table as he turned around again, raising his hand for the bill to be brought over. 'I don't think he saw me there, like' he mumbled, standing up to walk over to the counter to pay their bill.

Cavani knew this was his time to mention Declan, his time to try and get through to the same version of Eddie that he'd met on the plane.

'Listen, Eddie. I feel, awkward here, right.' Cavani was surprised that he actually didn't feel awkward, now that he was speaking, but maybe it hadn't sunk in yet, what he was doing – it seemed like the right thing to say though. He paused, letting his head clear, smiling, waiting for Eddie Reynolds to make some sort of joke, but there was a silence and a look that made Cavani hurry up

'I need a favour, right . . .' Cavani felt himself leaning forward and his elbows positioning themselves on the table. He had Eddie's undivided attention. 'Nothing dodgy, and I need you to promise me, nothing . . . right . . . you know what I mean . . .' Cavani began sweating as he realised that Eddie wasn't prepared to fill in any of the blanks for him.

Cavani looked to see who was nearby. The man whose after-noon had been marred by Eddie's strong language had gone to the bathroom or gone to complain about Eddie. Whatever, he wasn't there.

'I'm working on something, right. Siobhan's fine, she's going to be fine. She's got it all planned out.' Cavani looked to Eddie, sensing that this would draw a reaction.

'That's good tae hear. Great,' Eddie added, his arms folding, which Cavani took as a cue to get to the point.

'When she'd overdosed. The last time. That day on the plane.' Cavani looked away, sensing that he hadn't been as subtle as he'd wanted in referencing their conversation and Eddie's reflective, almost confessional tone. Eddie said nothing but blew some air through his nostrils as he tilted his head, slightly adjusting his view of Cavani.

Cavani wondered what he saw. His head telling him to hurry up. To end this one way or another.

'I met a young guy outside the hospital. He's been trying to get into screenwriting.' Cavani corrected himself, realising that he was maybe making Declan and himself sound pretentious, at least to someone like Eddie

'He looks up to me, that sort of thing.' Cavani made sure to laugh, to show that he was being modest or to try and remind both himself and Eddie who he was, at least to some people. He was surprised at how vulnerable he felt and he remembered how much easier life was from behind the celebrity façade. He'd only dwelled on the drawbacks, but the armour was something he missed now that he'd exposed himself, now that he'd wandered off alone. He spoke sensing he was about to be drowned in a fresh wave of doubt about everything that he'd thrown away and the uncertainty of what lay ahead.

'His mum came over to me and introduced him. He had his eye socket fractured, ribs broke – and all of that – off a couple of guys, a couple of dodgy guys.' Cavani nodded, apologetically, like maybe he'd used offensive terminology.

'Guys from down by, right, he grew up round behind the old red ash pitches. He went to St Catherine's as well or whatever it's called these days.' Cavani realised that he too was using the past as a safety vest, something to help strengthen the connection.

'He's a good wee guy anyway, right.' Cavani looked around, seeing that Barry Merson was walking towards the toilet. 'His stuff is, well, I think it could be brilliant. I want to do something with him. I see a lot of myself in there, but he's struggling, man, his head's a bit scrambled with everything and that's not helped. He's scared to leave his house. Scared to walk his dog. It's bullying, man, really. He got into an argument in the pub with his old mate who's . . . whatever . . . selling stuff. His mate's in debt, he got asked to look after something to pay it off – or however it all works.' Cavani paused to cringe at the emphasis he'd put on the word something, his head teasing him that he was already beginning to sound like a dad.

'After the argument in the pub his pals used that as an excuse to force Declan . . .' Cavani tried to act like mentioning Declan's name hadn't fazed him. Fuck. He'd made it a whole lot worse for Declan. Fuck. Maybe Eddie would come down on the other people's side. Solidarity with his fellow dodgy bastards. Or maybe there was more to it, he considered, for the first time. Fuck. Maybe Declan wasn't as innocent as he'd

353

KEVIN BRIDGES

seemed. What the fuck was he doing. He looked to the bag of books on the table again. His head shooting back to New York. Back to when he was a movie star. Now he was meeting with gangsters to try and sort problems for a young guy, a wee guy.

A father to be, meeting a gangster to ask a favour. He wanted Eddie Reynolds to interrupt him, to offer him a timeout, to offer him at least some sort of reaction.

It wasn't coming. He looked at his glass bottle of sparkling water, but it was empty, he looked at the crumbs on the table, at the mess Eddie had made, at how pathetic he'd looked, when his jaws were munching his two pineapple cakes as sentence after sentence made its way out through the dust. Cavani felt himself getting impatient, with himself, with Eddie, at the situation and at Declan's situation. He believed him. His instincts trusted him. His soul, or whatever it was. He thought of being a dad, and if his own child was in Declan's situation.

'They tried to force Declan – the wee guy I'm looking to start writing with – to look after whatever it was. Fuck knows. He refused and his mate attacks him, puts him in hospital.' Cavani was surprised at how angry he seemed to be getting.

'Now they're driving by him, laughing, trying to intimidate him, whatever. I genuinely believe he's done fuck all wrong and he's in a terrible state, and his poor mum too. They seem a good family. I just want to make sure he's going to be ok; I don't know, I'm worried about the wee guy. I want to do something with him but I don't . . .' Cavani leaned in further, his confidence had fully returned and his eyes looked straight into Eddie's.

'I don't want anyone to get hurt, right? I just want whoever is bullying him to cut him some slack. He wants into my

354

world, not yours.' Cavani leaned back, hoping his self-assertive confidence would hang around at least until Eddie spoke. He began wondering if he'd written too many scripts, and if he'd become so deluded as to believe that such a favour was possible. He looked to see Barry Merson walking back to their table.

'That's that sorted, lads.' He sat down, looking at Cavani and then to Eddie, sensing that he'd walked in on an unfinished conversation, sensing that Eddie was about to talk.

'Did they touch his dug?' Eddie asked. Cavani felt a solid clump of chewing gum from under the table where his hands had been sent as he'd been desperate to avoid folding them under his drenched armpits or rubbing them on his thighs, any sort of negative, nervous body language.

'I don't think so, no. Naw,' he answered, adjusting his own head to look at Eddie the way he'd looked at him, as though bracing himself for the follow-up.

'That's just as well, Jimmy. Ah canny promise no one would get hurt if they touched the dug.' Eddie Reynolds smiled, seeming like he'd had his fun, that he was back to being jovial and loud again, that he'd enjoyed watching Cavani – James Cavani – at his mercy. 'Do you know about this?' Eddie asked Barry Merson. 'A wee guy getting put in hospital for arguing with his mate in a pub and not agreeing to look after something.' Eddie laughed, enjoying placing his own ominous inflection on the something.

'Fuck sake, that lad that Tanser's got running around for him. It'll be him. Why?' Barry Merson looked at Cavani, surprised that they were having a conversation like this in front of him, in front of someone he'd only known from film and television.

'What happened?' Eddie asked.

'Eh?' Barry Merson looked at them both, like he was being wound up, like something had been conspired in his absence. Cavani made sure his face let him know that this wasn't the case. 'We were out a few weeks ago. Few drinks, wetting Chrissy's kid's head or something, there was football on. Tanser got this lad to drive us around. We end up in the lad's local and his mate comes in. His mate was fucked, like, proper mortal. They end up in a bit of something, the mate and Tanser. Just Tanser being Tanser, winding up some girl behind the bar who was his missus or his mate, or something, fuck knows, the lad gave Tanser a bit back, like, standing up for the girl, fuckin' fair enough, I thought – and that were that, just daft really, why?'

Barry Merson looked to Cavani for an answer, Cavani turned to Eddie.

'When are ye meetin' Declan again?' Cavani felt the guilt shoot through him once more at how Declan was now firmly on Eddie's radar, or soon to be.

'We're meeting tomorrow afternoon. About one o'clock,' Cavani answered, halting himself before his nerves allowed any further details to escape. This was the last time he saved someone, he warned himself. Thinking of Lisa, their child, Siobhan and her new life. Thinking of Declan and of *The Black Dog* and how they'd pitch it to someone, now that he didn't have an agent – he'd need to ask Johnny to get on the phone again, like the old days, he laughed, moving on to the next concerns, thinking of how they'd produce it, fund it, cast it. It was a huge risk, all of it, but he felt alive, so fuck it.

He wondered when Eddie would be in touch to collect his

debt. He smiled as he thought of how much Eddie wanted to see himself on screen or to see himself portrayed. It was cringeworthy and innocent almost. He thought again of the mess Eddie had made with his pineapple cake and of the night terrors he'd mentioned on the flight.

'Right, round up Tanser and the rest of them. Twelve o'clock tomorrow, behind the golf course. Usual spot,' Eddie instructed Barry Merson, who pulled his phone out of his pocket as they both stood up. Cavani took another look around the café again before joining them on their feet. What the fuck had he done?

'Ah'll phone ye and tell ye where to tell the lad to go, right. He'll know where.' Eddie nodded, aware of all the stories that went around about what went on at the local municipal golf course when there was a business dispute.

'Don't worry, Jimmy. Ah'm a man of ma word. No one will bother yer young padawan again . . .' Eddie laughed. '. . . and no one will come to any harm, ok?' He watched as it registered on Cavani's face that his thoughts had been read again.

'That's no' me any more. We spoke aboot this.' Cavani felt his hand being gripped at the first explicit reference to the in-flight conversation. He felt himself staring at Eddie Reynolds's eyes, at the past, and at the potentially decent person who lived in there.

'Good luck to you and Siobhan and with the new project, if there's a role for me, give me a shout before ah leave here for good. A fresh start.' Eddie looked down at his black fleece jumper, his hand strumming crumbs and icing into the air. 'It's hard to watch yer son become the arsehole ye used to be.'

Cavani thought back to a day a couple of years back when he'd been filming on the very same golf course where Declan was to head to tomorrow and of a run-in with a teenager who was said to have been Eddie's son. The scene had been abandoned as they couldn't get it right. It had been too difficult to pull off. He remembered how fired up he'd been that day and how intense he could become when he was working on something that he cared about.

It had been an attempted suicide scene that the executives had told him was too graphic, too heavy, and he'd let their feedback join with his self-doubt and together they'd taken over.

Too graphic, too heavy, that was exactly the sort of work that resonated and connected with people whether executives – or some people themselves – liked it or not. That was exactly the sort of work that he was going back to.

'I'm older than I wish to be, this town holds no more for me,' Eddie announced, watching as the memory arrived in Cavani's head.

'Oasis! Remember that night? Balloch Park, Loch Lomond. We bumped into you.' Cavani was surprised at how excited he'd sounded – laughing – conceding that he himself had fallen into the trap of talking about the glory days now.

The archive footage in his head played. Cavani and Johnny and the rest of them, faces he hadn't seen in years. They'd run into Eddie, who'd said he'd lost his pals, which could make or break your evening in the days before mobile phones. They'd been intimidated at first, hoping that his pals would show up and take him away, and then worrying about his pals showing up and their companies amalgamating.

Maybe Eddie had abandoned his pals on purpose, maybe he'd wanted to be on his own, like he knew his pals were pricks, bullies, there for all the wrong reasons. Cavani looked at him again, at the few diehard crumbs that had resisted the force from the back of his hand, thinking of how fortunate he'd been to have been in his twenties in the nineties. Standing in the sun, screaming out lyrics like someone had given you the words with which to tell your own story.

How small these memories seemed but how powerful they were when they picked the right time to ripple through your entire body.

'What a fucking day, man.' Cavani felt his hand being released.

'Take care, Jimmy.' Eddie Reynolds stood with his back to the café, waiting for Cavani to wander off, learned behaviour, maybe, from a life lived in fear.

'You too, mate.' Cavani hadn't worked out which direction he should head off in and whether he was headed home or to find a hardware store, enjoying instead the feeling of being back at Loch Lomond.

Like every other time he'd allowed himself to indulge in the warmth of the past, the harder he tried to add further clarity to the grainy images, the faster the melancholic nostalgia left him. He struggled through a brief roll call of who else had been there – of the class of 1996 – before being put out of his misery by Eddie shouting his name.

'Jimmy.'

Cavani turned, feeling his heart flutter like the way it did when he'd been woken up from a deep sleep.

'Ye forgot yer books.'

Cavani laughed and threw his head back in a horrific display of insincerity which Eddie looked like he'd expected. Cavani apologised as he passed him, sparing both Eddie and himself any comment on his forgetful nature or anything like that. It would require the full range of his acting skills to pretend to have been relieved at being reminded, to continue the charade of the books being the purpose of their meeting.

He smiled and thanked Eddie as he opened the café door to walk back inside, over to where they'd been sat, his books surrounded by the debris from Eddie's afternoon treats. He grabbed them, taking another look around the café, wondering if he'd seemed as suspicious as he felt. No one seemed to be watching though, no one seemed to be giving a fuck. He stepped back on to the pavement, noticing that Eddie and Barry Merson were gone. He focused on taking a breath, pulled out his phone, to check the time and then for a hardware store, and he'd call Declan on the way.

What the fuck, he smiled, confused, annoyed, happy with himself, walking to let the thoughts settle and decide how he should be feeling. He looked inside the bag again, his face looking interested – appreciative – as he wondered if Eddie was watching him.

PART 6

'Imagine he thought your script was that shite that he'd arranged for you to get done in,' Doof Doof laughed, turning to watch as his joke landed on Declan's face, immediately changing his tone in reaction to Declan, who hadn't even attempted to join him in seeing the funny side, the surreal side at least.

'Do you honestly think he's going to risk everything, for that? The papers and that. This would ruin him,' Doof Doof continued. 'He must think a lot of you, man, fuck sake, and he must think a lot of your stuff, man, and look, you can't live like that, scared to leave your house, he's right. Scared to go to the pub, to go to, whatever, having to watch where you're walking him . . .'

Doof Doof clapped Hector, *The Black Dog*. He rubbed his head. It was the first time Declan had really seen Doof Doof make a fuss of Hector, he thought, letting a smile break through.

'I don't mind never going out, honestly, man, fuck it. I just want left alone, whether it's in here or outside. I don't know. I'll move away or something.' Declan looked back to Doof Doof knowing that he'd sounded ridiculous.

'He's explained that he's got Eddie Reynolds on his case,

wanting to be in his films, wanting a film about him, they all want to be celebrities, man. Big Eddie Kardashian. His arse is fat enough anyway.' Declan tried to hold his laugh in, to seek further reassurance from Doof Doof that there was nothing to worry about.

He felt Doof Doof's eyes staring at him, tickling him, looking for him to let himself go, to trust him, to trust James Cavani.

'Eddie Kardashian,' Declan repeated, feeling his face warming up as they both laughed like they were in Doof Doof's flat, smoking weed and talking shite.

'He's seen something in you – you've read his book – he's seen himself in you. You're getting bullied, he knows the biggest fucking bully going. No one's to get hurt, he's clear on that, Eddie's clear on that. It's not my thing, this, it's not yours and it's definitely not James Cavani's, but here we are. We go here, that wee wank Jordan gets off your case and that big wank Gary Tanser. Aw man, fuck them.' Doof Doof drummed his hands on the steering wheel, laughing, reaching round to pat Hector again, to apologise for how passionate he was getting.

Declan had got over being hospitalised. The pain was still there but he didn't care about it, really, and a part of him needed it to happen, he knew. Something had to happen. Something that took him out of autopilot. It certainly hadn't been Jordan's intention though, for him to meet James Cavani and to expedite the breakdown that had been loitering around for a while. He hadn't smoked weed since and he hadn't drunk alcohol, and now he wanted to be released back out to the world, to life, to a life that he was going to make a good go at.

'We're getting it sorted and your life can get back to normal, well, better than normal, man. Declan Dolan and James Cavani, imagine that on the opening credits of something. Fuck me, man.' Declan nodded, staring out of the front window as Doof Doof started the engine.

'You ok, pal?' Declan rubbed Hector's head as they headed out of Declan's street.

'Fucking mental, man,' Doof Doof laughed, shaking the entire situation around his head as he slowed the car down before pulling out at the junction where Declan, Connor and Jordan used to meet to walk to school together.

Declan thought of Jordan, wondering what he was thinking and if he was already at the golf course.

He wondered if he was petrified. He probably was – he wasn't a gangster, he wasn't a hard man, he was a mollycoddled disappointment to his middle-class parents and maybe this was the day he could face up to it and decide too where his life was going.

The best things can happen in the worst ways, Declan said to himself, noticing a fresh bird shit on the left wing mirror of Doof Doof's van.

Declan turned to look at Doof Doof, who was still smiling, lost in his reflections. He wondered if Doof Doof's boss or anyone senior at the council would notice him showing up on his day off and wonder what he was up to, but he didn't want to ruin his moment by asking him. He thought of the car Jordan drove Gary Tanser around in and of the car that Eddie Reynolds probably drove. A Range Rover or something probably, and then he thought of arriving in Doof Doof's cooncil-mobile.

'What the fuck is happening, man?' he closed his eyes, trying to take himself somewhere else.

'What's happening is, we're going to see Jordan and the other prick, they're going to apologise to you, Eddie Reynolds has guaranteed that, and then I'm taking you up to James Cavani's house in the West End and the two of you are going to start writing a belter of a fucking film. You've done all your worrying, man, this is the hardest bit, I promise. Think of your mum coming to get you from the hospital, man. Think of going wherever you want, of going into the pub again, you can ask Georgie out.'

Doof Doof pulled off the main road, stopping the car to look at Declan, realising that mentioning Georgie had probably overwhelmed him further.

'I still need to see her, to apologise . . . about that night.' Declan threw his shoulders back into the chair, reaching out to pat Hector, whose head was resting between the van's front two seats. 'I'm fine, man, ok. Let's go.'

Declan nodded, feeling Doof Doof looking at him again, for confirmation that he was sure. 'Let's go, get it sorted.' Declan breathed in, filling his lungs as the van engine started back up, breathing out. He closed his eyes and spoke a few prayer-like words inside himself, hoping that James Cavani was right and that no one was to be hurt. He felt calm, he felt all right. He reached his hand back to grip Hector's harness as the van rattled along the road.

'Fuck me, man. It's like a fucking R'n'B video,' Doof Doof declared as four sets of eyes turned to look at the van, speaking to each other as Gary Tanser walked towards it. They hadn't been briefed on the purpose of the meeting then, Declan thought, feeling his legs shaking. Doof Doof had kept the engine running too, anticipating having to make a sharp exit. 'Where the fuck is Eddie Reynolds,' Declan asked, looking at Doof Doof for answers, noticing that he seemed to be panicking too. Only Doof Doof knew what Eddie Reynolds looked like. Declan only knew that he could see the Keogh twins, Gary Tanser and, of course, Jordan – who stood staring at his own trainers, chewing gum like someone who couldn't emphasise enough how much of a prick they were. Declan shook his head, almost regretting his prayer, regretting certainly the length of their friendship.

Declan noticed that his watch was proudly on show and the skin-tight T-shirt that he had on to showcase further gym efforts and probable steroid use.

'Look,' Doof Doof said, nodding past Declan to the left wing-mirror as a car came speeding along the path, a Range Rover, as expected, Declan thought, watching as Barry Merson jumped out of the driver's seat almost before the car had stopped, ignoring Gary Tanser, who'd tried to greet him.

Declan hadn't really thought of what he'd expected Eddie Reynolds to look like as he walked towards the van, taking a large gulp from what looked like a can of sprite.

'Will we get out?' Doof Doof asked.

'Fuck knows, man.' Declan felt his voice cracking as Eddie Reynolds chapped on his window, nodding for him that it was all right to get out. Declan turned to Doof Doof, who'd already opened his door, opening his own and stepping out of the car, noticing Jordan looking Doof Doof up and down, smirking as he made a comment to Chrissy Keogh, which was ignored. Everyone except Jordan looked as concerned as Declan felt.

'An old friend of mine speaks very highly of yer work, Declan,' Eddie Reynolds laughed. 'Relax. Ye'll never hear fae them again. Who's yer pal?' Eddie looked at Doof Doof and then at the van.

'Doof Doof,' Declan answered. 'Well, Raymond,' Declan tried to explain, frustrated at his own nerves, hoping that Eddie Reynolds would take it as a compliment that his voice was trembling, that his face was red and he was sweating, like he was paying respect to his reputation.

'Doof Doof!' Eddie Reynolds interrupted, buying Declan some time to compose himself, his voice cheerful, booming as he looked in the van, at Hector. 'He's a cracker, whit's his name, Woof Woof?'

Declan felt too terrified to laugh but he didn't not want to laugh. Fucking say something, man, he screamed at himself. 'Hector his name is,' Declan hurried, looking to Doof Doof, both of them considering that maybe Declan had been right, that this was a bad idea. If you touch him, I'll bite your fucking nose off. A voice in Declan's head made him stand up and straighten his shoulders, relieved that a set of balls had been located from somewhere inside him.

'Lovely dug. Right . . .' Eddie announced. 'Dec and Doof, we're having some bother, ah'm hearin'.' Declan didn't know how to respond. He looked at the scar near Eddie's eye and at Barry Merson who'd been present in the pub, who'd helped to calm the situation and who'd apparently been all right about it all.

'You, whit's yer name,' Eddie Reynolds shouted, walking across to Jordan, whose face looked like Declan imagined his own to look when he'd first met James Cavani.

'Jordan, mate,' Jordan answered, his confidence obnoxious.

'Hold that a wee minute for me, Jordan.' Eddie handed him his can of Sprite. Jordan looked at Eddie, confused, shaking the can to confirm that it was empty.

'Remember that yin, from school, when cunts would do that and ye would fall for it?' Eddie Reynolds laughed. Declan felt himself cringe as Jordan laughed along.

'Aye, all the time,' he added, managing to fully display his gullibility, his sycophancy and his stupidity in the first minute of meeting his hero.

'You're the wee guy that slaps himself, is that right?' Jordan's face turned red with shame, his heart broken that anyone had seen the videos of him, especially Eddie, his hero. Declan watched as Jordan looked round, trying to catch Gary Tanser's eyeline for an indication, a hint, of what was going on. He looked over at Declan and at Doof Doof.

'Fuckin' look at me. Right here. Every time you look away, yer gonnae slap yersel.' Jordan nodded, looking back to the ground. Declan felt sick. Worried that the promise that no one was going to be hurt was now a certainty to be reneged on.

'How long have you known him?' The back of Eddie's head tilted in Declan's direction and Jordan glanced up quickly, answering that they'd been friends since they were four years old.

'Since ye were four years old?' Eddie announced, looking

to Declan and then back to Jordan, who'd interrupted him to ask if he was to slap himself because he'd looked away.

Declan and Doof Doof looked at each other again, shocked with embarrassment for Jordan.

'He's a fuckin' cracker this yin. Tanser, get over here.' Gary Tanser shuffled across, standing next to Jordan.

'So, explain to me, in as few words as possible, as to how this here pal of mine ended up in hospital,' Eddie asked, folding his arms like he'd surely seen a fair few investigating officers do over his career.

'Ah never touched him,' Gary Tanser started, unable to look over at Declan.

'How the fuck did he end up in hospital?' Eddie screamed in Gary Tanser's face.

The reason for the meeting now seemed to be registering with Jordan as Declan noticed that his shoulders had begun to shake as his head bowed down further. He was fucking crying. Fuck me, man, Declan thought, almost rooting for Jordan not to humiliate himself as much. It was now impossible to feel anything other than pity for him.

Declan made eye contact with Barry Merson, noticing that their heads were the only ones which weren't bowed to the seriousness of the situation.

Declan found the whole thing surreal, fascinating, like a television show, exactly like something James Cavani would direct, which he had done, he reminded himself, returning a nod to Barry Merson, who must have known that he'd simply been drunk and made an arse of himself that night in the pub and that it hadn't warranted what had happened.

Fuck sake, he thought, looking back to Eddie, overwhelmed. It was already fair to say that Jordan would never bother him again. He turned to Doof Doof, who smiled, relieved that it was probably going to be all right and that Jordan was too pathetic to be slapped by anyone other than himself, let alone given a beating.

'Just a daft argument one night in the pub.' Gary Tanser looked to Jordan first of all and then the sneer on his face stayed fixed on Declan, as though he was trying to figure out the connection between Jordan's pal, the wee fat drunk guy from the pub, the Morrisons worker, and Eddie Reynolds.

'Don't fuckin' look at him, don't ever fuckin' look at him again,' Eddie Reynolds shouted at Gary Tanser, the hostility diffusing from his expression as he looked back to the ground. 'Say sorry, say, sorry, Declan, I will never look at you again.'

Gary Tanser, his eyes to his feet, mumbled the words he'd been ordered to say.

'That was yer chance, pathetic. Fucked it. Ah need to see a better apology, a real apology, and it's a shame because ah'm no' a violent man any more.'

'I'm sorry, I'm sorry,' Jordan announced from nowhere, pleading as the tears flowed from his eyes. What the fuck, Jordan, man, Declan thought to himself, looking to Doof Doof, who looked like he would have laughed if the atmosphere hadn't felt as volatile.

'Fuckin' embarrassin'.' Eddie Reynolds looked away from Jordan, like he was finished with him. 'Fuckin' embarrassin',' he shouted in Gary Tanser's face.

'So, this . . .' Eddie Reynolds nodded to Jordan's trainers, letting his eyes run all the way up to his snapback baseball hat. 'That . . .' He turned back to Gary Tanser, shaking his head as Jordan was now visibly shaking with fear. 'How did ye end up wae that and how did you or him or both of ye end up putting' ma pal in the hospital. Final fucking chance, Gary.' Declan looked around at the Keoghs, at Barry Merson, at Jordan, who was wiping his eyes and dancing around like he needed a piss and then back to Gary Tanser.

'He's in debt, owes me big. Sniffin' more than he sells, usual. Ah asked him to hold somethin' for a wee side job, he said he would but then he shites himself.' Gary Tanser cleared his throat and spat to the side before continuing.

'After the argument in the pub' – he nodded again in Declan's direction, careful not to look up – 'Ah told him to go and see if he'd look after it and that wis his debt halved. He refused to take it and then, well, there we go.'

Gary Tanser spat again, seeming to swagger whilst he stood still.

'Is that true?' Eddie Reynolds looked at Jordan, who could only manage another apology before his voice crackled again.

'Whit did he ask ye to hold?' Eddie asked him. Declan felt like he wanted to shout 'Objection!', like the witness wasn't in a fit state for any further questions. He was surprised at the sympathy, or more, the pity, he felt for Jordan, given what he'd done to him. 'A gun,' Jordan managed, shaking his head from side to side, telling Gary Tanser that he was sorry and shouting to Declan now that he was sorry and that he hoped they were still good mates.

'Aw shut the fuck up. Ah'm deadly fucking serious. If ah

never showed up here today would you be his good mate? Just shut the fuck up and stand still.'

Eddie turned back to Gary Tanser. 'Where is the gun, now?' he asked, looking to Barry Merson to make sure he was paying attention.

'In the café, under the floorboards,' Gary Tanser answered, wiping his nose with the sleeve of his jumper and lifting his head up.

'If ah never made a promise to a pal of mine, ye'd be in that fuckin' boot. Fuck sake. Right. Let me see. Ye're gettin' involved way, way above yer brain capacity, to the point wee guys like this – fucking whatever the fuck that is . . .' Eddie nodded to Jordan, who was now inconsolable and begging not to be hurt. Declan felt himself willing Jordan to be quiet, sensing that Eddie was really struggling with the non-violent part of the agreement and that the situation had grown considerably bigger than just Jordan's attack and harassment of him. 'Look at him. Imagine he gets caught with a fuckin' gun. The maw and the da straight doon to the polis station wae him and every single name and address he could give.'

'I would never grass, ever,' Jordan interrupted. Declan turned to Doof Doof, struggling to watch as Eddie Reynolds turned to Jordan again and then back to Barry Merson.

'Lad, fucking shut up, right, just don't say a word, nothing, right?' Barry Merson nodded for Eddie to continue.

'This wee guy wants to run around like he's in a film, daft wee cunt gets himself in debt to an even dafter cunt like you, so you start bullyin' him and in turn he starts bullyin' his pal, well, ma pal noo – ma pal who never wanted anything to do with anyone like you or anyone like me – but he ends up in hospital, is that fair?' Eddie Reynolds leaned over to slap the underside of the skip of Jordan's hat, sending it flying off his head and landing in the puddle behind him as a warning for him to remain silent.

'Rather than leave it at that, ye try and harass him when he's oot with his dug and intimidate him to the point he's fuckin' housebound, is that right?' Eddie turned to Jordan who looked affronted at the accusation.

'Don't fuckin' answer. I fuckin' mean it. Don't say a word.' Eddie turned from Jordan back to Gary Tanser, his voice becoming calmer.

'He's drivin' ye around. Ye're taking advantage of him and in turn he's taking liberties.'

'Ah'm sorry, Eddie, ah don't know whit to say, it aw got a wee bit oot of hand. I'll pay his medical bills or whitever ye want.'

Eddie Reynolds turned back to Barry Merson. 'He'll pay his medical bills, where are we, fuckin' New Jersey? Is that the car?' Eddie nodded at the BMW that had been waiting on Declan outside his work.

'Aye,' Gary Tanser answered, looking at the car and then over his shoulder to Jordan's hat.

'And the gun, is it still in the café?' Gary Tanser seemed too mortified to confirm that yes, it was.

'The café that's serving people all day long, old people, weans. A gun gets found there and . . . fuck me.'

Eddie looked to the sky like he was summoning every ounce of his strength to keep his promise to Cavani that no one was to be hurt.

'Were they two involved?' Eddie asked Gary Tanser, nodding towards the Keogh twins.

'Naw,' he answered.

'Right, Jedward, get doon to the café and get it closed. Get under the floorboards and make sure that the gun gets tossed in the Clyde. Nuttin' stupit, right? Simple job.' Eddie leaned into Gary Tanser's face, sensing that he was about to appeal this decision as the Keoghs both got in their cars and sped off without having said a word.

'You. Car keys.' Eddie held his hand out and Gary Tanser reached into his pocket and handed over the keys. 'Yer clothes, yer boots and yer motorcycle,' Eddie said out loud as he turned to check on Declan. 'Big Arnie.

'Let's see, a couple of bullies, eh, it's been a while since ah've bullied someone. Yer clothes, yer boots, that's an idea. The two of ye, get stripped, get in the buff. Come on, we'll get a laugh, a wee bit of bullying, eh?' Eddie turned to Barry Merson, who looked ashamed that it had come to this but he probably knew through experience that a simple verbal warning wasn't enough and that Eddie had taken this particularly personal given the respect that he had for James Cavani. He probably wanted word to get back that he'd done a fine job and that no one was hurt, at least physically.

'Get yer fuckin' clothes off and get them in the boot of the car or the two of you are going in the boot of the car,' Eddie shouted, laughing as he walked towards the BMW, studying the alloy wheels and the paintwork, opening the boot, nodding for Gary Tanser and Jordan to throw their T-shirts in and then their tracksuit bottoms.

Jordan looked at Declan and Doof Doof, his tear-stained face pleading with them to try and stop this. Declan heard himself speaking. 'Look, I don't want any of this, I just want to be left alone, man. I just don't want any trouble, or anything, ever again and that's all, it's all cool, man.' He looked at Eddie and then at Doof Doof, who nodded that he'd done the right thing, at least for his own conscience.

'Sounds like a good friend you've lost, Jordan. There's no' too many of them in life, let me tell you. Ah'm goin' to have to overrule you though, Declan, sorry.

'The full fuckin' buff,' Eddie laughed as they both removed their socks and then their boxers and Jordan started crying again. Fuck it, at least he wasn't going to end up in hospital. He thought of the pain he still felt in his ribs and the bruising round his eye, of Sharon from his work when she'd found him hobbling towards the bus stop, and the hysteria of the night of his attack, his mum. Fuck him, man, a little bit of humiliation would see him well in the long run.

'Right, let's see. How much does this young scamp owe you, Gary my friend?'

Eddie looked to be in his element now, like he was having a thoroughly enjoyable afternoon at work. 'About two grand,' Gary Tanser answered, his hands cupping his genitals as he looked around, like he was in the defensive wall for a free kick.

'Two grand, big money, high-stakes stuff, that could cover penis enlargement surgery. Get yersel back over to Turkey, see if the mob that done yer teeth will sort ye oot wae a new tadger.' Eddie turned to see if Declan or Doof Doof were enjoying this as much as he was, which they weren't quite, but they both smiled in the way they guessed that you smile when you want to show how grateful you are not to be on the wrong side of a fucking maniac.

'How far away is the café, Merse? Check yer phone.' Eddie Reynolds whistled as he waited for Barry Merson's answer. '1.2 miles away, it says,' Barry Merson revealed, putting his phone back in his pocket and adding that it was a twenty-four-minute walk, which indicated that he sensed where Eddie's head was at.

'Right, a wee race then, that's no' too bad, 1.2 miles. The two of ye, a wee scud run. In fact, ye can stick yer trainers on, since it's difficult terrain on the opening stretch and I'm a decent guy. Ah wouldn't want to see any of the competitors pull out early with an injury. In fact, let's get a wee warm-up done, come on, twenty jumpin' jacks, get the heart rate up and get a bit of blood intae that 'hing, Gary.'

Declan heard Doof Doof snort and realised too that he was trying to contain his own laughter. They both wanted to believe they weren't taking any real satisfaction from this – but then, maybe they were, it was funny, man, it was absolutely fucking mental and, well, Jordan was a prick. His meeting with his hero hadn't gone as well as Declan's had with his, and so, life goes on. It could have been a lot worse for him, Declan reminded himself again.

'Right, if Big Tanser here wins, you owe three grand, Jordan – and ah'll make sure it's paid. Believe me. If you win, which ye should do, a young man like yersel against this fuckin' clown, the debt is wiped and, again, ah'll see tae that.' He looked at the two of them, taking their silent dread as an agreement to the race and to the stipulations stated.

377

'The car stays here, with the clothes, and ah'll hand the keys in at the café, ok?' Neither man reacted. 'Oh, yer hat, my apologies, Jordan.' Eddie bent down, shaking the dirty water off of Jordan's snapback cap and placing it on his head. 'There you, go, what's it say?' He tilted the skip down. '"Icon!" Well, this should be fuckin' iconic,' Eddie cackled, playfully slapping Jordan's cheek.

'Right, we'll have a wee laugh, but most importantly, and fuckin' listen closely . . .' The hostility returned to Eddie's voice. 'After we leave here, the two of you have never to speak to ma friend again. You've never to look at ma friend again. If you're somewhere he is, you both leave and that's the way it's gonnae be, and me and Merse will make sure of that, ok?'

'Aye, but Eddie, come on, man, two grand! Please?' Gary Tanser pleaded, slightly breathless from his warm-up, looking down at his own naked body – doubtful of its chances in a mile-plus sprint against someone at least a decade younger – whilst Jordan looked to be planning his route to the café, confident of his chances of having his debt wiped, and, surely, adamant that he was going to keep on running, well after the race was won and the debt was clear, well away from the life that he'd dreamed of.

'On yer marks!!!' Eddie announced as he got into the passenger seat of the Range Rover and Barry Merson started the engine.

'And don't worry. Ah'll be drivin' alongside to offer some encouragement, to keep the spirits up,' Eddie shouted from the window.

Barry Merson reversed the car so that it was alongside Declan, 'Take care, Declan, and you, Doofer. He's a good man – our mutual pal – and I'm sure you'll be a success.' Eddie winked, a wink that let Declan know that he'd just watched an act – a performance – and that he was only a bad person when he needed to be, or whatever.

Declan didn't know what he should say, offering only an uncomfortable nod as the Range Rover pulled off and he and Doof Doof hurried back inside the van, watching as the two bare arses galloped out ahead of Barry Merson's car to the sound of its horn tooting and Eddie shouting.

'Holy fuck, man. That's probably the best thing I've ever seen.' Doof Doof laughed along to the sound of his van's engine starting back up, sending them rattling along the pathway. 'We'll follow for a wee bit, eh? See who wins.' He looked to Declan to make sure that this was all right.

Declan shrugged his shoulders and laughed. 'Ah fuck him, man, fuck him indeed,' he said, reaching in to pat Hector.

'Then I'll drop you at James Cavani's,' Doof Doof said as they pulled out on the main road to watch the runners descend the steep hill which led down to the café turned finish line. Declan noticed how relieved Doof Doof looked on his behalf and how delighted he seemed – proud even – every time he mentioned James Cavani's name.

Cars began slowing down to watch the race and horns were being tooted, it was a safe assumption that Jordan would be looking for a career change and that Gary Tanser's reputation would be in tatters.

'Look, fuckin' look, look, look.' Doof Doof almost mounted the pavement, managing to straighten the car just in time 'The polis! It's the fuckin' polis.'

Declan began laughing properly now at this latest twist as the police car pulled up alongside Barry Merson and Eddie at the traffic lights. 'Officer, officer! Come on now. That's a darn right disgrace that is, bloody deviants!' Eddie was shouting, his face purple – angry with laughter – his hand banging the dashboard like it was the greatest entertainment he'd ever witnessed.

'There's fucking . . .!!!' Declan looked as Doof Doof coughed and spluttered, struggling to release his words. 'His da—' Doof Doof finally managed, 'Wee Slam Dunc.'

'Holy fuck.' Declan lost control now too, as the lights turned green and they watched as Jordan had stopped, resigned to being arrested and resigned to having to begin to explain the unexplainable to his dad, only to see that Gary Tanser wasn't for stopping – his eyes firmly on the prize, remembering how high the stakes of the race were and deciding that it had to continue right to the bitter, naked, degrading end, regardless of intervention from parents or law enforcement. Jordan looked at Gary Tanser and then at his dad before breaking into a fresh sprint, hurrying to regain ground on the leader as they pounded down, towards the café, a police car in pursuit. Jordan's dad stood still, frozen to the spot, shocked, appalled, disgusted, failed.

Doof Doof and Declan took the turn towards the city and watched as Jordan, Gary Tanser, the police car and Eddie Reynolds and Barry Merson headed down towards the café.

Doof Doof turned the radio up and they both wiped the laughter from their eyes, granting each other the silence to play back and process all that they'd had the pleasure to bear witness to, until, finally, Doof Doof spoke, asking how Declan planned on spending the first night of his new freedom.

'We could go for a pint, once you've finished writing,' Doof Doof suggested.

'I think I'll stay off it, for another wee while anyway, but I'll join you though. I want to go in and see Georgie, and apologise in person – if she's working.' Declan felt himself blushing, resigning himself to Doof Doof laughing, laughter of encouragement.

'Ask her out, man. You're on fire at the minute. Untouchable.' Doof Doof seemed delighted to be witnessing Declan's come-back and excited to see what was coming next. 'Ask her if she wants to go and see that new James Cavani film,' Doof Doof laughed into his interior mirror as the van pulled out on to the carriageway towards Partick.

'I heard it's shite. But his next one will be a cracker,' Declan responded, his new confidence beginning to grow on him, beginning to suit him. 'Fucking right it will be!' Doof Doof shouted, tapping his steering wheel, his face still bursting from everything that had gone on.

'Here, make sure you put in a word with Siobhan Cavani for me,' Doof Doof announced, looking like he didn't know whether he was joking or not. Declan laughed, telling him that he would, wondering what the future held for Doof Doof and what his own plans were. He'd never had a friend like him, he thought, rolling down the window to let the fresh air hit his face as they cleared three or four green lights in a row, whizzing towards the West End of Glasgow, towards Cavani's, towards the future.

'Can I stick The Cure on?' Declan asked, turning to check that Doof Doof was as chuffed at the request as Declan had hoped he would be.

'What kind of question is that, ma man?!'

Declan turned around upon feeling Hector's breath on his ear as he'd climbed up on the back of the passenger seat to join them as they sang along to the lyrics of 'Boys Don't Cry' as the van carried them, celebrating, towards James Cavani. Declan thought of how the van was well out of its council jurisdiction and remembered that Doof Doof had mentioned before that the vans had a tracking device and that he wasn't allowed to roam around in it, but so fuck, Declan presumed Doof Doof's response would be, if he'd reminded him.

So, so fuck, it wasn't worth interrupting the tune for. They carried on, circling the one-way streets of the leafy neighbourhoods of the West End, Doof Doof driving and singing, Declan singing and patting Hector, whose tail thumped with excitement off the side of the van.

'Is it this one?' Doof Doof asked, leaning forward to look up at the sandstone town house. 'Serious fucking houses up here, man,' he commented, like he was trying to further motivate Declan.

'There he's there.'

Doof Doof nodded as Cavani and his wife and Siobhan were walking down the street, carrying shopping bags.

'I don't know if I should be nervous, or something, man. I

feel pretty cool about it which is makin' me feel like I should be nervous. Fuck knows,' Declan told Doof Doof, who didn't have a chance to answer as Cavani had spotted them and had begun walking towards the car.

Declan saw out of the side of his eye how Doof Doof had looked at Cavani, starstruck and like he himself was nervous, which further relaxed Declan.

'Jump out, I'll introduce you,' Declan told him, opening the van door and greeting Cavani, who turned to look to the driver's seat.

'The greenskeeper!' he announced. Doof Doof looked embarrassed, struggling to hide his delight that Cavani had remembered him, that the story he'd told and embellished so many times had now been validated, by the man himself.

'How did it go?' Cavani asked Declan, walking to the other side of the van to be away from Siobhan and Lisa, who were busy waiting for Doof Doof to open the back door of the van so that they could make a fuss of Hector.

'I think it's all sorted. It was mental but no one got hurt. Fucking hell though, man, you didn't have to do that.' Cavani held his hand out, an indication that it was never to be spoken of again, that he hadn't been proud of what he'd done, but that he was glad it was behind Declan now.

'I don't know what to say, but what do you owe him, or whatever, or what does he want from you?' Declan asked, lowering his voice and checking on Cavani's behalf that Lisa and Siobhan were occupied with Hector, who lay on his back having his belly rubbed.

'We go way back. I think, maybe, we'll write a role for him, or something.' Cavani rolled his eyes. 'He's always wanted to act, believe it or not. He'd be a good Ryzo, eh?'

Cavani laughed, looking at Declan, studying him, noticing that his eye had cleared up and that he seemed so much more content within himself than on their last meeting.

Cavani realised the full scale of the weight that had been lifted from him, which made him feel a whole lot better about his meeting with Eddie.

He waved for Declan to follow him as they walked towards the house and Declan shouted on Hector, who marched to Cavani's front door like the house was his own, like this was the house that he deserved to live in.

'I'll need to take him for a wee walk first though.' Declan stopped on the bottom step, embarrassed that maybe he'd seemed like he was taking the piss, that he was wasting Cavani's valuable time.

'I'll take him if you want,' Doof Doof offered from the side of his van, almost at the exact same time as Siobhan suggested that she could take him to the park. Declan looked at Doof Doof and then at Siobhan, who stood smiling with her hands in the air, conceding to Doof Doof's offer.

'We'll both take him?' Doof Doof suggested, which made Declan smile, impressed – inspired even – by Doof Doof's confidence. Fair fucking play, man.

'Sorted then. You're not a fucking weirdo though, are you?' Siobhan laughed along with Doof Doof, who seemed taken aback and like he fancied her even more now that he saw how confident she was. Something that he hadn't expected, something that Declan hadn't expected either. It was a small-town thing then, the inability to let someone grow beyond their reputation, beyond their past.

Declan felt guilty for any time he'd heard anyone talk about James Cavani's junkie sister, especially as she seemed like a genuine warm person and she showed no signs of her arduous past. Respect, he thought, as he handed her a couple of dog shit bags and a tennis ball and told Doof Doof that he would text him later, laughing as he shook his head, as a way of wishing him luck on his walk.

'What's your name, again? Doofy or something?' Siobhan let a smile pause on her face, waiting to laugh at Doof Doof's answer.

'I'm Raymond, but, aye, they used to call me Doof Doof.' He laughed, turning back to check Hector was good to go.

'Are you ready to get to work then?' Cavani asked Declan, clapping his hands together as Lisa opened their front door and asked Declan if he'd like anything to eat or drink.

He was both hungry and thirsty but he declined. He'd eat and drink when he'd earned it.

'Definitely, man.' Declan affirmed that he was ready to work, turning from the top step to watch as Raymond and Siobhan Cavani stepped back from each other, laughing heartily at something whilst Hector marched ahead, leading them with purpose to somewhere that he'd never been before in his life, somewhere that excited him.

'The Black Dog,' Cavani said, joining Declan in watching the three of them.

They looked across the street and out over the park and then even further than that, each of them reflecting on the journey that they'd both been on, that had led them to this, to maybe where they were supposed to be but fuck knows, the two of them seeming aware that no explanation was required – that an interpretation would do.

'Let's get crackin' then.' They walked into the house and towards Cavani's office, to the table that he'd decided against refurbishing.

It had lived and it had a lot more living to do.

Its chips and its scars and its imperfections were nothing to be concealed.

It was fucking life, man.

ACKNOWLEDGEMENTS

First of all, I'd like to thank Alex Clarke from Wildfire Books for first approaching me a few years ago backstage at the 02 Arena with the suggestion that I write a book. A book about my life that went down relatively well. We kept in touch and it was Alex who put the idea to me that I should write fiction, like, an actual book, a novel, like the one you're just a few more lines away from laying to rest in a drawer, to be boxed and handed over to a charity shop the next time you move house or break up with your partner.

I didn't believe I had a novel in me and so I made all the usual excuses, like a lack of time and whatever else, but then March 2020 showed up and slapped the world about a bit.

I made many a false start and gave up more times than I've ever given up on anything, but I'd far too much respect for real writers and novelists to ever believe that putting a novel together would be a straightforward operation, so with Alex's advice and encouragement I ploughed through day by day until I managed to stumble on to a flow and an energy that drove me to produce something that I'm very proud of.

A huge thank you to Celine Kelly as well, for her encouragement and for her excellent work in helping me edit my oversized – (single spaced!) – and slightly bloated manuscript, for pointing me towards the strengths and weaknesses and teaching me invaluable lessons about the craft of writing. And thank you to Mark Handsley for his thorough and masterful copy edit.

Thank you too to Doctor Hannah Mackereth and to my lifelong friend Claire Gallagher, who both kindly checked over a few chapters and kept me right on some of the finer details in relation to addiction, recovery and healthcare.

To Rick Hughes and his family, it's been beautiful watching you grow from wrestling with maps in hire cars on the way to arts centre gigs in the Highlands all those years ago, to now watching you negotiate with the literary industry whilst our friendship grows stronger and stronger along the way. A great agent but most importantly one of the best friends I've ever had.

As always, thank you to my own family. First of all to my wife, Kerry, for her time and patience in reading large sections of my first draft every week and giving her advice and support, and for keeping me from giving up even on the days when my self-doubts looked like they'd won. Your positivity and kind-heartedness always manage to salvage a victory over whatever gets thrown at them.

To Mum, Dad and my brother John – thank you for always being behind me in every single thing I've done in my life. Thank you to my mum for always encouraging me to read, my dad for always encouraging me to write, and to John for teaching me to think for myself.

To the people from my childhood who recognised that, for whatever reason, I was almost crippled with nerves, shy and seriously lacking in self-belief and who showed me kindness and helped to build up my confidence, namely an old teacher of mine, Mr Thumath, or Ronnie, as I now, slightly awkwardly, address him.

To my old English teacher Mr Ford, for the energy you put into your lessons and for sharing your own writing with the class, your own daft and beautiful short stories, I'll always remember how it blew my mind that someone could do that. You made writing seem accessible and human and I'm forever grateful that you did.

A special mention here to my dog, Annie – who would see herself in these pages, if she could read, of course – for every smile and laugh you've given me and so many other people, and for keeping me company in my office and in cafés and on our long walks together as I figured this thing out.

Finally, thank you for reading this, for taking a chance on what is ultimately a book by a first-time writer when there are thousands out there. I hope that the enjoyment and fulfilment I eventually felt when writing this story and creating these characters comes through and that it passed a few hours in your life and you took from it whatever else there was to take.

A big shout out to the real-life Declans and the real-life Siobhans and to anyone struggling; keep moving, keep talking, and if you see me about, please say hello.

I dedicate this book to my son, Liam – the single greatest thing that's ever happened to me. I hope that a love of reading and writing will help to fill your life with curiosity, knowledge and joy.

That's me for now. Heading back to my real job. Maybe I'll see you on the road.

Take care of yourself and again, thank you for your time.

Kevin